THE

BUFFALO HUNTER

Hunter

The Only Good Indians

The Babysitter Lives

I Was a Teenage Slasher

NOVELLAS

Sterling City

Mapping the Interior

Night of the Mannequins

**SHORT STORIES
AND COLLECTIONS**

Bleed into Me: A Book of Stories

The Ones That Got Away

Zombie Sharks with Metal Teeth

Three Miles Past

States of Grace

After the People Lights Have Gone Off

*The Faster Redder Road:
The Best UnAmerican Stories of
Stephen Graham Jones*

COMIC BOOKS

13th Night

My Hero

Memorial Ride

Earthdivers

True Believers

THE

BUFFALO HUNTER
Hunter

STEPHEN GRAHAM JONES

SAGA PRESS

LONDON AMSTERDAM/ANTWERP **NEW YORK** SYDNEY TORONTO NEW DELHI

SAGA PRESS

AN IMPRINT OF SIMON & SCHUSTER, LLC

1230 AVENUE OF THE AMERICAS, NEW YORK, NEW YORK 10020

First Saga Press hardcover edition March 2025

SAGA PRESS and colophon are trademarks of Simon & Schuster, LLC

For information about special discounts for bulk purchases, please contact Simon & Schuster Special Sales at 1-866-506-1949 or business@simonandschuster.com.

The Simon & Schuster Speakers Bureau can bring authors to your live event. For more information or to book an event, contact the Simon & Schuster Speakers Bureau at 1-866-248-3049 or visit our website at www.simonspeakers.com.

Interior design by Lewelin Polanco

Manufactured in the United States of America

1 3 5 7 9 10 8 6 4 2

Library of Congress Cataloging-in-Publication Data is available.

ISBN 978-1-6680-7508-1
ISBN 978-1-6680-7510-4 (ebook)

for James and Lois:
thanks for all the jelly

but the adversaries are treating the case in such a way as to show that they are seeking neither truth nor concord, but to drain our blood

—The Apology of the Augsburg Confession,
The Book of Concord

THE
BEAUCARNE
MANUSCRIPT

part 1

16 July 2012

A dayworker reaches into the wall of the parsonage his crew's revamping and pulls a piece of history up, the edges of its pages crumbling under the fingers of his glove, and I have to think that, if his supervisor isn't walking by at just that moment, then this construction grunt stuffs that journal from a century ago into his tool belt to pawn, or trade for beer, and the world never knows about it.

If this works out, though, then I owe that dayworker my career.

In January, I wasn't exactly denied tenure, but I was told that, instead of continuing with my application, I consider asking for the extension I'm currently on. The issue wasn't my teaching—*I'm* the dayworker of Communication and Journalism, covering all the 1000- and 2000-level courses—it was that my publications aren't up to University of Wyoming "standards for promotion." See: get a book under contract, Etsy, and then we'll talk.

And, if you don't? Then all your schooling, all your dreams of being a professor, they're smoke, and you're out in the cold.

Until that random dayworker reached into that wall. Until what he found wrapped in mouse-chewed buckskin wound up in the hands of Special Collections librarian Lydia Ackerman of University Montana State up in Bozeman, and she was able to read the scripty hand enough to glean a name from the very front page: "Arthur Beaucarne."

It's not far from there to me, that surname not exactly being common.

And, because technically that journal belongs to me—well, my father *then* me, but my father in his facility down in Denver's not exactly compos mentis—Lydia Ackerman's been sending me the digitized pages as they're processed, the original being a century too delicate to handle. But I don't think she does it out of kindness. It's to keep me from showing up unannounced again.

"Etsy?" she asked when I did show up like that in May, breathing hard from the stairs. She was looking from my ID to me, to see which was the typo. It's *Betsy*, really, I didn't say, but a boy with a speech impediment in kindergarten . . . who cares?

"The *last* name," I told her, as politely as I could.

So, I was led back to the workbench they conserve delicate literary artifacts on, was made to mask up, glove up, bootie up, and then sit like that through a lecture about the lignin content of old paper and the homemade inks of the late nineteenth century, and how this particular ink had aged into acid that was eating away the brittle old paper it was written on, meaning the individual letters collapse into hopeless crumbles from just the slightest breath—thus the case the journal's enclosed in. It's for humidity and temperature, Lydia Ackerman explained like giving a tour to second-graders, but mostly it's to keep any breeze from punching those black letters from the pages, effectively erasing this amazing find from history.

"It's also for *dust*," Lydia Ackerman leaned forward to say in some sort of confidence, like "dust" was a profanity in this particular room. "Even *dust* weighs enough to make the letters fall through the paper." To be sure I got how dire this all was, she heated her eyes up and raised her eyebrows.

"I'll be careful," I assured her, at which point she unlatched the glass case, both of us holding our breath behind our masks, I'm pretty sure, and, finally, I got to look directly at my great-great-*great*-grandfather's journal.

The workroom we were in smelled like my dad's chemistry lab on campus, sending me back to being ten years old, when I'd yet to betray him by choosing the humanities over hard science.

Sorry, Dad. Again.

I turned my back on chemistry, became an alchemist, yes, mixing facts with rhetoric and spin and encomium, all in hopes this or that speech will catalyze an audience, hopefully in what feels like a heartfelt way. Such is communication, which I long to enter into again with you someday, Dad—hopefully soon. I do get the reports from your medical team, after all.

But, as my great-great-great-grandfather says in his journal—okay, my *greatest*-grandfather—that's neither here nor there.

And, yes, okay, I'll admit it here in the privacy of this laptop: since I didn't inherit "science" from my dad, I'm here choosing to inherit journal-keeping from someone much deeper in my bloodline. Well, either "inherit" or "resuscitate"—I haven't kept my precious thoughts in a secret notebook since junior high, thought I'd outgrown that kind of stuff. Surprise, I guess? I'm still that awkward girl in seventh grade, except now the enemies I'm putting on my hate list are from my tenure committee.

But, Great-Great-Great-Grandfather, I know I'm nowhere near as practiced as you, with organizing my daily thoughts and recollections on the page. You were educated in the nineteenth century, when recitation was the order of the day. You could recite long poems and speeches, and I, who *teach* speech-writing, can barely remember a phone number.

Where we're also different: you were a pastor, and—this I did inherit from my dad—I'm more of a professional doubter.

I've worked my way through the first few days of your journal, though, and I'm coming to understand why Bozeman wants to pay to keep your writing in their collection. You were good, Arthur Beaucarne. *You* used my rhetoric and spin and encomium to come off sounding heartfelt, never mind the actual facts, but you had a documentarian's eye, too, didn't you? And a playwright's ear. You didn't have a camera, but you had a pen, and its nib was sharp enough to cut right to the center of the day, the year, the era.

You make your case better than I can, though. I'll paste in a news item from 1912, the year you disappeared from your church, and then showcase your more fleshed-out version:

"Is it happening again?" This is the question former cavalryman and current postal clerk Livinius Clarkson was said to be asking his patrons for the better part of Monday.

What L. Clarkson is talking about is the deceased individual found off the beaten path yesterday, out in the open prairie across the Yellowstone River, in the environs of Sunday Creek. Initial speculation was that this was some unfortunate who perished over the last winter, who was only just now thawing out due to last week's abundance of sunlight. This would explain the state of this person's remains. However, knowledgeable men involved with transporting the body into town assure the Star that this isn't frost burn or scavenging. They also assure the Star that while ice, when affixed to skin, can possibly remove it, this would seem to be something more pernicious and intentional.

This is cause for concern.

Are the Indians turning hostile again? If so, which ones? The Crow, the Nakota, the Ree? More farflung tribes like the Blackfeet, Gros Ventre, Snake? And, if this is a holdover from the depredations of older times, then what might be the cause of their ire this time? Does our government not provide them with beef rations, and land that they leave fallow and untended, not interested in working it as God intends?

When pressed on the matter, L. Clarkson, himself no supporter of the Indian, averred that what he was concerned about instead was similarity to a rash of grisly discoveries he claims went on nearly four decades ago, in Montana's more lawless times.

As for that supposed rash of mutilations, the Star talked to an unnamed source in the later years of his long and storied life. Once a miner, among other and sundry occupations, this source remembers this country when it was "young and open." Scoffing at L. Clarkson's sensational claims, this former ore-worker, treasure hunter, stagecoach driver and occasional cowpoke, who was young when the so-called "mountain men" were in their dotage, remembers that as the great buffalo herds were collapsing some 40 years ago, there were motherless calves left bawling out in the night, until finally the men of "Milestown" as he still insists upon calling Miles City, went out and dispatched them in a single night, leaving the humps skinned as a warning to any more disturbers of the night's peace. Apparently they drew all the calves together by draping a buffalo robe over a large bull borrowed from a certain rancher, also nameless.

The hides they salvaged from these calves, being too small for a robe and too golden for the milliner, were initially stored on a pallet in a shed behind the old livery, until they got too scabby to work soft. At which point they were fed to hogs. This recollector of former times assures the Star that this spectacle is what L. Clarkson is inaccurately recalling, as a buffalo calf weighs about the same as a grown man, and, dead in the grass in the state they were both left, it would be easy to mistake one for the other.

Of note is that the two dogs that accompanied the party to collect this dead individual both expired overnight, each of them chewing at the skin of their own bellies. But of course there is no shortage of dogs here in Miles City.

The identity of the deceased individual is as of this date unknown, save that he was male, and possibly a traveler, as his unmarred face isn't known around these parts.

The service for him will be private.

That's the just-the-facts version from the *Miles City Star*, dated March 26, 1912—microfiche, yes. Now, here's what my *greatest*-grandfather wrote into his journal the evening before:

Yesterday evening, word started to percolate around town concerning a man found dead out in the sea of grass that surrounds us. Martha Grandlin, Skeet Grandlin's second wife (his first, deceased) was the first bearer of this savory tidbit, being certain to contort her face in cultured disgust, and to not give the secondhand account her full voice, I presume either to keep it from being a real occurrence, or to keep from exposing herself as one who thrills in carrying such morbid news around town. Martha, kind soul that she tries to be, was bringing by half a loaf of German bread and some jam she claimed were spare, and clutching the week's mail to her side in case one of Skeet's many and farflung correspondences should blow away into those same grasslands.

According to Mrs. Grandlin, who held the tips of the fingers of her right hand to the hollow of her throat while pronouncing this, this poor man had had, there's no other way to say it, his skin removed "as if he were an animal!"

I ate the bread and jam in silence after Mrs. Grandlin's hasty departure, and considered whether a man liberated of his skin and left out in the grass was something that could still happen in this new century. Weren't such things supposed to be part of this new state's sordid past? And what would motivate someone to such an act? What could someone do to have such an act visited upon them?

The jam was huckleberry, with large chunks still remaining in it, and I found that if I had the patience to leave it on the bread for a few minutes, the juice from the jam would soak in and soften it, with the result being almost in the cobbler family, though I could hold it in my fingers if I was careful, the crust being stiff from yesterday's oven. I had told myself when Mrs. Grandlin handed this treat to me that I would make it last the week, that it could be the prize at the end of my duties, but once I figured out the proper soaking time, I greedily consumed all of it in a single, shameful go. God was watching, as he watches all, but assuredly he would allow a broken old man this simple indulgence, would he not?

And thank you, Mrs. Grandlin. This midafternoon delight was unexpected. As, of course, was the terrible news. This is Montana, though, I told myself. It's where things like this happen, isn't it? Or, as some of my parishioners might joke, "It's where things like this happen, n'est-ce pas, Pastor Beaucarne?"

In spite of my protestations about any immediate French ancestry, still these Prairie Deutsche like to poke and prod, which is why I write this in King George's English, not the German I deliver my sermons in, as curious eyes could then read it. But of course my parishioners' aspersions about their good pastor's Gallic name is all in good fun, and if the victuals continue to flow, then this non-Frenchman can only be grateful.

As to who the unfortunate man found dead a few miles either north or west of town was or is, or will be upon identification, Mrs. Grandlin had not an inkling. Though the intensity with which she watched me while delivering this served as explanation why I had been her first stop. As the clergy parishioners come to me with their problems and struggles and concerns, it stood to reason that I might have heard news about a husband, brother, or son who had tragically gone missing.

I had no knowledge of any such missing husband, brother, or son, and surely my expression didn't suggest otherwise, but, infected by Mrs. Grandlin's curiosity, I told myself to pay special attention. At the same time, not everyone feared to be on a drinking binge is actually drunken. Not everyone supposed to have taken work that pulls them suddenly away from home is actually earning a wage.

Eager about this find out in the grasslands, if for no other reason than that it broke the tedium, I buttoned my great-coat over the new and persistent huckleberry stain on the surplice I had thrown on when Mrs. Grandlin knocked——my only one!——and made my way out the side door and down to the lodging house porch, bringing with my personage, as it's unavoidable not to do, a retinue of raucous dogs of every color, size, and temperament.

As I approached with them barking around my feet, announcing my arrival to the whole of Miles City, the whole of Montana, I took pains not to notice the shuffling and scraping that always precedes my arrival to such a low place. I would be similarly unaware of any bulges in the mens' jackets that could or could not be bottles and spirits, and I held out hope that I wouldn't have to draw close enough for their breath to scald my eyes.

"The limping reverend!" Willem Thomlinsen called out with all the joviality he could muster, referring to my gait, impeded as it is by the three toes on my left foot that predecease me. I would expect the same from a ten year old boy caught antagonizing the chickens. Thomlinsen calling me by that appellation——Reverend——was a long standing hallmark of our interactions, my silhouette evidently prompting whosoever I encountered in my doddering perambulations to make joke upon joke at my expense. Such is the price exacted by these black robes, I surmise. By this craggy, thin silhouette.

Though I would wish it otherwise, Thomlinsen's was a joke that had over the previous year spread through his companions like grass fire, meaning I also had to endure as greetings from all these lodging house regulars a round of "Pastor" and "Preacher," "Brother" and "Bishop," and on into variations they had to mumble, as they had no real command of the terms, their childhoods spent in Quaker and Catholic pews so far behind them now as to be but fairy tales that happened to someone else.

"Father, Reverend," Thomlinsen rounded it all up with, apparently having had more training than the rest.

The humor of the west knows no bounds, respects no boundaries.

Nevertheless, I demurred and endured, grinning a sheep's grin at this camaraderie and acceptance, which is what I have to tell myself it is, every next time it's happening again.

As to why I'd chosen to submit myself to this good willed

badgering, it was that the porch of the lodging house was the catch basin for all news in and around Miles City. The gentlemen, or "denizens" if that's the more telling description, of the long, swayed bench that I've been assured was salvaged from a previous, temporary incarnation of my esteemed church, were irreverent and oftentimes in one stage or another of intoxication, but resistance to observing the niceties of society meant that they functioned as guards at a post, such as it was, not letting anyone interesting pass unless and until they had shared the news of the day with them. In such a way are tolls exacted.

Knowing that any corpse found either north or west of town would come in past the lodging house, I knew then also that such a parade passing in front of the lodging house would have been subject to inspection and interrogation. It helped that Sall Bertram, the quiet Ulysses Grant of these regulars, had, until 1899, been sheriff of Custer County, and that the current sheriff had been his deputy, so was still beholden to his former superior officer. Which probably in no small way explains why the porch of the lodging house was outside the law, as it were.

But that's neither here nor there, as I hear more and more of my parishioners saying of late——a verbal trend that worries me, as it sweeps things under the rug that should be dealt with in the light, rather than let fester. But this concern itself is neither here nor there, I suppose. Even a preacher pastor brother bishop father reverend of fighting age during the war between the states can join this bold new century, yes.

After describing for these regulars in great and delectable detail the bread and jam I had, tragically, consumed all of, I asked them about the poor man found dead and exsanguinated to the west of town, asking of myself meanwhile if

I wasn't, in own way, just as bad as Mrs. Grandlin. But no, I told myself. As shepherd of a flock, I needed to be informed on all goings-on that might affect that flock. It wouldn't do to look out over the Sunday morning crowd and have them whispering to each other about that of which I'm ignorant.

"The west?" California Jim spat in response, disgusted, answering the first of the two bluffs I'd built into my opening bid, for them to correct.

I've never inquired after the provenance of California Jim's name, but assume it has to do either with one or another gold rush or with another of his many former occupations.

"Ex-what, Preacherman?" Sall Bertram mumbled, leaning ahead to spit between his boots into a crack in the porch nearly crusted shut, from all the days he spends there.

"He had been bled, had he not?" I said with all false innocence, looking from one to the other, which prompted them, in turn, to look to each other.

"Your Lutheran god whisper that to you?" Thomlinsen finally said, which struck me odd, as I'd only proffered the possibility of exsanguination so as to be a babe in the fold for them, plucking at rumor and smoke, meaning they could correct me with the actual facts and thereby become authorities.

Men on in their years, whose sole job is to occupy a bench, like to feel important, I know. It's quite possible I suffer from a liturgical version of this myself.

"I suppose most of his blood did leak out when he were skinned like a hump," Thomlinsen said for them all, glaring me down as if challenging one so pure of heart to picture something so revolting.

If only he knew.

The depravity of man's heart knows no floor, and everyone in this hard country has a sordid chapter in the story of their life, that they're trying either to atone for, or stay ahead of. It's what binds us one to the other.

I wasn't there to publicize my own moral failings, howsoever, but to further hone Mrs. Grandlin's revelation. What I had so far, without asking directly, were "west" and "skinned"——and, now, possibly "exsanguinated," though that could very well be my misreading.

"To what end do you skin a person?" I asked.

"I seen a man filled with so many Indian arrows in him that he looked like a pincushion in a sewing parlor," Early Tate said, licking his cracked lips hungrily. "Sixty nine, it were."

"James Quail?" Sall Bertram either said or asked, it was hard to distinguish.

"Down on the trail," Early Tate answered with a shrug, yet holding my eyes, perhaps to see if I would challenge him on this.

The "trail" he spoke of was the deep ruts of the Oregon Trail, which he'd famously been a drover on in his twenties. In each retelling, his deeds and exploits become a little more grand, I should note.

I didn't doubt this pincushion man, though, "James Quail" or no. In the late '60s he spoke of, and into the bloody decade that followed, I had myself seen similar travesties, that still haunt me in my weaker moments, with only one candle remaining, the town around me long asleep. But you can build a wall around yourself with scripture and faith.

"Like a buffalo, you say?" I asked then, due to their use of the word "hump."

This question prompted more looks between the regulars. Looks and the shuffling of feet, the rearranging of certain jugs and bottles in this or that jacket. Finally Sall Bertram out and said it, immune as he was to legal repercussions.

"His face was even painted," he proclaimed, pulling his own fingers downward along his forehead and nose, down to his chin.

"Skinned and then painted?" I asked back, earnestly incredulous at this development.

"The skin on his face was still where it ought've been," California Jim said, forgetting for a moment I was there and instinctively taking a long pull from the bottle nestled against his chest. "Apology, Father," he added, wiping the back of his mouth with his sleeve.

"Forgiveness comes at a price, and none among us is immune to sin," I returned back to him, shrugging my thin shoulders and holding his eyes steady in mine, such that more words would have communicated less.

The grin spread among the regulars until California Jim shook his head in mirth and extended the bottle to me. After ascertaining no Puritanical eyes were trained on us, I took the bottle, tipped it up, and let that familiar fire into my chest for the first time since donning these robes, and for a moment I was in my thirties again, and my forties, and the first part of my fifties, swimming in such a bottle as this, looking out at the world, distorted into abomination by the irregular glass, and my own failing eyes, and the syrupy quality of my thinking. And my guilt.

"Preacher!" Thomlinsen cheered, holding his own bottle up.

"Reverend!" Early Tate chimed in, grinning so wide I could see the dark blood between the cracks of his lips.

"Yellow and black," the former sheriff of Custer County continued, such that I had to picture this "hump," the skin pulled from his back and presumably his whole torso and possibly his legs and arms, his face painted half yellow, half black.

You can't guess at what an Indian does, though, much less the why of it. Maybe Franz Boas can, but I'm no Boas. If anything, I'm more Boethius, trapped in my cell on these northwesterly plains, scribbling my earnest inquiries into this log, with hopes of finally arriving at some greater truth.

"Had a little dab of red in the middle!" Early Tate added with a satisfied chuckle, relaxing back into the pew, which creaked with the weight of his pronouncement.

When I looked my inquiry over to him, he waggled his blunt, somewhat red tongue, prompting Thomlinsen to fall into a coughing fit meant to direct us elsewhere.

I had the scent, though, and could make the leap myself, being no tenderfoot.

"His tongue was removed?" I said, awe quieting my voice to a whisper.

"What would be the use of that?" Sall Bertram said back, which I took to be confirmation, and when California Jim made to drink openly from his bottle, the former sheriff stopped him. The message he intended was subtle, but loud enough in this newly spawned quiet. Though I had previously, momentarily, been one of them in the brotherhood of spirits, and of flaunting it in the light of day, now, at this juncture, I was alone again, no longer a drinking companion, never mind that the long pull I had elected to imbibe was still a warmth roiling in my chest, and coursing through my thoughts, making me consider the sacraments of the Eucharist I have unmonitored access to.

"Gentlemen," I said to them with as much thankfulness and respect and lack of challenge as I could, and proceeded on my way, pretending for their sake that I had only stopped at the lodging house by happenstance, to pay my toll, and was now continuing on to my original destination of the post office, as if I had anyone in the world who might want to send me a letter.

I'm starting my transcription here, pretty much, as this seems to be when things get interesting. I'm trying to solve a mystery, I mean: What happened to Arthur Beaucarne in 1912? I've struggled an entry ahead of the transcription above, so I know he had, or planned to have, a series of fantastical conversations with an Indian man known in Montana in the late nineteenth century as "The Fullblood," but I don't know yet if this is causation or merely correlation.

And, yes, tenure and promotion committee, I know that this is more a project for a history professor, or someone from Ethnic Studies, American Studies, maybe Philosophy and Religious Studies, even the English Department, but . . . are any of the scholars from those programs *related* to the subject? That's my hook, I'm fairly certain. That's the thing that's going to get this junior professor a book under contract, and position her on campus for a long and comfortable career.

Like my dad, yes.

Like him, too, I wore a mask and gloves and booties for my work, at least the first time, sitting on my couch, my nose inches from the flickering screen of my laptop, Taz My Cat—full name, there—curled on the cushion over my shoulder. I was holding my breath, too—I was making a connection with someone actually *in my blood*. Being the lone daughter of a father with no siblings, my family tree has been more struggling vine than anything branching into a generations-wide canopy, so finding this unexpected relative has been nothing short of wondrous. In order to feel closer to Arthur Beaucarne, I even went to campus and loaded up the special-use paper from the back of the supply cabinet, printed the scanned-in images on what feels for all the world like card stock.

Those stiff pages are currently spread out across the dining room and hallway of my apartment, so I can walk along my greatest-grandfather's last few weeks.

He was never found after his last entry, no, and I admit I'm nervous about getting that far and having to say goodbye to him, watch him recede into history.

Last night I stood on the balcony of my apartment and peered out into the glittering darkness, and I whispered his name, *Arthur Beaucarne*, and then I closed my eyes, imagined I was hearing the rustle of his thick black robes when he raised his head out there in the vast darkness, hearing me.

As for the ramp to get to the entries in his journal, which I probably would have already laid out were I a historian: in 1912, the *Miles City Star* was in its second year; Trinity Lutheran Church was in its sixth. Miles City itself had only been incorporated in 1887—two years before Montana itself became a state, and some thirty-five years after Custer County was named that, in memory of the Battle of the Little Bighorn. Though the buffalo were long gone from Eastern Montana by 1912, and from North America as a whole, the memory of them blanketing the Great Plains lived on.

It's 2012 now, as I write this. The anniversary of my greatest-grandfather's disappearance. I have Lutheran blood in me, surprise. I'd always thought my family must be French a few generations back, possibly some of those French who came down through Canada, to trap and trade furs, but lineage doesn't mean much, finally, does it?

As for myself, which I should have said at the top of this document: I'm Etsy Beaucarne. Single, white, forty-two. I live on the second floor of an apartment complex where I sometimes see students from my freshman courses on the stairs, and my main source of conversation is my cat, Taz. It's short for "Tasmanian Devil," a cartoon character from my youth who was a force of chaos and destruction. You'd have to see the arms of my couch and the lower portions of the

drapes over my sliding glass door and the apron of my bed to understand why I named him that.

I love Taz like you love an only cat, though. We've been through
the fire of grad school together, through two live-in boyfriends, and
I've bathed him in the kitchen sink when he comes home with his
ears torn and his coat matted with blood.

But he means well. His gifts show his true heart, don't they? The
dead birds left on the kitchen floor, which he expects me to cheer for.
The mice he deposits outside the bathroom door—always there, I
don't know why. Because it's "the mouse place," I guess. Twice, now,
there have been moles, one of them still halfway alive, and suddenly
wriggling in bed with me. Most recently—and most out of place—a
prairie dog, this one completely alive.

Coming in from campus with that stack of printed-up journal
pages—so much heavier than I anticipated—I rounded the tall rub-
ber plant opposite the front door, deposited my shoulder bag on the
couch, and stepped into the hall, which is when we saw each other,
this prairie dog and I. He was a small form framed in the doorway of
my bedroom, mired in shadow, but I have to suspect I was as well, my
giant form blotting out the overhead light.

Slowly, this prairie dog stood up onto its hind legs and considered me, tasting my scent on the air, and then it charged down the
hall in its dromedary way, its yellowy, protuberant incisors meant
only for seeds and stalks, the rational part of me knew, but this wasn't
a rational moment.

I yipped, stepped neatly up onto the couch, and hugged a throw
pillow to my chest, but this prairie dog never crashed out into the
living room. After what felt like an hour but was probably two minutes, I gingerly stepped off the couch, still clutching that pillow, and
peered down the hall.

It was empty.

"Taz?" I called.

He didn't come, even when I broached into the kitchen, used the electric can opener on his food, a grinding sound he can't resist.

Two hours later, he thumped onto the balcony in his usual way, as if dropped from a low-flying blimp, and pushed his head through the cat door to look around like always, as if confirming this was the right apartment.

"There you are," I told him, and he slinked in.

He was, this time, coated in what I took to be antifreeze, about which I knew not to even ask. After he kindly left radioactive footprints on some of the journal pages, which were in their first configuration on the couch, I took him to the kitchen sink, got the good Dawn soap, and lathered him up against his will.

"I found what you left me," I murmured to him, scrubbing his coat clean, and for a moment I didn't want, my back straightened, because the floor had creaked behind me, exactly as if Arthur Beaucarne had heard me just thank him for what *he* left me—his journal— and had decided to step out of the ether, start mumbling a prayer in some dead tongue.

I didn't look around, though. You can't look around, every time you think you're not alone.

Once you start, you never stop.

Instead I'm just going to huddle here over my laptop, burn my eyes out trying to make sense of hundred-year-old script so light it's hardly there, and type it in after this the best I can, for however long it takes.

Here goes.

The Absolution of Three-Persons

March 31, 1912

He was there again today, the Indian gentleman.

This is only his second Sunday to attend, but in a congregation as tight knit as mine, I find a face I don't know out in the chapel to be . . . not worrisome, I should think of it as a gift, as another chance to fulfill a missionary's duty, and thereby inch myself that much closer to redemption. But his presence is disconcerting—— through no fault of the Indian's own. It's as if he's a face from either the past or my past, it's hard to decide which he might unintentionally represent.

Through the whole of my sermon, I longed to lob a pebble to his isolated pew at the back, to see if he would snatch that pebble from the air at the last moment, and then hold it in his lap for the rest of the service, worrying it between his fingers. And I would follow that pebble's journey further as well, to see if he let it fall alongside his right leg as he exited. Or maybe I would even follow him to wherever he's found or made lodging, to see if he examines that pebble by firelight, and perhaps slips it into the medicine pouch all of his breed carry on their person, close to their skin.

I would like to have that between us, I think. I would like to be part of the secret totem beneath his shirt, held close and important to his chest forevermore.

As for this Indian's appearance, well, he's Indian. The red skin, the broad face and wide nose, the hatchet cheekbones, that grim slash of a downturned mouth. A distinct amusement to his eyes about our proceedings in this house of worship, but a harsh, embattled cast to his face as well, speaking of many trials and tribulations, much hardship and loss. His hair is long and oily and black, suggesting he's not a product of Jesuit school, which is in contrast to the floor length black clerical robe he wears, about whose provenance I won't even hazard a guess, as it may involve some Man of the Cloth's remains moldering in a gulch.

As for his intention with arraying himself in this raiment, I have to think it's easily explainable. Surely, in wanting to come to a white man's church, this Indian gentleman thought it vital to attire himself after the same fashion he has to have seen white men going to church in. A failure to understand the hierarchy in these church walls, where the man behind the pulpit and he alone dresses suchly, is beneath having to excuse. Instead, I take this mimicry as the highest honor, and I'm thankful for the childlike innocence with which it's delivered——let the little children come to me, yes.

However, that robe is the only thing childlike about this Indian. While it's difficult to hypothesize the age of someone whose kind I'm not intimately associated with, I would put this gentlemen between his early thirties or late forties——well past the age where he would have been part of a raiding party in decades past, when such things were yet occurring, but, at the same time, he's perhaps older than individuals of his race usually make it to. I detect no silver in his hair as of yet, but I also know that the grey comes late among his people.

And, it's beneath saying, but the Indian's face is cleaned to shining, beardless and not mustachioed, and his hair, though long and heavy, is drawn back, which I take as a token of respect, as when a cur pastes its ears back along its skull in hopes of passing without drawing a kick or harsh word.

This is as well as I can draw him in the pages of this newest volume of my phrenic peregrinations. His bearing and posture this Sunday was the same as last, I should add——shoulders square, spine straight. I was initially discomfited with how his eyes tracked my every movement, as if I were one of his wags-his-tails, which I understand is his people's word for "deer," though of the big eared variety or the smaller variety with that white flag of a tail, I can't yet ascertain. But of course, his watching me like a deer he would roast on a spit actually makes perfect sense. Presumably familiar with enough English to accomplish simple commerce, he must be mystified by the Vater tongue I deliver my sermons with. His attentiveness, therefore, is but evidence of the concentration he trains on my words.

When everyone else reached for one of our few hymnals, he plucked one up as well, a strange flower to him, not understanding that the tome he held before him for the singing portion of the service was in fact a Bible——more evidence of his lack of formal education. Rather, he was surely educated in the Edenic hinterlands, where he can read the fowl and the fauna more closely than I can the very Scripture.

More interesting than his looks or comportment, though, are his reasons for attending my service. Is he hoping to suspend a delicate bridge from his people to mine, and so foster a unity where there's only been decades of division? Did he, in his youth, see a wagon train assembled before a Man of the Cloth, and wonder about the power wielded by that man at the front of the congregation? Has he heard tell of the white man's religion, and wants to see where it might line up with his inborn one?

Now that we've shared private and extended discussion over things so fabulous as to themselves be fables, I can speak better as to his reasoning, his reasons, but, reciting my service that first and this Sunday, I confess to having been mainly agitated about whether or not he was only here for a meal. If so, he would have had to make do with a thin white wafer. I'm ashamed to say that, during the Eucharist, I positioned myself so as to observe him. But, both Sundays, he limited himself to but a single wafer, glaring against his dark skin, that hand rising to his mouth and then coming back down, his eyes holding mine the entire time, as if to prove to me that the holy sacrament wouldn't smoke on his pagan tongue.

I would have allowed him more and of more substantialness, of course, had he but asked or made his hunger known. Had he stayed after that first service, I would have led him to my parsonage and broken bread with him——not Mrs. Grandlin's, that wasn't to me yet. But, had he been there upon its arrival, then we surely would have shared in that repast. I may be gluttonous in private, but in fellowship, I hope to set a better example.

When I would have extended such fellowship to him last Sunday, however, he stood with the rest of the congregation, holding my eyes across the congregants' as yet hatless heads, and I felt for all the world as if he had been there to judge me. Were I speaking to myself as I speak to my parishioners, I might portend that those who fear the presence of a judge may very well be carrying a secret burden of guilt they hope to unload. Yet, to be judged by an Indian, here in the new century? To have this twentieth century called to task by its predecessor?

Your fantasies know no limit, do they, old man? Leave anyone too long alone with his own thoughts, and every possibility will be not only explored, but poked and prodded until it raises its shaggy head, settles its lidless eyes on you. Such is the price of isolation, and that mulling that never ceases. Though of a different order, I feel I'm nevertheless a monk in his bare cell, with only a quill and scroll to converse with.

After this afternoon's proceedings, I suppose I now have this Indian to converse with as well, if I'm willing to lean in closely enough to hear his subdued voice.

But I was documenting his first appearance last week, which I neglected to write about that Sunday, I think due to my dim hope that he was but an aberration in my weekly routine, not worthy of committing ink to.

And even still I explore the fullness of language and distraction in the recounting, instead of daring to look directly at this Indian. But my ink pot is full, this candle is as yet tall, my back doesn't hurt too much yet, my nerves seem intent on continuing to twitch this nib across these evenly lined pages, and no one is immediately waiting for me to save their soul, so, what harm can there be? "Soldier on, Pastorbrotherman," the men on the porch at the lodging house might urge me.

It's to them I ascribe blame for the chalice of communion wine half in and half out of this candlelight. But, better it not turn to vinegar. That would be the actual pity.

This Indian, however, whom I know I need to find the strength to look directly at, at least on this unblinking page.

That first Sunday of his attendance, upon the service's conclusion, the Spirit moving through the congregation in a way that always fills my chest, he rose with a quickness that aged him down a full decade. Though when I would have forded the bodies to hold his brown hands in mine and look meaningfully into his eyes, he turned neatly away, lowering his face into the peculiar darkened spectacles I've seen travelers on the train platform wearing, to look directly into the endlessly bright sky.

He did look back once, confirming the pursuit he seemed to expect, his wildborne instinct keenly aware of such things, but by the time I reached the back of the chapel in my limping manner, this

Indian gentleman was striding away into the daylight, his Jesuit robe swinging around his long, purposeful strides, his hands tucked into the cuff opposite themselves, the dogs of Sunday morning giving him wide berth, which is the first time I've seen such a phenomenon in my time in Miles City. But surely it's the bear grease in his hair that forces them to keep their distance, or the scent of tragedy on his skin, or that he was keeping to the shaded side of the street, where the warmth isn't. Or maybe, not seeing his eyes, they don't know if he watches them or not, so can't guess his next sudden movement, can't anticipate his intentions. To them, he's a berobed, glassy eyed creature whose predilections are yet a mystery.

Over the intervening week, I convinced myself that in a place this far west, I should steel myself for visitors such as him, and not make of his presence anything portentous.

His sullen presence at the back of my church was a solitary event, I assured myself, a random occurrence. It tokened nothing.

But then, this morning at Service, he was back again.

When he stepped in at the last moment and settled himself into the last pew at the back and sat upon the aisle like a station his own, so there was no one between himself and me, I admit I lost my place halfway into the recitement of Our Father, which I know now as well as I know the contours of the roof my mouth.

Such is weakness. Such is blasphemy.

My penance will be long and just, I know. And it starts late in my life, with, I can tell now, this Indian gentleman, which I know is probably the first time one of his race has been referred to as such in ink.

This time, instead of staring into his darkened spectacles and folding himself into the busyness of the Sunday afternoon bustle, he remained in his seat while the congregation filed past, the women giving him wide berth, the men's eyes hardening upon realizing this relic they'd evidently been sharing worship with. Some of them, I know, as yet harbor memories of stock slaughtered, of horses stolen in the night, of women foully mistreated, children snatched away to have their pasts erased, replaced with a wildness they would use to fight their own kind when given the slightest chance.

But there was violence done on both sides, I would tell my parishioners consolingly. And there's the Lord's forgiveness, to wash all that away, start anew, so we can step together into this new century, absolved of the past, never mind what bloody footprints our boots yet leave. Walk far enough away from the scene of that violence, and your boots are like unto your neighbor's, shriven clean and born again.

As is my custom at the cessation of a Sunday service, I stepped out of my station as pastor, became an usher for everyone wading out into the bright sunlight, which is of course just a shepherd of different variety. And then I was alone in the dark, empty chapel with this Indian gentleman.

His stillness was offputting, if I'm to be strictly honest.

So as not to scare him away with interrogation or attention, I set to tidying the pews, my eyes flicking periodically to him. Usually I'm wont to hum with this task, so as to allay the oppressive silence, but in deference, I practiced restraint.

Did I think he was going to rise up, bury a stone tomahawk in my back? What I didn't expect was for him to finally say it, and in clear English, his voice exactly as deep as I was expecting in my heart: "Father."

I stilled my nerves, stood from the pew at the front I was currently pretending to straighten, then straighten again, and turned to him, my fingertips holding each other at my waist, my posture more pensive than a man of my years and station should adopt, but you can't always make yourself stand as you want.

"Pastor," I corrected him, attempting to strip the schoolmarm from my voice.

The Indian gentleman nodded once, accepting "Pastor" without question, but then he looked up to me about it, his eyes glittering with something, and said, as if correcting a mis-statement, "Three-Persons."

"Three Persons?" I asked back, about myself.

"Father, Son, Creator," he said, enumerating with his long brown fingers.

I didn't correct his conception of the Trinity.

"Do you mind, Three-Persons?" he asked then, holding his dark spectacles out between us, proffering both them and this new and complimentary appellation for a simple pastor. I let the name settle around me like a mantle, then commenced to prizing into what he might mean with these dark spectacles. When I could get no mental purchase——did he want me to polish them?——he clarified with, "This . . . the brightness in here." He moved his fingers back and forth by his temple, by his right eye, to mime the brightness so troubling him.

I looked around at the chapel I keep intentionally dark, so as to stymie conversation and focus attention to the front. I can't always direct the inner lives of my flock, but I can, in such small and indirect ways, control the bearing of their exterior selves. In quietness begins devotion, does it not?

"Of course not," I said in reply to the Indian gentleman, and stepped two pews closer, my hands still clasped in front of me.

He lowered his face into the dark spectacles and looked up at me through them, and I have to imagine that, to him, in the darkness of the chapel, I was but a shadow.

"I have an illness," he explained to me, tapping the side of his spectacles, and I nodded, stepped two pews closer.

"I knew a miner in Missouri who couldn't tolerate being indoors," I said in my gentlest, most understanding tone. "Not since the roof over a vein he was working collapsed in on him and his fellow workers."

"Like a big-mouth who wants for water but barks at it instead of drinking," the Indian gentleman said, as if to establish for me that we were, in fact, in communication.

"A . . . 'big-mouth'?" I was compelled to ask, however.

The Indian gentleman bored his gaze into a point above my shoulder, then nodded, seemingly to himself, and corrected with, "Wolf, as you would say it."

"Ah, a mad wolf, you mean," I said, taking the olive branch he would extend. As if talking to a child, I mimed foam coming from my lips.

The Indian gentleman grinned slightly to see me do this, looked away so as to let me preserve my dignity, and said, "Not the Mad Wolf I knew, no. Mad Wolf was Hard Topknot in my youth, who always stayed back during a horse raid, until his sits-beside-him wife finally walked away from him, telling the rest of the band that if she were a fine horse, he wouldn't have the nerve to follow her, lead her back to his lodge." The Indian gentleman grinned in a small way to be relaying this, suggesting it was a sort of running joke. "She was right," he added, which was perhaps the part in this retelling where those of his breed gathered around the fire in one of their tipis would nod and chuckle to themselves as one.

And I confess here that, while what he relayed to me held interest, what was even more fascinating were his ancient terms, only barely translated for me. "Sits-beside-him wife," "big-mouth" and their coyote brethren the "little big-mouths"——it's all so rational and easy, so descriptive and childlike. Over the course of our afternoon, this ancient language would pile up and up like a mountain of buffalo skulls——pardon, "blackhorn" skulls.

"Real-bear."

"Long-legs."

"Coldmaker."

"Sticky-mouth."

This last one I take from context to be not quite a bear but more than a weasel, perhaps with a mouth characterized by saliva?

Regardless, I hope to preserve these peculiarities on the page as best I can, as this may be their last uttering, the Indian gentleman's kind walking into the sunset of their day.

"So what brings you here today?" I asked him then, to prove to him that we were communicating clearly enough that I could sense he had more to say.

The way he, in response, stared past me, his head moving back and forward ever so slightly, as if he were on the deck of a steamboat in calm water, was, I believe, evocative of the difference in our two peoples. In his lodges and around his kind's fires, each word and each answer is surely considered before being spoken, so as to not utter anything unnecessary. To one who often listens to himself at the pulpit and wonders who it is speaking, and what it is he's saying now, this is a thing uncommon indeed.

As a pastor with some experience listening to his flock, however, I know I need must comport myself in these conversations by his guidelines and needs, lest he become impatient and remove himself back to his own people, denying himself the grace of God which I would so willingly share, and instruct him toward.

"What brings me here today," he repeated in the lips shut way he speaks, as if this question were a knot too complicated to loosen with a mere reply.

Behind his dark spectacles, his eyes closed tightly, I could tell, and I was able to study his face more closely than that view afforded me from the pulpit. I could tell now that his face and cheeks and jaw, while scrubbed to shining, were in fact pitted, telling of some encounter with the pox, in which he surely writhed for days in a flea ridden buffalo robe, some medicine man chanting and drumming over him and wafting various smokes, never knowing how useless those ancient practices were for this modern affliction.

When the Indian gentleman's eyes opened again, I let mine slide to the side, to give the lie that I hadn't been taking the opportunity to stare like a child.

He was as yet blinking from the brightness, however.

"Here," I said, and rushed around the chapel, pinching the few wicks out and carrying back the lone remaining candle, but being sure to place it far enough from us that it was less than the coals after a fire on a dark night, lending but the slightest underglow to our faces, the shadows of the hands I clasped between my knees probably exaggerated on the unpainted ceiling above us, but I dared not look.

"Thank you, thank you," the Indian gentleman said, pulling the spectacles from his face ear by ear, which required more head movement than I would have anticipated, the legs or arms of those spectacles being hooked nearly into circles at the back.

The spectacles folded neatly into one of his sleeves, which made me wonder what else he might have hidden up there.

"What I wish is to confess, Three-Persons," he said at last, holding my eyes in his, and, this being the first time I was seeing his eyes at this near proximity, I found myself mesmerized, like unto he held some animalistic sway over me. As I'd seen from afar, his eyes were inky, undifferentiated black, but the middlemost parts, usually a dot not dissimilar to a large period, were engorged as I'd only seen before in the dead and eternally resting.

Of course he needed it dark for his confession.

"You don't have a box we can sit in?" the Indian gentleman asked then, squinting around the chapel for the confessional booth. Then he corrected himself with, "A wooden closet we can speak in through the——the . . . ?"

He held his hands out in a plane between us, fingers spread across each other to simulate a series of chinks or holes, such that I knew he'd seen the latticework Catholic confessionals have.

"This is a Lutheran house of worship," I said as delicately as I could, as presuming him to know the varieties of the Christian faith would be uncharitable of me——and this on a day I'd just delivered a sermon about the Samaritan. "But yes, after reading the Commandments, we can go to the altar rail and . . ."

I swept my arm to the front of the church to show where I meant.

"You can unburden yourself there, if you so desire," I assured him, sensing either reluctance or a failure to comprehend——which, I couldn't tell.

"Can we do it here?" he said, staring at the floor between his polished black boots, which I could see now that his Jesuit robe had ridden up his lower leg from having been seated for so long. The boots were, unless I mistake them, of the cavalry variety, from when the cavalry was more needed. It put me in mind of the days when Indians would dress themselves up in the finery of their victims, both male and female.

I settled into the pew in front of him and to the side a bit, turning to lean a single arm over my backrest and thus indirectly face him, so as to not threaten this penitent with proximity, or challenge him, thus, in the limited way available, creating the privacy of the confessional booth.

"Of course, of course," I said. "What do I call you?" I asked then.

He nodded as if agreeing that this, indeed, was the place to start.

"In my youth I was Weasel Plume," he said. "As a man, I was Good Stab. I was a Small Robe."

"A small robe?" I asked, my words jumping the gate.

"My band," he said. "The Small Robes are a band of the Amskapi Pikuni."

He flashed his eyes up to me, to see how I was taking this, but hopefully not seeing deeply enough to know how I would, hours later, be spelling it, or failing to. However, I know what he was actually looking for. It was whether I recognized the name of his people.

I did, and do.

Though this is Miles City, the Pikuni, well north and west of us, are still well remembered.

"Glacier Park Indians," I said, that national land as yet less than two years old but the adjacent Indians already stationed in public lodges around and among it, as emblems of how these western environs were in their natural state.

The Indian gentleman nodded, the almost grin on his face suggesting what he thought of this designation for his people.

"Blackfeet," I said then, lower and more meaningfully, like a secret between us.

"Blackfeet," he repeated, nodding once as if accepting the burden of this name.

"Good Stab," I said then, our talk now a rock beginning to gather speed on its roll down the hill. "But your phrasing suggests this name, like your childhood one, is also behind you?"

The Indian gentleman looked away again, perhaps working through my words. I reminded myself to use simpler diction from there onward.

"Now my people call me Takes No Scalps or The Fullblood," he said, and the desultory, aggrieved manner in which he delivered this pronouncement spoke of the pain associated with, as I took it, the first of these two names, which, if my time shepherding a flock has taught me anything, had to be the source and cause of his visit to my church.

"Is that what you wish me to call you?" I asked.

He chewed the cud of this question for longer than I would have deemed necessary, long enough for me to register the anomaly of an Indian garnering a third and even fourth name, which must betoken special circumstances indeed.

"No one calls me either of those," he finally said. "They're just what I am."

"A full blood."

"It doesn't mean what you think it means."

"And one who takes no scalps."

He nodded a noncommittal nod.

"You must have earned that one by extending mercy and compassion," I said, my own scalp tingling under what hair I have left.

This caused him to chuckle, and press his lips together.

"Mercy and compassion," he repeated. "If that's what you would call it."

"Either way, the time for scalping is well behind us," I said. "This is a new day, is it not?" I lifted my arms, enveloping the whole grand chapel, and the civilized town beyond it.

"Or it's a single, long night," he said, looking the other way from the flickering candle, which I perceived was possibly still causing him slight injury.

I needed to be able to see his face, though. I needed to be able to ascertain where he was in relation to me. Anyone in close quarters with a savage would feel the same, I warrant.

"I don't expect you to believe my story at first," he said.

"I've earned this white hair," I said back to him. "I've heard a lot in my time, Good Stab, if I can call you that. Pastors are hard to surprise." When he was just looking at me about this, I added, "Hard to surprise, and slow to judge."

"I fast every month," he said then, the abruptness of this combining with his intonation to suggest that he was beginning to begin. "I fast every month, in hopes Sun Chief will take me back. In hopes of walking among the Small Robes again, what of them are left. Yet . . . yet I walk alone."

"Taking no scalps," I completed for him.

He looked up to me about this, and held my eyes with more directness than was easy for one such of my benign nature, inclined to peace.

"Taking no scalps, yes," he said at last, easing the tension some-what.

But not completely.

I believe this to be a hallmark of our conversations, which I put in the plural as he tells me he'll be back next Sunday, and the one after that, and on and on until his confession is told in full, and his great crime is revealed, whatsoever it be.

Such is the burden of the clergy.

The burden and the gift.

I submit willingly, O God. I am but Your servant in this and all things. With Your guidance, I can endure this and more, for Sundays eternal.

And, because I knew this new state when it was but a territory, and have comported with Indians before around fires and even twice in a smoky lodge of a kind that won't be seen again, the wind and snow howling outside in a way we see too much of here in the state of Montana, I knew what I had to say next in ceremonial fashion, to invite him to begin with his story.

"I listen with a good heart."

Good Stab looked up to me briskly upon hearing this, a joyful shine to his eyes, and I nodded the truth of my statement, and so he began.

The Nachzehrer's
Dark Gospel

March 31, 1912

I was born the year the stars fell. My father was Wolf Calf of the Black-Patched Moccasins, who was born at the end of the dog days and lived all the way through Starvation Winter but not as long as the Sweet Grass Hills Treaty or the Ceded Strip one, and my mother was Curly Hair Woman of the Small Robes, who had been taken from the Snakes as a child, and was my father's third and youngest wife. She died when I was born. I used to tell myself that, through the smoke-hole of the birthing lodge, she was seeing those long bright streaks in the sky that I only saw in Otter Goes Back's winter count, when he would unroll it every year and explain to us all the years before, his voice going up and down with them like a buffalo runner racing across the hills, faster and faster.

The last time I saw that winter count, a girl and her little brother were holding it above them to try to keep the freezing rain off, and, because I was an enemy to them, the girl was holding her hand tight around a long knife, not because that could have worked against me, but because she was Pikuni, and Pikuni fight even when the fight's over. That's why your Great Father still hasn't been able to stamp us all out like he wants, no matter how many soldiers he sends.

Also in that same year on Otter Goes Back's winter count was Spotted Elk getting his fancy uniform from the American generals, that started the bad times with the Kainais. This was before the Medicine Line cut the soldiers but not us off from the Real Old Man Country.

I was in my fourth winter when the white scabs came for us the second time, when we should have hidden from it in the mountains like the Crow. That's what these scars are from. They mean I lived. I was fourteen winters when so many of the Pikuni got baptized by one of you Black Robes, but I wasn't in Big River for that. I was sick from drinking whitehorn milk at the fort. My father had warned me not to, but I did it anyway. I was twenty two winters by the time of Lame Bull's Treaty on Yellow River that gave us our hunting grounds for ninety nine years, which still aren't over. This is right after the dry time when we had to eat dogs. I had two wives and two daughters and a son during these years, a full lodge, but they were all sent to the Sandhills at the same time from a raid by the Black Paint People. We made them cry for that, and never let them hunt Three Forks again, when there were still blackhorns there. Now they can hunt there all they want.

The next time the white scabs came for the Pikuni was the same winter the soldiers shot our elders and children sick in their lodges, but I wasn't in Heavy Runner's camp on the Bear River that morning, and I wasn't in Mountain Chief's camp either, which is who the soldiers were looking for. I was up in the Backbone of the World, dragging an iron cage to Ninastako, the Great Chief, Chief Mountain, which is so high that I still look for it from all the way down here. Or, I feel it watching me, which is how all Pikuni feel.

I can see your lips counting that I'm now nearly eighty winters, and I can also see that you don't believe this.

You will.

But first you need to know that this all starts with Owl Child, the Pikuni who killed the napikwan rancher Four Bears, who is Malcolm Clarke to you. He was married to Cutting-off-head Woman, who was Owl Child's family. Before that, it starts with the trappers and the traders and the whiskey and the smoke-boats and the wagons and the whitehorns and the many-shots guns full of greased-shooters. But the story I tell you now with Owl Child killing Four Bears with an axe in the forehead is where all of that left us, and it's where what I'm telling you starts, with soldiers getting sent out to find Owl Child at Mountain Chief's winter camp on the Bear, to put the axe back in his head.

Most of the soldiers went there following Joe Kipp and the other scout Joe Cobell, who pointed the cavalry's many-shots guns down at the wrong camp.

Most of the soldiers, not all of them.

Already Owl Child and the warriors riding with him, Black Weasel and Bear Chief and Fast Horse and Eagle's Rib and the others, had kept staying ahead of the soldiers, because the soldiers move all together at once, meaning their smoke and their sound of hooves and also their smell announce them a day or two before they get anywhere. Keeping ahead of the soldiers is like staying ahead of an old wagon with iron spoons hanging all over it.

But one of the napikwan war chiefs figured out that their soldiers were loud like that and couldn't sneak up on us. So, when the big group of loud, smelly, drunk soldiers went to the Bear, they knew Owl Child was going to have already left Mountain Chief's camp ahead of them. And, whenever a Pikuni needs to get away from the Long Knives, which is what my father called your soldiers, where do they run?

The Backbone, what you now call Glacier, from the ice-rivers high up there. The Pikuni's holy place. It's where Chief Mountain is, taller than Ear Mountain and Heavy Shield and Feather Mountain.

Taller than them all. Someday the Great White God will appear at the top of Great Chief and then it will crumble. So it's told.

This is what I tell you so you can understand where the people were that day. Mountain Chief and Heavy Runner were on the Bear in different but close camps, the big group of soldiers were coming up to them behind the two scouts, and I was up in the Backbone with Tall Dog and Hunts-to-the-Side and the old man Peasy. Hunts-to-the-Side and Peasy were All Crazy Dogs, Kunnutsomitaks, which is like your police. They had asked Tall Dog and me if we would help them do a thing.

Tall Dog's wife had left him to be part of Lone Bear's lodge, and since then the two of us had hunted together. We were just coming back to camp with a prairie-runner. Tall Dog had told me a trick for hunting them where we didn't even need a round-ball gun or a many-shots gun, which was good, since we didn't have either of those. I had a many-shots gun until the summer before, when I had let the boy White Teeth carry it around camp, but he'd put the wrong size greased-shooter in it. When it exploded in his hands he lost three fingers and his mother Last Stand slapped me across the face and told me I was nothing, that it was my fault, and she was right, so for all of winter I left my best cuts of meat for them, and for many nights I held the sharp edge of my knife against my own fingers like this, nodding to myself to do it, but never doing it.

A dream I used to have back then was of White Teeth's three fingers on the ground in the Sandhills ahead of him, and a dog trotting over, sniffing them, looking around, then eating them down. I don't know if that's how it works there, but that dream never came again. Maybe if I ever get to the Sandhills, then I'll know.

The trick Tall Dog knew for getting prairie-runners, he'd learned it from watching some Crows hunt once, from a high place he'd climbed to look for blackhorns. That the trick was Crow already made me not want to use it, since if you hunt like a Crow you might be a Crow, and start scouting for the soldiers, but camp was hungry. And it was a good trick. Prairie-runners are fast, not even a pack of big-mouths working together can catch them if there's enough room to run, so they don't even try, or they only try for fun, when they want to run and laugh, but now we had one, and there were just two of us, and no gun, and we felt like laughing too.

We were riding back into camp when Peasy looked up to us from the bowstring he was working in and out of the eye socket of a black-horn skull, and the way he looked up I could tell he'd been waiting for us. Tall Dog felt it too, I could tell from the way he slumped in his saddle, and looked everywhere but back to Peasy.

We sectioned that prairie-runner up, left it at two different lodges, packed some pemmican and one robe each, and set off with Peasy and Hunts-to-the-Side like so many times before, but if I'd known what was going to happen, I would have at least looked behind me to see camp one last time. The way the smoke curled up into the grey sky from each lodge. The dogs fighting over scraps, but their tails wagging while they fought. The two girls and one boy trying to throw an arrow through a hoop they were rolling across the crusted snow. The iron kettles hanging over fires, real-meat and turnips boiling in them. The woman whose name I can't remember coming up from the creek with a skin of water, her eyes set, lips shut, but she was hum-ming too. I think she was humming, but I don't know what. The day rider who might even have been White Teeth plodding in on his pony for a bowl of something warm. And the girl whose arrow finally went through that hoop, and how she fell to her knees and held her hands above her head and yipped and whooped until the other boy and girl tackled her into the snow, their tails wagging just like the dogs'.

But I didn't know to turn my horse to the side and watch for as long as I could, I thought it would never end, would always be the same, so all I have instead are hundreds of other days I have to steal that day rider from, and that woman carrying water, and those children, the dogs.

I've watched some of you napikwan at night around your camps, and I know you carry stacks of little paper cards with you, to lay out and study, trade back and forth, fight and laugh over. I've sneaked into camp when everyone's sleeping and studied those cards, laid them out in all different orders, but there's just marks and squiggles on them, not a woman carrying water, not a girl finally throwing an arrow through a hoop.

Those are what I carry on the cards I keep inside, that I lay out before me every night and study like I can go back if I look hard enough, if I remember it down to each flake of snow, each curl of smoke, each black hair lifting from each cheek in the wind.

But I can't see it that close anymore. There's something in the way, and I think it's all the bodies I've left behind over the years, which is why I'm here talking to you, so you can help me roll them out of the way at last, one especially.

So, I'm on my best horse that day, I'm behind Tall Dog, whose big horse made mine look like a pony, and we're riding away from camp with Peasy and Hunts-to-the-Side. I have my steel knife, my war club just in case, my parfleche and tobacco pouch, my short pipe, one robe already wrapped around my shoulders, and my eyes are slitted down like this because I'm already looking ahead, for how I can turn whatever we're doing into somehow getting a many-shots gun again. It was all I was thinking of. If I had one, I wouldn't have to use Crow tricks to hunt, and I could stay Pikuni in my heart.

It had been a good trick to get that prairie-runner, though. Still, ever since that day, I've only ever used it once, and I'm probably the only one left living who remembers it.

"Where?" Tall Dog called ahead to Peasy.

Peasy was wearing the same napikwan hat he always did, that

was tall like a chimney pipe and black like his horse, with hardly a brim at all. He said it was a target for enemies to shoot at, that it was good medicine, that it kept him alive, and he had lived longer than most, so he had to be right.

To answer Tall Dog, he pointed with his lips in the direction we were already going, and Tall Dog just shook his head and didn't laugh. Peasy needed us, but that didn't mean we were worth telling anything to.

"Wagon-road," Hunts-to-the-Side said in his deep voice without turning around to say it, so we could both understand what an insult it was that we didn't already know, just from being Pikuni.

Tall Dog and me nodded, knew not to ask more. The wagon-road to the south wasn't even a full day's ride. This meant that, by the next night, we might be back in camp.

Later on in the ride, when our order in line changed from going across a creek, Hunts-to-the-Side explained that a wagon train had been attacked, and we needed to get to it before any other wagons found it, to hide it so the soldiers wouldn't be even more angry with us than they already were.

"Owl Child?" Tall Dog asked, because he had done a lot more than just kill Four Bears, and was still out there doing it.

Hunts-to-the-Side shrugged and Peasy just snickered, tore a piece of pemmican off and chewed it.

I tell you this so you can understand why we ended up in the Backbone. The part of the wagon-road we were headed to wasn't there, was east of your Fort Lewis before it turns south. If that wagon train had been burned a day or two days after the turn south, then Peasy and Hunts-to-the-Side wouldn't have taken Tall Dog and me there to hide it, because then it could have been any Indians who did it, not just the Pikuni. But because it was so close, it fell to us to take care of it.

It wasn't the first time we'd had to do this. For four winters, since

Little Dog and one of his sons got shot by a group of napikwans for returning stolen horses, Peasy and Hunts-to-the-Side had been taking Tall Dog and me out to clean up wagons and bodies, and chase the leftover horses south, even though we could have used them. Peasy and Hunts-to-the-Side took us and no one else because we had no one waiting in our lodges for us, and that was good that he took us to do these things. It was right. But I think often of if that wagon train had been attacked just a day's ride farther out, even.

If it had, then I don't stay this many winters you see on me now.

I sometimes think the blackhorns were the ones who burned that wagon train, really. Because they needed a Pikuni like me. I finally couldn't stop what was going to happen to them from happening, what I didn't know then was going to happen to the herds, but I could make the hide-hunters cry for it. One at a time, sometimes in clumps of five or eight, and once even more than twenty five in a single night, because that's all there was.

But that's later. This is now, and I'm here after all of it, so you know it happened as I say it did.

Tall Dog and me are riding straight behind Peasy, who's behind Hunts-to-the-Side. With the snow like it was in the moon when jackrabbits whistle, our trail through it could be two riders or eight. A Pikuni could tell how many we really were, and Joe Kipp and Joe Cobell probably could too, the same way they knew Mountain Chief's camp from Heavy Runner's, but if a soldier found our hoofprints in the snow, he probably wouldn't look long enough to know how many we were.

We didn't know if there would be any soldiers moving around, but we were careful anyway.

We also didn't know that the napikwan war chiefs had sent a smaller group of twenty soldiers ahead of and to the west of the Bear, to be waiting for Owl Child when he made his escape ahead of the bigger group.

It's something our war chiefs would have done.

That smaller group of soldiers went too far, though. Instead of waiting on the big hill by Two Medicine, where they could see a rider coming from any direction, they went higher and farther, up into the trees, probably to stay out of the wind, since Coldmaker was making it blow that day. Or maybe it was so they could have firewood when they made camp, since dead wood burns hotter than blackhorn dung.

The reason for them taking to the trees doesn't matter. What does matter is that those trees are on the long slope leading up to the Great Chief.

Way down below them, we were just finding the wagon train. We found it from the smoke in the sky.

"Who told you about it?" I asked.

"Doesn't matter," Peasy said back, which I knew meant that it did matter.

There were three fire blacked wagons. Two of them were over on their side, smoldering, and one was on its wheels, hadn't caught fire. The two on their side hadn't been turned over by Indians, but to be shields. The six big-ears that had been pulling the wagons were all dead, shot by their drivers to hide behind too, it looked like. It didn't save them.

Thirty paces out from the wagons, my horse shied away from a dead napikwan in the snow, and when I looked down, I shied away too.

This dead napikwan was dressed almost like a Pikuni, in moccasins and leggings, but he also had a long blue soldier jacket on, with big brass buttons I wanted but knew Hunts-from-the-Side wouldn't let me keep, since they would tie us to this.

"Hold!" Peasy called out, and nodded to Tall Dog to go in alone.

Tall Dog handed his reins to me and stepped out into the snow and wagons and dead people, moving slow like a ground-deer, which is a many-legs to you, making its webs in corners and between stalks of grass. Of the four of us, Tall Dog was the best at putting together what had happened just from the tracks. The reason I was never as good was that I was always looking up to the sky, for the birds and the clouds if Sun Chief wasn't in his lodge, or the Seven Persons or the Poor Boys if it was already night. My father used to tell me that I needed to pay attention to where I was instead of looking farther away than I could see, and I know he was right, but knowing and doing aren't the same thing.

Sitting on our horses, waiting for Tall Dog to tell us what had happened, Hunts-to-the-Side made a disgusted noise about the deep ruts the wagon wheels were cutting into the ground. He wrinkled his nose and turned away to see something better.

I didn't know why it made him so mad. The cuts in the ground weren't wide enough to break a horse's leg. But I didn't say anything, watched the edge of the trees instead, for if a soldier was going to stand up and start shooting at us. I was always looking up at the sky like I said, but I was always looking for traps, too.

When Tall Dog came back, his face sweating from thinking so much and looking so deep into days before, his eyes twitching back and forth from how hard he had had to think to put the whole story together in his head, he climbed up onto his horse, wrapped himself in his robe again, and told us that the wagons had been headed east when the other napikwans who weren't really Pikuni started shooting arrows at them from the trees, which was where their horses were still tied.

"Why are they dressed like that?" I asked.

Hunts-to-the-Side made the same noise from my interruption that he'd made about the wagon ruts. He was right. It was rude of me to interrupt. But Tall Dog was skipping the important part.

"They're all wearing moccasins," Tall Dog said with a shrug. "But they're not Pikuni. They're napikwan moccasins, I think? Do they have them now, too?"

"It's supposed to be us who attacked the wagons," Peasy said, figuring it out first.

"That's why the horses . . ." Tall Dog said, trying to follow what Peasy was saying, "that's why their iron shoes are all hanging on a tree by where they're tied."

I had to hold the side of my fist over my mouth to keep from laughing at the picture of this in my head. All these napikwans unsteady and cold in moccasins, using tools to try to get their horses' iron shoes off, the horses stomping on their feet and shying away, blowing through their noses, eyes big.

"They were going to ride around through here, make it look like us," Peasy said, holding his hand up like a rider, weaving through the wagons.

Hunts-to-the-Side pointed with his eyes at an arrow sticking up from the bottom of one of the sideways wagons. I walked my horse over, reached down for the arrow and brought it back, handed it to Hunts-to-the-Side with the iron arrowhead pointed back at me. It had hardly been in the wagon's belly deep enough to stick, even, and it wasn't made from the right wood, hadn't been hardened over a fire, and the colors striped on it didn't mean anything. The more I looked around at these three wagons, the more of these arrows there were, all of them with their tails up, because they hadn't been shot straight from a strong bow but had had to climb high to go far, like from a boy's first bow.

"They used those at first," Tall Dog said, about the arrows. Then he pointed to the dead napikwan with his back against a tree, a bullet hole under his left eye like a dab of black paint. "But then that one pulled out his short-gun." Tall Dog opened his hand, presented the empty greased-shooter that came from that short-gun. "That's what killed the six in the wagon. All one after the other, no misses."

He was crouched down low and holding his hand in the shape of a short-gun, shooting fast down the line from one to six.

"Six?" Hunts-to-the-Side asked, standing as high as he could to try and see them all.

I'd only seen four, so far.

"They didn't expect him to have that short-gun," Tall Dog said. "They thought there were only going to be arrows, so they walked out in a line with their many-shots guns."

This got me sitting higher in my saddle, studying the grass for iron. This might be where I got a gun again.

"All men?" Hunts-to-the-Side asked then, because that didn't make sense either. These wagon trains were usually families, even though there was only one wife.

Tall Dog shrugged that there were no women, no children. We all stepped down, tied our horses, and started looking around ourselves, confirming what Tall Dog had said.

"This is Yellow Tail," Tall Dog said in his obvious way, pointing to a footprint in the snow. Yellow Tail had a limp, so his right leg always dragged at the first of his step. I told myself I would have recognized him just the same.

"He's the one who told us," Hunts-to-the-Side said, not happy to be having to admit this. But it made sense. Yellow Tail having been there first explained why all the many-shots guns I was hoping for were gone. And why the short-gun the false Pikuni with the fast hand had was gone. Yellow Tail had them all wrapped tight in a robe, tucked under a rock or a fallen down tree. He had caches all over, even women and extra blackhorns, he claimed, but that had to be a test, for if we'd believe him or not.

But maybe he wasn't lying, either. With Yellow Tail, you never knew.

"How many of these?" Peasy asked, studying one of the bad arrows.

"Arrows?" Tall Dog asked.

"Napikwans," Hunts-to-the-Side said, his voice impatient with Tall Dog, like Tall Dog had been trying to joke. "False Pikuni."

"Five," Tall Dog said, gulping while he said it.

Five false Pikuni to burn a wagon train of six napikwan and get us blamed, so it would be easier to shoot us in our lodges, or when we came in to trade robes.

We nodded, and set to hiding what had happened. Peasy and Hunts-to-the-Side ranged out to find all the dead napikwans who had been shooting from the trees, and Tall Dog and me dragged the wagon train men to the center of the ruts. They each had a buffalo robe coat as tall as they were, with high collars to hide their faces in, and they also had beards as thick and brown as a beaver pelt, so we could hardly see their dead faces.

Tall Dog inflated his chest and stood taller, and I understood. He was saying that these men were bigger than we were used to seeing.

But they died the same as any napikwan.

"No horses?" Hunts-to-the-Side said, looking around even though we already hadn't seen any.

"Only big-ears," Tall Dog said. We were used to the big-ears pulling wagons in their slow way, but your scouts and hunters would need horses, wouldn't they?

I shrugged, didn't understand this either. Maybe the wagon men had ridden two to a wagon, and they had enough guns and meat and water that they didn't need scouts or hunters?

Or maybe they were carrying the yellow coins Little Dog had gotten on a raid once but thought were just brass buttons, so buried them somewhere he never could remember. When the napikwans were carrying the yellow dust, they never went far from their wagons.

I held my hands up over my head like a big-ears, did my teeth out, and Tall Dog had to look away to keep from laughing.

Tall Dog led his horse over, tied his napikwan saddle to the side of the wagon that wasn't burned as much, and, with me pushing and his mountain of a horse pulling, turned the wagon back onto its wheels. A big breath of smoke came up when we did it, and we watched it climb and climb, announcing us to anyone.

"Over there!" Hunts-to-the-Side called, pointing with his lips to the cutbank Tall Dog should dump the wagon in, to hide it.

"He thinks we're too stupid to know that," Tall Dog said to me, breathing hard.

"Maybe I am," I said back to him, smiling a stupid smile where Hunts-to-the-Side wouldn't be able to see.

I was thirty seven winters by then, was too old to be making jokes, should have been grim with concern for all of the Pikuni, or at least with the seriousness of what we were doing, but I was never like Hunts-to-the-Side in that way, would always be the one trying the whitehorn milk, just to see what would happen.

While Tall Dog hooked his horse up to the front of the wagon, Peasy and me started dragging the bodies to the good wagon, to carry them away just the same.

All I was thinking about was the meat on the haunches of that prairie-runner, boiling in an iron pot back at camp, because the only thing we were going to have to eat that night would be cold pemmican, and maybe, if Tall Dog thought to bring it, some belly fat.

Instead of holding the hands of the dead napikwans to drag them, I stole a leather thong from one of them, looped it over their wrists so I could keep from touching their white skin. When Hunts-to-the-Side saw how I was doing this, he shook his head side to side like I was a child, even though he was only eight winters older than me.

When we had all eleven of the dead napikwans by the good wagon, Peasy reached up to pull its white-cloth hood off so we could load the bodies in over the side, and then he, with all his many years' experience, was falling back into all the bodies, and not even caring what he was lying in.

This is when we saw it for the first time.

"What?" Hunts-to-the-Side roared, his war club already in his hand, ready for the attack. I didn't even know he had the club, thought it was still on his saddle like mine.

Tall Dog skidded up on his horse, his eyes every direction, and then, finally, he looked into the wagon, where Peasy and me were already looking, and his horse took a step back, pulling at the reins like it wanted to wheel around, run back to camp.

I wish it would have. I wish we all would have gone with it, away from this place, this day, this whole winter. But it was like we were in one of your paintings, trapped in place, having to look at what was in the wagon, hissing at us like a real-lion.

It was the whitest napikwan any of us had ever seen, with the blackest hair long on his head but nowhere else, and it was locked in a cage big enough for a tall man to sit in. The cage looked like it had been made from the round, square barrels of your long-shooter guns, which we hadn't seen yet, but would soon.

Hanging all over the cage with rawhide strings and bits of twisted up cloth and braids of thin rope were dead-man-crosses like you have up there behind where you talk. Gold and silver, wood and iron. But these were little, and there were so many that at first I thought they were toy birds all grabbing onto the bars and trying to fly away at once, except their wings were too square.

"Ho!" Tall Dog said, more out of fear and bluff than to tell the thing to stay back.

This thing in the cage looked up to Tall Dog on his big horse, probably thinking he was our chief. It's what I would have thought.

The thing had a thin white face with intelligence to it, and at first I thought its chin and mouth were painted for ceremony, but then I saw that it was just that it ate like a sticky-mouth, where it made a mess, and then let that blood stay like it was proud of it, wanted all the other four-leggeds to see what it could do. Its mouth looked like it was pushing out too far, too, bringing the nose with it. But I told myself that was just because the dried blood made it look that way.

Its eyes were like mine, like I see you seeing, and its hair was hanging in its face, and it was naked so we could see it was a man, or had once been a man.

But it was no man, Three-Persons.

At first it hissed at us, and then it swiped at the air over its head. Like I am now, I understand it was swiping at Sun Chief's light, weak through all the grey clouds. By pulling the white-cloth hood off the wagon, we'd let that light in.

"What is it?" Hunts-to-the-Side asked, his voice small for the first time ever, but mad too, because he didn't already know the answer.

"Here," I said, and came back from my horse with my bow.

I walked right up to the wagon, drew an arrow back, held it long enough that this thing looked down along the spine of that arrow back at me, which was when I shot it through the bars of the cage, right in the center of the chest, through this flat bone here. From that close, I couldn't miss. From that close, an arrow hits like a greased-shooter.

"Now we can see it closer," I said, lowering my bow but not looking away from the cage.

"Good," Tall Dog said.

Peasy, trying to get his pride back from how the thing had startled him, stepped up into the wagon. But then he just stood there, looking down at whatever he'd stepped in.

"Go," Hunts-to-the-Side said to him. "Good Stab already shot it."

Tall Dog and me nodded that this was true, but we were also glad it was Peasy up there, not us.

Peasy took his tall hat off, resettled it lower on his head, and stepped forward.

The thing in the cage gasped all at once and sat up fast, pulled itself to the front bars, reaching with its claw fingers for Peasy, who backed off fast enough that his tall hat fell in front of him, too close to the cage for him to get it back.

The thing didn't just have a bloody chin like a sticky-mouth, either. It had the teeth, too, not as big as a black-bear's, but not as small as big-weasel's. These teeth were snapping at Peasy, daring him to come get that hat.

"What is it?" Hunts-to-the-Side said again, quieter, to himself.

We had no idea.

The thing hissed like a real-lion backed into a tree, and in my head, that was the first time I called him Possitapi, the Cat Man. Because he acted like one.

Now that he was snapping his mouth open and shut, we could see that the Cat Man had those sharp teeth like we'd already seen, but on each side right here he had longer teeth coming down from the top, and curled back a little, for keeping its prey in place.

It made me touch my own teeth with my thumb and first finger, like I was putting a whole turnip in my mouth.

"Its breath isn't right," Tall Dog finally said, and then we all had to see what he was seeing, that there was no white breath coming from the Cat Man. But his chest was coming up and down.

"What do we do with it?" I asked, looking to Peasy.

Peasy was just staring at the thing.

"Here," Peasy said, and took my bow, nocked another arrow, and shot it through the bars.

This time the thing caught the arrow in its hand and broke it in half by squeezing, staring back at us.

"This is what we do," Hunts-to-the-Side said, and sat the butt of his round-ball gun onto the ground to tip powder into it, and one patch of your thin white-cloth, one round-ball. After packing it down he held the gun up, waited for the barrel to get still, and shot the thing in the gut.

It threw the Cat Man into the back of the cage, rocking the whole wagon, and now none of us could hear, and we weren't breathing either.

We'd all seen blackhorns roll over dead from getting shot on the run, but then come back up, tearing a horse's belly out with their horns. It was how Yellow Tail's leg had gotten hurt. Tall Dog said he'd even seen a real-bear get shot by a trapper once, and the trapper sat down to sharpen his knife to get the hide, but then when he started in cutting, the real-bear woke back up, skinned the trapper instead. It was a good story. Especially when the real-bear put the man-skin on and boarded a smoke-boat, went down the river to the napikwan cities, to see what there was there to eat.

This was no story, though. This was happening for real.

It wasn't long before the thick, dark blood clumping from the new hole in the Cat Man's stomach stopped coming out and his hand clamped over that hole like any man's would, and then he screeched loud enough I fell to my knees, holding my hands over my ears because I thought there was a word in there, and I didn't want to hear it.

Tall Dog put his hand on my shoulder when the screech was over, so I could stand again.

Slowly, using the bars to pull himself up, the Cat Man sat on his knees like a Black Robe praying, like a little-grass-eater standing in its hole and watching for hawks.

He said something with sharp corners to the sounds, but none of us understood. Peasy knew some of your words, was always the one to speak for us with the traders, but I know now that what he knew was French, from one of the smelly trappers who had wintered with us when I was a boy.

This thing didn't speak French, which has more round sounds, and it wasn't your English either, that takes so many words to say a simple thing. I don't know what language it was.

"It doesn't die," Tall Dog said, in wonder.

"It's one of their gods," Peasy said, making it so.

"Burn him," I said to Peasy and Hunts-to-the-Side. "Cut him into many pieces, then burn him, then bury him. They'll be weaker without their god."

"Bury it where we hunt?" Hunts-to-the-Side asked back, insulted. He was right. I hadn't thought of that.

"It's a god, and it's white . . ." Peasy finally said, and the way he said it, we one by one heard what he was meaning. It was what I was already telling you, about how the Great White God would climb Chief Mountain, and Chief Mountain would crumble.

None of us knew what came after that, just that it had to happen, but Otter Goes Back had told us kids that when the Chief crumbled, it would leave a great hole in the ground, and the Pikuni could rush through there, and no napikwans could follow, not so long as we left all their kettles and guns and even their horses behind.

As a boy of eleven winters, I couldn't imagine not having a horse to raid with, a gun to make my enemies cry. But as a man of thirty seven winters like I was then, I knew I would trade all of those kettles in for no white scabs disease, no forts, no traders, no napikwans.

"This is him?" I said to Peasy, because I couldn't believe it. Things like this happened in stories, not to actual people. I knew Morning Star and Feather Woman and Blood-Clot Boy were all real, Napi too, the old man who shaped us all, and the world as well, I knew they had to be real because we were, but I never expected to see them.

Peasy shrugged one shoulder, didn't even look over at me. He had his hat again already, I guess from right after Hunts-to-the-Side shot the Cat Man.

"How else can we know than by taking him up there?" Tall Dog said, cringing to be offering this, to be agreeing with it, since it meant more days of walking through the snow, and not having time to hunt, even though we'd be up in the Backbone where the hunting is easy.

Peasy nodded, kept nodding, and finally, like a traitor to myself, or to my belly, anyway, I nodded with them, squeezing my whole face up.

But like Tall Dog had said, the only way to know if this was the Great White God or not was to test it. We could take this Cat Man up to Chief Mountain, open the cage however it opened, and maybe he would use his claws to scramble up the rock side into the sky, and then the Great Chief would sigh after all these years, finally crumble into the ground, opening up that hole the Pikuni needed, to finally get away from the napikwans.

And if he fought us instead of climbing up to be the Great White God, then there were four of us, weren't there? We could back up and keep shooting it until he fell, then cut him up while he was still shot, burn the pieces, take them south, out of our territory, away from Nittowsinan, and bury them in a string of places people never go, do ceremony over all those littles graves to be sure, and then come back every year, as long as we remembered, to dance the grass flat in all those places again.

It was a good plan, and I think it could have worked.

Except for what I did.

It started when we were going back and forth with the other wagon, carrying bodies to hide. Because four weren't needed for it, Peasy, looking ahead to our long ride to the Chief, dragging the Cat Man, told me to make sure the cage was tied down hard, so it wouldn't tip out. There was nowhere to grab those bars to lift it back, not if we didn't want him biting or clawing us.

I didn't want to do it, but Tall Dog was using his horse to pull the wagon and Hunts-to-the-Side was Hunts-to-the-Side, so I was the only one.

After they clattered off again, I nodded to myself that I could do this, and then I pulled myself up into the Cat Man's wagon to check the ropes. And I almost fell right back out. I knew now why Peasy had stopped when he'd stepped up. The bottom of the wagon wasn't your flat-wood boards, but soft instead, like I was sinking into it.

I lifted one foot then the other, afraid I really might be sinking, but then it was just beaver pelts lining that floor.

When I was young, ten beaver pelts had been worth a round-ball gun to the traders. But, being Pikuni, who can't kill beavers since their medicine is worth more than their fur, we always had to trade for beaver pelts to get guns, which made them cost even more.

For at least ten years, there hadn't been enough beaver left to stack them up and trade like the old days, and, anyway, the traders didn't want them as much. Just winter-coat buffalo robes, as many as we could bring in, so that we had to imagine all the napikwans in their big camps huddled in buffalo robes, making it look like the buffalo never went away, they just stayed in place, let the buildings and roads come up around them until they forgot they were grass-eaters, started standing in line at banks and mailing letters.

But these beaver pelts, since nobody brought them in anymore, someone bringing in ten of them at once might be able to get a many-shots gun for them.

Like Peasy had told me to, I checked the cage's ropes, which were really tight chains going to iron rings in the floor, but, trying to stay out of reach of the hissing Cat Man, I counted how many beaver pelts I was standing on.

Nine.

They were thick and healthy, were from some valley that hadn't been trapped out, but would nine be enough? Traders never liked numbers that were hard to add up, they said, and it was their post, their rules.

I considered this, considered it some more, then jumped down when the wagon came bouncing back, emptied again.

I helped load the last body, which was the first dead napikwan, the one with the long blue coat, and then we used dead branches to drag the snow back and forth, hide the blood, and then Hunts-to-the-Side drove four of the false Pikuni's horses out from the trees and we chased them south across the wagon-road, then sat there watching them run away.

"Look," Peasy said, about their tracks that were just hooves, not iron shoes. "Indians."

For the first time away from camp, Hunts-to-the-Side chuckled. Then he wheeled his horse around, we dragged more branches over the cutbank to hide the wagons and bodies and big-ears, which Tall Dog's horse was already tired from having to drag one at a time, and we tied the two leftover horses to the good wagon and set off for the Backbone, chewing pemmican in the saddle once the Seven Persons were up in the sky because none of us wanted to sleep with the Cat Man, god or not, watching us from between his bars.

Me especially.

The reason for that was that in the tall part of my right moccasin were two of the brass buttons from that dead napikwan's long blue coat. I was going to work them into the sheath of the many-shots gun I knew now I was going to get with those beaver pelts. They were hot against my skin, hot in a way I thought a god might be able to see.

The next day, after riding all night, we finally got to the top of that hill the soldiers should have waited on. Two Medicine was down below us. Peasy knew where it was shallow enough we could pull the wagon across.

The Cat Man wasn't hissing anymore. He just glared at us, had his sharp fingers wrapped around the bars like this, his face between.

"Look," Hunts-to-the-Side said, lifting his hand behind us.

Tall Dog and me looked, but there was nothing.

"Where are the birds?" he asked, because birds like to follow wagons.

"It's too cold," Tall Dog said.

"They still have to eat," Peasy said, studying the sky himself, now.

I looked from the nothing over us down to the wagon, then shook my head, didn't want to think about this anymore. The birds hadn't been picking meat from the faces of the dead napikwans at the wagons either, I realized. And the little big-mouths hadn't been sneaking in to fight each other for meat, and I'd seen the tracks of a sharp-back close by, but it had gone around the three wagons instead of coming in to eat. It didn't matter, I told myself. Soon this would be over, and I would have my many-shots gun, and wouldn't need any more Crow tricks to hunt.

"The Chief," Peasy said then, pointing north with his lips, reminding us what we were doing, and we turned to do it, but Hunts-to-the-Side was holding his round-ball gun up over his head like a war lance now, stopping us again.

He pulled with his gun for Tall Dog to come up. It was for how the snow was all turned over from hooves, where Hunts-to-the-Side was. From back where I was, it looked like a big herd of long-legs had passed. In the winter, they come down to the flats to uncover yellow grass, before they go back up to the north facing meadows to lose their antlers. In the winter they like the yellow grass as much as we like ripe sarvisberries, as much as you like your sugar bread, Three-Persons.

Tall Dog leaned down from his stirrups to study the tracks, urged his tired horse backward and forward to see the whole story.

"Soldiers," he came back and said, and told us there were maybe twenty of them.

I sucked air in through my teeth and straightened my back to see farther.

Soldiers all in a group means go the other way. Any Pikuni knows that.

But we were pulling a white god in a wagon, couldn't turn around.

"Soldiers don't look behind," Peasy said at last, deciding for us, and pulled his horse over into their tracks.

After a moment, Hunts-to-the-Side did too, and Tall Dog climbed back up into the wagon, and it felt wrong to walk where the soldiers had, but I fell in all the same, looking behind me for soldiers. For birds. For I didn't know what.

By the time I stopped watching like that, there was just swirling white flakes and the Backbone all around us, icy and steep. It was between night and day, and the wind was picking the snow up and blowing it against us so it stung like cold sparks wherever it touched. I tried to tie a piece of skin over my horse's eyes, but it was either not see where he's going or take the stinging snow. Some days that's the only way it is, in the Backbone.

I rode up beside the wagon. Peasy and Hunts-to-the-Side were a few paces ahead, so Tall Dog handed a bite of his belly fat over, covering it with the top of his hand like this.

"I knew you brought it," I said to him, chewing without moving my mouth too much, so the snow wouldn't get in and touch my teeth.

"Coldmaker," Tall Dog said, pointing ahead with his lips.

We'd all been seeing it, but nobody had said it yet. A hard storm was coming over the Backbone. That was good because it would hide where the wagon train had been attacked, and it was good because it would hide our tracks, doing what we were doing. But we each only had one robe, and I didn't know how many round-balls Hunts-to-the-Side had, for getting meat. But up in the Backbone, even in a storm, my bow would be enough. Tall Dog was better at reading tracks than I had ever been, but I always knew where the wags-his-tails liked to bed down. And we were Pikuni, and this was home. Our hands and feet might go black and dead from the cold and our eyes might go blind in the snow, but we would never starve, not in the valleys Napi had shaped for us.

You could never starve in one of your towns like this, could you? It's the same for us.

"The Lost Children," Peasy said, standing his horse still, to wait for us.

I looked up and there they were, glittering in the sky like always.

"All night?" Tall Dog asked, about how long we were riding.

Peasy didn't answer, just looked ahead of us.

"It's good we're fasting," he did say, though. "It's the best way to approach the Chief."

I swallowed what I had in my mouth, and it was big enough it made my eyes water, giving me away. I rubbed them, pretended to be looking to something on the other side from the wagon.

Ahead of us, two long-legs bulls walked out with their sides to us, and Tall Dog held up the many-shots gun he didn't have. The bulls looked at us like disappointed we were up where they lived again, and then they kept walking, their front feet dragging through the top of the snow, it was so tall already.

"It's a good sign," Peasy informed Tall Dog and me, about the elk not running fast away.

I'd seen the elks' sad eyes and faces, but I didn't say anything back to Tall Dog about it, but I did touch his wrist and then tap my own front teeth, to show him he had some black belly fat in his, that Peasy shouldn't see.

We'd been still in the soldiers' tracks until the trees, but now the blowing snow was wiping their tracks away. If we were walking ourselves, not riding, we could have still felt the icy ridges of their hoofprints under the top of the snow, but if we were walking, our moccasins would be wet. So, we rode.

The two bulls watched us from the trees, and we watched them back. I could have put an arrow in one, but in this up and down country, at night, tracking it down from drops of blood on the snow would take until morning.

"Go!" I told those two bulls. "Go!"

They just watched.

At the next steep part, the snow was tall enough that the wagon's belly was a skid. Finally we tied Peasy's horse beside the other two, to help pull, and Peasy rode in the front of the wagon, looking back every few steps at the Cat Man, who just looked back at him the same, and I say the Cat Man's eyes were like mine are now, but they were also hungry like a night-caller's sitting up in a tree, waiting for a dirty-face or red-back so it can swoop down on it.

We were the dirty-faces, I mean, our noses twitching, eyes always looking everywhere.

Halfway up another hill, the tallest one so far, the wagon got stuck where not even three horses could pull it with four men pushing and yelling.

"If we had those ruts to stand the wheels in," I said to Hunts-to-the-Side, my chest going up and down, trying to breathe.

Hunts-to-the-Side made a disgusted noise with his lips, turned away. Because I was right. But he still hated ruts.

"Another horse," he said just to me, and I knew it was an order. When I just stood there, looking to his and my horse, tied to each side of the wagon, Hunts-to-the-Side got my attention, hung his arms and shoulders over an imaginary piece of wood hooked over them, because we don't have a word that means one of your yokes, which is the word I know now. But I understood what Hunts-to-the-Side was saying with his arms, had seen your big whitehorns on the wagon-road pulling side by side harder than a horse or a big-ears, their necks and shoulders in wooden collars, with that thick wood beam curved above them to tie back to the wagon.

Hunts-to-the-Side was telling me to go find a deadfall still green enough, and the right shape, to be a yoke, to get us up this hill with four horses pulling.

Never mind the snow, the storm, or how weak with hunger I

was. On this raid that wasn't a raid, I was the boy, the assistant, even though I was thirty seven winters, had already had and lost my own lodge, my own family, my own herd.

This would all change when I got my new many-shots gun, I knew. I would stay out hunting, so these All Crazy Dogs could never pull me in like this.

Thinking like this, I nodded once to Hunts-to-the-Side and trotted off into the deeper darkness, taking my bow with me because all the wags-his-tails would be bedded down under trees so the snow wouldn't bury them, and if we ended up stuck too long, then our fast would have to be over.

Away from the wagon it was quiet, and there was hardly any snow because the trees were holding it all up.

I didn't want to go too far, because every step I took was a step I would have to drag the yoke I found back, so I took the first hill down I could, because that's where a fallen down tree would roll.

When the ground got soft under my feet, I knew there was a creek close by, and then it wasn't a creek at all, but a pond.

The kind beaver make.

I stood still, listening.

When I waded out farther, I saw the beaver lodge piled high, and then, past it, a white swift-runner up on his big back feet, his tall ears hearing me. It was watching me over a log, its nose twitching, and like I had to, I nodded once to it and held my face down for a moment, in honor. When I was sixteen, alone up here, my swift-runner had come to me just the same. Some warrior's helpers speak to them, but my swift-runner never scared me like that. It guided me just the same, would always pop its head up to tell me this direction, go over here, do this, not that.

I knew now that what it was doing was showing me the yoke I was looking for. It was standing right behind a tree that had fallen over but wasn't soft from rain and rot yet.

"Thank you," I said, nodding my head so it would know I understood this gift it was giving me. Or, trying to.

But I was weak.

Instead of going over to that log, freeing it from the ground and dragging it around the side of the hill back to the wagon, I was looking over to the beaver lodge some more. I was looking at it and hearing again the story about the beaver medicine bundle, where a brother spends the winter in Beaver Chief's lodge, learning all his medicine ways to bring back to the Pikuni. Beaver Chief in that story is as tall as a man. That was always the most wondrous part of the story, for me, I think because, when I was a boy, Otter Goes Back had shown me an old tooth his father before him had found in a crumbling away cutbank once. It was from a beaver, was curled and splintered and yellow like they always are from biting wood, but it was twice as long as my hand, meaning the beaver it had belonged to must have been taller than a man, must have been from Beaver Chief's tribe.

So, my swift-runner was showing me what I was here for, that yoke that would get us up the hill to deliver the Great White God to Chief Mountain, but my hand was opening and closing around the shape of a many-shots gun I still needed one more beaver pelt for.

Finally I nodded that I wouldn't be seeing this lodge if the beaver didn't want me to have his pelt, if he didn't want me to have a many-shots gun, so I waded deeper into the cold pond, humming to myself to try to make this holy and right. I can see that you understand this. That you have beaver pelts like this in your life, too.

I hope you're stronger against them than I was, Three-Persons.

And no, I don't remember anymore the song I was humming on the way to that lodge of sticks and mud. It's gone to the same place as the song that woman bringing water was humming. I do remember that I looked back when I was almost to the lodge. My swift-runner was still watching me, but its eyes were sad now, like my father's when he saw me drinking the whitehorn milk.

"Don't watch!" I called across to it, and when it still was, I reached down into the cold for a stone, threw it at the log. On the way to the log the stone crumbled through all the tree branches heavy with snow, so the snow fell down in a soft white wall.

When the air cleared again, my swift-runner was gone.

And that's the last time I ever saw it.

It was because I had turned my back on it, I know now, because I was turning my back on all Pikuni. We aren't supposed to kill the wood-biters. It's bad medicine to not just let them pass, and do what they're doing. But I didn't know how else to get a many-shots gun and be a man again, not a boy, so that was how I told myself this was all right, this one time.

It was my first step into the darkness, Three-Persons. My first step into this long night I live in now. When I waded into the cold waters of that pond, I was walking away from my life, my swift-runner, and I could never go back, no matter how hard I tried. It's like if you tore down your dead-man-cross up there and dragged it through the street, then burned it, and made water on the ashes. Your god would leave you, then, and your whole world. That's what was happening to me, and I didn't even know it, was only thinking about a many-shots gun.

Because beaver doors are underwater, I had to kick and pull through the top and side of the lodge until my hand went into warm air, and the beaver family thrashed up.

I only needed one, I yelled to them, drawing an arrow back.

They were already scattering into the water. All except the big one, slapping his tail hard and mad, like he wanted Peasy and Hunts-to-the-Side and Tall Dog to come running, see what this bad Pikuni was doing out here.

I shot this wood-biter in the chest just like I'd shot the Cat Man, but this beaver didn't get back up like the Cat Man had. His blood spread out in the water, but slow because of the cold. And, because he was a beaver, his blood was more red. This is how they swim underwater so long, my father had told me long ago.

My blood is like that now, too.

I skinned the beaver fast, washed my arrow in the clean part of the pond, rubbed my hands and face too, then rolled the hide tight and stuffed it under an overhanging rock. I balanced smaller rocks on in a line, so I could find this place when I came back alone, on the way to the trader's fort. The pelt would be stiff and frozen, but I could work it soft over the fire, stake it out and rub the flesh off, work it with brains and entrails of some other four-legged.

I nodded thank you to the beaver, thank you for the many-shots gun, which was when that many-shots gun said something back in its loud and cracking voice.

I stood up so fast I fell back down like I had been shot myself, but I wasn't. I had to feel all over my chest to be sure.

The next shot turned my head to where it was coming from, which was the other side of the hill I'd come over to get here.

The wagon.

After looking around to be sure I could remember these rocks, this creek, the slope above it, which makes me even more of a bad Pi-kuni, because I shouldn't have been thinking like that, I was running back through my own rounded off tracks, I was running and falling, holding my bow high to keep the string dry.

The first thing I saw was the dirty blue back of a soldier.

I spit the arrow I was carrying in my mouth into my hand and drove it into this soldier's blue back then dove past, already pulling the next arrow back in my bow, to let go into the face of the soldier who had been beside the first one, was just looking over to what was happening.

He stood up with the arrow in his eye, his hands on that arrow, and I left him dying there, ran into the open part past the trees, which was the way Peasy had said would be the best way up.

Tall Dog's big horse, maybe because it had originally been a napikwan horse, had pulled the wagon over to be a wall for us to hide behind. Except there were greased-shooters everywhere, coming in from all directions. It was the soldiers we had been following. They'd seen the storm coming like we had, and were backtracking to get down to where the snow wouldn't trap them up here.

I wished we had a medal from their war chiefs we could hold up, to tell these soldiers we weren't Owl Child, I wished we had a piece of paper like Heavy Runner did, saying we were good Pikuni. But all we had were each other, and one round-ball gun that was good for one shot, then would have to be reloaded, and maybe not even shoot then.

I slid behind the wagon Tall Dog had his back against, his long fingers trying to hold in the blood coming from his chest.

It was dark and thin, was from the liver, and there was too much of it to hold.

He shook his head no to the question in my eyes, and I rolled away just as a greased-shooter popped through the wagon where I'd been sitting, throwing splinters into my back and the side of my face.

When I stumbled a few paces out, it was because I'd tripped over Hunts-to-the-Side's body facedown in the snow, covered in all of his blood, his round-ball gun still in his hand, its powder spilled on the snow in front where its barrel had coughed it out. Meaning Hunts-to-the-Side hadn't even gotten his one shot off.

I rolled past him, knew this wasn't a fight anymore, that all I could do was run for Chief Mountain, ask him to take me, to hold me close, to save me, his Pikuni child.

Which was when a greased-shooter hit me in the left shoulder, high, right here, and spun me around, my bow slinging away, my war club still tied to my saddle, wherever my horse was. The bow landed on the crust of snow and slid until the string caught on a frozen branch, and I remembered Peasy two days ago, working his bowstring back and forth through the eyes of that blackhorn skull, and I wanted that again, please. Just daily chores to do. Meat to dry, wood to get, children to tie hoops for.

But soldiers were pouring from the trees now, leading with their many-shot guns, all of them yelling, their breaths white and cold, their eyes hot and mad, which is when Peasy stood shirtless from the snow he'd been hiding in there in front of the turned over wagon, his grey hair loose under his tall black hat, his death song in his throat, because Pikuni like him don't die like Tall Dog and me. Pikuni like him die like in the stories.

All the soldiers pointed their guns at him from the story they were in, which is your American story, and they shot at once together, over and over, so Peasy was dancing in place.

Seeing Peasy die like that, in a way that mattered, in a way even the soldiers would tell about, I knew I had to try for my death song too. But I couldn't get air inside, to sing back out. I was too scared, and the hole in my chest was cold fire, and it wasn't my death song anyway, I know that now. I know it because, since this night in the Backbone, I've sung it so many more times, over and over, this song you should only ever be able to sing once.

Instead of dying all the way yet, I was on my knees, I was reaching out for Peasy, the old man, who was already dead but still standing somehow.

It was because he was still doing his last thing, for all Pikuni.

It was to drag his hand down over the latch of the Cat Man's cage.

He was releasing our Great White God on these soldiers.

I nodded yes, yes, that this was how it had to be, this was all that was left. We were close enough to Chief Mountain, we had to be. This was where it could all start over again. This was why we'd found him.

Since we were all deaf from the shooting, none of us heard that iron latch.

But we all saw the Cat Man rush like a fast weasel over Peasy.

There were still thirteen soldiers standing when the cage opened.

The Cat Man, running on all fours, tore open the throat of the first and second soldiers before the third and fourth had even looked over, and then they were dead just the same, the first one's face gone, the second's whole head off, the stump of his neck welling with blood, the wet white of his bones and throat still bright for the moment, and the foggy yellow juice from his back spurting high, where his face had been.

I stumbled forward, fell over a dead soldier, came up with his many-shots gun, which was all I'd wanted from this.

I levered another round in, and it took me long enough that four more of the soldiers were already thrashing in the snow from the Cat Man, their blood spurting in the whiteness.

I wondered if those two long-leg bulls that had been off to the side were still watching.

I knew the beaver family was.

I screamed as loud as I could, even though I couldn't hear my own voice, and shot into a soldier who looked over, my greased-shooter folding him over at the waist, and then I levered again, shot the soldier beside him too, and the Cat Man looked up to the man he had his mouth to, had been drinking from.

He was breathing hard, his eyes wild, his whole chest and stomach red and shiny and steaming, so I could tell at last he was no god. He was just a four-legged. He even ran like one of them. But he could speak like a two-legged.

"You," he said in napikwan then, and I didn't know your tongue yet, but I knew enough to hear this like he meant for me to. Or maybe I saw it in his eyes, staring into me.

I nodded yes, me, and brought my gun over to him right as one of the two or three soldiers left ran his sword up through the Cat Man's heart from the front, while another shot him twice fast in the back, through what I knew had to be both lungs.

This had to be enough to kill him, I told myself.

I was wrong.

The Cat Man came around to swipe at them with his claws and I shot at him, aiming for his face, but instead got the last soldier right above his top lip, throwing his teeth out the back of his head, some of them going fast enough to stick in a tree, and then the Cat Man was rushing at me on all fours, the sword still in his chest, its sharp tip dragging through the snow.

On his way to me, I shot him twice fast, once in the top of his right shoulder, taking his arm on that side away, and once in the forehead at last, but then his mouth was opening over my face anyway and he was biting deep into my shoulder with his sharp teeth, making my whole side cold and nothing at once, which is when a soldier I hadn't seen, standing right behind me, said a napikwan word which I guess meant for the Cat Man and me to both look up to him, because we did. First at his mustache like brown wings on his mouth, and then at what he wanted us to see.

He had one of their cannons on tall wheels, which is the chief of all round-ball guns, their grandfather, Beaver Chief to all beavers, if beavers were guns, which I know now they aren't. This cannon didn't shoot one big ball, the Pikuni already knew. It shot handfuls of round-balls at once, not all of them round.

This cannon was aimed right at me, and then it twitched higher, its open mouth ready to scream at the Cat Man.

I tried to pull away, but the Cat Man just surged ahead, like to fight this thing the same as he'd been fighting the soldiers.

Before he got there, it shot with its deep cracking thunder. The ground and all the trees shook, my head too, and one of those pieces of iron left a hole burned through the hand I'd been trying to block this with.

I looked through that hole in wonder, because it didn't hurt, and saw the Cat Man's body flying back from his legs, off his legs, because he had been cut in half.

While he was still falling back into a hard snow drift, the soldier who had pulled the cannon string drew his short-gun from his belt and shot me twice in the chest, from close, but those last two greased-shooters were far away to me, happening to someone else.

I fell to the side, away from the cannon and the soldier, and because the Cat Man was uphill on his hard drift from me, the blood from his waist and his stomach where he'd been parted, it rolled in a fast steaming river down the top of the snow at my face, was warm on my lips but cold against my teeth, and when it got to my throat I coughed but had to breathe in to do it, meaning I sucked this blood deep into me like breath.

This is how I died, with the Cat Man's blood slithering down across the crust of the snow, filling my eyes and nose and mouth, my own blood leaking out of me from too many greased-shooter holes, and one cold bite deep in my shoulder.

The last thing I thought was if the birds and little big-mouths and a sharp-back or two were going to sneak in, pull the meat from all our bones, or whether they would leave us alone up here in the Backbone until some young Pikuni came up here after fasting for four days, and stumbled into us.

It didn't matter. I would be in the Sandhills already by then, in my lodge with my wives in their ermine and elk teeth, my children sleeping in a pile of robes, the smoke from the fire curling up and up, past the blackened ear-flaps and into the sky, silver lines of light always scratching across it.

Or so I thought.

This is my telling for today.

The pipe is empty.

The Absolution of Three-Persons

April 3, 1912

I'm just now finding time and mind to record this. Not because of Holy Week, but because another body, or "hump" as people in town have taken to calling them, has turned up.

This time they asked this local clergyman to accompany them out to retrieve it, so I wasn't at the church when the aptly named Lorelei Baker stopped by with a yellow cake. She's habituated to the church enough, however, her husband Roald having provided irregular maintenance, that she knew how to work the handle on the rear door so she could leave the cake covered with a cloth, along with the necessary note documenting this unexpected gift's point of origin——I begin to suspect my parishioners think they can ply in-dulgences out of me with victuals, that I'm, as they say, an easy man to give penance, knowing I should gain a good pittance.

If only I had such penance to dole out.

But I don't mind this horn of plenty tilting my way. I have yet half a slice of moist yellow cake on a plate above this very page as I write this, even, and I endeavor to dribble fewer crumbs onto these words with my next bite, as they seem to leave grease on the paper, which I take to be butter or pork lard. After the tragedy of last week's loaf of German bread having disappeared so quickly but lingered so long in memory, I am, with this unexpected bounty, limiting myself to one middling thick slice after lunch and one after dinner, and, so far, only a single thick slice betwixt lunch and dinner, as a crutch to get from one to the other.

Self-denial is fine and well when public approbation looms, but in the absence of such watchfulness, well. It's a very good cake, is more than an old man such as myself might deserve here in his solitary dotage. I'll let it rest there. And if I end up eating it with more haste and abandon than intended, it's only to insure that the mice don't steal bites in the night, the little thieves.

What did Good Stab call mice? "Dirty-faces," yes? I suppose it fits their character, but, too, all the terminology stirs together in my faltering memory in the most wonderful manner. His mixing and matching of terms and vocabulary I find intensely interesting, I mean, which is to say, I sense the distinct possibility that he adopts the more ancient constructions as a form of pitching intellectual woo at me.

Good Stab is more canny than he presents, I mean. There's a spark of intelligence to those black eyes, and a humorous glint as well. It's very much as if he's sneaking glances up to me between the tangled lines of his tale so as to evaluate how deeply it's lodging in me, and whether it's finding purchase——it is, Good Stab. Or, rather, it was.

What I mean to say is that, after your visit of last Sunday, telling myself it was but in order to confirm details, I rifled through an old trunk unopened for years, I rifled through until I discovered a weathered old letter I never expected to have been reunited with, a letter I'd mailed back to New Haven in my distant youth, a confession that languished unopened for three and a half decades awaiting my return since the recipient had passed before the missive reached him——a missive written by someone I'm not anymore, a man I hardly even remember, and would never claim relation to. Reborn in Christ as I most assuredly am, any sins guilelessly documented in that entry have been washed away in His blood, and are best not only forgotten, but denied. It was but a spasm of weakness that spurred me to dredge those pages up to flagellate myself with them until my hand was shaking, my face wet with tears, and this log as well.

Such is guilt.

But as the blood of the Lamb can take all that away, so could I in good conscience consign this letter from a less civilized age to the kindling hopper after all these years, to be fed into the fire as it deserves. My misguided impulse to conjure that past up from its moldering grave was but another temptation an old man was tested with.

As indication that I've passed that test, I've decided that this Blackfeet's sudden presence in my church has to be happenstance of geography, not yesterday's yesterday rising in judgment. Anyway, it's not man's burden to judge, but our Higher Power's.

As ever and always, I am at your mercy, Holy Father. Such is the wretched state of man. We're all but pigs in the sty, and our moments of repose when we can see beyond the filth and violence of our lives are few and far between, since we need must toil in the mud throughout our lives, snuffling in the refuse and waste for our next meal.

Unless of course the Lorelei Bakers of the world leave those next meals under a cloth for us.

Consider yourself shriven, Lady Baker.

And you as well, Good Stab, though you've yet to wend around to the trespass weighing so heavily on your everlasting soul.

And, yes, I have so far resisted prodding at the details of your story my station compels me not to question, though the chinks are obvious even to one with eyesight so poor as mine.

One example is that wagon train you and your tribesmen went

out to remove from the, unless I'm mistaken, glory days of the Mullan Road. As one of your party apparently had a musket from days gone past, then——and I know this first hand, have witnessed it after the fact——upon finding eleven men in isolation, each of them shot dead with what you insist upon calling "greased-shooters" from "round-ball guns" then the first task to have engaged in would be to cut into each of those wounds, in hopes of retrieving said round-balls, so you and yours could, with stones or other tools, hammer them back to their original shape, and thus use them again in the same fashion, against other men white or red, or even their sacred blackhorns. Scarcity demands such behavior, as offensive as those of us in the modern age might find it.

Similarly, that "cannon" you spoke of that the detachment of Baker's men are supposed to have had, that's of course the famed Hotchkiss Mountain Gun, which fired mortar shells, not grapeshot. This isn't the high seas, Good Stab, nor is it the era of the blunderbuss. Your over attention to detail may very well be the undoing of your story, kind sir, at least to those of us in the know of such things.

But of course veracity isn't what you're wending your way indirectly toward, I can sense that as well. Being a good confessor, I should let such trifles pass unmolested, in hopes of wading into more productive, and more honest, terrain, that being the rocky soil of the human soul, which I argue the savage actually has, even though his allegiance be to the dusky past, not to America proper.

As for the historical accuracy of this tale I'm being told, it's of course known that 173 Blackfeet were justly dispatched by the 2nd Cavalry and various armed citizens and scouts on the Marias River in that January of 1870, in response to various depredations these Indians perpetrated during the previous summer and fall, those depredations including the murder of Malcolm Clarke, your "Four Bears," but anyone with interest could have scavenged that from an old newspaper, provided they could read. And there's no record at

all of Major Baker having anticipated the killer Owl Child's move-
ments such that he sent a detachment of soldiers out ahead of him,
having already sent another detachment ahead to assure the safety of
a whiskey trader who did his business miles up from the battle——if
detachment after detachment is sent out, the main corpus becomes
itself a detachment, at least in number and effectiveness. But of
course Major Baker had received a brevet promotion during the war
between the states, and he was hand selected by Sheridan to deal
with the Blackfeet. So, far be it from me to impugn his capability as
a military strategist.

Yet, instead of charging directly at the Marias River in 1870 as
I initially thought you to be doing, Good Stab, you elect instead to
fabricate a massacre of a more intimate scale occurring, as near as I
can tell, practically simultaneously but a day's ride to the west, in the
high rocky mountains you call the Backbone of the World, an archa-
ism fetchingly antique, but I can't let myself be seduced suchly.

Stay instead in this century, Three-Persons, where another dead
man has turned up, this time to the south, and closer to town, perhaps suggesting his discovery was intentional.

Lacy Doyle, current sheriff, former deputy, requested in his
grumbling way that I accompany him. Not one to shirk responsibility, at least not with so many waiting at the hitching post, and hardly
immune to the allure of the modicum of respect due one of my station, to be seen by the citizenry of Miles City as part of this historic
party, I took the horse Doyle offered and mounted slowly, being fully
aware of the reaction my robes, when billowing about like the wings
of an enormous crow, can trigger in the equine set.

The ride out into the grasslands was more funeral procession
than any sort of retrieval posse.

"Look," Doyle's deputy said, tilting his chin up at the sky ahead
of us, over, presumably, this new hump. "Told you."

I hadn't been "told" as apparently the sheriff had, so all I could ascertain was open sky of the April variety, which, to be honest, I couldn't tease apart from the March variety or the May variety. But I don't have a stockman's eyes like all of these men do, so will leave such identifications to those better qualified.

The sheriff stopped his horse, grunted assent, and then spurred ahead, perhaps anxious to conclude this grim endeavor.

Instead of immediately falling in, I sat my horse behind them for a moment, yet studying the sky, waiting for enlightenment to dawn. When it finally did, I had to chuckle——it was as if Good Stab were sitting a horse beside me, waiting for me to realize this spectacle before my eyes.

There were no scavenger birds.

No coyotes either.

Not a single sharp backed porcupine.

A cold wind gathered itself and blew past, such that I had to clamp my flat brimmed and full crowned hat down onto my withered pate. As the sheriff and his men's horses were yet between myself and the poor deceased, I had to step down from the stirrups and ford the crowd, as it were.

"Father," Doyle said, removing his hat to hold it across his sternum, and his deputies and men comported themselves similarly, taking his lead.

I didn't correct his "Father" to the more appropriate "Pastor." The proceedings were too somber to introduce such trifling frivolity.

There was a man facedown in the grass before us, facedown and dead, the skin of his back and torso removed, as well as the skin of his upper arms and thighs, though I could see from the unpainted edges of his face that skin was pale unto Irish, if his hair was any indication. As for that paint, it was yellow and black, the black on the left side, the yellow on the right.

"He didn't used to paint them so careful like," Livinius Clarkson proclaimed, turning to the side to spit.

One by one, Doyle and his men, and our illustrious postmaster, settled their hats back onto their heads, some of them having to guide their uncut hair out of their faces first.

"Used to?" I asked back, my question scrambling over the gate before I could stop it.

Livinius Clarkson caught the eye of the sheriff, and Doyle nodded a curt nod.

"Used to and still both," Livinius said with me as his audience, it seemed, the rest of the men apparently already versed in this.

"He skinned them, you mean," Doyle corrected with all necessary dourness.

"Or they skinned 'em up," the main deputy added, or, rather, judging from his tone and emphaticness, reminded.

"Indians, you mean," I clarified, by way of asking that question.

General nods all around, and the shuffling of boots.

"They bleed 'em first, somewhere else," Livinius said, using his heel to roll the dead man away from his bier of grass so we could see its harsh, unmolested yellowness, which by rights should have been stained dark with blood, as skinless meat will of course seep for hours. And meat was most assuredly what this man had been reduced to.

"Father," Doyle said again, and I nodded, needed no more spurring.

Though not Catholic, complete with a kit for last rites, an old Lutheran pastor can still kneel by the mortal remains, hold two fingers to the dead's forehead, and mutter a prayer so quietly that the men gathered around, serving as wind block, don't feel compelled to repeat the prayer, never mind it be in a language none of them can repeat.

"Why paint them up so gaudy?" the main deputy said when my prayer was over.

I heard this question as if from another room, and I confess that at first I mistook it for "God-y," so had no immediate answer, lost in trying to make sense of the question.

"Heard an old buffaloer say that painting 'em up like that weren't the least bit un-usual," Livinius led off, giving dramatic pause in the middle of his last word so all could reorient to him.

"How so?" one of the other men asked. He was the man holding a dog on a rope, for purposes I wasn't yet privy to. I recognized the dog, however. It was the white one with a black circle over one of its eyes that had been pestering pedestrians on Main Street for days, now.

Livinius shrugged as if this were everyday information for one such as he, and set forth to regaling us with one of his tales of yore, as it were——I phrase it in such a way as I'm fully confident that's how Livinius himself would phrase it. But when you have his posture, can hitch the front of your pants up as he's wont to do, and can set the heel of your boot upon the very body we all came to view, then you hardly need vocabulary at all, do you?

The tale Livinius recounted, complete with sweeping arms and even more dramatic pauses and no small amount of leaning over to spit, was that an old buffalo hunter he'd known in the more unlawful days said, on his way down to the Territories so as to get away from a fate such as his fellow hunters were suffering, that twice in the last year he'd set up downwind from a herd and commenced to laying them over one after the next once he brought down the lead bull, such that the herd was no longer a single body, but milling cows and calves.

By day's end, his face blackened from powder, his shoulder dully aching from the harvest, it turned out he'd felled more buffalo than his two skinners could skin. After applying the strychnine to the ones already derobed such that any wolves coming in to feast would die for their efforts, he and his crew camped, feasting on tongue and passing a bottle among them in subdued celebration.

And of course, as was common and necessary practice, due to the dangers of their avocation, they assigned among themselves who would stand watch. Apparently, sleeping without guard in those days, you could wake up yourself derobed.

According to this buffalo hunter from back when there were yet buffalo to make an honest living from, their camp went unmolested this night, but when they woke and set to their skinning duties, the hunter himself even stooping to these felled beasts so as to expedite the process, they found that one of the cows on the downwind side of the herd had already been gutted, skinned, and had her meat spirited away——it was the stealing of the skin that was the affront, the meat intended to be left behind anyway.

How this buffalo hunter and his crew knew it was Indians of some breed was that the buffalo's face, like this dead man's, had been also painted in bisected manner, in honor of the gift it, not the hunter and his crew, was giving to these passing Indians. Never mind that this hunter had spent both lead and effort in felling the beast.

And then this happened to this buffalo hunter again the next season, Livinius said, punctuating it with a long string of spit. I have to assume that inside Livinius Clarkson there is only tobacco spit churning endlessly around, looking for an aperture through which to make its escape.

"Thieves in the night," Livinius said in closing about the Indians, flashing his eyes around to confirm we could all see the inescapable logic of such a designation.

No one objected, and all muttered assent. This buffalo hunter had shot these animals himself, and then the Indians had pilfered one of them, which is of course their way, to seek handouts instead of bending their backs to the plow. But that's neither here nor there.

What is is that it's now confirmed, at least by association and anecdote, that there remain some few hostiles out there even yet, and they're leaving missives for Miles City, and maybe for Montana itself. And they're applying their signature to their work such that those with eyes to see can't mistake the authorship.

As the Star asked, though, why? To what purpose? Was an Indian child trampled under a wagon, or in the wheels of one of the horseless carts to have braved Miles City? Did a homesteader divert a creek to his fields, as should be his right if he wish to feed his family? Or is this a more general complaint, on the order of agreements they surely would have also broken themselves, if given the opportunity?

These are questions I can't answer.

I don't have to, either.

My duty is first and foremost to my flock. Sheriff Doyle only asked me out there as a courtesy, to pray over the dead man, which I did, never mind if Lorelei Baker's cake was upmost in my thoughts at the time, my lips falling through the prayer that's so rote by now I don't even have to concentrate to dredge it and its many kin up.

I say this in the privacy of these pages, yet I know the Lord sees all. But, too, I have to imagine He's inured to the many and various frailties contained in His multitudinous children. Perhaps we're even amusing to him. Perhaps an old pastor fumbling through his prayer by ingrained sound rather than Divine meaning breaks the monotony of His days.

After Livinius's colorful story, the white dog we had brought with us was let slip from its rope. When it nosed eagerly around our feet instead of setting to its task, paying special attention to the spray of Livinius's spit, Sheriff Doyle removed a tin of what turned out to be bacon grease, which he slathered on the marbled buttocks of the dead man with the painted face, our carious "hump."

The dog, once it caught this delectable scent as I guiltily had myself, set to at first licking that grease off whilst growling, lest one of us intercede, but then, catching the meaty scent of the meal waiting under, it bit in as well, bit in and pulled, and we turned our backs so as to not have to remember this moment any better than we were already going to.

Sated after a few needlessly loud minutes, the dog padded around to us panting with satisfaction, was roped around the neck again, and, with the dead man wrapped in burlap and trussed with rope brought for that purpose, he was festooned like a deer across the rump of a mule, whose ears were, after hearing Good Stab's name for them, indeed big. We then walked in our own tracks back to town, an act that again triggered Good Stab's tale for me, in that I was near to expecting a garrison of soldiers to be coming the other way in those tracks——such can a story infect a listener's day, by rising up in ambush at inopportune moments, and coloring otherwise customary events.

Another way it can infect one such as I am is that, pinching up a stray crumb of yellow cake off this page, I happened to notice, as close to the candle as I am now, that the pad of my finger was shaded black, in which I saw the dense fur of the beaver in its darkened lodge, desperately beating its tail about this invasion of its winter home.

Upon inspection, the finger beside the black one was yellow, as if my mumbled prayer out on the prairie had seared this into my very skin.

After holding these two fingers over the flame, not too close but not too far, the paint was again glistening and soft.

I press them now into this margin, as proof of this day.

And, so as to not carry this burden around any longer, I should myself confess that the Sunday evening previous, after Good Stab and myself had sat head to head in the pews toward the back of the church, him relaying his tale, his "confession" as he would case it, I finally got around to sorting the offering plate. This is usually both a short chore and a relatively mindless task, which is why I save it for the end of the day's duties, when my powers of concentration are ebbing. Typically, there are a few coins at best, which I make do with, the clergy's vow of poverty being not only binding, but perpetual.

This evening, however, working by candlelight as I still do, even though there are oil lanterns stationed around the church, I had the simple offering plate in my lap, my knees together under my robe to keep it from tipping over, and I nearly gasped, seeing what I first took to be two Spanish galleons against that piece of felt we line these plates with, so that the tinkle and chime of coins against metal doesn't become a sound associated with status——something to be proud of. Rather, your offering should be private, between you and the Church.

But these, upon inspection, weren't galleons——too small, too thick, and not gold, just appearing so.

What they are is two brass buttons, most likely either from a military jacket from decades ago, or meant to appear as such to one such as I, who has been subject to the story I'd been subjected to but hours previously.

Two buttons, impaled on a single porcupine quill.

At which point, I confess I did drop the offering plate.

April 7, 1912

It's Easter, and the dog is dead.

This was the news moving among the congregation in the shuffling moments before I held my hands up for their silence, so we could begin worship as a single body united in holy purpose.

In Miles City, the passing of one dog when that one dog is instantly replaced by three more, already snarling and barking, is usually beneath mention. The dog in question this time, however, was the pestering white one with the black ringed eye that was taken out to the most recent, and hopefully final, "hump."

Apparently the sheriff, in his official capacity as shepherd of the larger flock that's our town and county, sought to confirm that the death of his personal dog the week before, in association with the first nameless man found skinned out in the grass, was causally associated with the condition of that poor soul.

"Poison" is the word passing from lip to ear in my pews.

The poor soul left out there as communication with us, he would seem to have been dusted with strychnine. If asked, I would hazard the guess that this isn't actually malicious, but results from the fact the Indians authoring these acts need the corpse to be found unmolested, so as to showcase their violent handiwork better. This would explain the lack of usual scavengers in attendance, would it not?

I cleared my throat, held my hands up to quiet the mumbling and looked down to the pages of my breviary open before me on the plush purple fabric that I consider an unnecessary but not unappreciated luxury. The words were swimming and darting amongst each other, the letters shivering, the blankness around them snow, skirling among burlap wrapped legs.

I cleared my throat again, which turned into a cough, one in which I lowered my face into my left fist, holding my right hand up to assure the congregation that I would gather myself on the nonce, that this wasn't anything consumptive or tuberculotic. At the end of it, my eyes were rheumy and watering.

Through such pellucid lenses, I saw an upright rectangle of yellow light open at the rear of the church, and a blurry form step through, its robes moving around its legs in such a way that, for a falling moment, I felt I was both standing at the pulpit and also just entering the church.

But of course it was him, the Indian, Good Stab, though in truth I don't know if he would answer to that name.

He was yet wearing his darkened spectacles against the injurious light, but otherwise he was the spitting image of himself a week prior. He nodded once to me and then took what was quickly becoming his usual pew, at first lowering his face to his hands to begin the complicated maneuver of peeling out of his darkened spectacles, but then, when the church was once again too bright for his delicate sensibilities, electing to leave them on instead, denying me his accusing——as I take them——eyes.

His posture was either that of one ready and willing to worship, or that of one who wanted me to believe as much. Yet, at the same time, I remembered how his opening salvo of last Sunday had ended with his own death.

This meant of course that I had to choose whether to believe my own eyes, that he was yet here, or believe his story, which assured me he couldn't be. Yet, had he not told me I would, in time, believe him? That his evidence would mount and mount until I couldn't clamber over it, back into my rational disbelief?

Listen to me, a man of God meant to instill faith but arguing reason and rationality when it suits my needs, when it palliates my fears.

It's late now, and Lorelei Baker's yellow cake has been long gone these past two days. All that's left of her generosity is the one long red hair that evidently fell into the batter, putting me in mind of another woman with similar hued hair I knew briefly, decades ago. And of course there's always the chance——nay, hope——that my shower of gratitude whilst shaking and shaking her husband's calloused hand will incite her to find her mixing bowl again soon. The Lord works in mysterious ways, does He not?

The Lord, not you, Three-Persons.

My ways are much more transparent, and probably less beneficial, in the final tally. But there is also the immediate tally, is there not? The one that would keep a man well fed and satiated, allowing him to do his work with more satisfaction.

So I sit here late into the night, a candle to each side of me due to my ever weakening eyes, attempting to transmute the flicking ethereal into these inky slopes and swoops. As if I'm Alexander Pope, yes. To err may be human, but to err in such a way as to make your own efforts grandiose, that, dear poet, is hardly divine, is perhaps the most human. Ecce homo indeed, Zarathustra.

In all humbleness, I hope only to record Good Stab's tale, as I feel it my duty as an American to attempt to capture these last exhalations of a people who won't be seen again in the world. One example that I fear I've forgotten to write down in the recording of his tale——so much that I crib it down where I can, now——is how these Black-feet, when setting up winter camp, their lodges being now moored to the prairie for much longer than usual, they know to surround the bases of their lodges with brush. According to Good Stab, the reason for this is that the snow can, otherwise, become a problem——one which the brush solves. But, living in Miles City as I do now, I have to also think that this brush serves a more immediate purpose, that being to keep all the camp dogs from lifting a leg on this meticulously painted buffalo hide that serves as wall of a home.

In ten years, maybe even but five, details and peculiarities such as this will have evaporated into the mists of history, and become irretrievable in this forward march of progress.

What use me preserving them in the privacy of this log, I know. But neither can I just let them drift past, not without attempting to stab the nib of a pen down through them. Had no one written the Gospels down, what would the world have lost then?

So I dutifully record this, The Gospel of Good Stab, in his own words. And that's what I will call his tellings in this log, so as to separate it from my own entries.

He is once again gone from the pews behind me, though his specter, I would argue, distinctly remains. Both his specter as well as the echo of his voice, his eyes boring a hole into the planks between my feet, such that I have to lean forward to hear the words he but mutters, I surmise either because he's ashamed of his broken English, or the state of his teeth are such that he would keep them hidden from these prying eyes.

It's a trait not uncommon in this new state, barbers being always late to put their bloody pole up in frontier towns, meaning the people of those towns' teeth often go unpulled.

I long for my parishioners to understand they need not be ashamed in my presence, but shame, being inbuilt, can be inescapable, even for those not part of proper society. Which is to say, after the congregation trailed out into their Sunday afternoon, and a beautiful April one it was, Good Stab was waiting, penitent, face lowered, in his pew.

"Do I keep you from your duties?" he asked when I approached.

"Only my repast," I said with a smile, and then immediately filled in the blankness I saw on his face with a quieter "lunch," as many are the perils of the educated holding their vocabulary over the heads of those without similar credentials.

"We can eat if you want," he offered.

"I don't have any . . . what did you call it?" I said. "Real-meat?"

"Buffalo," he said, hearing what I meant if not the playful manner in which I meant it, and I noted that, outside the perimeter of his tale, that was the word he chose, "buffalo," not the "blackhorn" I was growing accustomed to and even using internally myself, or the coughing word with all the i's in it that he had fallen back on seemingly by accident a time or two during our previous session, but declined to attempt to spell for me, as perhaps that would illustrate his ignorance.

"Though a parishioner by the name of Georgia Klein did leave for me a stew she said was made with a, um . . ." I said, pretending to feel blindly for the word which I had already at hand, "a . . . prairie runner, is that how you say it?"

"Antelope," he corrected, his patience with this game declining. Yet I continued to poke and prod, as shouldn't be my nature, I know. Yet, at the same time, and in spite of this agéd body I'm clothed in, I sometimes feel I never matured past my thirteenth or fourteenth year, when, much like Good Stab, I would also sneak around and drink the whitehorn milk.

"You never got to eat the one you and Tall Dog got with that Crow method of hunting, did you?"

Good Stab looked off, up at the cruciform Christ high on the wall I could feel framing me.

"What was that trick?" I was unable not to ask, thinking that, like the brush around winter lodges, this was another aspect of the past I could preserve in these pages.

Good Stab nodded again as if in internal conversation with himself, and when he looked up, it was to politely flick his eyes away from my fingers, which insist on rubbing against each other as if balling a dab of wax, lest they tremble in a fashion not conducive to the trust I hope to engender among the laity.

"Otter Goes Back did that as well, his last winter," Good Stab muttered about my fingers, either offering condolences or portending my immediate departure from this mortal coil, neither of which were comforting.

I tucked my hand out of his field of view.

"He said it was from a raid in his youth," Good Stab continued, quietly enough that I was to understand that this wasn't quite a believable excuse. "Is yours also from a raid? You were in the wars, yes?"

I nodded my grimmest nod.

Being born in 1839, I was, as he surmised with his savage maths, the right age. Or, some would say, if they could say any longer, the distinctly wrong age.

But, yes, my experiences on the battlefield are what's washed me up on this shore I've washed up on. Just as your pox scars mean you lived, Good Stab, so does my station at this church mean that I survived the red, frothing waters that would have pulled me under time and again. I also survived the amber and golden sea that looked also to drown me, one bottle at a time.

And, yes, I'm aware that, by your calendar, I'm but six years younger than you——according to Livinius Clarkson on our way back into town with this week's hump, those stars that fell the year you were born in that primitive lodge was the same year President Jackson rode a train, "18 and 33," as Livinius phrased it, which was apparently newsworthy, both trains and presidents being of limited quantity in those early years of the nation.

Six years younger, but much more stooped and grey, much longer in the tooth and weaker in the eye. And shakier in the hand by day's end, I admit, and oftentimes by midday as well. But a glass of sweet sherry settles that right down. And if it doesn't, then the next one surely does.

"Do you mind?" Good Stab said then about the candles, after having peremptorily steered me away from that Crow trick.

"Oh yes," I said, and swept up to douse all of them I could and still be able to see, as if in a glass darkly, his face.

When I came back, I also had two bowls of Georgia Klein's stew, and Good Stab's darkened spectacles had been secreted away in a sleeve or pocket.

"I believe it even has the turnips your people like," I said, offering him a bowl and spoon and a tear of bread that was old, but would soften if patiently soaked.

He took the bowl like a holy relic, nodded thanks, and studied the spoon, causing me to wonder if his people had had those.

Finally he said, "This day I tell you of, as you know, is the same day so many of my people died on the Bear, in their lodges."

"As I know?" I asked, my spoon nearly to my mouth.

"I told you the Long Knives were moving up the Bear behind their scouts Joe Kipp and Joe Cobell," Good Stab said, watching my eyes as closely as he ever had, apparently forgetting that that word for soldiers was his father's, not his.

I nodded yes, yes, the Marias River, Major Baker, the two scouts with the same first name, the third week of that frigid January in 1870, and then I slurped the hot stew in, held it in my mouth until it cooled enough to swallow down.

What Good Stab wanted me to acknowledge, and agree to, was

that one so-called massacre was happening down in the grasslands, at a bend of the river out of the wind, and one undocumented one was happening up in the foothills under his people's Chief Mountain.

At the site of that second massacre, as Good Stab would term it, though in actuality it sounds more like an unrecorded skirmish at best, he was, like his traveling companions and their Great White God, the Cat Man, dead in the snow, all because of the tenuous relationship between beaver plews and repeating rifles. Or maybe it was due to the boy White Teeth having ruined Good Stab's first rifle. Or maybe it was the indirect fault of the men he would have me believe were playing Boston Tea Party with that wagon train which was trying only to make its clandestine delivery.

Whatever the case, I took another slurping bite, set my bread in the stew to soften and did so with laborious slowness, so as to instruct Good Stab of the effectiveness of such practice, bread being foreign to his people, and recited very clearly the invocation I had to, to invite him to begin again.

"I listen with a good heart."

The Nachzehrer's Dark Gospel

April 7, 1912

I had killed one soldier before that day on the mountain with the Cat Man, where I killed five before getting killed myself. That one soldier I killed before had been when our hunting party found him wandering at the edge of a large herd of blackhorns. I was twelve winters, was just there to stay out of the way. I saw this soldier when my father pulled my horse over to his and pointed down and down at the herd until I saw this dirty napikwan hunched over, moving with them.

Our scouts had found the herd the day before, and we had planned to hunt just after Sun Chief rose. But this napikwan in his dirty blue coat and shiny black moccasins was too interesting. For half the day, the hunting party watched him from the trees, talking between themselves about what to do, or not to do. It was because this soldier was carrying himself like he'd forgotten he was a two-legged.

A boy called Nitsy worked his way to the man through the grass like a crawls-on-his-belly, and came back to tell us about the bullet hole in this man's face, right under his right eye. He had been shot days ago but hadn't died, but what had been shot out of him was his memory that he was a man.

My father had some of the hunters chase this soldier down and tie him by the foot to a tree, and I was left to watch over him, and then the hunt went on, racing two hills away, leaving me with this soldier. This was back when we hunted with bows, so I couldn't hear the hunters, had to lean forward and picture what was happening.

As I'd seen one of our warriors do once, I took all my short arrows from the quiver and stood them before me in the ground, so I could snatch them up and shoot all my attackers when they rushed up.

I was standing behind that fort of my arrows when the soldier grabbed me from behind, by the neck, in the bend of his arm like this. He had gotten free from his rope, as four-leggeds always do. When he pulled me up to his chest, it was like a night-caller had snatched me up, he was that quiet behind.

My feet were kicking in the air long enough for the soldier to stop my breath. The yellow grass in front of me was losing its color in my eyes, and the sides of my vision were already in the Sandhills, and it didn't matter how I kicked, the man squeezed tighter. His beard was on my shoulder and that was the first time I'd ever felt a napikwan beard. I didn't know what it would do, touching my skin.

I pulled and scratched at the soldier's arm but was just a boy, where he was a man. Finally one of my kicking feet caught an arrow's fletching between my toes. I pulled it up to my hand, could only see black by now, and with the very end of my strength I drove the arrow back beside my head, its side cutting my face here, making this scar.

A moment later I dropped to the ground, my throat too tight to let me throw up, and when I was finally breathing again, I looked around to this soldier, which is what my father had explained he was, the same as we were. He was balanced on his knees, dead. For a long time I thought that was how napikwans died, sitting up on their knees.

The arrow was stuck into the same hole where he'd been shot, but my arrow had gone deeper, into the four-legged part of him, killing it as well. I touched his beard with the back of my fingers like this but drew my hand fast away, sure that the hair continued under his shirt, over his whole body, and that that was why he'd been moving with the herd, because his curly dark fur was the same as the blackhorns'.

By the time the hunters rode back up in a swirl, yipping and spinning their horses, I had this soldier's head in my lap. His scalp was flapping and my knife was bloody, but I couldn't get his hair off. I'd been cutting too deep, didn't know how to do it right, yet, but still I could tell my father was proud.

That night around the fire I got the first tongue from the hunt, and the other boys looked at me in awe, the cut on my face not tended, and this is when one of the hunters told me that that had been a good stab I did with the arrow, and the rest of the hunters nodded with this, and when my father finally agreed with this, after looking long at me, that became who I was, Good Stab. I was the first of my age to get his warrior name.

It carried a responsibility with it, I knew. To show I understood, I shared that tongue with the other boys who had been brought along, and one of those boys was Tall Dog, but we didn't know each other yet, and I didn't remember him there, but he remembered me that day.

And that's the story of the first soldier I killed.

The second and third and fourth and fifth and sixth soldiers were there in the Backbone, fast, with the beaver family watching and the Cat Man hissing, but the next one was slower. I'm glad my father wasn't there to see me this time.

Like that first soldier from my twelfth winter, I had also forgotten I was a two-legged.

I woke up rushing over the snow on all fours, downhill.

I was just coming out of the trees and into the grass, and Sun

Chief had been in his lodge a long time, I could tell. Not from the cold, I couldn't feel the cold, I still can't, but I could tell how deep the night was from the color of the snow. I could see that the storm was over, and it had been over for at least a day. The snow was piled up but it had melted on top and then frozen hard enough for me to run on top of. That's what I thought at first. And there was ice at the bottom of the drifts, meaning Sun Chief had heated the snow up after it was iced, and the water had come slipping out the bottom like it does, which told me the storm must have been over for at least two days, but probably four or five, really. The more I looked and noticed, the more days had passed, and this didn't make sense but it didn't stop me from running either.

Soon enough I slid on some of that ice at the bottom of the drifts and went into the next big pile of snow but came out the other side still pulling ahead on all fours, not with my legs going one after the other like a big-mouth, but together and pushing and jumping like a real lion. I'd seen long-tails fly low and fast over the grass like a round-ball shot from a gun, and that's how it felt, this running.

Against the white of the snow, I could see that my arm and hand and the tops of my legs and my feet and the rest of me was black like dried blood. I scratched at it with my cheek to get it off but, instead, the skin came off like the bark of a quaking-leaf tree when it's been in the kind of fire that goes past fast enough that the tree can still live.

I had been burned like that. I was like a piece of meat that had spilled over the side of the kettle, been left in the embers for the dogs to nose out when there's just white ash.

But at the same time, I was alive. And running so fast I couldn't stop.

Also, there was a taste in my nose, which I know you can think means I was smelling, but it was more than that. I'd never tasted with my nose before. Not where every taste turned into a picture of itself. I could tell that a long-legs had passed here, and that a real-bear was sleeping there, and that a family of dirty-faces were living over there in a hole under a thick root. It made me dizzy and have to shake my head from having to know so much all at once.

But all those tastes weren't what was pulling me ahead, out of the trees and into the open grass, faster and faster. The taste in the air that was pulling me ahead was different. It was deeper, and wider, and more full. It was old meat and tobacco smoke, rum and leather and dried blood, and the picture it made in my head was a sound, was thunder but deeper, and I screamed with rage to hear it, because I was hearing it again, but I couldn't remember from where.

Like this I ran Sun Chief up. The palms of my hands were scraped raw from the ice and the sharp yellow grass, and my feet were too, because I didn't have moccasins on anymore, or leggings, or a shirt, or anything.

This is how we're born into the world, and this was what was happening to me. I was being born again, but not like the Black Robe said when he baptized all the Pikuni in Big River, when I was throwing up whitehorn milk and Wolf Calf was patting me on the back and smoking his short pipe and chuckling.

The one time I stopped, it wasn't from needing to breathe or sleep, it was to shove my nose into some of the grass and snow where there was piss. This was by Badger Creek, close to the fort buildings we call Old Agency now, but weren't calling the Ration House yet. I could see its tall part with the window to the east, and knew that the only reason the one who made water here hadn't gone over there was because he had passed in the night, and hadn't seen it.

I breathed the taste in again to know it better and then stood up on both legs and screamed again, and had to fall away because this was the first time I'd looked straight up with these new eyes.

Sun Chief was staring back at me brighter than he ever had, like the time the year before this when he turned into a black tunnel in the sky, a black tunnel with flaming wings to either side that were hotter than his middle had ever been. I flinched away, fell back and covered my face with my arms like this, and my legs wanted to take me back to the cool shadow under the trees, but my nose made me stumble forward, finally start running again, squinting and sometimes closing my eyes, because I didn't need them, this soldier was leaving so much taste in the air.

Dark was just leaking out from the Backbone when I caught him. We were almost exactly where my father, one year older than when I got my name, with Calflooking and some other boys, tried to steal the guns and horses from the Great Father's boat men, who shot Calflooking and counted coup on him after he was dead by putting a medal around his neck.

This soldier I'd been running after, I could see now, or remember, was the one who had pulled the string on the cannon and cut the Cat Man in half, finally killing him. He had a beard now to go with his wings mustache that made him look like he had the legs of a flapping bird in his mouth, meaning I had been dead long enough for him to grow that, but his eyes were the same kind as before, that can look dead and flat over a cannon.

He was pulling two long branches of dead wood up from a creek bottom that didn't have water in the winter, and the effort was making the taste all around him even thicker, so I could breathe in the smoke and ash and blood and fire on his hands and sleeves. Tall Dog was part of that taste in the air, and Peasy, but not Hunts-to-the-Side, which I could tell meant that he'd pulled Peasy and Tall Dog and me onto the top of Hunts-to-the-Side before burning us.

But there was a greasier, more dangerous smell, that it took me a moment to get a picture for. But then I did. This soldier had waited the storm out by backing into a hole left by the sideways roots of a tall tree that had fallen over the year before, and its roots made the roof of a cave, and pushed all the way into the back of that dark place had been a real-bear, sleeping its long sleep, and this soldier never knew.

This was the same real-bear I'd tasted on the air, running down from Chief Mountain.

I can see that you don't believe this, but that's all right.

You will.

The first soldier I killed, I was twelve winters. The next five were so fast it was like slapping flies.

This next one, he was different.

We saw each other, each on our own short hill, and I felt inside that I was my father and those other boys, seeing the Great Father's boat men on the opposite hill, each of them trying to figure the other ones out. The soldier was holding those two long branches he would make another fire from, and I was naked and burned, on all fours, my nose to the air, my eyes open all the way, now that the world wasn't so bright.

Instead of talking with signs and sitting around the fire like my father and those boys had done with the Great Father's boat men, we each already knew what the other was, didn't have to wait to figure it out. I don't like being this, what I am, but if I have to be, I wish I could have been with my father and those boys that day, so those boat men couldn't have told the Great Father to build forts in Pikuni territory, and fill it with soldiers and trappers and traders and whiskey.

But we did like the guns.

This soldier didn't have his on him, though. All he could do was drop his branches and dive away behind the hill he was on, to get back to wherever that gun was.

He didn't make it.

By the time he was down to where the creek usually is, I was jumping onto his back. All the times before I'd jumped on an enemy, it was usually off a running horse, so that part of it felt the same.

What didn't feel the same was I had no war club, no knife, no lance.

Also, I was leading with my open mouth, and this soldier, to me, he was moving so slow, like wading through mud, but the creek was dry, and had been probably since Cold Moon.

My open mouth bit into the side of this soldier's neck and all my weight was on his back, which should have driven him to slide on the ground, packing dirt and grass between his teeth. But the same way the crust of snow would hold me now without dropping me through as fast as I used to, this soldier could also carry me, at least for a few steps.

Until I started drinking.

At the fort, I once saw one of your generals drink a glass of what Peasy said was buttermilk with some of your rum mixed in with it, and the way it made this general breathe slow and close his eyes and relax into his own body, drinking from the soldier was that for me, but it was like the whole world was buttermilk and rum, and I'd never before had even one drop of it.

His blood filled me up, and made me more warm and alive than I'd ever been, even in my own lodge when I'd had wives and children and horses. My hands held his head like this and my legs were around his body, and I told you I was drinking from him, but it's really that I was nursing like a baby.

He kicked and jerked and scratched at me, but it was slower and slower, and nothing could hurt me, then.

The two-legged part of me knew I should save some of him, that I didn't want this going over so soon, so fast, but the four-legged part of me growled at this, couldn't even think about stopping.

It took the same long to drink all of his blood as it takes for a small piece of real-meat to go dark on the outside in the boiling water of an iron kettle.

This was my real-meat now, I could tell.

When the soldier was empty and dead, drank dry, my stomach was sticking out like this and I was breathing deep, but I couldn't stop suckling. I knew there had to be more in him. Finally, desperate for more, I cracked his leg under the knee against a tall rock in the bottom of the dry creek and then pulled the foot away, the leg bones in there open.

They fit perfect in my mouth, and I sucked the marrow out, clumped its thick wetness into my throat and swallowed so hard it hurt my eyes, and I was trying to break the longer leg bone open when that marrow started to come back up my throat, with strings in it that made me feel like I was choking.

This is because it was solid, not thin like blood. Marrow from the bone has blood of a sort in it, but that doesn't matter.

Anything I eat that's not warm blood, my body pushes it back up.

I backed away from throwing up, wiped my mouth with my arm, some more of that blackened skin coming off that I had to spit away, and I ran my fingers through my hair, felt for the first time that my hair was gone. Hair burns first in a fire.

This was good, I told myself. Because I would have cut it off anyway, to grieve for Tall Dog and Peasy, and even Hunts-to-the-Side. And for that beaver I knew now I shouldn't have killed.

That's what started all this. I've heard our elders and many-faces men and even chiefs say that it's the napikwans who are ruining the world, but napikwans are just what happens when we forget we're Pikuni. When we think a many-shots gun is more important than beaver medicine.

The soldiers ahead of us in the Backbone when we were walking up, they probably would have kept marching straight ahead to Chief Mountain and maybe the Real Old Man Country if I hadn't kicked into that lodge of sticks in the water.

This, what I am now, it's punishment, that's what I'm telling you. I deserve it.

There on that rise with my chest and mouth and hands and arms shining with wet blood, I laid my head back on that dead soldier's stomach and stared up at the Big Fire Star, thought I could hear it hissing in the sky.

I didn't have to try to know I couldn't stand yet. This is how it is after I feed. I have to lie down as flat as I can, so the new blood can move through my body, into all its new pouches. It's like carrying all the water skins you need, but carrying them inside you.

That hissing I was hearing wasn't the Big Fire Star, either, or Seven Persons, or the Poor Boys, or any of them.

It was the sound of a little big-mouth's front legs parting the yellow grass, two hills away. A mother.

She was watching me, and when my body started to shake me up and down, because this was the first time I'd ever fed like this, she laid her ears back but didn't leave.

She wasn't waiting to eat from the dead soldier, I could tell. She was hungry, but for real food, not food I'd touched.

She had never seen anything like me.

The lashback from the beaver medicine gone bad had turned me into a child of the Cat Man. I'm an atupyoye now, Person-Eater like the Pikuni have always known about, but I'm worse. It was good my wives and my children were already in the Sandhills. Now they wouldn't have to see me like this.

When the shaking stopped, I rolled over and cried into this dead soldier's chest, but because I was full of blood now, my tears were red.

The little big-mouth yipped, asking if there was anything it could do.

"Kill me," I told her, pointing my chin to the sky and closing my eyes, and I felt a mouth close over my throat then, and it was warmer and bigger and hungrier than this little big-mouth's, it was the night itself, but it just held its teeth there, didn't rip my head off like I wanted it to so I could go to the Sandhills, and I know now that this was Beaver Chief, showing that he could end my suffering if he wanted, but he wasn't ready for it to be over.

When I looked again, the little big-mouth was gone back to her pups, and I was alone.

Because I didn't have a knife of my own, I took the one from the soldier's belt.

I faced the east, nodded to myself to say I could do this, and then I pulled the sharp side of the blade across my throat, as hard and as deep as I could, and then, because I'd done it once to earn my name, I stabbed it into my chest with the last of my strength, all the way until the tip came out my back.

Like that first soldier I killed, I fell to my knees and balanced there, my new blood slipping down my chest.

If Tall Dog wasn't dead, he could walk in, read the tracks in the dirt and grass and snow, and know what had happened, tell my father what I did, to save the Pikuni. To save them from me.

But it was fine if no one found my bones and this soldier's bones mixed together. Let Sun Chief bleach them and dry them out until they turned to dust and blew into the Backbone, taking me home.

This is what I was thinking, there on my knees, that knife in me, my throat opened and spurting.

And then I felt it, behind me. Or maybe I heard it, maybe I tasted it on the air, or maybe I just knew, remembered, recognized what this felt like each time it had happened before.

It was my swift-runner, who had always hopped in, showing me which direction I needed to go next.

It had warned me about the beaver lodge, but I hadn't listened.

And now it had come all the way down here, and when it still had its white fur on for winter, so anything could see it down here, and eat it, or feed it to a den of yipping pups.

"Go away!" I said to it the best I could without turning around, but because my throat didn't work right, cut open, I held my hand behind me and motioned for my swift-runner to go back to the Backbone where it belonged, to find some better Pikuni to help, because this one was already dying.

I could tell that my swift-runner was up on its hind legs, its nose tasting what I had become, its eyes wet and curious, but sad, too.

Scratching across its black eyes, I knew, were the stars that fell across the smoke-hole of my mother's birthing lodge, and I cried again, tilting my head back to open my throat wider to the night, to let it all in, and I told Feather Woman that that magic turnip she was looking for to get back to her world, here was its top, right in my throat, she could just grab on and pull and pull, unwind me into the stars.

Please.

But she didn't.

And I heard or felt or knew the soft foot pats of my swift-runner, hopping away from me once and for all, so I would never know what direction to go anymore, would have to figure each step out on my own from here on out.

I told Tall Dog I was sorry, I told my father I meant to do better, I told my wives and children to keep the flap open for me, I was almost there, and then all the grass around me went black like blowing shadows, and I closed my eyes.

When I opened them again, Sun Chief was burning above me again, so that the skin of my face was stiff and dry.

I fell back, shielding my eyes.

I felt my throat, and it wasn't cut anymore.

I patted my arms, and the burned blackness was soft now, healed.

The knife was on its side between my knees.

I touched my hair, and it was trying to come back.

Dried on my face and chest was blood. The dead soldier's. Mine.

I stood, fell back down to a knee, covering my eyes with my left hand like this, and, just feeling, not looking, I tore some of the soldier's cloth shirt away, tied it over my face against Sun Chief, who the Pikuni can never turn their backs on. But I had to.

I had to lie down on my back to work my legs into the soldier's blue pants, and I had to pack his boots with dry grass to make my feet fit, and I kept having to stop to cry, but all crying did was get more blood on me, which was less blood in me.

Going by smell and memory, I staggered back up the hill I had jumped down, onto the soldier.

I knew I should be thirsty, that I needed to find water, but I was like that mad big-mouth you were talking about last time, when you weren't talking about Mad Wolf. Even thinking about taking water into my mouth hurt my throat and made my shoulders hitch up with gagging.

There's only one thing I can drink anymore.

It's why I'm here, talking to you. You Black Robes know about drinking blood, don't you? You make your people in these wooden seats do it every time they're here.

In that way we're the same.

But you're still a two-legged, even from drinking all that blood. Not me. What I am now is a four-legged, but with a man's memories, as punishment. And no arrow or bullet can stab deep enough to kill me, because Beaver Chief won't let them.

I didn't know that yet that first day after this soldier, though.

All I knew then was that I had to get away from Sun Chief. To do that without my eyes, I just had to keep the heat of him on my face, since it was already past the middle of the day. And I could smell all the places I'd touched, running down from the Backbone after the soldier.

I walked west like a dead man, and my hand on my stomach told me that all the blood I'd drank, that I hadn't bled back out, or cried from eyes, had found its pouch in me.

I knew I should go back, hide that soldier the same way we'd been hiding that wagon train, but I didn't. If any Pikuni died from the finding of that dead soldier, then that's one more person I'm responsible for.

One of so many, I couldn't count them in a moon.

By dark, I was stumbling into the first of the trees under Chief Mountain.

It was cool and dark.

I took the cloth from my eyes, let it fall away behind me. I still had to squint, but I huddled under a rock wall in the shade until Seven Persons came out.

I was shaking, but not from cold. To be a Pikuni and be alone is to not be a person anymore. I sat still long enough that the kind of dirty-face that lives in the Backbone jerked and darted past, seeing me too late.

My hand snatched it up before I told it to, and I cracked into its spongy ribs with my mouth, sucked it dry.

The taste wasn't buttermilk and rum for a general, was more like when Tall Dog had caught one of the silver fish from Two Medicine and we'd tried eating it even though we knew it was wrong.

I gagged but didn't throw up, and then I looked at the dead dirty-face in my hand.

From the holes bitten into its side, I knew to feel of my teeth with my other hand.

They were like the Cat Man's, these two, here. I was a man on the outside, but inside, even just inside my mouth, I was a four-legged.

But they're not always like that.

After drinking that one dirty-face's blood, the two sharp teeth pulled back inside. When I'm hungry, or eating, they come out, but when I've fed, they go back in. That's why they look flat like yours now, except white. It's so I can walk in the street. The red-back has that color on it so it matches the trees it lives in, so it can hide, even with its bushy tail. That same way, my teeth hide, so I can sit in the back of your church like everyone else.

When Sun Chief splintered his light through the branches the next morning, I shied away from it, smelled my way to the same fallen down tree the soldier had waited the storm out in.

The real-bear smell was so thick in there I could hardly breathe, but it wasn't dark the way it should have been. Not to me. Not anymore.

There were no colors, but I could see the dirt walls, the dull shards of rock that had never known Sun Chief, the hanging roots, the leaves, the pine needles, all of it.

This is where I live now, the night. My eyes are like a night-caller's, so I can see, and feed myself better. But, with these over my eyes, I can still come out while Sun Chief is still in the sky, even if he hates me now.

Instead of eating more, I burrowed deeper into the hole under the tree and slept, not because I was tired but because if I woke up again, maybe this dream could be over. But this sleep wasn't like I'd always slept. It was just blackness, and falling, and a great hollow space around me, with no edges. This is how sleep is for me now.

The next night, I stayed where I was, wasn't hungry yet. If I don't move, don't use the blood I've drank, I only have to eat once a moon, and can even go two or three if I have to.

Wags-his-tails and long-legs and long-tails and other swift-runners who didn't know me moved around, but I let them pass, was so still they didn't hear me, and I don't smell like a man anymore either, I don't smell like anything except maybe broken open ceramic, is that the word? That powdery glass your plates you eat from are made of, when they're not iron. That's what I smell like now. That's why the four-leggeds never knew I was there. The only way they could have seen me was my eyes, opening in that darkness, and tracking them step by step, jealous of their warmth, their families, and that they could still eat whatever they wanted.

With Sun Chief's next rising, I nodded off, moved my shoulders back into the frozen dirt crumbling over me, and when I woke at nightfall, I had moved deep back in my sleep. All the way to alongside the real-bear, down for the winter's long sleep.

It was breathing slow, and, lying with my chest up to it, my breathing went like the real-bear's, deep and slow, and the next time I woke, not even aware I'd been asleep, my mouth was latched onto the bear's hump, just biting in shallow.

My new teeth had punctured in, but not deep. Just enough for some of its winter fat shot through with veins of blood to coat my mouth but not go down my throat.

I closed my eyes, didn't pull away, and this was the only good thing to happen to me since kicking into that beaver lodge. I couldn't dream anymore, which is a banishment no Pikuni would choose over dying, but, with my mouth fixed on this real-bear, I could taste its dreams, which was all one long dream that never stopped.

It wasn't pictures and faces like mine had used to be, it was sounds and tastes, but what the bear was dreaming wasn't sounds and tastes, it was how those things felt. It was a fullness of smells, and snuffling, and rustling deeper, and the bursting of small, tight skins in a mouth, followed by coolness, and sweetness, and the satisfaction that there was going to be more of this, and then more after that.

What real-bears dream about, it's ripe berry bushes.

This is how I passed the winter.

But it only works with real-bears. It's because they used to be people. If blackhorns slept like that, all closed in, all winter, I would like to ride their dreams with them, I think.

If there were any left to dream with.

I woke in Geese Moon not biting into that real-bear anymore, but it biting into me. My shoulder was in that real-bear's mouth. The real-bear wasn't all the way awake yet, but it knew in its sleep way that it wasn't alone like it had been when it nosed down into this place.

It flung me side to side, against the top and bottom of this cave that was really a hole, that had been its winter den.

When I didn't fight back, it threw me away, then it shook its head all the way awake and roared, its breath hot on my face, the long lines of its spit splashing against my eyes and in my mouth, and a real-bear's first spit after sleeping through winter is like tree sap, but cold and stinging.

"Thank you!" I yelled back to it when it was done roaring, and pointed to Sun Chief's light past the roots of the tree. "Go now, eat!"

Instead, it charged at me with its mouth open, its long claws holding my sides and cutting in.

I was weak from the long fast of winter, and at first I didn't remember what I was now, and what I wasn't.

But the Cat Man in me knew.

It opened its mouth, roared back, into this real-bear's mouth, and I only weigh as much as a boy of maybe fourteen winters now, even though I'm this size, and I'm only as strong as I ever was as a man, but when I drove my hands down onto the tops of the bear's, holding me, its claws had to let go.

Doing it broke the bones in both of my arms, though.

I screamed from how that hurt and how it sounded, but the hurt was over almost when it started. Without meaning to think it, I knew it was my mother's hand coming down to cup over my broken bones, and take the pain away. I know I was wrong, because that would mean that the Cat Man had a mother to do that for him too. But he had been in an iron cage when I shot my arrow into him, not just tied with ropes to the floor of that wagon. This meant he had this same thing I did, where I wasn't strong, but what should hurt and tell me to stop, it wasn't doing that anymore.

It means I can pull harder, hit deeper, run faster, even if it breaks my bones or tears my skin.

All that can be fixed by the next meal, if I drink enough.

But it doesn't heal right away.

I was still the real-bear's plaything, my hands hanging down useless. When the real-bear came for me this time, I stepped a long step back. It took my other shoulder with its teeth and shook me fast like they do, like a dog does to a swift-runner.

When it let go, I flew out past the turned up root of the great tree we were under.

Because we were on a hill, I hit and kept rolling, then slid, and where I finally stopped was the edge of a pond.

It was the one the beavers had made. The one I'd waded through to get to their lodge.

The real-bear knew this, I know.

In the Backbone, the four-leggeds aren't just four-leggeds.

How I knew it knew was that, instead of lumbering down into the pond with me, to keep the fight going, this real-bear went sideways along the hill to the south, its breath heavy and deep, its great feet crashing with sound.

It was going to where it knew the berries would be in a few moons.

"Find them," I said to it. And then, forgetting my mouth was coated with winter fat shot through with blood, I swallowed, had to fall into the water to throw that back up. And because I couldn't hold myself up on my broken arms, my face went in, and breathed water in and down, which made me throw up more.

Trying to get back up, I stilled, hearing something.

It was one of the beavers, slapping its tail on the water.

It made me want to cry. But I was glad that one of the younger beavers had taken up that duty. I was glad that they had a new guard, a new warrior.

This is how it should be.

Finally, using only my legs, I crawled up to the shore, turned over, and laid there with my eyes shut against Sun Chief.

When a bird of some sort swooped past to see what I was, I bit up fast, onto one of its legs, then rolled over, trapping it to the ground with my mouth, so I could slurp its blood in. It was worse than a silver fish, but it was blood, so I could hold it in.

Hours later, my arms were starting to straighten back up, and harden enough I could use them a little.

The Cat Man had healed faster, but that's because he was older.

I was still new, having to figure everything out.

With the dark, I stood. Light as I am now, I hardly make a sound anymore.

This meant that, when I heard a long-legs grazing out into a meadow three hills away, I was able to sneak up behind her, clamp onto one of her hind legs with my hands, to keep her from jumping away. Instead, she kicked back hard with her other foot, hitting me in the face, knocking my nose and cheek in, and changing the direction my eyes looked, so everything had a shadow that was also itself, but with watery edges.

I held on anyway, my arms breaking again, and finally got my mouth up to the back of the long-leg's long leg enough to bite in.

I didn't kill her by taking her lungs or heart, or cutting her neck.

I killed her by drinking her.

And she had so much more blood than that soldier. I told myself again to just drink a little, let her leave, but, just like with the soldier, I couldn't stop until she was empty, her eyes clouded over, mouth open and dry.

This time my belly swelled so much that dark purple lines stretched in it, like I was going to burst open. My fingertips and toes swelled up, too full, getting fuller as the blood leaked from my belly out into its pouches, until finally I had to bite down on my wrist with my teeth, to let some blood out. It sprayed up as high as a boy of four winters, or a tall dog, and when some of it landed back on my lips, it tasted just as wrong as it had when I drank it in the first time. The soldier had been so much better.

But the long-leg's blood worked. The bones in my arm and my face healed by Sun Chief's next light.

I stood, staggered to a cliff of leaning out rocks, found a ledge I could shove myself under, and hid for the day, and the next night, and the next day, and finally came out into the darkness the third or fourth night. Only moving around at night, where Sun Chief couldn't see me, I was forgetting how many days were passing. It was all one long night.

Standing against that cliff, the Backbone was alive with sound, with tastes in the air, but I was full, didn't need to feed yet.

I went back to the long-legs who had given me her blood and she was still there. Nothing was feeding on her.

This is the way it is.

I knelt beside her and petted the side of her stiff face, then I laid down beside her and kept my arm on her and I didn't know what to do anymore. I didn't know how to die, or if I had the nerve to try to again, and if I went for starving, the Cat Man inside me woke up, ate anyway.

Four nights later, maybe six, the long-legs rotting where she lay, her taste in the air still good, I went two hills over and found the clearing where the soldiers had shot us.

Standing up under the melting snow was one wagon wheel, its spokes still in it, but cracking in long lines from freezing and melting and drying all winter.

In a pile of burn that was square because it was still the iron cage, I could taste Peasy and Tall Dog and Mountain Chief, and, I knew without having to dig in or taste that deep, the Cat Man. Not because he had been Pikuni, but because he wasn't a soldier. The reason I hadn't smelled him on the soldier I drank was that the Cat Man didn't smell like a man anymore. He didn't smell like anything. Neither do I. I can stand right behind you in the darkness and I'm light enough the pine needles hardly crunch under my feet, and my smell won't tell you I'm there either. If you feel my breath on your neck, it's too late.

I don't mean you, Three-Persons. I mean anyone.

If we'd met the Cat Man without his cage, none of us would have lived, and our bodies would have been added to the others at the wagon train, like they'd fought us off.

But because he had been in a cage, that cage was a grave box for him and Peasy and Tall Dog. It meant the soldier who did that to them while he was growing his beard, he knew their spirits would be wandering now forever. Their left behind bodies being in that iron cage, it was a joke, an insult. I wrinkled my nose up, tasting that the soldier I'd drank had made water through the bars of the cage.

I'd been in that cage dead when he'd peed there, I knew.

But, at some point after that, I'd woken up, crawled out, and ran after him, as long as it took.

All the dead-man-crosses that had been hanging on the bars all around had burned off in his fire. But they hadn't mattered anyway.

Over from the iron cage a little bit, under a crust of snow I had to scrape off, was the cannon. If I had powder I could stuff it with rocks and whatever iron was still around here, and stand in front of it, pull the string myself.

But there was no powder up there, and the cannon was already flaking with rust. No birds had taken the trigger string to make nests from, no dirty-faces had chewed it to sharpen their teeth, but they might, when the snow was lower.

I pulled the cannon's halter over my shoulder like this, to drag it under a tree for if I ever found powder again, and I pulled hard enough to almost break the wheels free from their ruts in the ground, but I could feel the bones in my arms creaking like they wanted to break again, which is the bad thing about not hurting enough.

Instead, I dug up all the soldiers' many-shots guns. They were rusted, and all but one wouldn't cock back anymore.

I laid them like Sun Chief's rays around Peasy and Tall Dog and Hunts-to-the-Side and the Cat Man, all shooting away from them, but then I decided the Cat Man didn't deserve that honor, so I dug into the cage, through the bones and leathery skin and hair and dried leggings and moccasins and, sort of under the cage, a belt Hunts-to-the-Side's second wife had made for him from iron studs.

All I found was ash.

This told me that, when my kind die, we don't leave bones and skin and hair behind.

I sang a quiet song over this snow grave, but my voice was raw and wrong and weak, and it was more an insult than anything that helped them.

My tears left red spots on the snow.

Finally I walked away from that place, telling myself never to come back. I could smell that the soldiers had been buried in shallow holes under a cutbank just over the hill on the other side, but I didn't go over there, didn't care about them.

For the next moon I watched the beaver family rebuild their lodge one stick at a time.

The whole time, they kept one of them watching me, even when I sat far away upwind.

In the day, while they slept, I covered my eyes as best I could and dragged sticks and limbs and dead trees closer to them, to help, but they wouldn't touch that wood, wouldn't let it be part of their lodge.

I understood.

I ran down a young long-legs who kept watching me through the trees, grabbed on to his spike horns and bit into the back of his neck, drank him as he ran and ran, until his chin had to dig into the ground and his hooves pushed back into the dirt slower and slower.

There was no snow anymore. Only in the shade, and high up the mountains.

Chief Mountain watched me from between the trees, his great rock face never smiling even once. I didn't know if I belonged in this holy place anymore or if I was an intruder, like the trappers we were always having to run down so they would leave enough fur for us to trade.

Two days after that spike, I ran down his father even though I wasn't hungry enough to yet, held him down and drank from his belly while he kicked at me with his hooves. His horns were already fallen off, but he still kept trying to hook them into me. I could tell he was the spike's father from his taste.

I cried while I drank him, and then I had to bite into both arms and both legs to let his blood back out. I laid in a pool of it and held my arms around my shoulders like this, like I was cold, and I tried to remember having given that bite of tongue to Tall Dog when I was a boy, but I couldn't.

Finally I ran away from Chief Mountain, down to Two Medicine Lodges, where Pikuni go for ceremony. It was where I had found my swift-runner, after I was already Good Stab, when I never pictured I could be anything but Good Stab.

When a wags-his-tail ran in front of me, going sideways uphill like they do, I chased it but not because I was hungry yet. I chased it because it ran, which was something I'd seen big-mouths do. You don't want to bite something until it doesn't want you to.

Instead of riding this wags-his-tail down like the long-legs, I grabbed on to the soft horns it was trying to grow and twisted hard, cracking the neck over.

I drank half of him before the blood went cold and dead, but I didn't know, so kept drinking. The dead blood didn't come up my throat like fat or food does, but my body pushed it up through the skin, so I was wearing that wags-his-tail. When that dead blood was in me, it was hot, it was cooking me from the inside, making me shake.

This is how I learned to only drink while the heart's still pushing.

Because I lost most of that blood, I ran down a young wags-his-tail, still with the white dots on it like hailstones, and was able to keep all of it down because it was so small. I'd been able to hold it in my arms like a child while I drank, even, and the small amount of blood was rich enough to last longer than a full grown wags-his-tail.

A week after that was when those same hailstones showed up on the top of my arms and the top of my legs. I tried rubbing them with dirt, and washing in a spring that had a rock blocking it, but they wouldn't come off.

By the end of Beginning Summer Moon, I felt two hard nubs on my head, here and here.

I was growing horns like a long-legs, like a wags-his-tail.

Because that's what I'd been eating.

If I ate only sharp-backs for long enough, enough to fill me up with their blood over and over, I would grow a quill bustle on my back, I knew. If I lived only on silver fish, I would lean over the water and fall in, never come back up on land. If I ran down a sticky-mouth and then all its brothers and sisters, then I would get those same white stripes on my sides, here, and would never be still, would always be roaming fast, hungry.

I thought about this for nearly a whole moon, not feeding at all anymore.

Was this why the Cat Man's mouth had been pushing out? In that wagon, the men carrying it had probably been feeding it dirty-faces and big dirty-faces only. So that's what it had been turning into, mouthful of blood by mouthful of blood.

If I wanted to be a two-legged again, or look more like one on the outside, I needed to stop drinking long-legs and wags-his-tails.

I needed to drink from someone who walked like me.

And the only one I knew about up here, I'd already chased him down into the grass, left him dead on his knees like an offering to Sun Chief.

Finally, nearly mad with hunger, I climbed to the top of Old Man Dog Mountain at night, where the wind blows up from all sides, and closed my eyes, opened my nose.

By dawn, I had the ugly scent I knew was a trapper. They wear the same leggings and shirts and boots until they fall apart. Even before I became this, what I am now, I could always smell them.

I slept that day under a cutbank, and I could tell it was Frog Moon already from all the croaking. Beside me in the hard dirt the creek had pulled away were the bones of a beaver hand, except they were big like mine.

I left the bones there.

Beaver Medicine wasn't for me anymore.

That night, the trapper's taste hot in my nose, I found him sitting by his small fire, singing to himself.

He was the first man I'd been close to since the soldier.

He didn't smell me or see me, but his shaggy black big-ears knew I was there. It whinnied and pulled at its rope. The man came up from the fire with a long round-ball gun sliding from its fringe sheath with beads. It was a Pikuni sheath, I could tell.

It made me hiss, that he had it.

I had been going to walk in, ask for some of his bitter black water, just to get him turning his back to me long enough, but now I just rushed in, jumping with one foot off the rump of his squealing big-ears, taking the barrel of his long gun in both my hands and biting into the front of his throat with my mouth, so that at first all I got was air he was trying to breathe.

But then the blood came.

I drank so hard from him that my back hunched up and down

like I was being sick, that's how good it is to feed on a two-legged like I'm supposed to. It's better than cold water from the creek after a long hunt.

With enough blood in me, I can see colors in the night, and I can taste those colors, and I can hear the roots of the trees, reaching one piece of dirt deeper in.

I knew not to drink the big-ears. Because I didn't want big ears.

Two days later, my horn nubs weren't shorter, but they also weren't longer.

I smelled another trapper, stalked him for three nights before jumping on him in the daytime. He was tall enough that the blood I drank from him came up around the edges of my fingernails, and he had something spoiled in his blood, that was making his nose rot away, but it didn't matter, inside me.

The next trapper, during Thunder Moon, was so drunk on whiskey that he smiled when I stood up on the other side of the fire from him. I left the traps he had in his camp out on Wild Goose Island in Walled-in Lakes. I left them out there so no other trappers could use them, and then I went back to the other trappers' camps, left their rusting traps there too.

Six sleeps after drinking that drunk trapper, I woke under a high ledge with my antler nub pressing into the side of my face. It had fallen off in my sleep. I worked the other one back and forth with my fingers like this until it cracked off too, left a smooth hard place under my hair right here, that's grown over again now.

I set both of those antler nubs on that high rock, and went down for another trapper, and another trapper. We thought we'd gotten them all years ago, but some of them had been deep enough in the Backbone that we couldn't find them. Or more were coming in, around us.

It didn't matter.

I went in circles around the drunk trapper's camp until I smelled his traps out. Four of them were empty, but a swift-runner was caught in the last one. It was mewling and pulling. It had its brown hair on, fine and soft.

"I can't drink you," I told it. "I can only drink two-leggeds. And I have to drink them all the way gone."

I couldn't drink this swift-runner, but I could open the trap.

The swift-runner tried to hop away, but both its hind legs were broken.

I sat with it through the night, and with Sun Chief's rising, I twisted its head over until the neck cracked, and laid it in a bright open spot, so some four-legged that could eat it might find it. I left the trap that killed it out on the island with the rest, and would always do that with any trap I found. I would have thrown them in the lake, but I didn't think the underwater people needed napikwan iron down there.

For sixteen sleeps after that, I sat high up on Face Mountain and didn't move, even when Sun Chief shone down and made my skin hard like dry leather.

I could feel the Cat Man rising in me, hungry, but still I sat.

I was thinking of my father, Wolf Calf, back in his lodge, tipping a drink of water out onto the ground for me. I was thinking of Tall Dog, buried in that cage. I was thinking of camp, and trying to do what I said and look back from my horse the last time I left, so I could save it all in my head, see it whenever I wanted.

By the twenty-first sleep, I was panting fast with my mouth, because I had used up nearly all of the trapper's blood I'd had in me.

I had to feed.

I stood, my burned skin cracking and the cracks showing blood that was too thick to come out. I followed a white big-head path down and saw two of them coming up the other way. They saw me too, and we stood there until I stepped away. Still they wouldn't pass, so I went down through the rocks and trees, crashing and falling and finally sliding, a sharp rock pushing through my side, leaking out the little blood I had left. It didn't hurt as much as it would have before, but it made me like a fire with no more wood to burn.

When I could, I stood, looked around. I opened my nose to taste the air, but without enough blood in me, I could only smell like a man, now.

Desperate, I stumbled forward, rubbing past trees that opened my skin more, Sun Chief glaring down at me, his heat searing the cuts in my side and my shoulders and the heels of my hands, so I had to hold my hands in fists to hold the pain in.

This is when I saw a two-legged walking up a clearing like a shadow, on the other side of the trees.

I fell to my knees I was so happy. I cried but it was dry, not even enough blood in me to make tears. I pulled forward through the red bushes, my eyes not working right anymore, and heard a black-bear snuffling under a log but didn't stop. He didn't have the blood I needed, and wouldn't have any dreams for me either.

I stepped out behind this two-legged I could only see the shape of, and I was so light he didn't hear me.

I didn't have time or patience to hunt, so just rushed ahead, my arms low to the ground, and, twelve paces back from him, I jumped, to come down on him like a night-caller, but he sensed me, turned, held his hand up to block my mouth, so that was where I bit, on his hand.

You can drink from anywhere.

I held his wrist in both hands and sucked and sucked, didn't even feel the hits coming down onto my back, the kicks in my stomach and hips.

I was staring into his eyes while I drank, and when my eyes came back, I saw what I was doing.

This boy was Pikuni.

I tried to stop drinking from him, couldn't.

And then I felt his fingers in my mouth better. I had more blood in me now, so could know more from touch, even with my tongue.

He didn't have nails on these fingers, and the fingers were just stubs.

Because they'd been blown off when he put a wrong size greased-shooter into a many-shots gun, and pulled the trigger.

White Teeth.

He was up here after fasting for four days. All his songs were in his chest. He was trying to turn into a man.

My eyes bled red but my mouth didn't stop, not until White Teeth's eyes fogged over, so I had to spit out the last mouthful.

I fell across him, rolled over to pull him over me like a blanket against Sun Chief, and I hugged him so tight I heard the bones in my arm creak like breaking, and I couldn't let go, because then I would have to see him.

When I woke in the night, he was stiff.

I looked up at the Backbone, seeing me like this, and I ran the other way. I ran through the darkness, and when Sun Chief started crossing the sky, I kept running, the land flattening out under me.

Soon I would be to the Blood Clot Hills.

I wasn't meaning to go to them, though. I was just going away from the Backbone. From myself. From what I'd done, and what I was.

Until my nose told me to stop.

I stood in the moments after Sun Chief had gone back to his lodge, when some of his light was still on the ground.

I knew what I was smelling, but I also didn't know.

I followed my nose up the hill, crested over it, and out in the grass as far as I could see were blackhorns after a hunt.

But no one had taken any meat from them.

Just the robes.

I walked through them, touching their haunches and sides and faces with my fingertips, not understanding this, and soon my fingers knew to feel for the greased-shooter holes, only one per blackhorn.

It was a whole herd.

I wasn't hungry yet, but I was breathing deep.

Beside me, one of the dead blackhorn's eyes was open. It was staring at me.

I walked over, fell to my knees, and pushed that eye shut, held it shut with both hands, and I looked all around, for who could have done a thing like this, which was when a greased-shooter hit me in the shoulder right here, from so far off I didn't even hear its sound. It spun me ten paces into another blackhorn, the sharp point of its horn pushing through my hand. Above me, the Poor Boys tried to hold in place but were shaking fast like my eyes. My fingers were curling shut like this over the tip of the horn sticking through my hand, either my hand or the horn so cold it burned, and I can still feel it but I don't know if it hurts or if I just remember how it hurt.

This is my telling for today.

The pipe is empty.

The Absolution of
Three-Persons

April 11, 1912

When did the Blackfeet learn about cats?

Good Stab calls the prisoner in the cage the Cat Man, but did his people even know about cats in 1870? Yet he delivered that term so naturally, "Cat Man."

Calm yourself, Three-Persons, lest you commence arranging angels on the head of a pin.

It's now been four days since Good Stab stabbed me to the quick with his tale, and I've spent those four days taking his story apart into its individual pieces, laying them out before me to study, and then attempting to puzzle them all back together again into a narrative I can begin to accept.

My provisional conjecture is that, disallowing the more fantastic elements, what happens in this tale is simply that a Blackfeet suffered a catastrophic loss of some kind, possibly even at the direct or indirect hands of Major Baker, so had to survive a winter on the mountain by himself. In that kind of perpetual isolation, his eyes and his mind played continual tricks on him, which perforce would, by degrees, become a series of tactics he used to stay alive. But then, due likely to starvation and privation and the aforementioned isolation, he neglected to keep straight which were survival tactics and which fantasy, so started to let the second step back into the territory of the first, such that the impossible became, to him, unassailable fact, as finally, to him, proven by his own survival.

It's either subscribe to this possibility or invest in the accuracy of his tale, where he was infected by this "Cat Man" and is now cursed to walk the Earth drinking blood whensoever he can, having senses beyond the ken even of animals, a healing resiliency in keeping with that grizzly he claims to have wintered with, and only being limited by his aversion to daylight and solid food, knives and bullets having only temporary sway over his mortal coil.

In addition, the inescapable torpor that overtakes him after feeding, that he would claim as peculiar, is hardly so. Some of us even anticipate falling into such a state of extreme satiation, as all thinking becomes but a low hum in the background, and we achieve a version of communion with Creation that speaks ineluctably of wholeness.

And, lest I forget, Good Stab need must drink each animal or person entire, due to the animal gluttony residing within him that's impossible to rein in, and if he strays overmuch in his feeding into those he would call four-leggeds, then he begins to express their various characteristics, which rhymes in memory with some ancient lay or another I read, complete with justice and chivalry, but can no longer conjure the precise details of.

He told me I would believe, however, did he not? That I even am logging these fantastic elements is perhaps the first step down that dark path.

The savage mind is more rhetorically capable than I would have given it credit for.

And, yes, as is evident by the state of the top part of this page, I would have written this all down the evening previous, if not for a disastrously spilling a glass of sherry. And, were that my first glass of the evening, I surely wouldn't have spilled it, but the deeper one gets into the dulling of his senses, the more mistakes he's prone to commit.

O if the Denizens of the Lodging House could have seen me last night, stumbling around this house of worship, having to right myself on the back of pews, making bold and then increasingly apologetic entreaties to the Man on the cross, looking down on me so beatifically that there was nowhere someone so base as I could hide.

Yet, the Lord forgives all, does He not?

Even old men in their cups, blubbering apologia.

Good Stab, I'm both glad you found me at this remote outpost, and I wish you never had. And, yes, if you ask, after you left last Sunday, I did make haste to the door, to track your meandering exit, folding yourself into Miles City one more time.

In keeping with your initial visit and subsequent egress, the roiling pack of dogs kept their distance. That oddity I knew and was prepared for, however. What I found out this time, standing in the doorway of my own church, was what I should have known all along——that you had only simulated partaking of the sacred Host, hadn't you?

It had been hidden in your palm when that hand rose devotedly to your mouth, after which it was presumedly tucked away in a sleeve, to trail out into the mud of the street and be sniffed by a black and brown dog but nowise eaten.

Did you dispense with this Sacrament due to its association with the white man's religion, or due to your inability to tolerate food so solid?

In God's eyes, it doesn't matter. The body of His Son left in the mud like that, it can only be the fault of His holy servant——me. I never should have allowed someone not of the Faith to make away with it so cavalierly.

Pilfering from the sacristy, indeed.

And, to add insult, where I would let you, Good Stab, finally eat that prairie-runner you claim to have had to leave behind before all this started, you would let that bowl of stew cool untouched in your hands as you spoke your tale, finally to be left behind on the pew, thereby, to you at least, proving the validity of the events you relayed, in that eating in front of me would pull down the edifice you would have me peer over, to better see your true self.

How hard must it be to resist warm food just to make a point, though? What devotion to a cause might that take?

More than this old man can muster, I warrant.

As evinced by the rapid and mysterious disappearance of the pease porridge Minnie Karl demurely passed to me under a cloth Monday morning, claiming it to be excess from the previous afternoon's repast, a claim she didn't need to make, as I could tell this was the afterlife for this sumptuousness by how she or someone in the Karl house had cut it into slices and fried it in butter, which is precisely to this old man's taste. Especially when dressed with sausage, as this pease porridge was.

However, as anyone who has experienced proper pease porridge of course knows, it has but a single afterlife——you can't continue to refry it in butter, as it quickly loses its best qualities. Therefore, though there was, strictly speaking, too much to devour in a single day, I endeavored not to let it go to waste, and managed to consume it all by evening vespers, which, as anyone who's similarly fallen victim to a failure of temperance can attest, meant that that Monday night's passage was stormy indeed, delivering me to Tuesday morn pale, gaunt, and spent.

Yet I had duty to attend to, so mustered as best I could, and presented myself whereso I was supposed to be——the funeral service for the poor man found without his skin better than two weeks ago.

I didn't inquire about any of Sheriff Doyle's reasoning for keeping the body of this man cooling in the spring house so long——though, a second one having turned up in similar state, perhaps his investigation would be aided by laying them all out side by side down Main Street to look for differences and similarities, or gauge the responses of those walking past, or as corporeal reason for retaliation?

This is just what Miles City needs, yes.

Whereas most indigent burials I officiate are attended only by myself and Doyle and the town's two gravediggers, this funeral, contrary to the privacy the Star had promised, hosted some twenty residents, which was an abundance of mourners usually not witnessed in the far reaches of the cemetery. However, the bulk weren't there to grieve, I warrant, but to participate in the continuing mystery of these poor souls, and perhaps snatch a tidbit or two to reheat and serve in confidence at some remote meeting, thrilling all involved.

I, wavering on my feet from the night's ill treatment, was hardly thrilled to be in attendance. Yet I processed through, speaking directly and perhaps overloud to the top of the hastily constructed pine box. And, though I chanced to peer up at the faces of those in attendance singly and in pairs, I failed to see the dark aspect I partway expected to see——Good Stab wasn't there. Which was just as well. Had he have been, it wouldn't have been for the dead, but to fix me in his penetrating gaze, such that I could detect the nascent grin about his mouth, there for reasons I'm reluctant to divine.

All of the faces but one were passing familiar, though.

The one I didn't know was a tall man stout of build, holding his neat bowler hat in his hands. He was neatly shaved and better dressed than is typical for Miles City, as if he could be that rare thing in Montana——a continental traveler, fresh from some class better than steerage. However, as I knew from Chance Aubrey's visit Monday morning, when he had been kind enough to deliver Minnie Karl to my door, the weather having been somewhat inclement, Mr. Aubrey having been fresh from the telegraph office as is his continual wont, the great ocean liner which is supposed to be like unto a whole town floating on the water was, on Tuesday, yet a day from launching itself across the Atlantic Ocean, so how could someone from that mammoth ship already be in attendance at this service on our erstwhile boot hill?

Ah, Three-Persons. Always jesting in the face of seriousness.

God watch over your soul.

After the abbreviated service, this tall, dapper man nodded once to me after putting his bowler back on, and then, with Sheriff Doyle convivially at his arm, he forged back down into town, leaving myself up on the hill with this man I didn't want to have to call a hump, as anyone deserves more respect than that, but finding myself unable to refer to him by anything else.

As penance for my errant thinking, I made myself wait to descend until the two gravediggers, in keeping with the dramaturgist's continual sketches of them, had the coffin covered with dirt and the bottle of rotgut they shared sufficiently emptied, such that they were singing in tandem, a song with words so bawdy they would make a man not accustomed to the frontier and its various barracks and bivouacs blush.

When the gravediggers, whom I believe in actuality to be twins, held the bottle by the neck to offer to me, up there in our privacy, I turned my back and studied the prairie opening up to the north and the west.

Surely, weeks previous, Good Stab had been a figure on that horizon, his black robes whipping around his feet, his darkened spectacles not on his face, because of course he would have made his entrance in the night.

Oh, to have seen his approach.

To have seen it and scurried away.

April 13, 1912

I admit here to studying my teeth in my shaving mirror this morning. In order to do so, I had to work a stubborn shutter open to get enough sunlight in, and then try various angles in order to see into my mouth, to judge the quality, the color.

Before Good Stab's comment about his teeth compared to mine, I'd never once given thought to my own ivory, as it were. He's not wrong, though. Even in the darkness of the chapel with one candle flickering, the pools of inky blackness he calls his eyes were able to adjudge the yolky varnish I must present wheresoever I go——and that's the better teeth, the show teeth. The remaining ones are best left undescribed.

Oh, Vanity, thy name is . . . is Arthur Beaucarne, evidently. A decrepit Narcissus holding his lanky old frame in the posture of a question mark in the small window of his own church to better study his own appearance, at least until the wax holding him together should soften and his limbs begin to sag, then fall to the floor.

But Good Stab's niggling, indirect assault on my appearance is just another test, I tell myself. In my station, in this post, I must not rise to such bait. Once you start taking remarks personally, you find yourself stripped of the objectivity you need to perceive higher truths, and diagnose accordingly.

I suppose, to his way of thinking, what he's done is count coup on me——he's touched the enemy in battle, and both he and the enemy know it.

Why I'm the enemy remains to be seen, of course.

His wide, dark face is new to me, except insofar as he carries the visage of every other Indian I've encountered, albeit he's the first one I've encountered who covers his eyes in those peculiar darkened spectacles.

O but if only he would visit me during the week, rather than only on Sunday afternoons, when I've spent my intellectual resources so thoroughly, giving all I can to my flock, which is their due.

We don't choose the shape or meter of our struggles, however. Our duty, insofar as this aging pastor can tell, is to simply endure them, and, when and if opportunity arises, overcome them.

I await that redemption.

Until that day, I shuffle around during the week, creating various errands to occupy my time. Yesterday, my errand was to visit and then interview Livinius Clarkson about what he said to the Star two weeks ago, but the post office was closed, the mail having not come for four days now——perhaps Chance Aubrey has the right idea, loitering around the telegraph office for his news.

According to him, whom I encountered at the butcher, that massive ship he's so compelled by is currently chugging across the Atlantic. The light in his eyes when he speaks of this feat unnerves me, as I can see in it hubris for the creations of men, which are but motes in God's eye, but the meat counter isn't the right forum for corrective sermons. It's important that I sometimes am just another citizen, not a shepherd.

This doesn't mean my presence at the butcher was for ordinary reason, mind.

I was there for a thick rasher of bacon.

When I'd queried the Denizens of the Lodging House about the presence in Miles City of any individuals of the Blackfeet persuasion, they had, after an overabundance of good natured chaffing which I dissembled to tolerate, directed me to a collection of canvas tents at the very margins of civilization proper, and managed to suggest that uncorking a bottle might be the best way to get this Blackfeet into a talkative mood.

Dragging my slow leg away, I considered this.

I had been asking after Good Stab, so as to make Sunday less an effort, in that we could go ahead through what he insists is a confession, but I didn't think that's to whom they were directing me, Good Stab not being, so far as I had any indication, the drinking kind.

He must then not be the only Blackfeet in Miles City, I surmised.

This I could use.

Specifically, I could put Good Stab's tale to the test by inquiring after cats with this other Blackfeet, could I not? And the rasher of bacon I had intended for Good Stab would be barter for this other Indian, I presumed, bacon being fundamentally desirable.

I had brought coin to pay for this provender myself, not with church funds, but the butcher insisted it be his tithe, which I take to mean he's paying ahead, as it were, for some sin he can see coming, that he can now enter into with less guilt, as he's already been shriven, as it were.

Such unstated economies do we of the ecclesiastical bent have to grin and nod about, keeping our silence the while, discretion being one of the many better parts of valor. I took the proffered bacon, I mean to say and confess, and, in keeping with my station, redistributed it where it could do the most good.

That was to the Blackfeet man I found at the eastern limit of town as the Denizens had portended, midst all the dingy canvas tents. He was huddled over a small fire of horse dung.

"Pikuni?" I said by way of greeting, which felt akin to approaching a horse and saying "Horse?"

This man looked up, and was perhaps in the environs of the age Good Stab would claim for himself. His face wasn't just lined with age, but it had been folded over and over into itself, and his skin was the darkest I had seen on a red man, and his black hair was shot through with white, yet, as with Good Stab, there was no stubble on his jaw.

"Amos," the old man said to me about himself, opening his hand to indicate where I should attempt to sit. "Amos Short Ribs."

He spoke surprisingly competent English. According to Sall Bertram, he had been a fort Indian in decades previous, which is what I chose to ascribe his accomplished manner of speech to.

As it turned out, Amos Short Ribs is in fact a Blood Indian, which is a distinction that matters among the Blackfoot and Blackfeet and perhaps adjacent tribes, but is tantamount to, in America, having been of Scottish or Welsh extraction thirty or forty years previous. It matters overmuch in their respective homelands and now, around their dinner tables, but is of little consequence in the broader sense, to the uninitiated.

Once some of the bacon was cooked on what I believe to have once been the door of a stove, which seemed a fitting afterlife for such a scrap, Amos Short Ribs said, in response to my convoluted promptings, that he had seen mountain lion cubs that small, yes, and he used that term, not one of Good Stab's more antique ones. Were these cubs what I was asking about?

Sitting on an upturned crate, he held his hand near his ankle to show me the height of the animal he intended.

Finally, after processing through bobcats and straying into animals whose validity I can't attest to, I, in frustration, removed myself from his camp to procure an actual cat as example, finding one in, at long and painful last, that house of ill repute which I would otherwise never visit. My hope is that any citizen seeing me approach that den of iniquity understood I was on a religious mission, not a personal one.

The cat lounging inside the door was orange and fat, and I promised the lone woman lounging similarly on the faded divan with crusted over spittoons at either arm that I would return it. In reply, she swept me away with the back of her hand.

I held this small beast out to Amos Short Ribs and he stood in reverence, walked all around it, studying it this way and that, evincing both that he was unfamiliar with the house the cat was from as well as the fact that this indeed was his first experience with such a domestic animal, thus, as far as this pastor was concerned, ending the poorly considered interview.

Exiting stage left, however, unpursued by any real-bears, Amos Short Ribs asked after a man he called "The Fullblood" he thought he had seen leaving my church.

I stopped by the trough, holding the cat along my forearm, the cat purring for the attention, and turned back to Amos Short Ribs, considering him anew.

"Fullblood?" I asked with as little urgency as I could.

Amos Short Ribs stared at me, chewing his bacon, then looked out to the street in Indian fashion, his kind not preferring the continued eye contact that civilization depends upon for its continual re-assessment of itself.

I oriented myself alongside him and faced the street as well, him holding his bacon, me holding the house of ill repute's mouser. I was familiar with the term halfblood, it being but a minor variation on halfbreed, which anyone in the west is familiar with, such mélanges and mulattoes being not uncommon in the least.

Amos Short Ribs finally nodded yes to my question, which was no answer at all.

"But I thought he was already——" he finally said about this Fullblood, holding the blade of his hand out sideways before him and slicing it outward, which in some wordless fashion communicated "death" to me, meaning he thought this Fullblood was already dead, just, he was too respectful or too superstitious to phrase it as such. Then he added, cryptically and in confidence, "I thought they finally got him, I mean."

My impulse was to press him on this "him," but I chose instead to say, "Got him for what, pray tell?"

Amos Short Ribs, having himself surely the first solid food in a while, as opposed to the more liquid diet those of his station and location depend upon, held a piece of this all too rare bacon out for a dog trotting by. I warrant, I'll never understand the mind of the Indian, who would give away that which he himself most direly needs.

The dog, ever untrusting, a stance probably well earned from the various kicks directed toward it on a daily basis, growled, but was growling at its own desire to draw close enough to take that bite, his instincts telling him that this was a trap.

Amos Short Ribs tossed the bacon out for the dog, which snapped it up and swallowed without chewing, which I suppose is a thing I can identify with.

"They wanted him for what he was doing to the buffalo hunters," Amos Short Ribs said with a sort of savage grin, sneaking a look up to me to gauge whether I knew of what he spoke.

This is what Livinius Clarkson would educate us all on.

"What was this Fullblood doing to the hunters?" I asked, ducking with all delicateness into this promising discussion.

"So he was in your house there?" Amos Short Ribs prompted, pointing to the side of town the church is on and forcing me to realize too late that I had confirmed Good Stab's presence with me there.

You should always be careful around Indians, I'm learning.

I nodded once, squinting the while, and asked again what this Fullblood had been doing to the buffalo hunters.

Amos Short Ribs, instead of answering, pointed with his lips and chin out into the prairie opening up beside us, such that I saw some warrior in full regalia from decades ago, hectoring a camp of buffalo hunters across the grasslands in a one man war, its inevitable result already written.

But then, still looking out there, instead of seeing my own romanticized notion, I for a moment saw the hump Doyle had taken me to witness, such that I didn't see the grand pursuit that delivered this poor soul here without his skin, but such that I had to see that lone warrior, evidently not a halfbreed, sitting his horse in the distance, to satisfy himself that his work was being seen by those whom he would have see it.

"Is he the one painting——?" I turned to ask Amos Short Ribs, only to find him no longer in my presence.

Instead, it was the man I had cast as the continental gentleman earlier in the week, at the funeral service.

He was looking out into the prairie lands as well.

"Arthur Beaucarne?" he finally said, my unfinished query about "painting" yet hanging between us.

Behind the continental gentleman's jaw, near to his ear on my side, there was yet a line of shave cream, from the barber's.

"Pleased to make your acquaintance," I said, adopting my pastoral tone, extending my hand so we could comport ourselves as the civilized sort, not as black robe and savage.

"Dove," he said about himself, just that one word.

"Mr. Dove," I said in polite greeting.

"Just Dove," he corrected.

"You knew the unfortunate?" I said about his attendance over the grave, and winced at the directness of my question, when we had only just traded names. But I had to move us past the question I had tried to swallow back down.

"Came here from San Francisco, on the stage," he said, finally rubbing at the vague irritation apparently occasioned by that line of shaving cream, and rubbing it in deeply enough that I could finally let my eyes rest elsewhere.

"We're honored by your visit," I informed him, my weight unaccountably on my heels, as if I were a young boy in the presence of my father, never mind that my age has to be at least twice this Dove's. Such is the authority some men introduce into social situations.

To add to it, Dove produced his credentials in a timeworn manner that whispered that he had been doing this for years.

"A Pinkerton," I said, duly impressed.

"That your cat, Father?" he asked, his cheeks cupping his eyes so as to prepare him for my answer——perhaps I was to be the kind of old man who brings his pet with him to all places, speaking closely into its ear, lest someone hear our secrets.

"It was . . ." I began, unsure how to conclude, finally settling on "I was but showing it to an acquaintance, and will be returning it to its rightful owner shortly."

"It's a healthy one," Dove opined, suppressing his grin.

I hefted the cat on my arm in agreement.

"Is there aught I can help you with?" I asked then.

"There may be," Dove said, nodding to himself. "There may be, Father, yes. I'm here on the trail of . . . I can't say for sure. But I do know that a family I was tasked to find——"

"Out of San Francisco?" I interrupted.

He nodded as if it pained him to do so.

"And as near as I can tell from various orders of lading," he said in his deliberate manner, as if measuring each word, "they're now in or around Miles City." He looked over to me about this, and held my eyes to register the effect of what he said next: "Parts of them anyway, Father. I can't say for certain where their skin is."

April 14, 1912

Chance Aubrey's floating village of a ship is due in America on Wednesday of this week. It's all he can talk about, as if this titanic hull will slide right past the pier and into shore, cleaving America in twain so this monstrous ship can sail on through to the Far East. From the state of Chance's eyes and the tremble in his fingers when he relates these unasked for but infectious facts, I daresay he's even losing sleep from the tension and excitement, as if he's gambled all he has, including his happiness, on this crossing.

My fingers, now, are trembling similarly.

Usually of a Sunday, instead of scribbling the day's events down like this, I elect to retire with whatever dish has been kindly left for me.

I'm still reeling from yesterday's encounter with the Pinkerton man, though. Three times since then I've sat here to relay that conversation lest it find a dark corner of my memory to lurk in, until, like a mushroom, it sends fibrous tendrils out into the more vulnerable parts of a humble pastor, and three times I but rise and circle, wringing my hands and wiping my brow.

The Pinkerton man Dove wasn't just passing the time of day by talking with me, I daresay. He was interrogating me, I came by degrees to know. It was no accident he found me out by the tents——he would have found me wheresoever I had been. And it was probably no accident that Amos Short Ribs made himself scarce with Dove's encroachment, Indians having an inbuilt sense to avoid anyone in uniform, or with credentials granting them authority.

If only Amos Short Ribs had pinched my sleeve, pulled me into the close safety of his tent with him, I would have continued to bring him rashers of bacon for days on end, until there were no more hogs in all of Montana.

Instead, Dove and myself and the abducted cat strolled directionless along the streets of Miles City, our conversation carrying us whereunto Dove had all along intended.

The particulars of the case he had been assigned——those he could share in strictest confidence with me——was that an established man of middling high society in San Francisco, who stood to inherit part of the newspaper there, had been taken from his family's grand home some five weeks ago.

In the week leading up to this unnamed socialite's sudden disappearance, he had been seen having long meetings with a man in black robes.

I stopped, my free hand latching onto Dove's forearm.

"Surely you don't think I——?" I pled.

"Younger than you by a fair bit," Dove said back, suppressing what I take to be the grin he gives when proceedings are proceeding his way. "Darker hued as well. And, you don't have any of those sunglasses either now, do you?"

I blinked and swallowed to get this term to register, to translate, to situate itself in me, and then——of course.

I shook my head yes at first, that I understood of what he spoke, but then I immediately corrected that to an emphatic, almost desperate no, no I didn't have any darkened spectacles, the sun being no particular enemy of mine, or, the world being already quite dim enough from my advanced age, thank you.

"But it could have been someone of your order," Dove went on, leading us ahead into the day.

"Lutheran?" I stammered.

"Bible people," Dove clarified, which he meant as no reduction, I could tell, nor did I feel insulted, being of a group with the other denominations. Really, my rejoinder, if it even rose to such a status, had been merely to keep our mouths moving while, in my head, I was seeing Good Stab in San Francisco of all places, luring this would-be heir into his thrall afternoon after afternoon, until——

Until what?

For very immediate, personal reasons, that was my prime concern.

"Was this missing heir the abducted man that we buried?" I had to say, just to have it aloud between us.

Dove nodded as slightly as possible.

I swallowed again, the sound a deafening thrush in my ears.

"So you found him as you were assigned to, then," I added, needlessly.

"We'll have to exhume, of course," he said with all attendant exasperation. "There's an empty plot waiting in California."

"And you need me there for that exhumation," I replied, barely giving it utterance.

Dove looked up to me as if to ascertain he was hearing me correctly.

"I have a commitment to those I help inter," I explained.

He nodded that he could accept this, even though I was pulling it whole cloth from the air. Such are the steely nerves of Man, who would act guilty even when preemptorily cleared of any association.

"To what end was this poor soul . . . ?" I asked, unable to give voice to the violence done to him.

"Yet to be determined," Dove said.

We were passing the house of ill repute to which the cat belonged, forcing me to shift her to my far side, lest she vault from me and run for her true home, giving the lie to this Pinkerton man that there be some sort of traffic between me and the women on that porch, two of whom had already lifted their hands either to us in greeting, or to their favorite mouser.

Dove lifted a hand back and grinned, already ducking away, his eyes yet flashing under the short brim of his bowler.

"A family, you said?" I asked then, bringing his eyes back from their brief dalliance.

"The next morning, his three sons also turned up unaccounted for——missing," he said. "The father would be the one you provided the service for. The youngest, the last of them spirited away, as near as our investigation can conclude, he had been . . . with a young house maid, who, ahem, had only just stepped out to freshen up. When she came back, this, well——"

"Her paramour," I filled in, using all my powers of discretion.

Dove nodded, liked that enough for temporary use. "When she came back, the young paramour was gone," he said, squinting into the distance as if seeing again that empty bedroom, its sheets and coverlet surely mussed, the house maid beside herself not only to have lost her one true love, as she would surely understand the dalliance, but to now have to, in order to attest to his absence, admit to a thing she would otherwise rather keep hidden until the eventual grand announcement of their pending nuptials.

"So, four in total," I led off.

Dove nodded. He was studying a dog who was intent upon studying him in return, as if the two were reuniting now after many a long year, and both were the worse for wear, but they could yet rise to their old acrimony at the drop of a hat.

Or maychance I bring my own perturbations into this fraught interrogation.

But this man beside me had announced himself to the sheriff, I knew that so far. As well, I knew that a Pinkerton always gets his man. I had nothing to fear in that regard, not being that man, but nevertheless I felt the bacon being offered to me on outstretched hand, and I was growling inside because this had to be a trap.

Dove looked over to me then, holding my gaze until I had to break away, say it as if out into the street, but loud enough so he could hear.

"So the second man we found out there, he was . . . one of the sons, then?" I said, an abreaction almost, though I measured it out as if recondite unto ignorance.

In reply, Dove, with a beleaguered sigh, reached into the interior chest pocket of his fine but sturdy jacket and produced a small photograph. I took it, studied it at arm's length, my sight being what it is, and tried to associate the benign features of this young man with the face of the poor soul I'd prayed over but last week.

Perhaps if I could have used paints to color one side of these features and then the other, I could have recognized him better.

"It's him," Dove assured me, returning the photo to his jacket.

"So there won't be a service for this one," I decided out loud.

"We'd just have to dig him back up," Dove said.

"Yet you allowed the father to be interred?" I asked, genuinely stymied.

"Was but fresh from the station," Dove said with a shrug that indicated to me the fruitfulness, or lack thereof, of this line of questioning.

"And I can help with your efforts how, sir?" I got up the nerve to inquire.

"Your, um, position within the community," he informed me.

I swallowed, watched a bird soar across the top of the grass without flapping its wings once, and then, finally, nodded.

"Your sect does include confession, doesn't it?" he prompted back.

"I am bound by Luther's Small Catechism," I had to regretfully inform him.

"So . . . yes to confession?" he asked nextly.

"I can say that my congregation is of largely Germanic stock," I explained to him, not using my lips overmuch to say it. "Not from the auld country."

Hearing my intonement, he caught my eye, had to grin.

"But if I hear anything I can relay," I added, "I now know whom to relay it to."

He digested this.

"He's from . . . California, yes?" I went on, hoping to unmire us from this undesirable moment. "Whoever spirited this family away?"

"Until I know," Dove said with a sort of harrumph, "he's from anywhere."

"Or they," I amended, calling the quarrelsome deputy to mind. "They're from anywhere."

"They?" he asked back, squinting at this quibbling distinction.

"A tribe, a band, a clan, a society," I said, probably too eagerly. "If the deeds here are Indian."

"Because of the . . ." Dove said, doing his fingers over his own face, to mean "paint."

I nodded, added, "And the violence, of course."

"Can't forget that," Dove agreed. "This is someone who knows how to use a knife."

"And places low value on human life," I said with all due reverence.

"Or a higher value on himself," Dove said with a shrug, ending this derivation we were involved in, I wasn't sure why.

"Sheriff Doyle knows how to get in touch with you?" I asked as a way of initiating our farewell from each other.

"Lodging house," Dove said, and I felt confident that the toll the Denizens there took from all passersby was, in all likelihood, not being successfully extracted from a man so taciturn.

"You should talk to our postmaster," I said then. "He claims the men being found out there are in keeping with certain incidents from the woolier days."

Dove chuckled, liked that enough to repeat it: "Woolier." He nodded, took his fixings out for another cigarette, and said, "Like a buffalo hide, yes?"

He offered me the cigarette he neatly rolled and I declined, suddenly certain that sharing tobacco with one such as he could only lead to perdition.

Dove drew deep on his neat cigarette, held the smoke in, his eyes near to watering with pleasure, and then he blew that smoke back out, indicated the prairie to the north and west with his chin.

"How far is Fort Benton?" he asked, and I could tell by the way he didn't look over to me that we were in uncharted terrain, here——that he was speaking with me now as a person, as a man, not as a subject, or unwilling font of information.

It felt good to be blundering out the other side of this interrogation. My humors aren't sufficient to that anymore, if they ever even were.

"One man, one horse?" I asked back, about the ride I gathered he was proposing.

"How far?" Dove repeated, pinching his cigarette from his lips and studying the lit end.

"Six sleeps, as the Indians say it," I answered.

Dove let slip a dismissive hiss, turned away.

"Does Fort Benton factor into this . . . San Francisco situation?" I asked.

Dove shook his head no, said, "Standing orders, that's all. Any Pinkerton in Montana Territory——"

"We're a state, now," I was and am vouchsafed to mutter.

"Any agents in Montana," he went on, riding roughshod over my correction, "we're to telegraph back any information we happen to find concerning the missing si——a missing transport."

At which point he turned to continue our stroll back the way we'd come.

I hustled to keep up, my bad leg its usual hindrance.

"Missing transport?" I repeated.

Dove glanced over with only his eyes, as if deciding on my worthiness.

"My flock has a long memory for such things," I said, using his own imposition. "Many of them have lived here since before the Indian was tamed."

He nodded, seeing the sense in this, and drew again on the half a cigarette he had left then dropped it hissing in the mud, a profligacy foreign to these parts.

"Could be some of them remember this, then," he led off with. "1870. Half dozen of our top agents were transporting a large package west in a pair of wagons, and the last word of them is from Fort Benton. After that——" He held his fingers up and opened them wide to indicate how two wagons and their cargo can just vanish in a land as wide and empty as the one we were standing in.

"Six men, you say?" I clarified.

He looked from the cat in the crook of my arm up to me, finally nodded.

"I was under the understanding that your agency only offered security for money and the like, during transport," I heard myself saying.

"Did I say it wasn't money and the like?" he asked right back, watching my eyes much closer now.

"Just——isn't gold and currency usually carried by train?" I offered so, so weakly as to be embarrassing.

Dove didn't offer any explanation.

"Well, the snow can be deceptive up here . . ." I said with a shrug of commiseration, just to fill the silence, but then found myself standing alone in the street, Dove having stopped in his tracks.

I looked back and he was reevaluating this old man.

"I say it was winter either?" he asked, a distinct note of challenge to his tone.

"When else can six men as capable as you disappear without a trace?" I asked back, hopefully without too much of a pause.

Dove considered this, considered me, then stepped forward so we could continue whatever this was we were deeper and more involved with, now.

After a longer count of silence than I thought I could suffer, he stopped in front of the lodging house, signaling the end of our time together.

He extended his hand and I took it, and we shook, the Denizens sniggering in their way about the cat I was yet holding, but holding their jibes for the moment, due to the august company I kept.

"There was no horse," Dove said to me quietly, almost in farewell, and I realized in a painful wink that he had saved this back for precisely this parting moment, so as to catch me unaware, like the stinging couplet at the end of a sonnet, which is where the fatal turn resides.

"No horse?" I had to ask.

"No hoofprints at either of the two men found out there," he said, his lips hardly moving, his eyes blue and intense in mine. "For when you're asking your church people if they know anything. Anything about the gentlemen from San Francisco. You can preface it by saying that whoever did this, he must be strong enough to carry a grown man over his shoulder, and still leave no boot prints."

"Of course, of course," I said, shaking his hand even more, like a man being walked to the gallows but still hoping for mercy, and then I walked away into a haze of brightness I couldn't escape for well on half a day. Not until I found myself again at the pulpit this morning, that tall door opposite me opening to admit its slab of daylight, and a single Indian, his eyes hidden behind darkened glass.

Good Stab took his seat, Lorelei Baker looked over her shoulder to assure herself he was drawing only that close and no closer, and then I heard myself reciting the sermon more than actually delivering it, I daresay.

But my soul can burn later.

For now, it's all I can do to keep this nib in control enough for these words to be legible, for my later consideration. If I don't finally write them down now, however, I fear some might slip permanently away, and that those might, in retrospect, have been key.

After the congregation had trailed out into what I knew for them to be another ordinary afternoon, I tidied my way over to Good Stab's pew, where he patiently awaited me.

"I looked for you in town earlier this week," I said by way of greeting.

He provided no explanation for my not having discovered his lodgings.

"If you want," I led off, taking the cue of his darkened spectacles to rise and extinguish the candles again, making me have to speak louder from across the chapel, "you can stable your horse here for no charge. I have no mount of my own, as I don't have need of one, yet the church in its generosity has——"

"I have no horse," Good Stab said.

It nearly took my breath away.

I came back to him holding a single candle, which I again positioned more on my side of our conversation than his, so as not to unduly blind him, and make him feel at a disadvantage.

"No horse, and you're a Blackfeet?" I said with what I admit here was mock incredulity.

For the first time in our weekly meetings, Good Stab seemed to wince in such a way that I could clearly discern his shame.

"I can no longer dream my own dreams," he said quietly, into his hands clamping tighter and tighter onto each other between his knees. "I can't live among my people anymore, I can't eat real-meat or have a wife or children, I can't hunt the blackhorns since the blackhorns are all gone, and horses know me for what I am."

He chuckled a mirthless chuckle, one that portended grief more than anything.

I almost extended a hand to place upon his, resting on his knee now, to show him that I could take some of this burden of grief from him. To show him that he wasn't alone.

"You're still Blackfeet," I assured him. "Blackfeet is in here"——I opened my hand on my own chest——"not . . . in all the trappings."

He neither accepted nor denied this. What he did do, I had to note, was force himself to stare directly into the white hot flame of the guttering candle, until he had to snap his face away all at once.

I fully expected smoke or steam to waft up from behind his darkened spectacles.

When it didn't, he slowly removed them ear by ear, folded them and slid them into a sleeve, then crinkled his nose up, slashing his newly revealed eyes back and forth across the pews, the intensity of this new carriage causing my own hands to clamp onto my assigned pew.

"What is that?" he demanded, a ferocity to his voice I hadn't heard before.

I looked around with him, unsure. The ash cakes Grelda Koch had left sitting in her pew as she does, as if handing them directly to me would somehow sully the transaction, were yet in their place. Since Good Stab wouldn't partake, it seemed lacking in manners to eat something so delectable in front of him.

The ash cakes weren't what was prompting this response in him, though.

Sitting but a single pew from me, he peeled his lips back from his teeth in a most animalistic way, only remembering at the last moment that he wasn't alone, so must need keep his mouth more shut. Or perhaps he saw my eyes leering at his teeth, tracing them down to see if they were flat now, or had those points he had intimated.

He grinned a wicked grin, wiped his lips with the back of his hand, then nodded.

"A cat," he said with a knowing grin.

I had forgotten about her. All through service, she had been wending and winding through people's legs, a distraction I was grateful for, today's sermon being more rote than from the heart.

Yet, now, for all her friendliness, Cordelia had evidently made herself scarce.

I told myself that, living in the wild as Good Stab had to, the forest and the plains being natural to the Indian, he probably had a keen enough nose to detect a whole host of animals in his immediate area.

"She's a hunter," he said then, nodding appreciatively, and I grinned as well, only registering a moment later his use of the feminine. But of course there are many who would consider all dogs male, all felines of the female persuasion, perhaps working off the proclivities or dispositions of both.

"Do you want me to put her outside?" I asked back. "If she offends, I can——"

Good Stab shook his head no, that Cordelia was of no concern.

As to whether that's her given name, I know not. But, being a cat, she only responds when she wants, so I don't see it mattering much what I deem to call her.

I stepped away to pour myself a tin cup of water, and, feeling it rude not to at least offer the same to my guest, I came back with some for him as well.

He took it, held it between his knees as he had held the stew the week before.

I opened my mouth to jest that, if he preferred, I could enact the transubstantiation on this water, and turn it more to the color of his liking. This would debase both my religion and his belief, however, so I instead took a long, contemplative drink myself, savoring it more than one should savor tinny, tepid water.

"So we ended last Sunday with you getting——" I said, holding my hands up around the idea of a long rifle, and, though I didn't necessarily mean to, I could hear the tone in my voice. It was as if I were talking to a child at bedtime, and inviting them into fairy land, on the other side of which lies the sleep they need.

Good Stab raised his left hand from his cup and massaged his shoulder, in what I took to be memory of that bullet boring into him.

"It hurt?" I asked, investing in his reality as apology for my dismissive tone.

"It always hurts at first," he said, his eyes following something I couldn't see down the side of the wall on the far side of the church. "She's about to get one out there," he said appreciatively.

"One?" I asked.

"A mouse," he said with what I would have to call a sibilant thrill, proving to me that he did indeed know that word. And, I believe, he saw this register in my unguarded expression.

I tried to hide it by studying the dark wall harder, but then decided Cordelia had again left the chapel, was indeed outside the church, using as passage some hole or chink I've yet to discover, my eyes being so dim, my frame so bent.

However, I also reminded myself of the various snake oil men I'd seen in years past, who were equally fond of making unprovable claims. Were Good Stab and I to rush out, I knew, there would be no cat, no mouse. Or, rather, I suppose, there would be one of each there, now that Good Stab and myself were outside.

"How long do we have?" he asked then very politely, as if not wanting to impinge on my afternoon, though that's precisely what he was already doing, and had been doing, and would, I surmised, continue to do, until I was ground down to meal.

"As long as you need," I said, lifting my cup to toast him along.

He nodded, didn't toast me back, apparently unfamiliar with that custom, and, after breathing in as if to reorient himself in his own tale, he looked up to me to begin this again.

Taking my assigned cue once more, all the world being if not a stage then at least a farce, I cleared my throat and intoned my line as if it were gospel truth.

"I listen with a good heart."

The Nachzehrer's Dark Gospel

April 14, 1912

I had been shot before, like you already wrote down, by the soldiers in the Backbone, but never by a gun like this. Those greased-shooters before had been children's arrows. This was a war lance driving through me right here, under the bone. The shot lifted me up and carried me back and back, my feet higher than the rest of me.

Since the cold no longer touched me, I hadn't cut new moccasins out. I didn't have leggings or a shirt anymore either. I didn't need them. But, away from the protection of the Backbone, moving among two-leggeds again, I saw myself as naked for the first time.

Thrown back against the hard side of a skinned blackhorn bull, I held my hand that wasn't bleeding over the greased-shooter hole like this, hard, to try to keep White Teeth's blood in. That I had killed him was bad enough. To waste what I'd taken from him was even worse. But the blood wouldn't stay inside. At first I could taste White Teeth in the smell of that blood, and it made three of the fingers of my right hand hot, but when more and more kept running out, my nose forgot the world, like it had been stuffed with mud from a lake bottom. When I breathed in, I could only smell like I had been able to smell before the Cat Man, which is like you can smell now. The world around me got smaller.

I closed my eyes to hear the boots that had to be walking up but my ears were dull now too.

I was emptying out more and more. And without more blood, I couldn't heal.

My body bucked like this, my back swaying in. The hole in my shoulder from the greased-shooter was enough that I could have pushed my fist through it, then opened my hand behind me, spread my fingers wide on my back. The arm on that side was dead and loose, not mine anymore.

I pushed hard with my heels to stand, to run, to find whatever I could to feed on, just to get my nose and my ears back, and my night eyes too for when Sun Chief went down, but I only pushed back instead, harder into the blackhorn bull. But blackhorns are always there for the Pikuni. We've always known this, but over the winter, dreaming the real-bear's dreams instead of my own, I had forgotten.

But then this bull breathed in from me pushing on it. Its breath was raspy and wet.

I rolled over and its great black eye looked into who I was, the Good Stab part, all the way through to Weasel Plume, and maybe even to Wolf Calf and Curly Hair Woman. Then its nostrils flared like this, smelling the Cat Man in me, and it straightened its back legs fast, trying to get away. But this blackhorn bull couldn't stand and run anymore. It had been shot once through the liver, enough that it laid down to die. Then, while it was taking the sleep before death, tasting again the grass of the moon when the strawberries get ripe, watching from under its heavy eyes as a golden calf kicked and kicked, learning its own legs in the safety of the herd, this bull had been skinned of its robe, its tongue cut out, and then it had been left there.

We have a story of this, the Pikuni. It's from the dog days, before the horse and the gun, before the white scabs and the black pox, before the trappers and the whiskey. It happened at the old blood-fence just north of Old Agency, on Two Medicine Lodges, in the moon when the snakes go blind. We had driven the buffalo over the edge and now were moving among them with the knives we had then to get the meat and robes, the tongues and tails, the horns and hooves.

But then one of the last of the buffalo to have fallen raised its big head like this, scared, because it had landed on all the other buffalo instead of the ground, which had been soft enough that it didn't die like it was supposed to from falling.

Right when it did that, Kills-for-Nothing had been kneeling over it. She jerked back but it was too late.

On that blackhorn's horn now was her face. The tip of the horn had gone through the cheek right here, like this, and then pulled all the skin away in a single tear, up to her hair line, down to her throat, back to her ears. Otter Goes Back told us that this was before he was a boy, even, but he saw the winter count from then, and the many-faces man who had recorded this hadn't drawn her face without the skin, because that would have been disrespectful.

Without her face, Kills-for-Nothing ran a day and a night away, just running from the pain, but then, because it's where we always go, she realized she was running for the Backbone. Once there, she jumped into Running Eagle Lake, and Otter Goes Back told us how she still lives there with the underwater people but can't ever come out again, because Sun Chief would burn the meat of her face.

The skin she left behind with that blackhorn was in a medicine bundle that Never Laughs kept, that they said was going to be one of the main medicine bundles one day, but when the white scabs found them there was no one to pass the bundle to, so it dried out on its tripod behind one of those lodges of the dead. Tall Dog told me this after he found the Never Laughs' winter camp when he was up there fasting, looking for his vision. It was close to where the Small Robes winter, but it was small and well hidden, and old. Tall Dog could have taken the bundle, but without the songs, no one could ever open it. When the strings around it let go after another winter or two, the bundle would open anyway, and spill what was inside onto the ground for the rain to wash into the river. Since all the waters are one water, Tall Dog said, then Kills-for-Nothing could find her face floating on the surface and rise to it with her chin up and eyes open, finally walk onto shore at last, and be his wife.

This was how most of Tall Dog's stories ended, with him getting a wife.

But no one tells those stories anymore, even ones like Tall Dog's, that are just for one night. The stories in the lodges now are all about when there was real-meat in every iron pot, not whitehorn meat locked up in the ration house, crawling with worms.

I'm not talking about that, though, Three-Persons. Everybody knows that already, and it would take too long anyway, and I would have to stand and walk back and forth because some things you tell you can't sit still for.

What I'm telling you right now is when that big greased-shooter came through my shoulder, and I was losing all of White Teeth's blood into the dirt by a blackhorn bull that had come back from the Sandhills to help a Pikuni, because when it saw me from over there it couldn't smell the Cat Man on me yet.

Now that it did, it wanted to get away, be dead again, because dead is easier, but it was too late.

Using the sharp tip of my finger, where the nails grow harder than they used to, I slit this bull open from its chest down and I pushed my head in first, then my good arm, up by my head like this. With that good arm I pulled the rest of me into that wet darkness, kicking out the guts to make room.

I didn't mean to do this part, but when the blood inside this blackhorn touched my lips, I jerked all up and down from the taste and opened my mouth, started drinking and drinking.

The blood was still warm and alive, and it brought my nose and ears back, so I could smell and hear the right way again. I couldn't eat the real-meat, and this blood wasn't the blood I needed, and it had the white-powder poison at edges of how it tasted, but I could drink it and keep it down if I really tried. I tried. I kept drinking and sucking, just all around in the darkness, like a dirty-face pup dropped into a pile of guts.

That blackhorn blood kept me alive. It brought me back.

Now I could hear boots crunching in, taking a few steps and then stopping to listen, and coming on again, because the Indian I was could be anywhere.

It was napikwans. Two of them. I don't know what they were saying because I didn't know how to talk like this yet, but they were standing where I had been when that greased-shooter found me.

They didn't know to look inside a blackhorn. They didn't stop to ask why this pile of guts was shiny and wet.

Inside the blackhorn, I was still sucking on the meat between the ribs, to get all the blood, but it was slower now. My belly was tight already, but I couldn't stop, kept finding a new place where the blood still was, until two things happened at the same time. The first was that the blood went cold. That meant the bull had died again, this time for good. I spit out the last mouthful. The second was that my side split open right here, from drinking too much.

Like with my shoulder, I worked my good hand down to try to hold this blood in, but it wouldn't stay, and I was slowing down anyway like happens after I feed, where my eyes open and stare at nothing and my mouth moves like a silver fish dragged up into the air to drown.

The same way you bury your dead in a wooden box, I was sleeping open eyed in a blackhorn. Otters Goes Back used to tell us about great hunters who had done this in winter when they were far from camp, but it had always been a thing the amazing people did, not someone like me.

If the two napikwans had found me full like this but unable to fight, to run, to even raise my hand, they could have cut me in half over and over until I was pieces, then dropped those pieces into the coals of a fire and captured the smoke from that in glass bottles, to bury in holes far from each other.

I had been burned before and come back, but this would be different.

But these napikwans, they gave up, they crunched away, each of their boot steps making me jerk in that blackhorn like I was walking in a dream, except I wasn't dreaming. I was in that big darkness, falling and falling, my breath leaving me in fear over and over, because each next moment was when I was going to land.

I woke a full day later, when Sun Chief was just reaching back to close the door to his lodge in the Backbone, so the Poor Boys and the Lost Children could come out in the darkness.

Because I'd forgotten where I still was, I tried to stand at first, and when that didn't work, I stood harder, and harder, and finally burst up through the side of the blackhorn.

I was covered in blood and guts, and breathing hard.

The first thing the Cat Man part of me did was open my nose, taste the world.

I was alone, now. Alone in a herd of dead-on-their-side blackhorns that had been skinned and left. I felt like Napi walking through the Blood Clot Hills, each blackhorn another hump of land.

Moving among these red and white hills were the calves whose robes weren't worth anything, so they hadn't had greased-shooters wasted on them.

The calves bawled at me for milk, and because I was wearing that bull now instead of leggings and shirt, they couldn't smell the Cat Man in me yet, so they drew close, their wet noses touching my hand over and over, then finally taking my fingers into their hungry mouths.

If you ask why I did what I did, why I became what I became and went to war against the hide-hunters, then watch me right here, letting these calves suck on my fingers in the darkness, and knowing that the few of them that didn't starve, the big-mouths were going to pull them down, and the one or two that got away from that were going to starve, still calling for their mothers.

Finally I pulled my fingers back, made my hand into a fist.

For the first time since I woke in the Backbone after being burned, I hissed like the Cat Man, and I stared in the direction that greased-shooter had come for me, daring another one to try, because I would get back up from that too, as many times as I had to.

I walked the direction the shot had come from and gagged from the taste of these napikwan so thick in the air it stung. They hadn't bathed for moons and moons, and they hadn't changed their leggings or shirts or boots either, or swam in the river like they needed to, so their hair and beards were matted with flecks of blood and food and worse, and their breath was like the oil from your burning lamps, but before it burns.

Wolf Calf told me once that the first trappers to show up in Pikuni territory were like this, from how long they had to walk to get to us, down through the Real Old Man Country. I thought he was talking about men who smelled like the trappers I'd been feeding on in the Backbone, who I could taste on the air from two valleys away, but these napikwans were worse.

When I was walking, turning this way and that way so I wouldn't have to insult a dead blackhorn by climbing over it, all the calves were following me, bawling.

I stared straight ahead, led them on.

Instead of walking in the thick air where the napikwans had, I walked upwind of it, only dipping in to where they had been to be sure I was still going the right direction. I could see the snow they'd stepped in, and that was easy enough to follow.

It was eight hundred paces from where they'd shot me. This was longer than any many-shots or round-ball gun could go. I didn't know any gun could go that far and still hit something hard.

These napikwans' campfire was still burning, and two of the napikwans were sitting by it with a boy, resting against their saddles and talking to each other and passing a bottle back and forth, and making the boy drink. But then they heard the calves moving in and stood with their guns.

From a hole in the ground that was the door of a dugout, six more men came, and then more after that, some of them holding the long-shooter guns. It was the first time I'd seen these guns. They were almost as long as a lance, and their barrels weren't round but had corners and edges, and the mouths opened wider than a many-shots, meaning the greased-shooters that came out had to be that big too, and then even bigger when they hit.

Hanging on a rack away from the fire were at least twenty boiled tongues. Two of them were frying in a pan over the fire, and I could smell that what they were frying in wasn't fat but your hard yellow whitehorn milk, like on those breads in the bowl over there that the woman left. The tongues popped and sizzled. I had eaten tongue roasted on both sides over a fire, but never from a pan.

There weren't any dogs, but there were two wagons.

The napikwan were talking loud to each other, and motioning big with their hands. I think that, seeing the calves, they thought the big-mouths were tired of the poison meat, were moving in for some meat without poison. But then one of the calves bawled loud and long and desperate, asking to feed, saying it was scared, and the napikwans all laughed, turned back to the fire. One man raised his long-shooter gun toward the calves but another man pushed it back down with his hand.

I didn't know your napikwan talk yet, but I know that he was probably saying that greased-shooters cost too much to waste on calves they can't even get good robes from.

Years later, Wolf Calf told me that, when the soldiers came for Heavy Runner's camp on the Bear, the soldiers didn't want to use their greased-shooters up that time either, so killed the men with axes, the children with the butts of their many-shots guns, the women with the same knives they opened the sides of the lodges with.

That was a long time ago, though.

But the Pikuni still remember.

If there were any blackhorns left, they would remember fields like I was walking through too.

Instead of shooting these calves, these napikwans set their cups and plates down and walked out into the darkness with skins of water. They had dropped your hard yellow whitehorn milk into the skins first and held them over the fire. They went out in pairs, one man holding the open corner of the skin high for a calf to suck from, the other reaching under fast, to cut that calf's throat, so that when the blood slipped down, it would have some of that whitehorn milk with it, because the calves would keep drinking even after they were dying.

The calves were too hungry and scared to understand what was happening, so they were climbing over their own dead to get to those skins of whitehorn milk.

The taste of their blood on the air made me dizzy, even though it would taste wrong. I finally had to fall to my knees, my right hand touching the knotty line on my side that had burst open. It was beating like a heart, so I kept my fingers there.

With my eyes like this, I could see these napikwans like Sun Chief was out, only riding behind clouds. The napikwans, to my eyes, were in the Sandhills, were grey and dim, but still living their lives, doing what napikwans do.

Because their noses were dull from their own smell, I didn't bother moving upwind. And I wouldn't have smelled like anything to them anyway.

When they came back into the light of the fire from killing all the calves that would come to their water skins, I was standing there in front of the flames, and they stepped back and one of them shouted, probably because I was still wearing the insides of that blackhorn bull everywhere except my eyes, which were open and staring hard. And I could feel that my teeth were sharp when I hissed at them.

All their guns were leaned against the wagons, from when they'd got the water skins that had been hanging there.

Their chief stepped forward and made a speech to me, pointing all around. His voice was deep and booming, but it was like the treaty the Pikuni had signed two winters before. It didn't mean anything.

Finally when he pointed to the east, to the Backbone, and I looked, he drew out the short-gun he had in his belt.

By the time he shot it at me, I was already gone. His greased-shooter hit the fire that had been behind me, and coals and sparks went up everywhere, along with smoke after, and the napikwans were shouting and diving for their long-shooter guns.

I watched them from under one of the wagons, through the spokes of one of those tall wheels.

One of the napikwan walked close enough I could touch the fringe on his leggings.

When he hung his water skin back on the side of the wagon, I lowered it down, emptied it on the way back out to all the calves with their throats cut. I could smell that they'd fallen down before bleeding all the way out, meaning there was still some blood in them. Enough.

I filled the skin with it, wrinkling my nose from how dead blood tastes in the air, and it didn't matter that these napikwans sat up three men to watch the darkness for me.

I slipped past them in the grass, pinching the open corner of the skin and not letting it go until it was into the mouth of a napikwan sleeping with his head on a saddle.

His eyes opened but before he could cough or sputter, I drove my hand like this down into his throat and squeezed the sound part in there shut in my fist, and then watched his eyes the whole time he died, my left foot finding his right shin, to keep his heel from scraping the ground like he wanted to, like his foot could be a beaver tail slapping the water, warning the other beavers.

The next man I woke with blackhorn calf blood in his mouth, my knees already on his arms, he had a Pikuni mother. I could smell it. I could smell her through his skin.

Like me, he didn't have a beard.

"Good Stab," he said, so I could understand it, and then I knew him. He wasn't Joe Kipp, but he was like Joe Kipp. His dad was a napikwan trader who had married a Pikuni, Kicking Bird Woman. I remembered this man now, from when he'd come through camp once, dragging a sledge of fresh mink and otter and muskrat, because he'd found a valley in the Backbone that had never known traps.

Everyone had stood in their lodges and watched him until he got to my father's lodge, to tell him that the soldiers were walking through on the wagon-road, so no Pikuni should go that way for ten or twelve sleeps.

We let him live, that day.

Not this one.

"Yes," I told him about who I was, and then, instead of pushing my fingers into his throat, I held my hand over his mouth and nose like this, so he couldn't spit the calf blood out. He drowned in it.

And then a tomahawk hit me in the back, between the shoulder blades, and I rolled away, stood up already running, and went back into the night.

The tomahawk was iron, and deep in, and cold when I thought I couldn't feel cold anymore. It finally dropped me to my knees when I was back moving through the dead blackhorn herd. I fell onto a robe staked out to dry, hair down, and remembered the women of camp working days and days, scraping the flesh from other hides, of blackhorn we honored, didn't just leave to rot.

I wanted to go back to those days. I hadn't watched them with the right eyes, when they were happening.

I rolled over and the tomahawk pushed deeper in, made my legs stop being my legs.

I coughed and threw up blackhorn blood, enough to fill a just born calf, and gave up, told the napikwans behind me to do whatever they could to kill me, to see if it would work. I didn't even know which one had thrown the tomahawk into my back where I couldn't reach it.

They were already coming. I could hear their boots, their breath, their voices calling to each other to be sure they were all still there. The one giving the orders to the others sounded like a soldier.

I nodded that this was good, that at least I had gotten two of them.

But then a calf they hadn't got licked the side of my face with its rough, long tongue.

I jerked away.

Because it was a calf, was supposed to have a mother and a herd to protect it, it didn't know to be scared of me.

I touched its jaw, held its face, and knew that if the men found me like this, they would kill this calf they'd missed.

I shook my head no about this, that not even one more blackhorn could die, and pushed the calf away hard enough that it fell down, and then used my hands and arms to pull myself over to a big cow, her robe stretched out beside her. It was slick enough I could pull across it fast, to her side.

I held my mouth to the meat of her side and thanked her for being here for me, and then I bit into the ribs, making a hole. I made it bigger with my fingers and then turned around, pulled myself up to her backwards, and screamed when I got the handle of that tomahawk into the hole I'd made.

I pulled forward all at once and the tomahawk popped out, even more of that blackhorn bull's blood spilling down and out of me.

I turned around, got the tomahawk in my hand, did it like this to know its weight and its balance, so that when the first of these napikwans got close enough, I threw the tomahawk spinning fast across between us. It went into his shoulder right here, like where they'd shot me.

I could have put it in his face, but I needed him to be alive long enough for me to drag over to him, latch onto his throat with my mouth, his hands beating at my shoulders and back and head. I fed from him harder and faster than I had since that first soldier.

The napikwan screamed while I was doing it, and it was loud enough that one of the long-shooter guns boomed to this side of me. That big greased-shooter pulled through my new hair but went past, and my teeth were bitten in deep enough that my mouth stayed where it was. I clenched up for the next shot, because I couldn't stop drinking, but what I heard then was this napikwan reloading his long-shooter gun, meaning they were like the round-ball guns the Pikuni had, that only shoot one time.

I sucked harder, faster, growling into the man's open throat, his blood splashing even into my eyes. All around was screaming, and two of the napikwans had torches, because they couldn't see in the darkness like I can. Like your cat out there can. Like the dirty-face it's eating now could.

In that flickering shadow light, the napikwan with the short-gun, who sounded like a soldier, saw me and shot, the little greased-shooter hitting me in the side, the blood I was drinking from the other napikwan spurting out already, and I hate that this soldier who had shown the others to put the hard yellow whitehorn milk into the skins was the one saving my life this night, but he was.

If he hadn't shot me, then they would have had me, because after I feed, I have to lie there for a sleep, so the blood can move out from my belly. But this man was already letting that blood out again, meaning the blood was already moving out, faster than it wanted to.

The shot pulled me away from the dying napikwan, my mouth holding on last, the Cat Man part of me screaming because I wanted more, I needed all of it. And even though I needed to run, to fight, to not die, I couldn't help crawling back to this napikwan to finish feeding.

He was cold and dead now.

I stood without drinking more, had my legs back.

Blood was pouring down my side, out of me, and was still leaking from my back, and the rest of me was shining and covered in it. Another story we have is of Blood-Clot Boy, and how I looked now is how I always saw Blood-Clot Boy in my head, the way Otter Goes Back would explain him, his voice whispering so all us children would lean in to hear better.

But Blood-Clot Boy was a hero in all the stories.

That's not what I am.

I'm the one who killed Beaver Chief's people. I'm the one with the Cat Man inside me. I'm the one who has to drink the blood of my people, just so I can keep drinking that blood.

And now there were seven smelly napikwans standing around me, two of them holding burning torches, one of them trying to hold his short-gun steady on me, the rest of them raising their long-shooter guns, three of them screaming because they didn't know what I was.

What I am is the Indian who can't die.

I'm the worst dream America ever had.

When that short-gun finally shot, I wasn't there anymore, so that little greased-shooter went into the hip of the man behind me and he fell over, shooting before he fell. It was into the knee of a napikwan with a long beard who was standing beside the one with the short-gun.

Three of the long-shooter guns shot with one booming voice, one of them burning a line along my calf right here and then hitting into the ground, but I was already running into the night, naked and covered in blood, my eyes crying it too, my side open to the night right here, and the Pikuni are fast, the fastest, we always have been, especially when running for the Backbone, but this night I ran like no Pikuni had ever run, and on the way out of the light of those two torches, with long-shooter guns booming behind me, their greased-shooters burrowing fast into the darkness around me, I scooped up that blackhorn calf that had licked my face and held it close to my chest, because I couldn't leave it there to have its throat cut, and it wasn't until Sun Chief rode into the sky that I could see that this calf was dirty white.

My heart is empty now from telling this, Three-Persons.

So is my pipe.

The Absolution of
Three-Persons

April 18, 1912

I don't have time to be writing this.

Chance Aubrey was found in the wide doorway of his barn, hung by the neck. Not in the usual way, from the rafters, but strung between a post in the barn and his saddled plow horse. Chance Aubrey had jammed his left foot all the way through a stirrup so it wouldn't come out unless it was slack, and then he'd used a quirt to skin the horse's rump so it would pull hard against the noose around his neck, tied to that post.

The bones of his spine had been broken so thoroughly that skin was the only thing holding his head on.

When Sheriff Doyle arrived, he unlimbered his revolver from its tooled holster and shot the horse where it stood, then walked forward continuing to shoot into it until his pistol was empty, and then had to make his way to the fence where he stood looking the other direction.

This according to Martha Grandlin, because her husband was the one Chance Aubrey's wife, whom I don't know as she's never attended worship, had run to for four miles in her nightgown, for him to go to town, bring the law because, she said, whoever was skinning men and leaving them out in the grass had attempted to do the same thing to her husband.

Doyle, of course, being versed in the myriad and sundry ways of self destruction common to man, knew this for the self immolation it was, and there was naught he could do. Except to the horse. Which I would forgive him for, both in my official capacity and in keeping with my personal druthers.

That was Wednesday morning, meaning Chance Aubrey had hung himself laterally from his horse Tuesday night.

Later in the afternoon on Wednesday, the Star told me why Chance Aubrey had done this to himself. The ship he had invested so much of himself in had sunk partway through making its maiden voyage.

There was a count of the dead in the article which is more than the population of Miles City, maybe more than all of Montana, not counting Indians.

As to why Sheriff Doyle emptied his pistol into that horse, who had itself only been scared of the quirt, knew nothing of ships, part of it must be that the Pinkerton man Dove was found mangled on the tracks a mile west of town. It was the children of Miles City who found him. Not because anyone had claimed him missing, but because one of our constant retinue of dogs was trotting down Main Street with the right hand and forearm of a white man.

By mechanics beyond the ken of a pastor cloistered in his church, these children, being conversant in the ways of dogs, ultimately found the Pinkerton man. According to the talk circulating up and down Main Street, Dove had apparently been in his "nice California suit" when the train ran him down.

Sheriff Doyle had been called to this travesty as well. The next train was stopped for an hour while the deputies used blacksmith and farrier tools to extract Dove's remains from the tracks. This was out of respect for the dead and general propriety, of course, but it was also to keep the dogs from returning there to pull meat and bone from the railbed, which passengers didn't need to be reporting back east about, Montana already having more than enough sensationalistic episodes to keep the genteel folk thrilled for a decade or two.

No one knows what business this Pinkerton man could have had on the tracks, that far from town. I surmise he was yet looking for the "Missing Six," as he almost called them. Which, in retrospect, I perhaps could have provided him some help with locating.

Then just this morning, the proud American flag Livinius Clarkson faithfully tends in front of the post office, raising it each morning and lowering it each dusk, which had unaccountably been left flapping in the darkness of night for some three nights in a row, was found defaced in a trough at the south end of town.

I fear the fabric of our community is fraying.

In Miles City now, all the shutters are drawn.

Main Street belongs now to the dogs.

And even though the mail bags arrived by rail Monday, for once arriving on their assigned day, no one has as of yet received their parcels and missives.

So far, there are no indications where Livinius Clarkson may or may not be.

Not from me, anyway.

Not until I can appeal to Doyle's rationality, and his lawman's insistence that this all stop, which is to say, not until I can prompt him with a tale less fantastic than the one I've been hearing from Good Stab.

Until then, the shutters of the church are closed now as well, which it's not in my nature to do. As it transpires and develops, however, the most reasonable course of action for aging Lutheran pastors this week has been to fret among his pews and in his parsonage.

If the two weren't connected by the covered walk, I would have had to select one or the other, as my nerves would wither under the open night sky, but the Lord is merciful to old fools and Indians, and I admit to being one of those.

The only solace to be had has come from Grelda Koch's kindly left ash cakes. As Good Stab intimated, which is as anyone seeing them could have guessed without having a preturnatual sense of smell, they did indeed have a generous amount of butter to them. And, perhaps to better insulate them against the seat of the pew, or possibly to insulate the pew itself, Mrs. Koch left the basket of ash cakes on a pad of neatly folded buckskin. When unfolded, it revealed itself to be a neat pouch of sufficient size for a Book of Concord.

I need to remember to thank her, both for the sweets and for the labor it took to soften this hide so well, and then stitch it where needed. And I should also make an effort to express such gratitude in the presence of her husband, so as to make the suggestion to him that she's deserving of tenderness and kindness, not the back of his hand, which she too often shows evidence of, both in her face and in her wincing walk.

But woe to the clergy who would step between a husband and wife. I advise, but I never presume to intercede.

Except, of course, in the case of those ash cakes, which I interceded upon such that, by Tuesday, they were but crumbs I would have to clean up or not myself, as there are no longer any mice to act as house maids in this hall of worship. The ash cakes were surely meant to last the week through, but Mrs. Koch couldn't have anticipated the embattled, fearful state we would all find ourselves in. But yes, when my Judgment comes as it must, I plan to aver that I ate so not out of greed or gluttony or the absence of self inhibition, but I did so consciously and willfully, so as to better grieve for those poor souls drowning in the cold waters of the Atlantic Ocean.

Because warming my belly also warms theirs, yes.

Regardless, and in spite of what I take to be Mrs. Koch's best and purest intentions, I believe that, instead of hiding my guiding text in this buckskin pouch, I instead will secret this very log in it, and thereby tuck it away from any eyes that would pry.

What I mean is that I was listening, Good Stab, when you mentioned, forgetting your dark intent but for a moment, that I was writing all this down.

But Cordelia would surely tell me, were an Indian creeping in here after sleep, to peruse a log it's impossible he can even read.

Would but that I could believe that. I can't even convince myself the front door of the chapel is adequately locked, however. Time and again I find myself rattling it, assuring myself of its impenetrability, and then, shuffling back up the pews, dragging my poor leg, I hold Cordelia close and whisper to her that we're safe in the House of the Lord.

When she opens her mouth back to me, I can smell plundered open mice on her breath. But she is warm and solid, and her purring is a comfort I don't deserve but hoard all the same, as it fills me with life, and satisfaction, and wards away the loneliness, which I would have previously termed solitude.

And when Cordelia, like an owl, swivels her head to a wall distant from both of us, I tell myself she's but tracking another rodent, skittering desperately along the outer wall of the church, staying close to the wall as that immovable proximity hampers the owl's wings.

On Tuesday, that being the day after the hubristic ship found its fated iceberg in the darkness, the night Chance Aubrey would saddle his plow horse, a Pinkerton man's macerated remains cooling already in the spring house, the redheaded woman who I take to assume claim or dominion over Cordelia stood at my door knocking loudly, for any passerby to witness.

I crouched behind a pew, my cupped hand on Cordelia's head

lest she mew, and eventually the knocking crescendoed, punctuated by a string of invectives, and then both abruptly ceased.

I wasn't crying, but neither was I not crying.

Why must her hair be red?

All the candles in the place were alight, so as to blind anyone with delicate eyes. Were the shutters not drawn, I avow that some citizen would have stopped to inquire what was going on in the church.

"Nothing," I would mutter through my hand. Meaning, of course, "Everything."

Why has Good Stab chosen me of all people to tell his story to? How would he know to choose me? Are there no men of the cloth in his people's territory? Am I Job to be tested thusly, dragged across the coals of life solely to see how his skin will blacken and crack, revealing whether or not a glowing faith resides within?

Good Stab assured me I would believe his tale, so . . . is Dove intended to be proof? Is Miles City the source of Good Stab's ire, actually, and I but a representative of it, meant to spread his dark gospel?

And, Sheriff Doyle might ask me, what proof do I have for or about these suspicions I harbor?

"None," I would have to tell him.

But, where words fail, perhaps action can suffice.

Maychance it's fortunate these shutters are already drawn.

Forgive me for what I intend, Lord, but it's the only recourse I can muster, weak and fearful as I am.

I return anon.

April 22, 1912

I would apologize for having lied about returning presently, but would not that apology be only to myself, and thus as hollow and insincere as I am?

"Much has transpired" is what I should instead have opened this entry with.

Much indeed.

First, instead of regaling the public on the sordid events of yesteryear, Livinius Clarkson is instead now become a hump in the story he longed to be known for telling.

He was found out toward the badlands, along with another unnamed soul, probably, if Dove's Pinkerton instincts were on point, one but recently spirited away from San Francisco, and reduced to the same mockery of the time honored practice of buffalo hunting.

But to what purpose?

The local saloon is already festooned with the staring faces of three of these woolly former kings of the prairie, locally referred to as "The Judges Three," and the lodging house features at least one buffalo head on its wall as well. Were I to take a tally, I don't doubt that many of the former herd are now mounted both publicly and privately all over town——trophies, yes, but less ones waxed nostalgic over as emblems of longed after former times than what business owners and dinner hosts long to show off in pride, as assurances of the eradication of the Indian menace.

It's best that I now hide this log away in its buckskin pouch, lest any casual reader see what devious industry seethes within the heart of the local pastor.

Cordelia knows wherein I tuck this away, but she keeps my secrets.

Yet, too, she has her own secrets. Or, I should say, she now has one less.

Late into the night but a day ago, not yet half an hour after Good Stab's most recent confession, as he insists upon terming it, I was sitting in a pew as a congregant, alone in my own church, trying to reconcile in my thoughts this latest sordid chapter, when a scuffling above and behind me forced me to flinch forward from my seat and latch onto the pew in front of me, my knees bracingly to the hard wood of the floor, my bladder a gasp away from releasing, my heart clawing its way up into my throat.

Cordelia mewed long and sonorous as is her fashion, letting me breathe once again, in halting flutters.

"Girl?" I said to her, looking here and there for her, and finally finding her in the rafters well above the front door.

I didn't know it yet, but up there is a small window meant for heat to escape in the summer, a window that's been my wiley Cordelia's means of ingress and egress since she took up residence here.

After gathering my wits as best I could, and turning the lantern up to its brightest, I braved the darkness and freed the weathered ladder from its years of weeds behind the parsonage. I have to suspect the builders of the church hammered it together for the higher work on the church and then left it behind, it being of a length not convenient to the bed of a wagon. After working it inside in a most complicated and unflattering manner, I propped it up over the front door, giving it my weight slowly and unsurely.

"Watch over me, Lord," I muttered, and commenced to climb, Cordelia watching from below, her long tail swishing back and forth.

As it transpired, the window up there has high pivots on both sides which allow it to swing back and forth, resting shut in the middle if not propped open by the forked stick tied to the frame by a length of thoroughly cobwebbed twine.

It's cleverly constructed and well hidden, and will come of use in the coming summer, last summer's Sunday sermons having been brow mopping endeavors. From my station at the pulpit, this transom is hidden from view. From nearly every vantage point in the chapel, it's occluded. By design, I assume, it being merely functional, not in any way ceremonial. Upon swinging it in, I could see that the glass on the exterior had been painted to match the outside of the church, so it would admit no light, and be undetectable from the street. Ingenious, really.

I swung it back and forth, impressed, and then turned to make my careful way down to terra firma, at which point I saw that which I would rather never have had to.

The rafter nearest this ventilating window, its length divided by an upright timber reaching up to the point of the roof, thus forming two triangles atop the rafter, a girding system that repeats the length of the chapel, up to and over the pulpit, was on one side coated in dust as fine as that on a moth's wing, as was everything up in this undisturbed aerie.

Everything save the left hand triangle's base, from where I sat. That is, the side nearest this window. The top of that rafter is as free of dust as the day it was installed, exactly as if someone has been sitting there.

"Oh," I believe I heard myself say, and, forgetting for the nonce my lofty perch, I brought my hands to my mouth as if to keep my fears and certainties from spilling forth all in a rush.

Apparently, my hands on the upright portion of the ladder had been carrying enough of my slight weight that, when they were removed, that weight was transferred to the rung under my feet, which had been freezing and thawing and drying in the harsh sun for years.

That rung parted with a muted crack, delivering me instantly down to the next, which held me but for a moment, and so it went, rung by rung, my hands grasping for the uprights again and filling with splinters until my feet stood again on the floor of the chapel.

In wonder at not being harmed save those slivers of wood embedded in my palms, I unthinkingly loosed the uprights I'd slid down, so as to inspect the welling stigmata of my hands. The ladder's erstwhile uprights each fell slowly to the side, clapping the wood floor resoundingly as one, the candles close to them wavering, but finally holding on to their flame.

Unlike me.

I collapsed slowly to my knees, my hands a bloodied steeple over my mouth, staining my lips red. Partly for the fall and my unearned deliverance from grievous injury, but moreso because, when I'd thought myself alone, bent over my log with all fastidiousness or stumbling with sherry from pew to pew, or scampering here and there, lighting every candle, flinching from every sound, I may well not have been.

Yes, that hidden ventilation window is, I believe, just wide enough to admit a small man, or even, possibly, one of my size, committed to the effort enough to lead with an arm, thus narrowing the breadth of his shoulders, his head turned sideways, the skin of his face stretching and scraping.

It's the "committed" part of that which gives me pause.

Good Stab, I fear, has been making a show of his exits so as to blind me to his returns.

Because . . . does he hunt after the manner of Cordelia, for whom it's not enough to corner a mouse, but she first then must also watch it panic and soil itself, batting it back into the corner each time it would escape?

I know not, and so can only play this farce out to its terminal point, ever awaiting grace to snatch me up. I know not, so I scribble on thusly, and thusly, the candles lining the chapel guttering again, their shadows ducking and cavorting like Walpurgis Night, forcing me to stand on a pew to see the ventilation window for if there's a new breeze being admitted, along with a leering face, black hair draping around it.

In my course of studies at the Collegiate School——before it became the far less descriptive Yale University——none of my academic or ministerial training prepared me for this. The Indians in the east were already tamed, however. No one in the whole of New Haven could have anticipated Good Stab.

Nor me, I suppose.

Yes, I came to the cloth late, but that's only because having experience in the world of men could benefit my eventual flock.

I speak as if my twenty year old self had such foresight, lighting out for the grand and untrammeled west. I speak as if all that experience I would mine for the benefit of others wasn't in fact a labyrinth I had to hack my way out of over the course of decades, surprised at the end of it all that the education I had received was mostly intact, if thoroughly soused, as well as the various languages and texts I had been schooled in so rigorously.

None of which particularly helped me on my peregrination to the lodging house, whilst Doyle and fully a third of the town's citizenry had absconded to the prairie to witness the two new humps, which is the second of three items I mean to record here.

Doyle and the townspeople should have stayed back so as to enlarge the spring house, such that it can accommodate all the dead this season brings, but their absence was my chance.

After securing Cordelia in a closet and telling myself this was to save her from association with the house of ill repute she's wont to return to as it's certainly filthy with vermin, I locked the church door from the outside and made my way down to a certain porch, which is also not of upstanding repute.

Willem Thomlinsen was the first to note my limping approach.

In the absence of either law or townspeople, the Denizens were openly partaking, and my presence didn't curtail their imbibition this time, tokening perhaps a new stage either of our relationship or their boldness——perhaps both.

"Gentlemen," I said, doffing the hat I wasn't wearing, the wrapping on my hand momentarily untucked, so its tail whipped in the breeze.

"Brother," Sall Bertram said, leaning over to spit but holding my eyes the while.

I knew that, being of similar vintage to me, sallying out into the heat of the prairie without cause would be overly ambitious for this lot.

"Here to shear us?" California Jim said with a snigger and a slurp.

Over the course of one of my previous encounters with them, they had gotten onto the line of jest that concerned my being shepherd of a flock, with all the attendant duties and peculiarities of such a herder, including, which was hilarious to them, constant buggery, and buggery in return——"But never on Sundays, mind!"

I already regretted having to come to them for help.

"Not the season," I said in return to California Jim. "You have to let the wool accumulate."

"Saying that's what we're doing here, Padre?" Early Tate asked, running his already crusty finger under his nose. "Spinning wool?"

"Only vital deliberations and pronouncements here, I'm sure," I answered back to all, nodding my head forward once, meaningfully, as if giving benediction.

"Got that un right," Willem Thomlinsen said, though I could tell he wasn't certain I had been complimenting them.

"The Pinkerton man was staying here, was he not?" I asked, peering from grizzled face to grizzled face, and finally landing on their leader, Sall Bertram.

Word is he spells his name thusly to avoid confusion with any kings from the Old Testament, that being the prime holy text for certain races he wishes no association with, as he would neither lender nor borrower be, as that would surely lead to some sort of usury.

"Walked him here yusself t'other day," Early Tate said with a shrug I took to be the challenge it assuredly was.

"Why you asking?" California Jim asked, peering up at me.

"Someone should mail his personal items back to his family in San Francisco," I said, narrowing my eyes as if that expression could make my statement true. "I believe I'm the only person in town he trusted with his mailing address, as we were going to continue our correspondence."

"Livinius gonna sell you a stamp, there?" Willem Thomlinsen said with a chuckle.

By this time of afternoon, we all knew the fate of our postmaster.

"I'll send it with the conductor," I said, that not being common practice, but practice all the same, for those he deemed worthy.

"Why ask us?" Sall Bertram asked. "Crockett's the one, ain't he?"

Deuce Crockett, one time gambler and layabout, being the current hotelier, who has some unknown relationship or agreement with these Denizens which, apparently, allows them to idle——or, rather, idyll——on his porch.

It's none of an honest pastor's business, I'm sure.

Neither is it my business.

"The church's coffers aren't, um, sufficient for dealings with Mr. Crockett?" I answered as delicately as I could, meaning that Deuce

Crockett is of course known for hoarding items left behind in rooms to sell later at his discretion, which discretion of course lowers as the coins gather, as they say.

In short, I didn't want to have to pay for Dove's personal belongings. Not so much because of the poor state of the church coffers, but because doing so could lead to questions from other Pinkerton men which I would as well not have to answer.

"But of course any other transactions would be met . . ." I said, exposing the illicit bottle I had acquired on my slow walk over——again not having to pay for, as apparently Miles City is lousy with those in arrears on their tithes.

And so did the liquor change hands, and so did Early Tate lead me duckingly into the lodging house whilst the rest of the Denizens stood guard on the porch, assuring us they could adequately delay anyone attempting to gain entrance. I had been certain to select liquor of tempting enough proof to keep them honest, or thereabouts.

Passing through the sitting area was when I saw the one buffalo head I now know to be there. It watched our clandestine crossing, its visage as timeless as an oak tree's, and as imperturbable. On the way up the back stairs, Early Tate explained that the Pinkerton man's tab was still open——that was why Crockett hadn't cleaned the room out yet. He was aiming to charge the full and excessive bill to the Agency, which would be but a trifling expense for them, but a windfall for Crockett.

In the small room in the upmost corner, Dove's room was as yet unmolested save by his own hands, Deuce Crockett apparently confident he had time to collect his booty.

Woe to him, as they say.

I made a show of first gathering his spare suit and bowler, treating them with the respect they were due, as they might very well be his graveclothes, and then, as if an afterthought, I slid the various envelopes and papers on the desk into an unwieldy stack, which I immediately tucked into an inner pocket as best I could whilst looking elsewhere, for what other there was to gather.

"Get all what you want there, Preach?" Early Tate said to me, as if we were in cahoots.

"I'm sure his family will appreciate anything," I said, and, to cut off any further implications Early Tate might want to smuggle across, I quickly dropped to a knee and lowered my face in prayer.

When I stood again, using the bedpost to hoist myself up, Early Tate was standing in the doorway, one of his hands to his scalp, scratching deeply enough that he then had to lower his hand, inspect his fingernails.

"Ready?" I said to him.

"I think my . . . my head's burning in this sun, Reverend," Early Tate said back, loading enough meaning into his statement that I couldn't help but gather his meaning. It was a cloudy day, to be sure.

"Perhaps this would help," I said, extending Dove's bowler hat. Early Tate snugged it onto his head, ran his fingertips around the brim in appreciation and smiled wide and gaptoothed, even stepping forward to peer into the foggy cameo mirror hanging low on the wall.

"Dapper," he said. "Casewise Widow Boone comes around."

"She'll have to, now," I told him, and was studying the room like the investigator I'm not when the clatter of hooves in the street made its way up through the window, meaning the party had returned.

"Time to make an honorable exit?" Early Tate asked with a grin that opened an aperture through which I could see him at ten years old, up to mischievousness.

"Honorable and fast, please," I answered, already moving.

Halfway down the stairs, we could hear California Jim doing as Sall Bertram had said and drawing whoever hoped to gain entrance into one of his long winded tales about the time he was tied to a flat rock to be sacrificed by savages, but then a wagon wheel on fire rolled in causing a commotion, and, and, and——

Early Tate ushered me quietly but urgently out the back door of the lodging house, and when I looked back one last time, he tipped his very much present hat to me, his grin leering under it, and I had to ask myself if a man must be judged by the company he keeps.

Back in the privacy of the church with my boon, I lit one of the lanterns, sacrificing my dear supply of oil in order to see better.

Dove's hand was small and cramped, his notations wandering and not of a single throughline, as these were but preparations toward a final report, meant only for his own seining and sifting, but, with attention and my spectacles, I deemed I could eventually make sense of them, if there was indeed sense to be made.

More immediate, however, was the small, much used envelope of photographs. One of them was the face Dove had already shown me. Another was the first man found in the prairie, whom I had performed the funeral for. He had a good bearing——strong jaw, waxed mustaches, and eyes that stared directly out, unwavering. His hair was oiled down, still showing the parallel channels of a comb, and his suit and vest sported the light striping that must be the fashion in port cities. As I hadn't yet seen, nor did I expect to, the latest hump, laid alongside our postmaster, I can't say for certain which of the two remaining photographs perhaps matched, but I feel confident one of them must.

I returned to the father of the three, tilting the photograph this way and that, but I knew him not, I was certain, though there was something of an aunt of mine in the mischievous cast of his eyes, which is to say, that mischievousness is a benign failing shared across time and oceans, in Man. So as to keep this father from staring up at me, I turned him facedown beside the papers, which is when I saw the light writing on the back of the photograph, in a hand not Dove's.

Quickly, I turned over all the other photographs to find the same.

This family, evidently, carried the surname "Flowers." Benjamin the father and his three sons, Archibald, Milo, and——I gulped my surprise down——Arthur.

It's a common enough name, though. There are at least two other men in Miles City who carry it as I do, and we three consider it a private joke of sorts.

I now fold these photos into these pages, making of it a family album, I suppose.

Thirdly and lastly, then, that being Sunday. Yesterday.

In order to draw Sheriff Doyle in for my morning service and thereby deliver Good Stab into his presence and possibly his judicial purview, I, the previous afternoon, sent none other than Martha Grandlin to him, with word that I had a pressing matter requiring his immediate attention, about which the less said, the better. Speaking in such vague but thrilling terms being her special inclination, I felt confident she could deliver this with the urgency and suggestiveness I intended.

What I produced for Doyle when he sauntered in, looking all around this chapel I doubt he's ever set foot in, was the tin cup I had offered Good Stab water in, that he of course had left untasted, sitting on the floor in front of what I now call his pew.

Doyle hefted it in his hand, scowling about its supposed import my delicate handling portended.

"There, right there," I believe I told him, here in this holy place.

Doyle rotated the cup in his hand according to my direction, stopping only when the faint yellow and black smears on the side rolled into his view.

"Well well well," Doyle said, recognizing those colors.

I then commenced to explain to him how an Indian man I didn't know had come to my door asking for but a drink of water, and I hadn't noticed what he'd left on the cup until he was gone. But, all was not lost. This red man had asked what time Sunday services were, as he had been a resident of an Indian school in his youth, and yet appreciated Christian teachings, as he had abandoned his people's pagan beliefs.

He held the cup like the evidence it was, never mind the actual source of those yellow and black smears, and thanked me for it.

Yesterday morning, then, though hardly a speaker of German, the good sheriff was in attendance for the first time, his hat sitting in the pew beside him, crown down, his revolver at his belt, his hair not so much combed as, judging by the deep furrows, plowed.

Arrayed outside, he assured me in passing when he leaned in over our handshake, were his retinue of deputies, and some willing citizens as well, all of them armed.

"Thank you," I told him in earnest.

"We don't need any more Californi'ns turnin up skint," he said.

Meaning that Dove had opened his case files to the good sheriff as well.

"Californians?" I gambled, squinting to suggest a mishearing on my part, as I didn't need to be later connected to Dove's missing papers.

Doyle held my hand a moment longer, considering me, and then moved along, being certain to, as instructed, leave Good Stab's pew empty.

After publicly greeting our esteemed visitor for the congregation, who resituated themselves with straighter backs to be in the presence of such constabularity, I leaned onto the pulpit, the meat of my thumbs to the soft purple stole as ever, my breviary open before me, and fell into the sermon with all my heart, even stopping periodically to prompt the sheriff in the English he needed, to keep him in step with the service. Instead of nodding off between those promptings as Doyle probably could have, he instead remained attentive throughout the sermon, as I presume the men positioned outside were.

At least three times to my notice, but more I'm certain, Doyle scratched his scalp in order to peer back to the door I had guaranteed an Indian was going to be slouching through. Yet Good Stab, time and again, failed to present himself, even when I extended the sermon by a full half hour, testing both my congregation's patience and their bladders.

Foregoing another handshake afterwards, Doyle clamped his hat on his head, flashed his eyes to me about this wasted morning, and made his way out with the rest, leaving me and my apologies alone in the chapel, and, as it went, leaving me alone for the afternoon and evening as well. I tried to assure myself that Doyle and his men were out there yet keeping their vigil, but I know they had no reason to do so.

Even Cordelia kept away.

I swept the chapel twice, I straightened the pews which were already straight, and I endeavored to discover from what portion of the floor I might best see the hidden window above, or the rafter before it.

Finally, I sat down with the sausage that Erna Schmid had so graciously handed over after the service, along with both a half dozen brown eggs and the long and winding story of the sausage's source, making, history, and sentimental worth, which this log has not enough pages for me to repeat.

Suffice it to say that the sausage was still warm when she left it for me, and it warmed up again quite nicely, once my stomach was settled enough to partake. Being savory, not sweet, I told myself that this week my proffered dish could last at least until Thursday, which didn't, as I'd hoped, preclude my immediately setting to and eating both today's and Tuesday's portions, rationalizing that I needed to fortify myself.

Against what, I found out when a creak behind me announced itself.

Good Stab was seated in his customary pew, never mind the locked door, the late hour, the absence of an invitation.

If Good Stab's senses are as keen as he claims, then no doubt he heard my sharp intake of breath upon realizing I wasn't alone, and felt through the floorboards my heart. Mayhap he even tasted the sudden sheen on my skin, and the hot tears gathering in the inner corners of my eyes.

They gather again, now.

I carried my plate dutifully back to the pew before Good Stab's, was chewing when I settled down in what I'd come to consider the confines of this confessional box I was trapped in.

Good Stab nodded for me to continue, and I nodded thanks in return, endeavored to swallow, and apparently this is how captors and captives communicate——with belabored civility, masking the violence that longs to spill forth.

"We missed you this morning," I finally was able to tell him.

"I had gotten this . . . muddy the night before," Good Stab said, pinching the chest of his black robes out. "It was drying, and I have no other to wear."

I nodded about the sensibility of this. We can't have naked savages coming to Sunday service, after all.

Though the care with which he selected "muddy" whispered to me that mud had not in fact been the soiling agent.

"You camped north of the river?" I asked conversationally, taking another bite of sausage.

Good Stab pondered this much longer than seemed necessary.

"In Pikuni territory, you mean?" he finally said back, having adjudged that that was the silent question cloaked under my spoken one.

According to the Blackfeet's treaty, the Yellowstone is the southern border of their assigned land. North of it also being where the first hump had been discovered, this meant that this poor soul had been left in Good Stab's home. On his doorstep, as it were.

He isn't the only one who can lay traps. But he did indeed see the question I was attempting to smuggle across, too.

"You need a horse to drag a lodge," Good Stab said in reply, returning my parry with one of his own.

"How did you know I spoke this?" I asked then, with intentional abruptness, so as to catch him out. "English, I mean. That first Sunday."

"You do speak it," Good Stab replied.

"But my congregation——"

"Do not all napikwan?" he interrupted, tangling slightly in the lines I'd laid, perhaps realizing or remembering that he had previously told me the old man Peasy spoke a few words of French, not English.

"Most here do speak English," I agreed, not wanting to belabor this, as I'd already gotten what I desired. Then I tilted my head slightly back and inhaled deeply through my nose with my eyes theatrically shut. When done, I looked back to Good Stab, asked, "How does the world smell today, my friend? Is it full, or is it barren?"

This was a question I hadn't meant to confront him with until what he'd said about his sullied robes, which I knew had to have had blood on them, not merely mud. Meaning that, were I to subscribe to the particulars of his tale, then he had gorged such that his senses must now be enlivened, taut as the string of a violin.

"The world is always full," he said in return, vaguely.

"You don't——?" I asked, holding a bite of sausage out between us, and Good Stab only looked across the aisle to the pew mirroring his, his eyes tracking something I knew not to turn my head for, as it would be either beyond my ken, or another ruse meant to anchor his tale, as invisible rodents and their like are easier to pretend to track than it is to mime recovery from a mortal injury, or extend teeth into fangs.

I took the proffered bite of Erna Schmid's storied sausage myself, had to close my eyes it was so enjoyable. When you expect each meal to be your last, you enjoy it so much more. But then, not wanting to be rude, I rose to douse the candles, so we could begin again.

"Why do you walk like that?" Good Stab called behind me, using the exact same conversational delivery I'd attempted to weaponize against him but moments previously.

"Because of the life I've lived," I told him glibly, my fingers pinching a flame out. At the next candle's smoking, I said, "Three of my toes had to be clipped off to save the foot, the leg, the life entire."

"Snow," Good Stab said, understanding.

"I'm glad to still be able to walk unaided," I said, sitting back down and leaning across the back of my pew, the plate of sausage in my lap.

"You also know the words Peasy did," he said to me then, which only served to make the bite of sausage in my mouth expand with each chew.

Good Stab was still ruminating on my question, it would seem. Suggesting it was the aging pastor who had stabbed well and deeply, this time.

"French, yes," I said after a painful swallow.

"Like your name," Good Stab said.

"My grandfather I never knew was a Frenchman, yes," I said, confessing to this Indian what I never would to my congregation. "But we are German still, from the old country."

"The old country," he said, unable not to grin. "That's where the Pikuni are from as well. Maybe we're German like you."

I gave this the perfunctory chuckle it warranted.

"We?" he asked, then, yet teasing apart my words.

"My mother and myself," I explained. "Though she's long passed, of course."

"No other of your name?" he pressed.

"It's difficult to spell for most," I said back in deflecting jest. "And even more troublesome to pronounce."

"I mean——sons, daughters," he corrected.

"Oh, of course," I said. "I never married, no."

Good Stab started to press more on this, but instead pressed his lips tighter, nodded to himself that my answer was sufficient. Either that or he couldn't formulate an ensuing question——he'd most likely only had contact with Jesuits, so my saying I could have married may have been quite unexpected.

As for me, I longed to ask him whether his travels had ever taken him to California, but could find no way to broach my way that far west, being mired down in spellings and marriage.

I breathed in to deliver my ceremonial invitation for him to begin his tale anew, but before I could utter the first word, Cordelia darted out from underneath a pew across the aisle from Good Stab.

Being a cat, she is of course fast, but Good Stab, in this flurry of a moment, was faster.

His hand grabbed the skin over her neck and lifted her up quicker than a snake striking.

Clenched in her teeth, carried in from outside, was a struggling mole, its feet slow, its doom already a foregone conclusion.

"It's bright in here, yes," Good Stab said not to Cordelia but to her prey, and, when in her panic she dropped the mole, perhaps hoping with it to buy her life back, Good Stab snatched it from the air with his other hand.

Cordelia he let go, whilst inspecting this mole. She careened down the aisle in her scrabbling escape.

"I apologize," I said to him, standing to take care of this crude interruption myself, but before I could, Good Stab drew this slowly kicking mole to his face, clamped his mouth onto the thin skin of its belly, and, watching me the while, drank it in over the course of half a minute, the mole, to my eyes, steadily deflating, my own teeth clenched hard against each other, hard enough to, in spite of their flatness, surely bite through the belly of a mole if I needed to.

As I had to presume Good Stab was doing at the moment.

When done, he slung the sack of bones and organs and meat up the aisle behind him, such that it lodged against the front door, and he wiped his red mouth with the back of his left sleeve, holding his arm there a moment longer, instantly regretting having sullied again the robe he had only just cleaned.

Unless that too was a lie.

"I'll take it with me when I leave," he said, having never looked back. "If, that is, men with rifles aren't out there."

I gulped, only registered later his use of "rifle," not "many-shots gun."

We're now some forty years after the events of his tale, though. Perhaps he's taken in new words since then.

"How is your heart, Three-Persons?" he asked then, leaning forward to look into and through the windows of my eyes, into my very soul, a drop of blood yet dripping down his chin, from the corner of his mouth.

"It is weak, Good Stab, it is weak, but it is willing."

Then I said it, as I must: "I listen."

The Nachzehrer's Dark Gospel

April 22, 1912

I didn't know about what the soldiers did to Heavy Runner's winter camp on the Bear until four winters after it happened.

Another boy had come to Two Medicine Lodges, his sides drawn in from fasting, his eyes empty and scared, waiting to be filled. He was bent over some grass he was trying to start a fire with, but it was only smoking and dying, smoking and dying back again.

By his fourth night, he was on his side holding his sides like this and crying, saying his mother's name over and over. I don't tell you his name, or his mother's. I do tell you that, by when the wind died down, I had a horn of embers I had kept banked all day, for this boy.

I don't need fire like I did before, but I still make them. Across the flames I can see Tall Dog sitting there laughing through another of his stories about getting a wife, or Wolf Calf smoking his pipe and watching me like he always did. I can still remember my two wives and my children in the warmth of our lodge, wrestling with each other while I smoked my pipe and watched them, knowing better the eyes Wolf Calf had watched me with.

The starving boy had all his fingers. I counted them over and over from the trees, because if he was missing some, then it might mean I had stepped through, wouldn't be in the world anymore.

But I was.

I could tell from how much it all hurt.

I had some soft leggings I had made from a long-legs, and some boots like these, that I can take off faster than moccasins, for if I need to run, or climb. Back then I kept these leggings and boots in a parfleche under a rock by a spring I knew, but not too close to it, because people might come there to drink.

I wasn't staying on Two Medicine Lodges then, was only passing through when I heard the boy singing, his voice cracking and falling into itself.

I hadn't seen my swift-runner for four winters, but still I asked it to come help this boy if it would. That it was right that it turn its back on me, but this boy needed guidance. He needed not to be alone like he was.

When my swift-runner didn't come in, I did.

I walked out of the trees in my leggings and soldier boots. I had rubbed my hair with grease and braided it in three so he'd know I was Pikuni, and my face was painted white with black hailstones on it and a line from here to here. I want to tell you I saw in a dream where the line should go and how wide it should be and whether it was straight or jagged, but real-bears don't dream of paint, except the juice of berries smeared around their mouth, and I already had that stickiness around my mouth whenever I fed.

I walked out of the trees carrying in one hand that horn of embers, held by my shoulder high like this, so the boy could see I didn't have a lance, and in my other hand was a rope braided from grass, so I could lead Weasel Plume beside me.

I didn't mean to name that buffalo calf that, but once I said it I couldn't take it back. But Wolf Calf told me when I was young that a real Pikuni gives away what's closest to him, and my childhood name was the one thing the Cat Man and the soldiers hadn't been able to touch. So I had to give it away.

Weasel Plume was white when I'd stolen him from the hide-hunters, and he was still white, but now he had a heavy head, his back as tall as me, his horns still pointing straight up as it is with bulls.

I had painted him with black lightning and then dipped my hand in red, pressed it on his forehead above the eyes. When we stepped out, he shook his head and blew through his nose, so the boy sat up, still holding his sides. By the time we were ten paces close, he was standing and breathing fast, his mouth opening and closing but no sound coming out.

I held my rope hand out, opened to him with the palm first like this, guiding him calm.

I stuck the tip of the horn in the ground and backed off with Weasel Plume.

Slowly, the boy approached the horn. When he saw what was inside, he pulled some grass over, balled it up loose and pressed it down into the horn until it flared back up high, which isn't how you do it, but it's how he did it.

I laughed and wanted to cry, but blood coming from my eyes would scare him, so I held it back.

Weasel Plume pawed the ground. Blackhorns don't like fire, because it can go any direction all at once, and can run faster than the herd.

In a few minutes, the boy had added green branches, so the fire was smoking. On my first hunt, when I killed that soldier who had forgot he was a two-legged, one of the hunters had sorted the wood I had brought back to camp, throwing away the green, keeping only the dry, and as he did that, he explained how Crows can see smoke pale in the sky at night, that burning wood that isn't dry means you can't sleep that night, or you'll wake with your best buffalo runner gone, and maybe your throat also.

I let the boy's smoky fire burn anyway. I wasn't scared of the Crow anymore, and I didn't have a horse to worry about getting led away.

The boy sat out of the direction of the smoke and opened his hand for me to sit.

I reached fast into the heart of the new fire, took the charred horn back and used it to stake Weasel Plume down a few paces away, so he was at the edge of the light. He could pull the horn up if he wanted, but he wouldn't. I pushed the grass away from the horn so it wouldn't catch fire. The grass the rope was braided from was still green, so it wouldn't catch at first.

When I sat down across from the boy, the hand I had reached into the fire was smoking so I rubbed it down. The skin was burned, but it was only like the skin on a roasting turnip, when it's hardly started roasting.

I had forgotten how to be, around people.

I had forgotten what scares them.

The boy watched me, studying my paint, my hair, the way I tied my leggings. Down along the side were brass buttons from a napikwan who had come to Walled-in Lake with a many-shots gun and a wife.

Neither of them ever left. The gun I threw in the lake, for the underwater people to puzzle over, and cover with silt like will happen to all napikwans someday.

"You're Siksikaitsitapi," the boy finally said, lifting his chin at the end the way young men who want to be tough do.

His lips were cracked and bleeding, but I told myself not to taste that on the air.

I nodded that I was of the people, yes, and I told him I was Pikuni by doing my hand like this, watching his face while I did it. I think I was looking for if they talked about me, living up here, or if I'd just gone missing with Tall Dog and Hunts-to-the-Side and Peasy, never to be found again.

I wanted to be missed, I think. It would still be some connection. I could feed on that for the next winter, maybe even the next two winters.

I started saying my relations and clan and band so the boy could know not to be scared of me, but when I got to New Breast the boy looked fast away like a spark had flown at his face.

"What?" I asked him, because this fire wasn't popping yet.

The boy did his eyes like this, like it hurt, and explained how New Breast, my father's sister's last living son, married into Heavy Runner's band, had ridden into a fort in the daytime in his medicine shirt, singing his death song and holding his lance high, and it took six soldiers shooting over and over to finally hit him.

"Why?" was all I could think to ask.

"For what they did to Heavy Runner," the boy said with a shrug.

When I only stared at him, he told me about the soldiers standing high over the Bear and shooting into Heavy Runner's winter camp when they already had the white scabs, and how Heavy Runner had his name-paper that would keep him and all of them safe from the soldiers, but they shot right through it. And that name-paper was supposed to be big enough for his whole camp. Heavy Runner was the first to die that day, and if only they hadn't shot him, the boy said, then maybe none of the rest of them would have kept shooting. Everybody knew this. But they did shoot him, and nearly three hundred Pikuni went with him. And the ones the soldiers let go, after burning all the lodges and robes, they were let go into the coldest part of winter, so most of them died the same, with jackrabbits whistling at night.

"Why did the soldiers not read the name-paper?" I asked.

The boy didn't know. But he said, "They were looking for Mountain Chief, because of Owl Child."

This I did know.

"Did they find him?" I had to ask.

"Just Heavy Runner," the boy said.

It made me breathe deep, and all the blood inside me came to my skin so I was hot and cold at the same time.

"Where was Little Two Bulls?" I asked, my voice small. "Why did they not shoot him too?"

Little Two Bulls had been New Breast's name when we had been boys together, playing with hoops and arrows.

"Hunting to the west," the boy told me. "All the men were hunting that morning."

I nodded, knew this meant that when the hunters came back with meat, everyone they knew was dead, burned in piles, the smoke probably still rising. Then I was seeing New Breast riding into a fort in his medicine shirt after thaw, and making one last stand he knew could never work, that would only get him shot into again and again.

"I would have ridden with him," I said to the boy, and wiped away the blood leaking down my face. It smelled like a hide-hunter who had had a red beard and yellow hair, and had been crying the whole time I was biting into his neck.

The boy saw the red on my cheeks and around my eyes and pushed back from the fire.

I shook my head no, that he didn't have to be scared, that this wasn't even really my blood, that me having this blood just meant I was a real Pikuni, fighting the napikwan for the blackhorns.

But when I opened my mouth to start to say this, I think the boy saw my teeth. They'd come out when I'd accidentally thought about what if I had been there on the Bear that morning. About what if I'd seen that first soldier about to shoot Heavy Runner, starting all the shooting that morning. About what I would do to that soldier, or whoever told him to shoot.

When Heavy Runner fell, the ground shook under all Pikuni's feet. The only reason I didn't feel it was I was dead in a cage, and on fire.

"No!" I called to the boy, but he was already falling away, running.

I lowered my face, stared hard into the fire, burning my eyes more and more until I could hardly see, and then I swept my arm forward all at once, scattered the burning wood so I was standing in sparks and smoke.

All around me the grass was crackling.

It came up with flame all at once and Weasel Plume snorted behind me, but still didn't pull the horn up.

I did it for him.

I led him away, dropped the coals in the horn in the creek we were walking through and kept going, and then left the horn too. Behind me Two Medicine Lodges was burning bright against the night, making its own wind and its own stars, and then I stopped.

The boy wasn't a man yet, was too hungry to think right, didn't know what to do.

I unlooped the rope from Weasel Plume's neck, told him to go back to the herd at Face Mountain, or stop by Walled-in Lake, or the falls at the head of the lake, it didn't matter, I would find him, I would find him.

But first, this boy.

I ran back, around the edge of the fire, my eyes still only seeing like through water, from how long I'd stared into the fire.

The skin on my hand was already getting soft again, but my eyes always take the longest to come back. And now, with all the smells mixed together, the sound just crackling and popping, now was when I needed my eyes.

I ran and ran, hoping the boy knew to go sideways to a rocky place the fire wouldn't be hungry for, or that he would follow a hill down to a creek and then down that creek until the glow was far behind him.

Where he was was fallen down from breathing smoke.

I would have scooped him up without stopping, but there was

a raven sitting on his back, staring at where I was before the smoke even blew away to show me.

I had to smile.

This was what the boy had come up here for. This was what his many-faces man had told him would happen. He would sing and starve and dream, and finally, when it was supposed to happen, it would happen.

When I ran in because the fire was too close now, the raven flew off loud like they do, scolding me, complaining about everything in their funny way they take so serious. It wanted to protect the boy it was now with for life, and I wished I had a piece of liver to leave for it, but I didn't.

The boy was lighter than Weasel Plume had been when I ran with him, and he didn't wake up the whole way down to the Fat Melters camp, which was where his taste in the air was. When I left him at the door of his lodge, Sun Chief was already sending straight ribbons of light up into the darkness. I licked the one black feather that raven had left behind and pressed it on the boy's forehead, so all would know, but most important so the boy would remember. So his many-faces man could explain to him what this meant, that he was going to be a powerful one. His feet had blackened in the fire but would heal, his lungs had smoked down but they would come with each breath he took. What was important was that now he had the wisest of the birds to whisper to him for his whole life. Every time he needed direction, all he would have to do was ask.

I miss that.

All I have now is the Cat Man, buried inside me. And he only ever tells me one thing.

Instead of going all the way back to Weasel Plume and the other grown up calves I had been saving back from the hide-hunters, I sat a distance off from the Fat Melters camp and watched it wake. The women were going for water, the men were walking off to water the grass, like Wolf Calf used to say, the dogs were trotting from lodge to lodge, stopping to nip at each other and then run away, and the nightriders were coming in from guarding the herd, their chests high because no one had stolen any.

This was what I could never have anymore.

My face was dripping red by the time I came back to Weasel Plume, and I knew I was leaving blood on his shoulder from pressing into him.

The sixteen other buffalo I had with him watched me, always two of them keeping their eye on me while the rest grazed, like black-horns do, but they knew I was more like them than the two-legged I only looked like.

The only people who came up this high were Snakes or Black Paint People, sneaking over high for a raid because Big Gap to the south usually had Pikuni watching it.

Snakes and Black Paint People and one old trapper.

I found him sitting among the buffalo one morning, not long after that boy. Weasel Plume was rubbing his nose on the trapper's shoulder, and the trapper was scratching under Weasel Plume's chin. This was my fault. I hadn't taught him he should be afraid.

I made my hands into fists and walked in, stood over this trapper.

I didn't need to feed so soon after my last raid against the hide-hunters, but I could.

But this trapper grinned and held his hands up, and then he spoke my language to me.

"You're the one started that big fire the other night," he said.

I just stared at him, my eyes hot.

With my eyes I was telling Weasel Plume to leave, that he didn't want to see this, didn't want to see me do what I do. But this old trapper was still scratching under Weasel Plume's chin.

"Why didn't you shoot them?" I said, nodding around to the herd. "They don't know to be afraid."

"Too much meat for one old man," the trapper said, and reached up for one of Weasel Plume's horns, to pull himself up. He was old enough that standing wasn't easy for him. Weasel Plume tilted his head over the other way, helping pull the old man up. "Anyway, me and this one, we're friends. Known him since he was a little white calf, still bawling for milk." He held his hand down to his waist to show how tall Weasel Plume had been then, and that made my lips peel back.

"You live in the Backbone?" I said, showing my sharp teeth.

The trapper looked away from them but not like he was insulted. It was more like he was trying not to laugh.

This made me tighten my hands into fists, my sharp nails pushing holes into my palms so that blood came up through my fingers.

"Lived here longer than you have, Takes No Scalps," he said.

It was the first time I'd heard that name.

"Who?" I asked.

"You, boy," he said back, turning to look at me from my eyes to my feet, which was his way of telling me he knew me, that he had been watching me these last four winters.

I shook my head no about this. Because it was impossible.

"Think you're the best hunter there is, don't you?" the trapper said, patting Weasel Plume between the horns. "Think you're the only one knows to be quiet, to not smell like anything."

I tasted him on the air, sure he was another Cat Man somehow, that he was going to smell like me, like broken open ceramic.

He didn't. Mostly he smelled like the dirt up here that never has any shade. That and the snow that doesn't melt.

"How do you know to speak like this?" I asked.

"How do you?" he asked back, which was his answer. It meant he had lived with one of our bands for a winter or two.

"Come on, big man," he said to me, and turned his back.

He was walking away, leading me somewhere.

I glared at Weasel Plume, telling him he was a traitor, that he was no Pikuni. But who am I to tell anyone that.

When Weasel Plume stepped forward to follow the trapper, I was there stopping him, pointing him back. The other buffalo all looked up to me about this. Their eyes were black and heavy, their coats golden on top from Sun Chief, so close to the peak of Face Mountain, and they were all watching me, seeing what was going to happen.

"I'll go, not you," I told them all.

I followed the trapper down a fold in the mountain I never had taken, even though I'd been everywhere in the Backbone, and the creek down there had beaver dams all along it, and ermine in the water, and weasels in the grass.

This trapper hadn't taken all their fur, even though it would be easy.

He was just living here, like I was.

"I see you sitting on him like he's your war pony," the trapper said about Weasel Plume. It made me bare my teeth at his back. "He would be a good one," the trapper added.

"I'll never take him down there," I said back, trying to control my voice.

He nodded like he could understand that, like it made sense.

"In here," he finally said when we were lower down, in the quaking-leaf trees. I didn't like to walk in them, since the way my eyes are now, it always looks like there's napikwans standing every-where in the black splotched pale trunks, walling me in.

I think the trapper knew this. It was why he lived here.

He didn't have a lodge but a hole in the side of a bluff, like those first hide-hunters when I found Weasel Plume.

"It's not a big dugout, but I'm not that big either," the trapper said, standing at the door, holding the flap open for me. It was made from a wool blanket, had red and green stripes on the field of almost

white. On the side of a lodge, stripes up high were clouds in the sky. I
didn't know what stripes might mean to a napikwan, though.

I stared at the trapper, not trusting this, but finally I ducked
down, giving the back of my neck to him if he wanted it, and went in,
standing up fast from the wool blanket scratching on my back.

The air I'd tasted coming from those first hide-hunters' dugout
had been rancid and thick, telling me I never wanted to go in there.

This dugout only smelled like the trapper. Not even like smoke.

He had robes for sleeping, a book like yours, and some spectacles
like these, but clear like water, not dark.

"You watch me?" I asked when he came in, sat across from me.

He pulled a piece of pemmican out, said, "I would offer you
some, but I know you don't eat like this."

I just stared at him, and his home.

"I do watch you," he said at last. "Who do you think guards
Whitey from the Snakes when you're down there?"

He tilted his head west, meaning the grasslands, and how I went
out there once or twice a year now, to make the hide-hunters cry.
And because if I had to eat two-leggeds to stay up on two legs myself,
then that meant they didn't really count for people.

"Whitey?" I said back to him, raising my lip in disgust like this,
like I had to.

"What do you call him?" he said.

"His name is Weasel Plume," I said, angry.

"Weasel Plume is a boy's name," the trapper said. "I knew a man
once, a Pikuni like you, who had a boy named that, I think."

"You saw this boy?" I asked before I could stop myself, my eyes
about to cry.

"Wolf Calf only told me about him," the trapper said with a shrug.
"I didn't go all the way down there to meet boys, but to smoke with
men. His story about the boy was good, though. It was about how he

made his own pipe, and then tried to smoke it, but didn't have any tobacco, so used pine needles he crushed up small with a rock."

I still remembered that taste. I was spitting for the rest of the day.

"Is he still alive?" I asked.

"The boy or his dad?" the trapper asked, watching me over a pulled off piece of pemmican. It smelled both good and bad. Good in memory, bad in the back of my mouth.

"Wolf Calf," I told him.

The trapper shrugged, said, "It's been many winters since I was with the Small Robes."

"You knew Peasy, then?" I asked.

He was the same age as my father. They had been boys together.

The trapper's eyes were shiny like he was making a joke on me. This was how I knew he wasn't a napikwan at all, he had only made himself up to look like one, to trick me, to have his fun, because that's what he does, that's how he is.

We all thought Napi had come up here after shaping the world and laid down to sleep from how tired he was.

But he was awake now.

He saw me figuring this out and shrugged like it didn't matter that I knew.

"I call you Bear Sleep," he said, holding his chin up to swallow the big bite he had. "But Bear Dreamer might be better, yeah?"

I just stared at him.

I was shaking almost, from seeing Napi, from sitting with him like this. It should be any Pikuni but me.

"But you're also the Tender of the Dead," he said, like that didn't matter either.

I lowered my face in shame from this.

What he meant was all the Pikuni dead I moved among during the night sometimes, in their places in the trees and scaffolds where we leave them. I wasn't watching over them like he said, though. They can turn to bone without my help, and then blow away. I went there and moved among them because I might see where they stepped through, to the Sandhills.

"Not those dead," Napi said, and my whole body jerked with fear.

He did say he had been watching me. What he was talking about then was the hide-hunters I brought back with rope around their neck and kept in a low cave, and fed to keep alive, until I needed another one. It meant I could stay up in the Backbone longer. They were my whitehorns, penned up.

"They're not even men," I said to him, about what I did.

"They're man enough," Napi said, and reached out with the back of his hand, rubbed it down the line of my jaw like this, so I could feel the scratch. At first I thought it was dried blood from crying, but when I felt closer, with my hand, there were stubbly hairs.

I pushed back against the dirt wall and kept pushing, scared, breathing too fast, but I couldn't get away from what was happening to me.

"It happens," Napi said about my beard with a shrug, looking away so I could keep my dignity.

What he meant was what I should have figured out, what I should have already known, what that raven boy probably saw and didn't understand. I had been drinking the blood of so many hairy napikwans that I was turning into them. Soon I would be like that first soldier I killed, who had forgot he was a two-legged. I still remembered his woolly face hair scratching on my neck and shoulder when he was choking me from the back.

I shook my head no, no, and my hand dropped to my belt for the knife I didn't carry anymore, to cut this hair away.

"It would just come back again," Napi said.

"What do I do?" I asked, my eyes filling with blood.

"What do you think?" he asked back. "Figured I best tell you before you ended up looking like me."

He rubbed his straggly grey beard like it was the softest thing of all, like he loved it.

"I had to put that fire out myself, too," Napi said with a shrug like it had been nothing for him.

I was still touching this new roughness on my jaw, and also on my throat right here, and here, and all around. It was also prickly over my lip. I wanted to run and run until I was a different person.

"But fire can help too" was all I could say back to Napi, about the one he'd had to put out, that I'd left.

"Helped you, didn't it?" he said back.

I looked at him about this because I didn't understand.

"When the soldiers burned you," Napi said. "You and your friends, and that other one."

"The Cat Man," I told him, making my lips thin and mad.

"That's what you call him?" Napi asked back with a grin like I was still a boy.

He looked so much like a napikwan trapper that I kept forgetting what he really was. But then he hissed like a cat, clawed at the air with his pemmican hand and fell forward laughing from it.

"You called me a name," I said when he was done.

"It's what the People call you now," he said. "Because you don't."

"Don't take any scalps," I finished for him.

"The Pikuni aren't blind, are they?" he asked. "But you think the buffalo men will never find Whitey and them?" He balanced an imaginary long-shooter gun and sighted down its top.

"They won't," I insisted.

"When the starving times comes, the Pikuni will have to trade the Backbone for food," Napi said. He was eating something from a napikwan jar, now. It was berries in a paste, I think. But it was golden, and its taste in the air wasn't anything I knew. "If your herd, or the children's children's children of your herd, if they're still in the Back-bone, well, the white-man hunters will be looking all through here with their rifles, won't they?"

"The Backbone isn't ours to trade," I told him. "And we never would, anyway. And if those napikwan hunters come up here," I said, baring my teeth again to show him what I would do.

Napi shrugged, digging two of his fingers deeper into the jar.

I wondered what his blood would taste like. How long it would stay inside me.

"Try," he said back, not even looking up to me.

When I didn't, he said, "You'll stay here with me this winter, not with the bears. They're getting tired of you sucking their dreams, but they're too sleepy then to stop it. When they wake, they remember lodges and camp, and your wives and children, and they shake and shake their heads like rattles but they can't shake the memories all the way out, even though they're making trouble when they go down, try to live in the camps. One of them won't stop talking like Tall Dog, even. All day long, he's telling stories about how he found a wife over here, behind this tree, and then one came up from the creek, and, and . . ."

"Don't," I told him, when he was already stopping from laughing anyway.

Napi was licking the jar clean now, his tongue longer than any man's tongue. Or maybe the curved side of that glass jar made it look bigger.

"The leaves are dry now," he said, smacking his lips and putting the lid back on the jar, trapping his breath in there just like one of the stories Otter Goes Back used to tell us. "You go down one more time, now, eat what you know you need to eat. I'll watch out for Whitey and the rest."

"Weasel Plume," I said.

"I'll watch out for your little boy," he said, making fun of the name, "and when you come back, we'll winter inside here this time, and you can stay awake like a man, and leave the bears to their own dreams."

"I don't want to be awake," I told him.

"You're not a bear," he said back to me.

"Why do you care?" I asked, standing.

"Maybe I don't," he said.

"What if I don't come back to this hole?" I said.

"You will," he said. "You'll have to."

"To talk in circles with you all winter?" I asked.

"You will," he said again, bored with my pushing back, and was already digging around for something else to eat, which is how Napi is in all the stories about him.

On my way out, I stopped with the flap on my shoulder, said, "Don't call him Whitey."

"Whitey Whitey Whitey . . ." Napi said, facing away from me, making it into a song, and I let the flap go.

Ten steps away, I looked back and the flap was gone, was just crumbly brown rock again, that kind that's like blankets folded on top of each other and laid flat, with their edges showing on the side.

I went back to Weasel Plume and the herd, who were all safe and eating, then I checked the main choke points to get up to Face Mountain. They were all still clogged with brush and logs and rocks like I'd done, to keep people out. I'd also started, the last two years, putting long-legs and wags-his-tails that died in winter there, like a warning.

Next I dropped down into the opening of the cave that was my whitehorn pen.

The one man left in there was in rags, and couldn't see from being in the dark so long.

I grabbed him by the wrist and led him out, pushed him ahead of me but when I went too fast, he fell forward over a rock and a broken limb from a fallen down tree went up through his throat like this, and out the side of his neck.

The taste of his blood in the air made my teeth come in fast, my breath go deep, but I shook my head no.

I didn't want a beard. I didn't want to have to be a napikwan.

I left the man there for the sticky-mouth I knew was moving through, higher on the mountain. Sticky-mouths make big circles over and over, eating whatever they can as fast as they can. This one had already smelled this blood. Soon she would stick her whole face in, and fight off any real-bears or ravens that tried to steal it from her. One sticky-mouth, not this one, had even tried to bluff me off its kill the winter before, but I ran back at him, snarling and laughing.

He's still out there ranging around, avoiding the traps, not eating the poison the hide-hunters leave.

Instead of following a creek down like I would before the Cat Man, I moved along the spine of a ridge. I was thinking if the old trapper I'd been talking to at some point earlier in the day or the week would try to get that sticky-mouth's hide . . . and then only barely remembered that it had only been a little bit earlier I had talked to him, and he wasn't a trapper at all. But that's how it is with Napi, I think. Probably all Pikuni talk to him at some point, but it goes flat in our heads and we remember it in ways that make sense, and the blanket flap of his dugout is just rock again, and we never know we can walk through it. The only reason I remember now is that I did come back, spend that winter with him.

Trying to keep it in my head, who he had been and still was, it made my legs swing hard through the tall stiff grass. It made my eyes glare straight ahead.

I could smell our camps from far enough off to walk all the way around them, because I didn't trust myself around the taste of all that hot blood under the People's skin. If I could just drink from five or six in one night, that would add up to enough, I thought, but I also knew that I couldn't stop with just one drink from each of them, so they might live through it. The Cat Man takes over once my teeth bite in, and drinking becomes like gulping air after being underwater. I can't stop.

I didn't know where I was going, either. Just away from the Backbone, away from the camps. Maybe to not ever come back. I don't know what happens if I go too long without feeding, and I still don't. Every time I try, I wake up with my mouth around someone's neck, and it's never who I would have wanted for this, it's always the worst person it can be.

I had never before been glad my wives and children were already in the Sandhills, but I was then. Because I would still be sneaking in to watch them, I knew, and watch over them. Meaning my feet and my nose would remember where they were, and then one morning Sun Chief would find me holding my son in my arms, drinking him dry, and I wouldn't be able to stop, even though his blood would be crying back out my eyes, and my heart would already be on the ground.

I walked east because that's what I'd been doing for four years already, to find the hide-hunters. There weren't any this time, though. I went all the way to the Blood Clot Hills and didn't see any of them. I started to think they were going away, that their time was over already.

But then, around the edge of the Blood Clot Hills, I heard the shooting. They weren't killing buffalo now, but big-mouths. They had them trapped against a bluff. The hides they had from the days before were bundled up high in a wagon, and I could taste on the air that these napikwans were sneaking some little big-mouths into each bundle.

Circling their camp at night, tasting the air and wrinkling my nose, I felt like a big-mouth myself. When the four big-mouth hunters went out to shoot more the next morning, I walked into their camp, sat where they had sat, and finally broke a piece of wood from the wagon and pushed it into the coals from the night's fire. When it finally lit up, I carried that flame to the bundles of hides, left them burning, their two big-ears kicking through camp, stepping through the kettles and pans. The two many-shots guns the hunters had left behind, I'd already laid them in the coals of the fire.

None of this filled me up, but I liked it.

Five winters ago, we had told the soldiers' war chiefs we wanted Owl Chief caught too, because he was causing trouble for both sides. But now I was Owl Chief.

I wondered if he was still alive, maybe living up in the Real Old Man Country where the soldiers couldn't go.

I wondered if I was still alive.

A night later, I realized where I was going. It was to get another calf for the herd, for Weasel Plume to knock around and teach about how to live up high all year. It's not easy or natural for a blackhorn, but it's better than getting cut into a robe and having your tongue cut out.

The night after that, it felt like I was the only person left, and it felt the same the next night, making me ask how long it was I had been in the Backbone.

But then, on the fourth night after the Blood Clot Hills, I walked into a field of skinned blackhorns almost too big to get across in a night. I fell to my knees in the middle of them and while the Lost Children moved across the sky I just stayed still, not able to do anything.

The hide-hunters had brought a whole herd down and only taken the robes and tongues. This much meat could feed every band of the Pikuni through the winter, and even longer.

But I didn't let myself cry.

I needed the blood I had inside to stay inside, for what I knew I was going to do.

I took off the leggings I had put on, left my boots there in the grass with them, remembering the taste of the air right there, and because I was doing that, I tasted something else, barely there.

It was a band of White Clay People.

I went low to the grass and worked over to them on the other side of the herd, stopped at the two cows they had cut the meat from already.

Their fire was low and small so the hide-hunters wouldn't see them, and they had just started roasting the meat over the flames, but one man couldn't wait, had already been eating it, even though the others were joking and pushing him back and forth. It didn't stop him eating. Hunts-to-the-Side had been like that. He always ate real-meat when it had hardly been cooked, and the children in camp would watch him with wonder, and dare each other to take a bite too early like that.

I shook my head no, for this White Clay hunter not to do this, not to eat this meat, but a few minutes later he was stumbling out to throw up from the white-powder poison the hide-hunters used to leave on the blackhorns, to kill the big-mouths. I don't know how these White Clay People didn't know about that. Or maybe they thought they had rubbed it off enough, when really that was just rubbing it in deeper. Or maybe that's how hungry they were, because the hide-hunters were shooting up all the blackhorns.

The White Clay hunter was out in the darkness on his knees and his hands now, throwing up and choking. He couldn't stop throwing up, and he wasn't breathing good, and it was too late for him, I could tell. When another man from the fire called to him, a joke I could tell, I rushed in, moving as fast as I could, and kicked through the fire, scattering their meat.

I was a naked Pikuni doing this, so the men all grabbed for their many-shots guns and their bows and their knives, but I was already gone, and they were trying to control the horses that had smelled me and knew what I was.

Because they had forgotten about the throwing up hunter, the dying-already one, I went to him and kept him between me and what was left of the fire, and I drank and drank, hard. His hands came up and held my wrist that was holding the other side of his neck, and it was the same way my daughter had used to hold on to me when I carried her, but I kept drinking, couldn't stop.

Then an arrow made its loud noise, tearing through the air at me.

But I had blood in me, now. My hand that was free caught that arrow from the air before it could hit, dropped it to show how useless it was, and now I was staring at this White Clay hunter with the bow, who was staring back at me.

He said something in his language to the other White Clay People, I felt the hunter I was drinking from finally die, I spit the last drink out, and when the rest of the arrows came, I was already running away. The reason they didn't try to get me with greased-shooters was the same reason they hadn't been singing scalp songs. They didn't want to tell the hide-hunters that they were there, stealing.

Because I'd done it before and knew it was the best place to hide, I cut open a blackhorn cow and burrowed in like a calf not born yet, and I stayed there the rest of the night and also the whole day, letting that White Clay hunter's blood go all through me like it has to.

In the darkness between those ribs the next night, I ran my hand along my jaw but it was still stubbly. It had taken four winters of drinking napikwan blood to do this to me, though. One White Clay Person wasn't going to fix it. It would take a whole band of them.

I spit the dead blood from my lips and kicked with my heel to climb out, but the stomach wouldn't open.

I kicked again, harder, and it still wouldn't.

This is when I panicked, turning every way fast, trying to find a way out, back into the night. Finally, using my sharp nails, I cut under the ribs enough that I could push a finger through, then a hand, then my arm, and both arms, and stand up, pushing hard with my legs, the broken ribs scratching and cutting me the whole way.

All around the blackhorn cow was rope, tied over and over, thick enough it was like a second robe.

The White Clay hunters had tracked me here, and trapped me in. They would have burned me too, I knew, but a fire that big would bring the hide-hunters and their long-shooter guns.

I stumbled ahead, tasting everything at once, but mostly all this real-meat, starting to spoil, and that was when the first lines of Sun Chief rising broke to the east. I had only meant to stay inside that cow until dark, but now it was almost dawn again. This was how thirsty my body was for Indian blood. It made more time go past than I meant.

I pulled up the first robe I could, its stakes falling away, and wrapped it over my head like it was winter and I was just going to the river, but there were cuts all through the robe, letting the hot light in.

I walked out of this robe, got another, but it was the same.

Every robe I tried, it had been slashed and cut.

It was the White Clay People, doing what war they could.

Good, I told myself.

I should too, if I was a real Pikuni. If I really was Siksikaitsitapi, like I'd told the boy with my three braids, the way I tied my leggings, how I spoke, who I remembered. How it hurt, about Heavy Runner and his winter camp. How much I hated whoever had shot first that day.

I sat under my ruined robe all that day, and the long-shooter guns shot and shot.

When the big-ears pulled the wagons around slow to collect the robes, the skinner boys picking them up screamed and threw the robes, seeing how they were ruined. They weren't mad, I could tell. They were scared.

Their breath still smelled like the tongues they had fried in your hard yellow milk the night before, and eaten almost until they were sick.

I would cut their tongues out too, I told myself.

Once Sun Chief was in the Backbone again and the Seven Persons were in the sky, I worked my way through the grass like a crawls-on-his-belly, like Nitsy had done on my first hunt, and instead of waiting for the men to walk out to me, I went into the last place I ever wanted to go.

The dugout.

Its air tasted like a real-bear den tastes after all winter, when one of the real-bears that don't sleep had broken in, ate the haunches and hump off, left the rest of the sleeping bear to rot.

At first the men's voices were angry and yelling and they were passing a bottle around, one that was making their voices louder and angrier.

Good, I said to myself in the foul darkness where they would come to sleep.

But when they came in, it wasn't to sleep.

Two of the hide-hunters were dragging one of the skinner boys in, and he was crying and fighting and drunk from what they'd been making him drink.

The hide-hunters pulled the boy's pants down and bent him over one of their knees, and the other one dropped down behind him, was untying his pants that were sticky with blackhorn blood. The hide-hunter smelled like greased-shooter powder and smoke and death and hard yellow milk, which he had a handful of, to use, and when he forced his way into the boy, the boy screamed like his throat was full, like it had a whole fist in it coming up from his belly, and his eyes cried and red shot through them in cracks all at once, and the other hide-hunter laughed and patted the boy on the back like to help him through what was happening to him, and that was when I came at them.

I tore the man in front's throat out so deep that his head fell behind and touched his back, and he hadn't fallen over yet when I bit into the chest of the hide-hunter who had smeared the hard yellow milk on himself. But then at the last moment I remembered that I was Pikuni, and wanted to stay that way, so I couldn't even start to let his blood into my mouth, because I wouldn't be able to stop.

Instead I grabbed his jaw and pulled it down hard and fast, tearing it off except for one side of skin, and he tried to scream but could only stand to try to get away from the pain. When he stood it brought the boy up with him, until the boy fell off onto his face.

When another hide-hunter called in asking a question that sounded like a joke, I pushed my fingers into the jawless one's eyes and pulled both ways, splitting his head down the middle. His body jerked, both from dying and from finishing, and he held his bottle upright without spilling the whole time he was dying.

When the boy was crawling away bleeding, I stepped forward, drove my knees into his back, pressing him to the ground, then pushed his head into the ground hard enough to make his face go back into his head.

I was breathing deep and this arm was broken from how hard I'd had to use it to pull the third hide-hunter's head apart, but I was hardly started, and I couldn't stop.

When the next two men came in, laughing about something, I don't know what, I used a knife from the first hide-hunter and cut both of their throats so they bled out together with me hunched over in the short dugout, watching their eyes. I wanted them to know who was doing this to them. I wanted them to know and not understand. If I would have planned better, I would have cut a yearling blackhorn's head off and hollowed it out, pulled it over mine, because, for what I was doing, I didn't need my mouth.

I would like them to think that the blackhorns they shot were turning around and coming for them now.

Maybe I wouldn't even have to open their throats and faces, then. They would just drop in their tracks, and I would walk through like the blackhorn chief, my horns pointing up to Sun Chief, my shadow black ahead of me.

Until then, I could do it this way.

By my count, there were still four hunters and thirteen skinners out with the fire. It was the biggest party of hide-hunters I'd seen so far, and there were too many hunters for how many skinners there were, and it didn't matter.

The next one came in alone. He was the first man with black skin I'd seen up close. But he was still a hide-hunter.

I stepped in behind him and held my hand over his nose and mouth so he couldn't breathe. He kicked and stood up hard enough to push me into the top of the dugout so it crumbled around me, but I held on until he jerked and died from not having any air.

Before I could remember, I lowered my mouth to drink the last of his warm blood, even though it was probably too late, but stopped right before biting in, with my lips to the neck of his skin, my teeth pushing all the way out, longer than I'd ever felt them get.

I shook my head no, that I couldn't, that I wouldn't, even though the taste of all this blood in the air was making me dizzy with hunger.

I pulled the sleeve from one of the dead hide-hunters and wrapped it over my mouth, tying it behind my head, some of my hair in that knot. It was for the next time I forgot.

There were still more hide-hunters to pull down and walk over.

The next one didn't step in but called in, because all of them out there knew something was happening, something was wrong.

When there was nobody to answer, he threw a burning chip of blackhorn dung in. It landed on the pile of dead, and it lit their clothes.

The dugout smoked thick, and I was glad my mouth was covered. But my eyes were burning.

When the unspilled bottle they had been drinking from blew up in the fire, which I didn't know they could do, I had to rush out.

It was into two long-shooter guns waiting for me, and one short-gun.

This time, they only shot where I'd been, even the short-gun that had more greased-shooters. I was moving fast. That White Clay hunter's blood in me was making me remember who I was, what I could do. I hadn't realized that the other hide-hunters I'd been feeding on like they were whitehorns was making me dull and slow like they were.

With this White Clay blood in me, I was starting to be Indian again.

I hooked the sharp nails of my left hand into the crotch of the first hide-hunter and opened him up, pulling so hard I fell forward from it. His blood splashed down all at once, and I'd gone deep enough the bone of his hip showed for a moment, black like they are before Sun Chief makes them white. When the next hide-hunter stepped back to point his empty long-shooter gun at me, I took it by the barrel and hit him hard enough in the throat with the back end that his throat cracked and he fell to his knees, dying.

The man with the short-gun shot one more time, digging a line in my side right here but going on by, then he turned, ran.

He was the fastest of all of them, or maybe he wanted to live the most, or maybe he'd seen what I was, and was more scared than any of them had had time to be. None of that mattered. I was on him before he was to the wagon, was riding his shoulders and back, twisting his head sideways until the neck cracked over and he fell as limp as a child's doll.

I stood covered in blood and naked, knew that only my eyes were clean anymore.

The skinners were running off through the humps.

They were just boys, but I ran each of them down just the same, and buried them in the blackhorns they had skinned, and then I found the one hide-hunter left curled up under a staked robe, saying your three-persons prayer over and over, like if he said it right I wouldn't find him.

I found him.

Then, with Sun Chief rising again, staring down at what I had done here, I went from robe to staked out robe and cut them with the skinners' own knives, cut them to shreds and nothing, so even if more hide-hunters came, they still couldn't get anything.

When this still wasn't enough, I pulled all the dead hide-hunters out of the dugout and skinned them just like the blackhorns they'd shot and threw their skins hissing into the fire.

I cut their tongues out too, and threw them in the fire that was burning high now from all the stakes I'd collected, so they couldn't be used again either.

The day was bright enough that I needed to hide, but not yet.

I also took all the long-shooter guns and stood them like lodge-poles against each other over the fire, so the barrels would melt together. I even pulled all the spokes from the wagon wheels and burned them, so they could never be stakes.

Finally, my head pounding from Sun Chief's light, the blood all over me dried into leggings and shirt that cracked with each step, I walked out.

This was when I saw the White Clay People.

They were just watching me.

Two of them were painting the face of one of the hide-hunters yellow and black, and this was good, I knew.

They held their hands up to me, telling me they knew me, and I wanted to hold my hand up to them and be known, but I was too ashamed. And my arm was broken anyway.

I turned, walked away, Sun Chief right over my head. I made myself walk backwards and stare at him until I couldn't see anymore, which is when I started running.

The next night I did the same thing to the big-mouth hunters, except they didn't have a dugout, and I hadn't fed, so my arm was tied to my ribs with a piece of green robe like this. One of them stabbed me in the leg with a sword he had, one of those with a guarded handle like the horse soldiers use, and then one I thought was dead already shot me in the side with a short-gun that fit in the palm of his hand, it was so small. I lost most of the White Clay hunter's blood from the sword and that little greased-shooter, was weak like a blackhorn with an arrow in its liver. I ran away from the Blood Clot Hills and the big-mouth hunters' smoking camp. I was falling into the grass over and over, my trail right there for whoever wanted it. The White Clay People could have walked right up to me and done me like I'd done the hide-hunters. But they hung back and hung back, until they could see I wasn't going to where their camp was, to the north. I could smell it blowing down in the gusts. There would be so much blood there, easy for the taking. But I didn't want to. I didn't want to have to.

I was going west now, for the Backbone, because that's where Pikuni know to go, but I was only walking, and falling down sometimes, having to talk myself into standing again and walking some more. If I didn't get more blood soon, I didn't know what would happen.

No, I did know, but I didn't want that thing to happen. I didn't want to wake up latched onto the closest living two-legged. Not unless I was in one of your towns, like here. But then I would get all the blood I'd just pulled in shot right back out, wouldn't I?

I couldn't go back to the herd on Face Mountain this hungry and hurt, either. I might bite into one of them, even Weasel Plume. It would burst my side open again, trying to drink all of a blackhorn bull in, but I would do it, I knew. And when all that blood leaked out, I'd go for the next blackhorn standing there watching, and the next, and then, from that much of their blood, I would finally start to get those horns and that hump I knew would scare the hide-hunters.

I couldn't, though. I wouldn't use my little herd like whitehorns. They were my new band. I was Siksikaitsitapi with them, now.

Finally I fell down on my face and couldn't get up again.

Night was cool on my back.

On the hill to my north, a little big-mouth tasted me on the air and padded away, making a wide circle to get around, and looking back the whole time, because I might be tricking him, just pretending to be hurt.

And then my hearing and my smell started to draw back in close to me, leaving me even more alone.

I didn't know if I could stand back up, but I knew that, as much as the Pikuni move through these grasses, one of them was going to find me. And when they did, the Cat Man crouched inside me would pull them down to my mouth.

It could be a boy like my own. It could be a great chief we needed.

I did it finally, I stood, went back and forth like this, about to fall down again.

Farther away than even a long-shooter gun could shoot was the glow of a camp.

I stumbled that way, shaking my head no the whole time, not to go there.

But I was.

When I was close enough to see the painted lodges in the center, ringed by all the unpainted ones, I could tell these were the Small Robes.

It was my band. What used to be my band.

My lodge would have been on the outside if I could still be there. On the outside, but close enough, still in the circle of the People, which was the main thing I'd ever known.

I wanted to be there so much that my body jerked and I fell to my knees. I was shaking my head no, that I couldn't. That I wouldn't let myself. That I would be no better than the soldiers who shot down into Heavy Runner's camp if I did. Only it would be worse, because I was one of them. They would be glad to see me at first. Hunts-to-the-Side's first wife would run to me, asking about her husband after all these years, and the children would crowd around, touching me on the leg and then pulling their hands fast away, like counting coup. Like being sure I was really there again.

I turned, stood into the best run I could, because I wouldn't be able to keep myself from their blood for long.

The Backbone. If I could just make it there. I would even drink the beaver family if I had to, if it kept me from the Small Robes. What worse could Beaver Chief do to me? What was he saving back to hurt me with?

I was just past seeing the glow of the camp when I saw one lodge, like it had been left behind.

It had been.

From the markings on it, this was a lodge of the dead, was a lodge no one would ever sleep in again. One of our elders had told camp it was time, they were ready, and so the women had stood an old lodge up for them to die in, to keep from slowing the rest down, and then one of them had painted it, telling any Pikuni to stay away, and I could tell it was an old woman or maybe all of the old women who had painted it. I could tell how high they'd been able to reach the paint up.

Inside the lodge, the fire that had been burning was gone now, so the sides of the lodge weren't glowing. The smoke was swirling around, hardly even going out.

I'd moved among the scaffolds of the dead in the lower hills of Badger Creek, but this was different. Up there, the dead were already dead. Whoever was in here, they were just dying. Maybe I had been doing it wrong, watching the Pikuni we'd already buried. They weren't going to show me the way to go.

This one could.

I pulled the flap back and was so weak that I fell through when I only meant to look.

An old woman with a wrinkled face and grey hair turned her face to me from the thick robe she was lying down in. She was so small she could have been a girl of ten winters, and her eyes had a coating in front of them like happens to the oldest ones. I knew she could see my shape, but that was probably all.

"Who is it?" she asked.

"Me," I told her instead of my name. It was rude, but I knew that my name would scare a Small Robe, and I didn't want her to have to be scared.

Tied from pole to pole above her was a small bundle, open at the top. In it were a napikwan comb and a mirror and two black braids of Pikuni hair.

I stood over her and touched the comb, not the hair. I drew the mirror up slow, moving it this way and that, and finally, fast, saw my own face in that shiny glass, even though it was dark in the lodge.

I slowed the mirror, did that again, looking into it.

My hair wasn't black anymore like the two braids in the bundle. It was brown like the blackhorns' backs on Face Mountain, when Sun Chief draws the color out of them.

It was because I had been eating napikwan for four years already. There was even some red in the hair.

I fell to my knees.

I threw the mirror out the lodge door, heard the grass take it.

The woman's old hand, shaking, found my knee.

I covered her hand with my own, opened my nose to her taste on the air.

She was dying, would be dead the next time Sun Chief came up. She had already seen him for the last time. When she woke, it would be in the Sandhills. Meaning, she was about to know the way. She could lead me there, if she trusted me.

Even though it might scare her, even though I didn't want to say it, I did.

"My name is Good Stab," I told her, my voice hardly working.

"Yellow-on-Top Woman," she managed to get out, her hand still under mine, and I fell forward over our hands, my head pressing into the ground, my tears staining the robe with the last drink of the White Clay hunter's blood.

This was Tall Dog's mother. His father's third wife.

I remembered her chasing us kids with a willow limb once, when we'd been sneaking bites from her kettle. She'd been chasing us, just hitting the grass around us to scare us, and our mouths had been full, and she had smiled when she saw that's what we were doing, and we did this all afternoon, stealing bites from her kettle, not for the bites but for the chase, for the running.

"I was with Tall Dog when he died," I said, turning my face sideways so I was lying right by her. "He was brave, and he sang his song, and he's in the Sandhills now."

She closed her eyes and grinned a little, her hand patting mine.

"You're him," she said. "The one who doesn't take the scalp."

Her other hand was on my forehead now, so she could feel when I nodded, even though I hardly moved. She was blind, then. It's why her eyes were so milky.

"I'll see him tonight," she said about Tall Dog.

"Tell him he left all his wives behind," I said, my eyes trying to leak blood but I didn't have enough left. "Tell him they're behind every tree in the Backbone, that they're standing in the creeks blocking the water up. Tell him he needs to come get them, all the four-leggeds are complaining because they can't get any sleep with all these women crying for their husband."

She patted my forehead again and I tried to ask her to tell Tall Dog that I needed him too, but I couldn't make the words.

Her body jerked, starting to die, and I want to say the Cat Man made my mouth bite forward, into her shoulder.

But it was me.

I bit in and drank the very last of her, and, just like when I'd fed on that first dirty-face in the Backbone, her blood wasn't enough to make me full and sleepy. It just made me more hungry.

I sat up after drinking all of her in. I was swallowing over and over, telling myself I had to not cry her blood out, that I needed it to get back to Napi in his dugout, so we could winter together, and then I smelled tobacco smoke, the napikwan kind. But that didn't mean it was a napikwan smoking.

Outside the lodge, someone was sitting there with a pipe, with their back to the tent, meaning it was someone who had known Yellow-on-Top Woman. They knew not to come into one of those lodges, not to even look, but they didn't want her to have to be alone.

But who was old enough to have known her when she was a girl? To remember her like that?

I tasted the air with my coming-back nose and sat up straight like this, scared.

It couldn't be.

But it was.

I came out on all fours, the flap resting on my back so my knees were on the robe, my hands on dry grass.

"Father," I said.

Wolf Calf was sitting a few paces away, his back to me. He was looking at the Poor Boys in the mirror, moving it back and forth, and smoking his short pipe.

"So it's true," he said, holding his smoke in like he used to, then breathing it out into the sky and watching it turn to nothing.

I stood, walked over on two legs, sat beside him.

He lowered the mirror between us.

"It's true about me, you mean?" I asked.

He nodded, and I was glad that, in the dark, he couldn't see my napikwan hair, or the blood still dried all over me, or the blood still wet on my chin, and around my mouth.

"Is she gone, then?" he asked about Yellow-on-Top Woman.

I kept nodding, my face down from shame now.

My father pulled more in from his pipe.

"We found where the soldiers fell on the four of you," he said, pointing with the bowl of the pipe up to Chief Mountain. "We counted the bones, and yours weren't there."

"Tell me again about the Great Father's boat men," I said.

My father just sat there at first, but then, after another smoke, he nodded to himself and told the story again, just like when I was a boy. Him and Calflooking and some of the other boys were driving horses back across Two Medicine, south and east of where we were sitting then, and the boat men were the first napikwans any of them had ever seen. My father wanted to go around, keep the horses safe, make his father proud like that, but Calflooking made them go in and talk, and eat their napikwan food, and camp. Then, after the fire was dying, Calflooking and two of the others got up to take the round-ball guns and the horses, because everyone in camp would be in wonder that boys could do what men sang songs about. But then the boat men woke, started chasing and shooting, and, and . . .

My father stopped the story there, but I was still with him, back when he had been a boy. Horses were still new. Round-ball guns were still magic. Cooking pots were buffalo stomachs, not iron kettles. Knives were stone.

As a boy, I had never understood how we had made it through winter like that, with so little, but we always had, farther back than anybody could remember, back to when Napi shaped the land.

Again, like every time my father told the story, I pictured what would have happened if him and Calflooking and the rest of the boys had cut these boat men's throats while they slept. Then they could have taken all the guns, all the horses, and the boat men wouldn't have gone back, told the Great Father to send soldiers and trappers, to build forts, and we could have stayed like we'd always been.

But they hadn't. And maybe they couldn't have, I don't know.

With my face still lowered, I laughed to myself because, even though I wanted to be, I wasn't a boy anymore.

I was a child, but not my father's. I was the Cat Man's son now.

Behind me was my friend's mother, the marks of my teeth on her neck deep enough that they'd touched behind her windpipe. Her blood had woken my nose and my eyes and my ears. My arm was already unbreaking, making me want to itch it. The sword cut in my leg was already closed up, and my side where I'd been shot was pulling tight over itself.

I reached down before it could close all the way, pushed my fingers in, got the greased-shooter out.

I held it up between my fingers, against the sky.

"Are you going to kill them all?" my father asked, watching what I was doing. I had to be a shadow to him.

"The ones killing the blackhorns?" I asked, still studying the shape of the greased-shooter.

"The napikowaks," he said, holding his smoke in. The same way he still called your soldiers Long Knives, he still used the older words the right way.

"There's too many," I told him, settling the greased-shooter down on the mirror. "They're like the blackhorns. There's always another one."

My father looked over to me about this, said, "You think that? That the blackhorns can't all die?"

I looked down at the grass between my feet.

Of course the blackhorns would always be there for the Pikuni. They always had been. Even the napikwans couldn't kill them all.

I couldn't push back against Wolf Calf, though. He was still my father.

"Tell me about Curly Hair Woman," I said to him then, my mother. It was another thing I'd always asked for when I was boy.

"You're not a child anymore, Good Stab," my father told me back, quiet.

"I don't know what I am," I said, and he might not have even heard.

He clapped his hand on my wrist like a hug and held it there, and I shook my head no, not to cry out Yellow-on-Top Woman's last blood, but some of it slipped out anyway.

No Pikuni had touched me like I was a person for five winters, now.

I licked the blood from my eyes back in. I hid my face and shook my head back and forth, and told my teeth to stay where they were, that this little taste of blood didn't mean anything.

"She once got in a fight with that one in there," my father said, tilting his head to the lodge and smiling.

When he handed me the pipe, I took it.

My father kept smiling, couldn't stop. "They were pulling each other's hair, and then your mother got a little log from the firewood and stood over Yellow-on-Top Woman and she was about to bring that log down, but then she didn't. After that, Yellow-on-Top Woman and Curly Hair Woman never fought again."

I grinned to hear this one last time, and brought my father's pipe to my mouth. It was barely still burning, but it was burning enough. This was the same pipe Wolf Calf had passed me the night I killed that first soldier, when he told me I was a man, now, that I had a man's name, and so a man's responsibilities to his people. The pipe's stem was blackened wood and the head was green stone, and my father had a certain song he would sing in his chest when he was fitting the two pieces together, and that's the best way I remember him, humming that song I never knew the words to and being careful with his pipe, because it was from his father, who had gotten it from his father, who had never seen a horse or a gun or anything made from iron.

I pulled the smoke in deep, held it, my eyes filling with blood from the warmth in my chest, making me feel Pikuni again, for however long I could hold this breath in.

But then it went bad.

I had breathed in fire smoke before, but this was the first napikwan tobacco I'd had since the Cat Man got inside me. All the Cat Man inside told me was to eat, though. He never told me what.

The smoke in my chest was hardening, I thought at first, but that was wrong. It was choking every creek and river inside me that the blood used. It was squeezing them down, and when they were squeezed down like in a fist, they felt hard and stiff and dry, like I was dead, like the spring they came from had been packed with mud and rocks.

I pushed back and stood up, waving my arms around, and my father's pipe fell from my hand and the green stone broke open on the only rock in the ground, probably the only rock for twenty paces in every direction.

I kept falling back, into the lodge. The stakes holding the bottom of it to the ground held at first, but then the first came out, and the one beside it, and I was falling in, the lodge folding over me but I didn't care.

I couldn't breathe. The tobacco was choking me, inside. Not just where the blood goes, but it was taking my air too.

I slung the side of the lodge away, fought out, and looked down at my arm. It was so cold because there were black lines tracing through it like probably happened to your toes before they had to get cut off.

My father had pushed back the other direction. I don't even know if he knew yet about the broken pipe. There was just me, his son, dying years before he was supposed to die, years after he had already died.

I screamed loud enough that people from the camp might come over, and I fell to my knees, jerking and drawing in like this, like a dead man in the snow.

My whole body was cold now, and I still wasn't breathing.

All of Yellow-on-Top Woman's blood was coming up in drops through my skin, dressing me in red.

I shook my head no, that this wasn't supposed to happen, not from something as simple and Pikuni as smoking my father's pipe, and then, because the pain was making me back into a boy again, I looked up to my father, held my hands out to him for help. He was the only one.

The last thing I saw was him reaching down for me, his face scared but also mad, and the next time I could see anything, it was him leaning over me, cutting into my chest with the broken stem of the pipe, digging with its sharp end into my skin, and then pushing my ribs apart.

It didn't hurt my chest, it hurt deeper, because now he had to know his pipe was broken after all these years.

The cut he was making was big and ugly like the hole you kick in the ground for your own dung when you're raiding, but my father finally got deep enough into my chest I could breathe, sort of. Through the pipe he'd stood up in me. It was like your chimney over there.

I gasped in deep but not deep enough, just deep enough to be alive. I shook my head no because this wasn't going to work, and then my father stood, looked over to the camp.

Camp had heard me. People were coming.

"No, no," my father said and kept saying, and everything went black for me.

When I could see again, it was in pieces, and it was all stars rushing past, leaving their light smeared behind. Stars and my father's grey hair.

He was running with me in his arms, to keep me away from the people. To keep my teeth away from them. My hunger.

We ran all night, his legs as old as mine are now, but always know that a Pikuni can keep going all night when they're going toward the Backbone. Yellow-on-Top Woman could have stood from her death lodge and done it too, if she'd heard Tall Dog calling her from over there. Some of the kids the soldiers killed that morning they killed Heavy Runner could have also, if they hadn't had their faces crushed in with the butts of guns.

Someday, when Chief Mountain crumbles into itself, all the Pikuni will run like my father did that night.

By the time Sun Chief was making the sky light, there were trees above us.

I don't know where my father was taking me, but it didn't matter, because I was already home, with him holding me to his chest.

But then he stopped, and I could feel his voice even if I didn't understand it.

He was talking your French language, the few words he knew. He was talking it to the trapper, and the trapper was saying it back but faster, until it became words I should have been able to understand, but now they were too far away and quiet.

My father handed me across to him when the talking was done, and I could see past the trapper's thick arm, I could see behind me to my father, watching me leave with this funny old napikwan trapper, and I tried to lift my hand to him, to point to the white lines scratching into the sky, opening it up like the night I was born, but I couldn't even move my hand.

"What'd you get yourself into down there, son?" the trapper who I didn't think was really a trapper said to me, breathing hard from going uphill, and I shook my head like this because I didn't know. But it hurt.

The stem of my father's broken pipe was hitting on the side of the man's face with each of his steps, and it made the other end dig deeper into the hollow part of me in my chest.

When I got too weak to draw air through it anymore, the trapper turned to the side, breathed his own hot breath into it, waking me up again and again as we climbed higher and higher.

My chest was full with the breath he gave me, but it was emptying fast, too fast, like you can hear me breathing now.

But I won't cry in front of you, Three-Persons.

Not you.

My pipe is empty now.

The Absolution of
Three-Persons

April 23, 1912

And now all the sausage is gone, as I didn't want it to go bad. My writing hand is leaving smudges of pungent grease on this paper that make it opaque, admitting the previous page's words through into this one, which is emblematic of the past rising, pushing through, insisting on making itself apparent to all.

As for why I saved the sausage by eating it so, it's due to Frieda Zimmerman, wife of Heinrich Zimmerman, both of whom only bothered to learn enough of the American tongue to get along in town. Frieda Zimmerman who but recently concluded her weekly visit, if I can call it that.

In actuality, I couldn't convince her to step over the threshold into this chapel she's been in every Sunday for the last two years. To accommodate her obvious hesitation, I held my arm out to the whole afternoon awaiting us, and made suggestions that I had been about to step out anyway, to close my eyes and feel Sun Chief on my face and let Creation warm my soul.

"Excuse?" Frieda said, kindly as ever, but her eyes betrayed the inner turmoil my falling unwittingly onto pagan terms had caused her.

"The sun, the glorious sun," I corrected, tilting my face up to it as if luxuriating in its ineluctable warmth.

My life is a charade beneath even the lowliest mummer, yes.

"I don't——" she said, looking this way and that for passersby who could witness the farce we were engaged in.

"We're still in God's house," I assured her in my most consoling manner, even blinking my eyes overmuch.

Frieda Zimmerman gathered herself, gathered herself again, and finally said, "That sausage Erna left for you?"

I nodded sagely, or attempted to affect that mien, after which Frieda Zimmerman relayed that it was her who implored Erna Schmid to dress her sausage with those eggs. The eggs, being raw to my shaking, had indeed struck me as odd, but of course I'm never one to turn down future repasts.

"Do you still have them?" Frieda asked.

They were as yet on a cloth in the parsonage, awaiting cooking.

Frieda Zimmerman quietly requested I retrieve them, which caused me to insist she come inside and rest her legs, please. She couldn't be convinced to, however.

I limped away, moving at the only pace I have left, and returned minutes later with five of the eggs, the sixth having broken in the delivery, between the pews. Frieda hissed about this as she would at a child's sorry comportment.

As for Frieda Zimmerman herself, I need must establish her character. She's one of the flock who remember and depend upon the superstitious ways of the Old Country, even when they by their nature refuse to reconcile with the Faith. I of course can't condone this, yet I also know that when Frieda Zimmerman dies, so much knowledge will go with her——both cultural lore and experience midwifing. Yet, this afternoon, she still had one delivery to make.

She held the eggs in the cloth I had delivered them in and looked both ways down the street again, as if for anyone attempting to hear what she was about to tell me.

"Two Sundays ago," she said, having drawn near for confidence though any German words making their way into the street would fall on deaf ears, "I suppose you saw Heinrich drinking from his flask during service?"

I stepped back as if aghast at this revelation, but of course I have been fully aware of her husband's tendency to sip from his poorly hidden flask. I assumed it was to keep his hands from trembling, which I can very much look past, suffering from the same cure myself, but evidently this pastor wasn't being charitable enough.

"It's not what you think," Frieda hissed, hitting me with the handkerchief she was using to cover her lips when she spoke, reminding me with that simple gesture that, though a pastor, I'm still but a man. "His stomach has been bad for years, and, as he refuses the Chinese cure"——her euphemism for laudanum——"he carries the morning's milk with him, to take sips from when the need arises."

"Would that he had not to suffer," I said, holding both my hands around one of hers and gazing imploringly into her face, like I would take her husband's stomach malady onto myself, if but I could.

Frieda shook my condolences off, as there was something more pressing.

"What, Frieda?" I said, using her given name, which, for a woman of her era, is either an overstep or an invitation to honesty.

"It had turned," she said, her whole torso hitching to say it, as if desperate to be rid of this.

"Turned?" I asked, softly.

"It was fresh at that morning's milking," she said, her voice even lower now. "And it was fresh through the first half of your sermon. But . . . but then it wasn't."

I continued holding her hand, unsure how spoiled milk was as dire as she was making it out to be.

"But you had more at home?" I ventured.

"Yes, no——that's not it, Pastor," she said. "Here."

And she proceeded to carefully unwrap the eggs.

After confirming yet again our relative solitude on the stoop of the church, she dropped one into the packed dirt just beyond the wooden planks. It crunched open as any egg would, exposing its yellow interior to the daylight.

No sooner had it fallen open than a rangy tan dog with black shot through its ragged coat was upon it, slurping up not just the yolk, but the shards as well.

"I had to see," Frieda said, and dropped another.

It cracked as well, and was stolen by a small reddish dog that had been able to strike forward through the tall dog's legs.

"Good, good," Frieda mumbled.

She dropped another, which the tan dog and the reddish one were instantly fighting each other for, with the result being that a third dog, white with three legs, stood over the egg and, instead of eating it all at once as the other two had, delicately licked it up while growling savagely to keep the other two at bay.

"Maybe you're wrong, maybe you're just foolish," Frieda said to herself, and dropped the last two at once, as if cleaning her hands of this mission she hadn't wanted to be in on in the first place.

The lead egg hit the ground, starting another row among the dogs, but the last one never hit.

It was snatched from the air by an overlarge terrier of a sort I hadn't seen before, as I would remember eyes such as these. They suggested an intelligence I wasn't completely at peace with.

The dog stared at us with those all too human eyes, holding the shattered egg in its mouth.

But then it opened its mouth, let the egg run out uneaten.

"Oh," Frieda said, steeping her hands over her mouth and stepping back alongside me, though what protection I could offer, I know not.

This egg's yolk and its clear barrier were oily black.

The egg had turned just like the milk had.

"Nachzehrer," I heard Frieda mutter, only once, but once was enough.

Having grown up with a mother who herself was filled with folk beliefs, I knew dimly of what Frieda spoke. The nachzehrer rises nightly from the grave to subsist on the lives of the living, and it does so until stopped.

Before I could stop her, Frieda was scurrying away, distancing herself from the church.

Because, to her, and possibly for me as well, it's infested.

I shook my head no, but was already asking myself if I could still subscribe to a secular understanding of Good Stab's tale.

No, tales have morals, don't they?

What he would lay at my feet instead is a dark gospel.

Instead of writing more this night, I will instead be moving backwards through this log, to retitle all the portions of the savage's story. And while I'm at it, I'll also scratch my own name off the front, and inscribe deeply what this account is actually becoming, page by page, visit by unholy visit.

Behind me now, Cordelia is mewing long and plaintively, and I know she's asking for another fresh egg like was dropped between the pews but previously, which I've been trying not to hear her lick up bit by bit while I write this, her tongue a metronome of meat, steady in its hunger, implacable in its need.

There are no fresh eggs anymore, dearest Cordelia. I most humbly apologize.

All we have left here is rot and decay.

April 25, 1912

I have, for the first time during this, my first and last posting, circulated word that there will be no service this Sunday, the Feast of St. Mark.

Instead, gentle people, your pastor may himself be the feast.

I chuckle at the reversal. He who would aid in the transubstantiation of wine will himself be sublimated into a meal of blood.

This must need be Good Stab's indirect objective, mustn't it?

His breed is known for such daring acts, "counting coup" I believe it's called, which French derivation I initially took to be another jibe having to do with my surname, but further deliberations whisper to me that this is what he's been doing to this poor old man every Sunday last for near on two months——counting coup. Touching the enemy time and again as a show of power over him before finally striking the mortal blow, thus not only killing him, but shaming him en route to that eventuality.

All that remains is that mortal blow.

Unless I can convince Sheriff Doyle of the threat in his constabu-lary, that's already dispatched our postmaster, a Pinkerton man, and the better part of a family out of San Francisco.

Cordelia sits now in my lap, watching these words appear on the page from——in her limited perspective——out of the ether. Never mind the color, dear cat, this isn't ink I write in. These are my tears on the page.

And I apologize beforehand for the tight and darkened confines of the closet I take you to again but shortly. I would leave you a can-dle, but I fear returning to my church ablaze. I fear, I mean, that I would look up at those flames, not considering their heat but nod-ding about their familiarity, and then, this being the proper home for one such as I, step up, duck in, and pull the tall door shut behind me with finality.

April 26, 1912

My efforts to convince Sheriff Doyle have resulted only in isolating me more.

I check the rafters continually for Good Stab, but if he's up there then these old eyes can't detect him. I would trust Cordelia's better sight, but the moment I opened the door of the closet upon my return, to grievously announce my not surprising failure as regards Doyle, she screeched past me with such desperation that I had to return with a candle to inspect the limited environs of the closet. It was empty. As is the chapel, the various storage spaces, the rafters again, and, presumably, though I am not of steely enough nerve to brave the walk as of yet, the parsonage.

Yet I feel distinctly observed, and, as Cordelia has made her temporary escape, I can't trap her in my lap to serve as my better ears.

And so I sit here alone, uncaptured yet captive.

Was this afternoon's sally my last walk about town?

I think perhaps, yes.

As finding Doyle is a continual matter of chance, his patrol having no set path, Custer County being large and wide, I of course went first to his office. Though unlocked, it was absent of any lawman who could direct me.

The porch of the lodging house was my next gamble, as the Denizens there would have hallo'd the good sheriff had he passed there. I never made it to the lodging house, however. Instead, over the back of a cart whose driver wasn't at the reins as he was inspecting the forehoof of his horse, I saw a neat bowler I recognized with a start, and no small degree of both hope and trepidation.

I had set out to find the local law, but was there now another Pinkerton man in town, to find the one now missing, just as the one missing had been curious about the six lost decades before?

I worked my way around the stalled cart to call this man down, but saw he was already ducking into the second of our local saloons, where I had acquired the bottle I traded to Sall Bertram and his cohorts.

Mose the taverner nodded to me, limping in from the daylight, but I was already fixated on the bowler hat that was ducking through the back door. At the last moment, however, the wearer of that Pinkerton hat chanced a look back, and of course it was Early Tate, yet in possession of Dove's headwear.

He tipped it to me, flashed his smile of rotting teeth, and slipped away, I think to the jakes immediately behind the saloon.

"Reverend!" Sheriff Doyle said then, from the table he was holding court at.

I winced at this appellation but sat down regardless.

The two business owners he'd been deliberating with rose, made their excuses, and stepped back to their establishments, the discussion, evidently, having been not meant for the ears of a Man of the Cloth.

"What brings you to this . . . this . . ." Sheriff Doyle said, struggling for the right term.

"Den of conviviality?" I supplied with forced lightsomeness, as Mose was surely within hearing, and you always want to be in the good graces of the Ost, as a certain group of travelers call the tappestere.

Doyle shrugged maybe to my conviviality prod and slowly rotated his hat counterclockwise on the table top as if attempting to dial the hands of time back to before my interruption.

"He came back," I led off with, having no time to set the plate out for what I intended to feed him.

"This Indian," he said, using, I believe, the same paternal tone that judges the breathless testimony of a child, frightened after dark.

"He was the one responsible for the——the previous humps," I insisted. "The ones Mr. Clarkson knew about."

"You know this how?" he asked back.

"He told me," I assured him. "In his youth, he slaughtered whole encampments of hunters, and skinned them just like these are being skinned."

"Just one man?" Doyle asked.

"He claims to be more than that," I told him, not blind to how that must sound.

Doyle absorbed this, his eyes moving across the empty saloon.

"Drink, Father?" he said, pushing the bottle he was working on nearer to me.

"You have to stop him," I said, or, rather, adjured with all the desperate conviction I had. "He still has——I know he still has one more of those San Francisco men out there in a dugout somewhere."

Doyle was staring right at me, now.

"Dugout?" he finally said.

"He's——time and again, in his . . . his confessions, he keeps mentioning dugouts," I said. "I think he does that as a way of telling me where he is, should I wish to find him?"

"Do you wish to find him?" Doyle asked.

"I don't need to," I told him. "He comes to me."

"And you're sure of this dugout?" he asked. "You would, um, swear to it on your good book?"

"I and my congregation both," I lied, the unspoken portion of that being, I'm ashamed to say, a threat of sorts. Bringing the body of my congregation into this was my indirect way of forcing Doyle to count their votes, as it were. And what his next election might mean, with or without them.

"A dugout," he repeated.

"Just go look?" I begged, prostrating my voice if not my corporeal self. Then, lower, I added, nudging the bottle back his direction, "You could make an afternoon of it, could you not? At my expense, of course. I can settle up with Mose."

Doyle considered this, judged the remainder of the bottle, and finally, without affirming his course of action, as he wished it to be his decision rather than a result of my urging, he stood, the neck of the bottle in hand, and made his exit.

"Settle up, you say?" Mose called from behind the bar, washing a glass with a cloth that hadn't been white for years, I daresay.

"Of course," I told him, and waited at the bar for him to collect his talley of debtors, to which my name would now be appended. In his search for a pencil, as well as the talley itself, I leaned back against the bar and studied his place of business.

There was the customary buffalo head mounted over the door, and, wherever possible, there were the rifles and pistols riders of the range find nearly daily out in the grass, rusting into the earth. It would seem that Mose provides a free drink or some such for these trophies of yesteryear.

Tracking a line of pistols, all in the same configuration, up the wall, I found myself enchanted instead by the chandelier hanging from the tall ceiling.

It was an agglomeration of Sharps rifles that had, at one time, all been leaned together at the barrel over a fire, such that they melted and sagged together to finally achieve the visual effect of straw that's been cut, raked, and bound together at the top, in wait of collection.

The chain they dangled on was thick, perhaps nautical.

The chain back to Good Stab's dark gospel was even thicker.

I scurried away before Mose could find that prophesied pencil, and, out in the bright daylight of the street, was apprehended by Amos Short Ribs. Well, I claim "apprehended," but in truth he was merely watching me from the trough he was washing his shirt in. I believe it was a shirt, as he wasn't then wearing one.

I was holding his amused eyes——amused by what, I had not an inkling——when the door I had but stepped through opened into my back. It was Early Tate, fresh from the jakes, his step both lighter and less urgent, a detail I deplore having to stoop to capture on this greasy page.

"Preach," he said in passing, turning to get past me.

When he was ducking past, I chanced to see the oily black feather he had jauntily worked into the silken band of the bowler.

I snatched it as a boy might snatch a sweet from a tray passing by at his level.

With Early Tate passed, I could see Amos Short Ribs was yet watching me, as if waiting for something.

What I did, I did by instinct, not planning.

It was to lick one side of the feather and press it into my forehead.

Amos Short Ribs stood quickly, no longer amused, and, though this limp precluded me catching him, I was standing in the doorway of his canvas tent but slightly later.

This time, instead of bacon, I had procured another bottle from Mose. For this he had found the tally, the fabled pencil. I am in deeper with him than I would wish, yes, but that matters not to a dead man.

"Tell me," I said to Amos Short Ribs, touching my forehead again with the feather, which refused to maintain its perch on my brow.

Amos Short Ribs eyed the bottle, turned away as if in pain, or reluctance, but finally he faced me again. A moment later, he had the bottle, was uncorking it, and drawing deep.

Instead of asking, I waited for the spirits to have their multiloquous effect.

As Amos Short Ribs's manner of speech declined over the course of the gifted bottle, I here deliver his recounting in my own words.

Yes, that feather, it reminded him of someone from the before days. It was a renowned medicine man named Happy, who had gone to the mountains for his vision and had one unlike any other. As with all things Indian, it came in fours. First, the Morning Star appeared with a spirit buffalo. Next, this Morning Star placed his hand in the fire without injury. Third, sad for the fate of his people——what had happened and what would happen——the fabled Morning Star cried blood at one point, which is where he got his name among the Blackfeet, The Fullbood. As in, he was so full that it was spilling out of him. Fourth, he burned the Backbone and his spirit buffalo both, but walked through the fire for the boy who would become Happy, and flew with him back to camp, leaving a single raven feather to assure Happy that he would never be alone in the world.

When Amos Short Ribs was done, and nodding off over his bottle, I said to him, "This Fullblood Blackfeet, he takes no scalps, does he?"

Amos Short Ribs looked up to me, his eyes watery and unfocused.

"Two different people," he said, obviously, one a divinity, the other a monster.

I didn't correct him.

April 28, 1912

Good Stab is gone again, and I remain whole and intact, possibly because, in addition to the bottle I delivered to Amos Short Ribs, I also got onto Mose's tally for the pack of Chesterfields he had in his chest pocket, not including the one he had tucked behind his ear. I haven't smoked since the day of the quirly and the cheroot, when tobacco perforce replaced meals for long and painful trudges through the gathering snow, but my lungs remembered what Poitevin's thinking self had forgotten——any Frenchman I must hide under their nom de plumes——and I relaxed into myself for the first time in days.

In addition to the instantly felt medicinal benefits, this Chesterfield, being mass-produced, was easier to draw through, and the straightness of its shaft was comforting in that its regularity suggested a modern world where order reigned supreme, each cigarette like the previous one, in a line extended back and back——soldiers in a column, advancing steadily and implacably forward, to bring civilization to the savage wilds. Better yet, there were eighteen more in the troop after this one, and their inhalation wouldn't be stymied by tapping leaf out and rolling it with unsure hands, then licking it shut with a tongue long gone dry.

Whatever was now due Mose for this, it was worth it. To say nothing of the fact that its vituperative tinge in my blood, cogito, has to be the sole factor that kept Good Stab's teeth from my neck.

I know not why mere tobacco, inert as it is, would deal so violently with the otherwise resistant constitution he claims, but I do know that any effort to tempt him to smoke with me, thus incapacitating himself, would only hasten my inevitable end.

But I can use these Chesterfields as ward, I warrant. Against his teeth solely, I mean, not to forfend his corrupt and corrupting presence. As illustrated by . . . well. Smoking that first Chesterfield and thereby joining arms with the contemporary world for a moment, I wasn't as alone in the chapel as I assumed I was. Peering through the smoke I was exhaling, I finally, as must happen when sitting in a pew, looked higher, to that which I no longer see, due to His constant presence.

I speak of course of Jesus on His cross, looking down on us all, His pain and suffering graven in wood, His skin not pale and sunless like mine, but leathery and brown from His long walks across the deserts of His world.

As I watched, He spasmed forward and coughed from my exhaled smoke.

I turned to run and of course fell with the first step, my bad foot betraying me as ever, so I didn't see Good Stab extract himself from his cruciform perch, leap all that distance down and retrieve the robe he must have secreted in the pulpit. Neither did I hear him, which made his descent even more ominous. I did apprehend him standing in the aisle at the end of the pews, however. Waiting for me, his dark spectacles already covering his eyes, his hands hidden in his sleeves.

I collected myself as best I could and stood, dusting off the knees of the white robe I was now wearing, and this Christ-who-wasn't removed his darkened spectacles ear by ear, the leftmost one getting momentarily caught up in his long hair, which caused him to let it all down and then recapture it, smooth it into the gathered tail that ran down his back now.

Not the three short braids of the Blackfeet, the pedant in me noted.

"Allow me, Three-Persons," he said, and while I gathered myself, leaning on a pew and coughing, the pack of Chesterfields in my hand like a shield, he went from candle to candle around the chapel, pinching the flames away but delivering the last flickering one to me so I could place it where I would, not stranding us in the complete darkness I troth he would prefer.

I used the candle to light my next cigarette, then drew deeply, turned to the side to breathe it away.

"Do you miss it?" I asked, about the smoke swirling and eddying above us.

Good Stab nodded reluctantly, perhaps bitterly, that he did miss smoking, yes.

"All the things that made me Pikuni are like that now," he said, dissipating the smoke with the back of his hand.

"Including death," I said.

Not expecting an answer to a statement as rhetorical as this, I held my hand out to the side, offering the same pews we'd previously stationed ourselves at.

Good Stab considered me a moment more then nodded, took his customary seat, his hands now clasped again between the knees of his robe.

"So you start to believe," he said about what I was smoking, and how poison it was to him.

"Those fifty caliber rifles you left over that cook fire," I told him. "They're hanging in an establishment down the street."

"Melted guns are what proves it to you?" he asked, either impressed or incredulous.

"The nail in the coffin, you could say," I said. "I'm sorry I have no food to offer," I told him. "For you to decline, I mean."

"Do you not hear?" he asked back.

I tilted my head as if to listen to the subtle, Divine mechanisms of the universe, but all I heard was the pregnant emptiness of the chapel.

"Out there," Good Stab said, about the front door.

"Do you mind?" I asked.

When he didn't, I rose to inspect and found on the church's stoop some eight or nine formerly covered dishes, most likely delivered en masse, so I might have or at least have access to the strength necessary to either recover from whatever malady I suffered that was causing me to forego services, or, if word of Erna Schmid's spoiled egg was being passed along, then these meals were of the sort left after funeral services.

It mattered not.

The dishes were formerly covered because all the dogs of Miles City were feasting on them, the towels the food had been under scattered, the dishes either broken or currently breaking, the dogs delirious with this gift. Not wanting their attention, I closed the door but gently, and locked it firmly.

When I returned to the pews, Good Stab was looking up at the now empty crucifix on the grand wall behind the pulpit.

"Where did you put Him?" I asked.

"Napikwans must hate him," Good Stab said back, still looking up there. "Every chance you get, you pin him up there like that at his worst moment. Is it to remind him of his pain, should he ever return?"

"Return He will," I informed Good Stab with all the confidence my station provides.

"Not if you don't find where I put him," Good Stab said, holding my eyes.

"I know that boy's name was Happy," I told him then. It was a blundering ambush, but it was all I could muster.

Good Stab considered me long about this.

"Does the secular nature of his spiritual awakening say anything about the validity of what you call your religion?" I asked, fully expecting this to be the thing that killed me. It would have been a good death for a Man of the Cloth.

"Does the absence of your savior tell you anything about yours?" Good Stab asked back, however, either unfamiliar with the term "secular" or dismissing it entire. "Is he not insulted if his head now sits at the bottom of the trough out there in the street?"

"Like Livinius Clarkson's flag," I added, dourly.

"Was it only his?" Good Stab asked back. "I thought it was a blanket for all you Americans to hide under."

"One you would rip away," I muttered, swallowing to be so bold.

"It flew above the Bear the day they killed Heavy Runner," Good Stab said back without pause. "It flies above every camp of dead Indians. I will always pull them down. You put your reminders of pain on the wall and pray to them. We still hurt, so we don't need that reminder."

"Why are you here?" I asked then. "Why me? Can you do me that dignity, at least?"

"Do you deserve my attention, Three-Persons?" Good Stab said more than asked, if I'm to be honest.

"Do you really wish to be absolved?" I said back with the same intonation, or lack thereof.

"Do you?" he said to me.

I said, "You say you've killed some fift——" but he interrupted me with "I'll give you the count when the count is done."

The meaning I take from that, and that I took in the moment as well, is that I'll be among that number.

"But know that it will be more than the number of toes you lost in the snow," he added.

"You've killed more than three in the last two weeks alone," I told him.

"One," he corrected, holding his finger up to show he meant a single week. "But thank you for sending your sheriff out into the grass-lands."

"Does he still have his skin?" I asked.

Good Stab just stared at me, but then he finally said, "Two of the dogs at your door are pregnant, both by the same father." He raised his nose and sniffed to show me how he knew. Or, rather, to let me know how acute his sense of smell was in this moment, which served as answer enough about Doyle, though a scratch of beard on Good Stab's jaw could have done the same.

It takes a while for such characteristics to present themselves, I know. And, I presume, he knows as well, better than I.

To the contrary, however, a single cigarette had already quelled the trembling in my fingers, its effect felt immediately. Of course, more Chesterfields will be required by midday tomorrow, I expect.

And yes, I do indeed feel the guilt of having directed Doyle out to some imaginary dugout, where, isolated, Good Stab could do vi-olence to him. However, corollary to this is the necessity that, while I was considering the first of my Chesterfields, Good Stab, but re-cently returned from his fatal errand out on the prairie, had to have been moving like a spider across the ceiling above me, and maybe more than once, as he would also have to remove the statue, behead it, and deposit that head in the trough.

I would like to say I've since collected that sacred visage, wooden locks and beatific mien and all, but when I opened my door to test whether I had the mettle to do so after Good Stab's departing, that head had already been returned from whence it came. Or, to the church's stoop at least.

I trust this was boys in the street who didn't want to be accused of having done anything wrong or sacrilegious, yet knew that if they were seen with such a holy artifact, dripping a mix of water and horse mucus and the leavings of Amos Short Ribs' ablutions, they would taste the switch, and possibly the strap.

Oh, to be so young and easily punished again, if only for one eternal afternoon.

Sitting with Good Stab earlier, however, I was as yet unaware of any such return. I was still being forced then to picture Doyle skinned out in the prairie, and my unwitting complicity in such an abhorrent act.

"Just take me in their stead," I finally said. "They've done you no injury, no insult."

"You want to be up there yourself," Good Stab said, about the crucifix.

He wasn't as wrong as I would have preferred——what Man of the Cloth doesn't harbor such private fantasies?

"Then let the last one go, the one from California," I pled with all the earnestness I could express. "As a favor to me."

"If there is another," Good Stab said with a devious grin, "you don't even know him."

"Any life is precious," I muttered, my quiet objection meant to be more compelling the less loudly I delivered it.

This caused Good Stab to actually laugh, such that he had to turn away, cover his mouth.

When he came back to me, his eyes were rimmed red.

I had to suck air through my teeth.

Good Stab understood what I was seeing, what he was showing, and blinked that redness away, drinking it back in, I have to believe.

"Your cat man was able to die," I said then. "Why are you so different than him?"

"Am I?" Good Stab said, then shrugged, added, "I still had the hide-hunters to make cry."

"The men who were shooting the herds," I said.

He didn't have to affirm this, but I did note how the fingers of his hands clenched together in response. In memory, perhaps.

"So you kept doing that?" I asked.

"They're the ones who kept doing it," he said, looking directly at me for a moment.

"But the buffalo were all gone by the eighties," I said to him.

"And so were . . . many of these hide-hunters," he said with a lecherous grin.

"They were just making a living," I countered.

The chuckle this elicited from him was no longer an expression of mirth, but something more violent, and dangerous.

"Let me ask you something else, then," I began. "You say horses are skittish around you, because of what you . . . are. Because they can sense your true nature. Yet these buffalo you raised from calves became accustomed to your presence?"

"Are you now accustomed to your missing toes?" he asked back. "Do you fall every second step, or are you able to make it up and down this aisle?"

The answer to this was beneath giving voice to.

"But could you, in the same way, raise a horse from a foal, and accustom it to you?" I pressed.

"And when I return to him in the night, covered in blood?" he said back. "When he rears and slashes his hooves at me, would I let him run away, forever haunted, or would I, in anger or betrayal, cut the back of his leg, or slash his eyes? And how would I live with that betrayal?"

"How do you live with having drunk that old woman?" I asked, weakly.

He nodded that this was the crux, yes.

"She's not the only one," he said, as if punishing himself with the confession.

"Not the only old Blackfeet?" I asked.

"If you ask why I hate myself," he said, "I'll tell you it's because, by taking the lives of the elders, I'm stealing wisdom from the Pikuni. They're the only ones who remember the old days, and the old ways."

"Them and you," I said.

"The people might listen to The Fullblood," he said, "were he ever to walk down from the Backbone. But they would never listen to Takes No Scalps."

"What about Good Stab?" I asked. "Would they listen to him?"

"They don't remember him," Good Stab said. "I wouldn't either. His life was thrown away. He didn't matter at all, to anyone. He couldn't even protect his wives and children. It's good that Beaver Chief made him cry."

"Cry red," I added.

"On the inside," Good Stab said, "my tears, they're like yours, Three-Persons."

"How do you know I cry?" I asked.

He looked up to me in a way that told me how weak this question was.

"I can hear your stomach making its hungry noise," he said.

"The dogs are eating my dinner," I said back with obviousness, and made sure he observed the next deep inhalation of smoke I took, so he could clock how long I made myself hold it, hopefully suffusing my very essence with the dread tobacco.

"Do I need to put this out?" I said with false imploringness.

Good Stab shook his head no but slowly, watching me the while.

"I would like to see your missing toes for myself," he finally said.

It made them cold in my boot. Their ghosts curled in, trying to hide.

"So you can draw blood through them as you did the boy's missing fingers?" I dared to say back.

It should have been the thing that killed me, I know. Again and again I was asking him to reach across with the nails he claimed were sharp and hard, draw them quickly but surely across my throat, letting flow the blood I judged he was here for, so this could finally all be over.

"You think I've done something to your little hunter," he said back, about Cordelia, nodding to himself. "I haven't, and I won't."

"Kindred spirits?" I asked.

"Cats eat doves," he said back. It was peculiar enough that I, as surely intended, unpacked it exactly as he meant me to.

I disallow him a sophisticated vocabulary, yes, but his acumen I can't question, except insofar as it seems to be tempered by a certain playfulness. In a poet or other writer, this would be an admirable trait, a defining characteristic. In a savage with nefarious intent, I have to take it as merely another weapon to wield against an old man.

"Why are you here?" I finally had no choice but to ask, in hopes I could at least assign a purpose to my coming death. However, in my phrasing I detected the undercurrent I would never intend, but which Good Stab had now made me sensitive to——"My God, my God, why hast thou forsaken me?"

To which Good Stab might in keeping but reply, "I thirst."

Good Stab was right, however. My stomach does speak to me about its hunger, now, these hours later which have passed like the merest of minutes. And the dogs, the last time I checked, have stationed themselves on my stoop, as this is the place where food once appeared. It may yet again.

The only time they slunk off, tails between their legs, ears flattened to their skulls, eyes averted, was when Good Stab walked out the front door, parting them.

As to his answer to my question about his purpose for seeking my company, he considered the question for a long moment, then finally looked to the side, said, "Because you remember too, though you pretend it never happened."

I swallowed, the sound roaring in my ears.

"I'm here to remind you," he said.

His fingers were wringing each other again.

"Then please do," I said to him, waiting for his eyes to find mine again. When they did, I placed my right hand over my chest, said——

"You listen with a good heart?" Good Stab interrupted with a sharp cornered grin the likes of which I would only ascribe to the Pit.

"I listen with the only one I have," I told him.

The Nachzehrer's
Dark Gospel

April 28, 1912

Rising from the pipe I had smoked with Wolf Calf took two winters. Two winters with Napi the old trapper mumbling to me in the dugout. His words were like the splashing of a stream that never freezes. The stories he told and kept telling were from before he made the world, about how the stump left behind when a beaver chews a tree down looks like a little Pikuni lodge, and they were from that afternoon too, about the berries he wanted being reflected in the water, about bobcats having tails and then not having tails, about when the stars fell from the sky and who went out to catch them, who hid from them, and all of his words rolled over rocks and dipped under branches, and they carried me through my long cold fever, and I can't tell which moon it was when he started switching in a napikwan word for a Pikuni one. But that's what he was doing. At first it would be buffalo instead of the right way to talk about black-horns, but then he would trade in two words instead of one, talking about a buffalo bull now after I already knew buffalo, and then, like he was forgetting we were in the Backbone, a whole mouthful of American at once, where I could only hear a word or two, and have to figure the rest out. After doing this he would laugh in his old man way that's mostly a wheeze, and he would look over to me, his eyes the eyes of a boy or girl getting away with something, and wanting to keep on getting away with it for a little bit longer.

This is how he pushed me from the camp of the Pikuni to the town of the napikwan. It was slow at first, like he was walking ahead of me but looking back to make sure I was keeping up, but then it happened all at once in a single afternoon, fast enough that I threw up red onto the floor of the dugout. Your American words were coming over me like heavy wet snow sliding down the mountain, not caring what was in their way. The words picked me up and carried me with them, inside them. They were all around me. When I opened my mouth, they were the only thing I could breathe. Taking them in burned inside at first, but then, like bees coming back to their nest, each one found its little hole to sleep in, that it fit in, and having them inside wasn't cold or hot anymore.

It's why I can talk to you like this.

I think Napi wanted me to be able to.

Because he saw you, Three-Persons.

He never knew your name, he never sat across from you like this in one of your holy places, but all the way up in the Backbone he felt what you did, and it made him cry.

It makes me cry too.

I'm still crying, in here. I always will be.

You were saying the Cat Man could die, so I can the same. I know this, and I know how. I could eat only dirty-faces for three winters, for four winters, handfuls of them every day, drinking one and then another, and at the end I wouldn't be a two-legged anymore. My nose would twitch, I would scurry alongside things to stay away from open sky, and I would forget who I used to be, would just be a big dirty-face that keeps eating other dirty-faces, and so I would become more and more one of them, and never know to come back. But I haven't done that yet.

It's because I had to wait, Three-Persons. I had to wait for you to come back to Nittowsinan. That means Our Place, Pikuni territory, where we've always lived and always will live. Now you have that word inside you like a bee, but because it's Pikuni, it probably will sting you the whole way in, until it dies from it. You can write the word in your paper book like the rest of this if you want, that book you keep in that square of skin I left you, but I only know how Nittowsinan feels in my mouth and my ear, not how it looks in a book.

But I'm telling you about those two winters with Napi, in his dugout.

When I could sit up again on my own, he was at the kettle, poking the fire just to watch the sparks, I think. I never figured out where the smoke from his fires went, but two days' walk from the Backbone I've seen springs that bubble like a cooking pot, and I think that under them are Napi's cook fires, because he has dugouts all over. It's how he keeps from being bothered. It's how he hid where we were, those two winters, and all the moons between them.

"Ho, welcome back!" he said without turning around.

"What happened?" I asked, touching my lips like scared of them, because it was your napikwan words coming out of them. At first I thought I'd eaten enough hide-hunters that all their tongues were swimming in me now, but then I remembered Napi's steady voice talking for so long.

"That tobacco squeezed you inside for two winters," Napi said with a shrug. "It didn't want to let go."

"Two?" I asked back, this time in Pikuni, to be sure I still could. To be sure that I hadn't lost that, along with everything else Pikuni that was already gone.

Napi turned around, said in your American, "It would have been three, if my old friend Wolf Calf hadn't brought you to me."

This is when I remembered my father, running with me.

I had to look away from Napi, but still a red tear fell down my face. I touched it with my finger and put it back on my tongue, and the taste, it wasn't White Clay People, it wasn't Pikuni, it wasn't napik-wan, it was . . . it was long-legs and real-bears and blackhorns and wags-his-tails and big-mouths and little big-mouths and long-tails and quaking-leaf trees, and everything that lives in the Backbone.

No, that's not the way to say it.

It was everything the Backbone is shaped from.

When I turned back to Napi, he was watching me figure this taste out.

"You're hungry again," he said, and walked over to me, held his arm out like this, showing me the part here, above the inside of the wrist. Already there were marks there, from teeth. It was nothing but scars all over each other like knots tied in the skin.

I didn't want to, but my body remembered, my mouth remembered. My teeth were already coming out.

I latched on, drank deep, and Napi sucked air in his nose but I didn't stop, I couldn't stop.

The only reason it didn't kill him like the rest was because he can't run out of blood.

But it did hurt him.

When my side was starting to bulge in the weak place where it splits when I drink too much, he hit me away with this part of his other hand, breaking my mouth off his wrist. I fought back for more, because the Cat Man in me is still trying to kill me, he always will be, but Napi pushed me back into the robes I'd been sweating in and freezing in, turned back to what he was cooking.

"That's the last time," he said, his eyes hot from how much I'd drank. "Now you can feed yourself again, can't you?"

"I don't like that way," I told him.

"You hunted for your food before this happened to you," he said back to me.

"Blackhorns," I mumbled. "Not people. Not Pikuni."

I didn't have the taste of Yellow-on-Top Woman in my mouth anymore, but I had it in here still. It made me keep having to turn my head to the side, in shame.

"I can smoke another pipe," I said, like a child would.

"You think I'll tend you better again?" he said back, which was telling me he wouldn't, that he already had once, and it took two years of him staying in one place.

"Thank you," I told him.

"It wasn't for you, Good Stab," he said, tasting what he was cooking and nodding about it with his eyes shut. "It was for the buffalo. The buffalo and the Blackfeet. And the Backbone too."

"But you said we trade it for food," I said like a question.

"Just because they put a fence up and call it theirs doesn't mean it is," he said back with a shrug. "They don't belong to it."

"We do," I said. All Pikuni know this.

Napi nodded, slurped another spoon of his soup in and held it in his mouth for a long time before swallowing. When he turned to fill the bowl, the Cat Man in me, but probably me too, we came for his back, because if I drank and drank from him, maybe I would never have to again, but I was too full already, and sluggish from it, so couldn't move fast enough.

Before I could get my teeth into him, he stepped to the side, balancing his bowl away without spilling any, and he watched me fall, looked down on me unable to get up, now that I was slowing down more and more, the blood in me trying to find where it went, my eyes losing his edges so he was just mixed colors, then a big grin hanging against the dirt wall, then he closed his mouth, was gone.

"Sleep, Good Stab," he said from I couldn't tell where. Inside of me, it felt like, but also around me, like the dugout was him, and I was in it, safe.

I didn't know anything again until Sun Chief was in the sky again. I could tell because the flap of the dugout was open.

I didn't dream that night because I can't, but Napi's blood was strong enough that I stayed awake a little bit, like when the white scabs brings its fever and you don't know if you're alive anymore or dead. I was back under Chief Mountain again, and the soldiers had already shot Hunts-to-the-Side, and my leggings were wet from the beaver pond I'd been in, and when I looked to the soldiers now, yelling at each other in the cold, their breath white clouds, I was watching their lips, because now I knew their words.

They thought Hunts-to-the-Side was Mountain Chief. They'd been sent to be ready for Owl Child to make his run for the Backbone, but instead of catching him, they'd caught our main war chief, trying to hide away to make war later.

One of them was yelling to the rest that the old one was for him, that he wanted that grey hair hanging off his saddle. Another was screaming about the Cat Man in the cage, asking what he was, what he could be, what he looked like, and another soldier, this one with sad eyes and a thick black mustache on each side of his mouth, was saying a word for the Cat Man I didn't know, because Napi had never said it. What I do remember is that, while I was seeing all this from so long ago, when I was standing there again about to die, I heard a slapping and looked behind me for what it was, and it was me, I had a big flat beaver tail, and was hitting it on the snow hard and fast, trying to warn Heavy Runner on the Bear, to tell him that his name-paper wouldn't save his camp.

Then I was sitting up, shaking, the robe around my shoulders like this. I hadn't fallen with the robe, so this meant Napi had laid it down over me. I looked around for him but the dugout was empty, the kind of empty a cave or den is in summer, when nothing's slept in it for many moons.

Napi was gone. I could tell because he'd taken his iron kettle with him. And because he'd drawn one day of a winter count in the dirt of the wall.

I kept the robe around me and, not needing fire because I'd just fed and my eyes were like this, I read the story Napi had put on the wall. It was a river with a long hill and then another hill by it, and in the water and in the grass were napikwan soldiers, all of them dying or already dead. At first I thought it was the Bear, that this was Heavy Runner like that boy had told me about, but the hills he had drawn aren't on the Bear. Where Heavy Runner's camp was shot, there's a tall crumbling bluff, like this, straight up and down. And the soldiers weren't all dead, there. It was us who were dead, that day.

And then I saw the Necklace-People sign Napi had drawn for the Indians killing the soldiers, which is how I knew they weren't Pikuni, and then I stepped back fast when I remembered Napi telling me the story of this as he drew it, when I was sick. It had been a way for him to make me talk like you.

He called the war chief dead on the side of the hill Son of the Morning Star, even though he was just a napikwan with long yellow hair and fancy clothes.

This is how I learned about all the soldiers we killed at Greasy Grass. It made me proud, it filled me up, but it also emptied me back out. Because you can't kill all the soldiers. Whatever ones you do kill, there's always more of them getting off the boat again, and even more of them being born, back where you napikwans are from.

I rubbed the drawing of them out, pushed dirt over the embers of the fire, and stepped out into the light, the robe still wrapped around me like this even though I didn't need it.

When I looked back to the flap, it was already gone, was that soft brown rock again.

How had that old trapper even gotten in there?

I touched the rock with my fingertips to be sure, and when I held my hand there, I remembered it had been Napi, not a napikwan trapper.

It took me years to be like this, where I can remember it. It's because I carry a piece of the Backbone with me, this smooth rock from a creek. I can touch it whenever I need. For the first few years, every time I went out into the grass to feed, or to make the hide-hunters cry, I would forget those two winters. The way I would remember them instead was that Wolf Calf had left me there against a tree to die, but I lived like a weasel, eating whatever little four-leggeds I could from the grass, always starving but never quite dying, until I finally pulled something bigger down, something with enough blood that I could get something bigger than that, and finally started finding people to latch onto, so I could get strong enough to go on two legs again.

But then I would place my hand to the ground up in the Backbone, to a tree, to a long-legs that died in winter, and those two winters would come back to me so fast that I would have to suck air in my nose.

After those two winters, I knew stories Otter Goes Back had never even known, that Peasy had never known, that my father never knew, that his father's father probably never knew. And I knew more about Beaver Chief now, because he had been a friend and tor-mentor of Napi, depending on which moon it was, and how Napi was acting, what he was doing to stir things up, but I couldn't tell any of these stories at camp, because they wouldn't let me walk among the lodges, they wouldn't let me sit by the fire.

You ask why I don't eat dirty-faces like I was saying, your little hunter's mice, and that's another reason. When I die, all of Napi's stories die with me. Tall Dog was sad about that bundle he'd found in the camp of the dead, and how he had to leave it there to blow away and become nothing, and now I'm that bundle, sitting in the camp of all the people I've had to feed on since the Cat Man. Their dead eyes watch me.

Someday I will dry up and blow away like they're waiting for, I know.

But not today, Three-Persons.

Not yet.

Anyway, your little hunter has taken all the mice from this place, hasn't she? You napikwan, you call a place your own and you bring a cat like her in to keep other things out. You say this is yours, and nothing else can come in.

The Pikuni should have learned from you, when your trappers first started coming in. When the Great Father's boat men were there on Two Medicine that day for Calflooking and Wolf Calf.

We never called this place ours like that, though.

But that didn't mean it was yours.

Put up all the fences you want. Pikuni know what to do with fences, Three-Persons. And we know what to do with the napikwans who hammer them into the dirt, too. When Chief Mountain finally crumbles, all of you will see.

I don't like the Cat Man being inside me, but if it means I get to live long enough to see that, well.

I will watch.

And until then, I'll keep feeding, and talking to you, telling you my confession.

The next part is what I did after Napi left.

I went south along the Backbone, and could have crossed to the east anywhere, but I waited for the Big Gap, because it makes me feel like a Pikuni, going across there like we always have.

It was the whiskey fort over there I needed.

I moved in the trees above it, watching it from all sides over the day. There was a camp of nine Rabbit Men at the back wall. I had never seen Rabbit Men on this side of the Backbone before. It meant there were more napikwans to the east over the last two winters. Even the Rabbit Men were having to come this way. And they must have known where the Big Gap was. I didn't like that.

When the Rabbit Men, who were all men, no women or children, when they followed a wagon two big-ears were pulling to the front of the whiskey fort, I sneaked in. I didn't want their food, their many-shots guns, their robes. And I didn't open any of the holy items they were carrying either. But I did take the round mirror hanging from a buckskin string inside their canvas tent.

Back up the hill, I found a place where the moon shined, so I could see myself. Since my hair had turned the color it was after eating so many hide-hunters, I didn't know what I might look like now. My jaw was smooth and there was no hair on my lip or my chest, but I could only feel the hair on my head. When I pulled a piece out, all alone it still looked black, and when I pulled it around like this it looked black. But I couldn't see all of it, and I needed to be sure.

I nodded to myself when, in the mirror, it was how it had always been. Even though I'd been drinking from that old trapper for two winters.

No, I told myself, dropping the mirror into the grass and dropping fast to catch it before it broke, meaning my knee hit the ground of the Backbone and connected me to it again. No, not a trapper. Napi. He was the reason I was still Pikuni. It's because that's what he is, under that old napikwan skin he wears because it's funny to him.

I nodded thanks to the Rabbit Men for having the mirror I needed. It meant I didn't have to break into the whiskey fort. I had only been under a big roof like you have here three times before in my life, and I didn't like it any of those times.

Two days later, after one of the Rabbit Men killed a soldier at the whiskey fort and ran uphill into the Backbone, he broke his leg crossing a creek, and would have been eaten by a real-bear that was higher up than us, but would come down for easy meat like this, that he only had to dip his head down for.

The Rabbit Man said something in his tongue but when it was nothing to me, he used his hands to sign, and told me about how his band had died from the white scabs, and they were coming over the mountains for something I couldn't understand, but I think it was the black sky iron he was talking about, sky iron that could bring their dead back, if they went far enough north to find it on top of all the ice where it fell.

I used my hands to tell him that was three moons away at least, and there would be white real-bears up there, which Wolf Calf had a story about from his dad, from when one of them had gone down into the Backbone looking for its two cubs, and hearing this made the Rabbit Man's eyes narrow, trying to understand what a white real-bears could be.

While he was still trying to make a picture of it in his head, I picked him up and he held on to my neck, but instead of carrying him back to his camp, I buried my teeth in his throat, drank him dry. He should have been dead already, I told myself while sucking him in. It didn't matter if it was a broken leg or a real-bear that killed him, finally.

It could be me, too. Dead is dead.

And eight Rabbit Men could find their sky iron the same as nine could.

But I didn't think it would bring their dead back. If it could, our many-faces men would have told us this long ago, so we could stop crying. I would bring my wives and children back, and Tall Dog, and Heavy Runner's camp, and so many more.

I laid the Rabbit Man along a cutbank, painted his cheeks under his eyes with two fingers of mud on each side, and pulled dirt over him. I didn't need to eat so soon after Napi, whose blood lasts longer, but I needed to prove to myself that I still could feed the normal way. The normal way to me.

I couldn't only take Rabbit Men, though. Even mixing them with Snakes and White Clay People and the rest wouldn't be good enough. I would look Pikuni, but inside I wouldn't be anymore.

The only people I can drink and stay Pikuni are Siksikaitsitapi. Make that one look on your paper the same as you did when I said it to the boy with the raven. It's not like anybody's going to read it, right, Three-Persons? Not as good as you hide it every night?

It would take a person who can taste the air like a big-mouth to find it.

That Rabbit Man lasted inside me all the way until the moon when the snakes go blind.

Mostly then I was just staying with Weasel Plume and the herd, on Face Mountain. The brush stops I had put at all the ways in and out had lasted through the two winters, and had gotten even thicker without me. And there were calves in the herd now, which meant it could keep going without me. The calves weren't white like Weasel Plume, but they were his. I could tell by their taste on the air.

At first they were scared of me, but when Weasel Plume pushed the boss between his horns into my shoulder and lifted me up, they knew who I was.

I pushed him back and then hugged him with the side of my face in his white hair.

For a whole moon, I stayed with them, playing with the calves like my daughter used to play with a puppy. For the next moon, I ate a wags-his-tail that kept following me. The taste almost made me spit her blood back out, but I didn't.

But I couldn't eat too many of her, I knew. I didn't want horns sticking up through my hair again. I didn't want my eyes to have to get big and round like that.

It was already the moon when the jackrabbits whistle at night, the moon the Pikuni starve getting through. The snow in the Back-bone was deep and tall, and I had been sleeping down on the dirt and old needles under the trees, with their branches up there holding all the snow from falling down any farther.

I told Weasel Plume that I would be back, and when I told him, his hump was only as high as my waist, because the frozen snow won't hold a blackhorn. Just me and the birds, and the swift-runner with big feet that don't fall through. I had been going down to carry armfuls of grass up for Weasel Plume and the herd to eat, and it was spread on the snow like the world was upside down.

From fifty paces off, all I could see of him in the white was his black horns and his eyes and his nose. He was watching me.

I told him again that I would be back.

How I knew where I was going was that I followed a raven down-hill. It wasn't my swift-runner, it was the boy's helper, but it wanted me to go behind it, so I did.

It led me to the Fat Melters again.

It flew in and perched on a meat rack, and I had to sit far away.

If anyone saw me without a shirt, with just the new leggings and moccasins I had made from that wags-his-tail, they would know I was dead already, because the dead don't care about the cold, since they're already cold inside.

But nobody saw me. They were all in their lodges by their fires.

I remembered. It almost made me warm like them.

That night a noise by the creek drew me in.

It was a nightrider probably fourteen winters old. Not the raven's boy and not White Teeth, but he looked like both of them.

He was chopping at a big-leaf tree with an iron axe, and his horse was tied a few paces away, digging in the snow for grass.

When the boy finally fell to his knees, the axe still in the tree, I stepped in so he couldn't see my face and finished the tree down for him. It fell along the creek, so it didn't block it, and that was good.

This was when the boy saw my face.

When I tried to step through the snow to be like him, it was hard for me to do, and the boy saw this too.

I shook my head no, he didn't need to run back to camp about me.

Before knowing if he would stay or leave, I started peeling bark off the big-leaf tree. In the winter, horses can eat that if there's nothing else for them. I don't know if you napikwans know that.

After a few pulls of bark, the boy started on the other side of the trunk.

I threw a long piece over to his horse and the boy watched the horse smell of it, and open its lips around it but not eat it yet.

"It takes them a while to figure it out," I said, at first in napikwan, which made the boy's eyes big, but then I said it the Siksikaitsitapi way.

We kept pulling the bark.

Doing this with the boy was the most Pikuni I had felt since I died from the soldiers in the Backbone.

"You can chew on it if your tooth ever hurts," I said to the boy about the bark.

"I know," he said back, insulted.

I grinned into my chest.

My son would have been like him, I knew.

"Does it help with anything else?" he asked then.

I pulled a long strip slowly away from tree. From the way the boy had stopped pulling bark on his side, I could tell this answer was important to him.

"Why?" I asked, not looking up.

He shook his head no, that it didn't matter.

"You're Kainais, Siksika?" he asked.

These are the other two Siksikaitsitapi.

Because we had the same words but he didn't know me he thought I had to be from above the Medicine Line. I told him I was Pikuni like this, like I showed you before.

"Small Robe," I added, about who I was. Or had used to be.

"Why are you here?" he asked, then.

"To help you," I told him, and stood with all my bark.

He stood with his too.

"You're not cold," he said about me.

"In here I am," I said, trying to touch my chest to show what I meant, but my hands were too full.

"We can tie it on there," the boy said about the old cavalry saddle he had on his horse.

He led off but I didn't follow. If I did, the horse would rear up, slash with its hooves.

"I'll carry it," I told him.

He looked at me about this but didn't say anything, just tied his bundle of bark on and took his horse by the reins. I followed behind, being sure to walk in the horse's hoofprints so I didn't have to push down through the crust of snow.

The herd was over the hill, maybe two hundred of them.

"There," the boy said, like I might not understand.

When he walked out into the middle of them and they all smelled what he had, started moving to him, I watched him doing this, and it hurt as bad as when the big-mouth hunter stabbed me in the leg.

I set my bark down, was gone the next time the boy looked back to me.

I was already running east on top of the snow, leaving no tracks.

Hours later, the closest hide-hunter's fire was tall, like they wanted me to kill them. But then I thought they made the fire like that because they knew about my eyes, and that I would be blind if I came close.

I was standing in another field of skinned blackhorns.

It wasn't a trap, but somehow they knew about me enough to have hunters hiding in wallows they'd scraped out under the staked robes. I should have smelled them, but the air was thick with the dead blackhorns, with the powder for their guns, with the tongues they were cooking, and with their bitter piss, splashed over everything.

The first of them stood up from under his hide and it stayed over him, and the front part raised like a flap when his long-shooter gun came up.

I dove to the side right when he shot and felt the greased-shooter pull through the air by my shoulder.

Before that hunter could get another shot ready, I was to him, running past without stopping, my hand like this, to open his belly to the night.

Twenty steps later, the taste of that blood in the air stopped me, made me look back.

I pulled my hand to my nose to be sure.

It was Pikuni blood.

The hunter behind me was on his knees, trying to catch everything that was spilling out of him. It was steaming in the cold.

Another greased-shooter hit the ground between my feet.

I looked down to it then up to a Pikuni warrior with a war club. He was flying through the air, had pushed off from the side of a dead blackhorn to jump high, come down on me.

I stepped to the side, watched him hit and then roll to his knees, ready with his club.

These were hide-hunters, but they weren't napikwan.

I never would have believed Pikuni would do this to the blackhorns. Because it was doing to themselves.

I shook my head no, I must be tasting that blood wrong, and slipped away just when two more greased-shooters hit the dead blackhorn that was behind me. Instead of running away, I dove into the wallow the first of them had been hiding in.

His war bag was in there, and his short pipe, and his tobacco. I pushed away from the tobacco, didn't know yet that it was only breathing it in straight from the pipe that hurt me, not just touching it, or breathing someone else's smoke.

When Sun Chief broke into the sky, these Pikuni were gone.

I had shot more blackhorns than I could eat too, when my wives had been alive, but that was to trade robes for iron pots and round-ball guns. But when we did that, we took the meat, the horns, all of it, like we always have.

These Pikuni weren't doing that. But they were probably doing it for pots and guns. And I can't say that, if I didn't have the Cat Man in my blood, I wouldn't have been with them.

I found the man I'd cut open lying behind a dead blackhorn. He'd been left behind.

"Takes No Scalps," he said when he saw me standing above him, Sun Chief to my back because it hurt too much to look at him.

"Siksikaitsitapi don't do this," I told him.

"They don't do what you do either," he said back, grunting from how he was dying.

We were both right.

"We don't leave the white dirt on them," he said, jerking from his pain. One of the backs of his feet had kicked a long scrape in the ground. He'd been there all night.

"I won't take your scalp either," I said to him, and I didn't. But his blood kept me from having to find another Pikuni until the end of Tricky Moon. It was the longest I'd stayed away from the Backbone since the soldiers killed me.

I followed the Pikuni hide-hunters. They were hunting their way east to here, I think, to sell the robes.

The night they camped upwind of a small herd, I went ahead into the blackhorns and got them running like to a blood-fence, to go falling off the edge of a cliff. But I was just driving them away, north to the Blood Clot Hills, that we call the Sweetgrass Hills now. So you can know where I mean.

The big-mouth hunters' camp was under the snow now, almost flat again, along with the hunters.

I would have made water on them, but I only have to do that every few days, now, and it's just the clear part of blood, after my body's taken all the red out. It doesn't smell bad, is like the water when you break into a four-legged's spine, so it's hardly an insult. And if you're wondering if I could have another wife up in the Backbone, to grow old while I didn't and finally get scared of me and try to stab me in my sleep, she would leave me before it even got to that. The only way I can have children now is like the Cat Man made me his child, with his teeth, but I'll never do that.

But biting, and drinking, it feels as good as the other used to feel. Better, even. When the blood is gulping down my throat so thick I have to breathe through my nose and my eyes roll back to look inside, I'm not hot and I'm not cold, I'm hanging in water that's like thin mud from a lake bottom, but it's clear, and it's the same hot and cold I am, so I can't tell where it stops and my skin begins.

It's like being big and small at the same time, like being alive and dead together, and I hate that it feels so good. I hate it because it means I can't ever stop.

I left those four big-mouth hunters buried in the snow, but I took their knives and their iron pots and kettles. They were rusting, but you could rub the rust off with sand.

I left them all by the nightrider boy's horse while he was making his normal water in the grass.

When he saw them, he melted up onto his horse as fast as any Pikuni ever had. He pulled the horse around and, instead of riding into camp, he ran for the far side of the herd.

Horse raiders, the first thing they do some nights is leave something for the nightrider to carry back into camp, so everyone will see how important he is. While he's being important, they drive the herd off.

This boy had been taught well.

When he came back, I was sitting on the big iron pot. It was turned upside down.

"You," he said, still on his horse. It was snorting and trying to pull away from me.

"They're for the Fat Melters," I said about the pots and kettles and knives.

"Why?" he asked, finally sliding off his horse and letting it run off into the herd.

"Because you need them," I told him.

"You're The Fullblood," he said back to me. "Happy tells about you."

"Happy?" I asked.

"You saved him," he said.

The raven boy.

I nodded yes to that.

"The hunters will be back soon," the boy told me, when he saw me looking into the glowing lodges of camp. He was warning me.

"The hunters going after the blackhorns?" I asked.

"You saw them?" he asked back, and from the way he sounded like a child when he said it, not a boy almost a man, I knew his father had to be among them. I opened my nose to the boy's taste on the air, from his piss still steaming in the grass, to see if his father was the one I'd killed, but he wasn't. But it had been someone's father, someone's husband.

I looked away from him, to the east.

"You keep the herd safe," I told him. "Your father will like that."

"Fifty of them are his," the boy said, his chest raised.

I nodded. I too had once had fifty horses. My second wife's oldest little brother had been nightrider, then. I didn't know where he was anymore.

"What do you know about Heavy Runner's camp?" I asked.

"I know that I was there," the boy said, and flung his head to the herd, all of them watching me, because they knew what I was. "I was there doing this."

"You must have been nine winters," I said, impressed.

"Eight," he said.

"Tell me," I told him.

"You don't know?" he said, not believing that every Pikuni didn't already have that day in their heart.

"I don't live down here anymore," I said.

He considered this, looked away, then nodded to himself, shrugged, and said it all at once: "The soldiers caught me and Bear Head when we were up on top, coming back to camp. There were so many horses that we had to split them into two herds. When we saw the soldiers, the rest of the boys ran off, but Bear Head told me to stay, that we had to watch the horses. The soldiers held the reins of the horses we were riding and told us they wouldn't kill us if we didn't holler. The soldiers went to the edge of the bluff and laid down to shoot. The soldier holding Bear Head's horse backed up to go around and be at the end of the line of them laying there, but the soldier holding my horse led us right up to the edge between two other soldiers. They had to move over to not get stepped on. Joe Kipp was telling them all that this wasn't Mountain Chief's camp, it was Heavy Runner's, but they kept pushing him away like this, and finally had to hold him by the arms because he was going to run out and warn the camp. The other scout knew this wasn't Mountain Chief the same, but he went down on the side where you can walk. He went down partway with a tall soldier who had brown bags tied around his legs, and the bags were frozen so the soldier had to swing his legs and walk funny from being heavy with ice. The soldiers already had two Kainai roped by the neck. I don't know what they were doing below the Line. When Heavy Runner came out with his paper, the soldier with his legs in bags was talking to the napikwan scout and then that scout raised his rifle fast like this and shot, and held his gun up the whole time Heavy Runner was falling. And then the soldiers beside us were shooting because the scout had, and they all were shooting for the whole morning almost, and that's what happened to Heavy Runner. They burned his name-paper after, on the same fire they were burning all the lodges, and all the dead people."

From the way the boy said this all at once, and especially from how he ended it, I knew he had said it over and over, probably to the other boys, but maybe also to the war chiefs.

"Who was that scout who shot Heavy Runner?" I asked.

"The napikwan one," the boy said, and touched his chin to show that this other scout had a beard.

I nodded.

It would be too late to do anything by the time I knew this other scout's name.

But I wouldn't have drank him. I wouldn't want his blood in me, even if I hadn't fed for two moons.

"You can come," the boy said, standing, using his head to tell me he meant camp.

"You did good that day," I told him, about the Bear.

"They stole all the horses," the boy said.

"But they didn't shoot you," I said.

"I was supposed to be watching them," the boy said, still about the horses. "That's why they were really there. Everyone knows. Pikuni have the best horses."

"I can't go there," I told him, about camp.

"Because of Happy?" the boy asked, watching me.

I finally nodded, lying to him.

"The horses don't like you," he said.

"Horses are smart," I said.

The boy grinned about this, huffed air out his nose like how horses talk to each other, then said, "Are you hungry?"

I nodded that yes, I was hungry.

"I'll bring you back food," he said, and trotted off.

I wanted to collect his horse, tie it down for him, but if I went into the herd, the boy would get blamed for letting it scatter.

Instead I watched the lodge he went to.

When he came back, I wasn't there.

He left the cold whitehorn meat he'd brought anyway, balanced on the big-leaf tree we'd pulled the bark from.

I took it so he'd know, and that night when I went into camp, I tore it into pieces and fed it to the dogs that rushed me, trying to bluff me away. When they smelled what I was, they whimpered and ran off, the two brave ones taking the meat with them and chewing it with their mouths like this, because my smell was still on it.

The boy was out with the herd already, and would be until Sun Chief came up.

I stood by the lodge he'd gone into and pushed the flap in just with my hand. When no one inside said anything, I pushed again to be sure. I could hear them breathing in their sleep in there, and their breathing didn't change.

I looked around, saw one dog watching me. I told it to be quiet and ducked into the lodge, saw why the boy had asked about what else the bark could do.

A young girl whose blood smelled like him was lying with her eyes open by the fire. Her forehead right here was still shaped like a horse's hoof. She'd either been stepped on or kicked. Her eyes were open but she would never see anything again, or say anything, or know anything.

I could have taken her then and nobody would know, but this was my first time back in a lodge since Yellow-on-Top Woman. But that had been a death lodge. This was a family all around me. It was warm, and it smelled like them. The boy's sleeping robe was piled against the north wall, and his mother was sleeping with her back to the fire. His father's other wife was sleeping on her back with her mouth open.

I sat by the fire almost until Sun Chief was starting to come up and stirred the dying fire and my face was red from crying, and finally I did it like I knew I had to, I leaned down over the girl and bit into her throat right here, over the air and the voice. I didn't think she could scream anymore, but I didn't want her mother to have to see this.

I drank her fast. There wasn't much blood, but I could tell already that it would last longer, probably two or three moons. I didn't have to breathe as much to keep it alive, and I didn't have to sleep after her, because I wasn't the same kind of full.

When I broke away, she was dead, and I saw that my hand had been holding hers.

I stood too fast, into something they had hanging from the poles. It fell to the pile of robes loud enough that I had to fall out the flap, run with my chin and mouth red through camp. It was just starting to wake up.

I ran the opposite way from the herd and made myself stare into the heat of Sun Chief until I was blind.

This was when the Rabbit Men found me.

They weren't looking for their sky iron anymore, to bring their dead back. They were looking for me, for killing one of them.

The first one's lance ran through my back and came out here, and I looked down to it, because it should have hurt worse than it did. Then a tomahawk went into the side of my head here, cutting my ear in half and making my jaw open like this.

I fell over and they stood back to watch me die.

I coughed and jerked and then went still with my eyes open. My eyes were easy, because I was blind, and I had the girl's blood in me, so didn't have to breathe as much. And I felt dead already from what I'd just done in that lodge, so that part was easy too.

They pulled their lances out, turned me over onto my stomach and started cutting here, to take my hair. It was because, at the whiskey fort, they could trade my scalp in.

I let them have it.

They cut my back with their knives, rode their horses back and forth over me, and left me there, broken like a doll left behind after camp's already moved on.

When the girl's blood I still had enough of finally brought my eyes back, and I could open and close my mouth again, the raven was sitting on a rock, watching me. I rubbed my ear that was still cut in half and stared back at the raven, the bones in my chest trying to fix together, my head trying to pull skin over the bones, right here on top from where I'd been scalped. I had never healed this fast, but I'd never drank someone so young, either.

Then a skinny leg stepped in front of the raven.

It was the boy they called Happy. He was a man now. He was wrapped in a red and black blanket with thunder signs on it, and his breath was white from the cold.

He was different than he had been, I could tell. He was a many-faces man.

"I knew you would come back," he said. I didn't know if he was talking about me coming down from the Backbone or the lance not killing me. It didn't matter.

"I told him, I did," the raven squawked.

I sat up, my arms around my knees like this.

"Yellow Kidney said you were here," Happy said.

I nodded, said, "You tell them I'm The Fullblood."

"You are," Happy said, and opened his hand to the grass and dirt stained black with my blood. "Except for all this blood not filling you up anymore."

That's how many-faces men are. The world is funny to them. Or it's funny how it all fits together, and it's funny when it doesn't.

I shrugged.

"But last night," Happy went on, "Yellow Kidney's sister died, from someone biting her neck at the front, right here."

"She was already dead," I said, because that's what I'd had to tell myself to kill her.

"You are The Fullblood," Happy said.

"And he takes no scalps, no scalps!" the raven added, hopping from foot to foot.

I ran my hand over my head. I could feel that bare bone under my palm.

"They went deep," I said.

"They couldn't have killed you if they took all day," Happy told me.

"They could feed me dirty-faces," I said, because I'd already figured that out.

"You eat the mice?" Happy asked, looking at me in a different way now.

"Why did you find me?" I asked.

"I found you, found you!" the raven said in its bird way.

"He says you used to be a Small Robe," Happy said, either about the raven or the nightrider Yellow Kidney, I wasn't sure.

Either way, I nodded that this was true.

"I found you because Wolf Calf told us to," Happy said.

"He's still alive, then," I said.

"He'd the oldest Pikuni left," Happy told me.

"He saw the Great Father's boat men when they first came," I told him back.

"I know," Happy said.

"I won't be back for two moons at least," I said.

"What do I tell Wolf Calf?" Happy asked.

I stood. The air was new on the bone of my head.

"Tell him his son is dead," I told him, and walked away. The raven fluttered up like it was going to follow me, keep saying things, but Happy called it back.

The whole way through the grass, I could feel both of them watching me.

That night I slept at the edge of a beaver pond in the low hills of the Backbone, but they kept talking about me being there, so I finally had to leave.

I didn't come back to the Fat Melters until the next winter.

The girl had lasted me three moons, even with the Rabbit Men splashing so much of her blood out. Her blood made other blood taste bad, compared to it. But I made myself drink it anyway. A trapper who might make me grow a beard. A Snake who had been banished by his band. I could tell from how he wore his clothes turned around backwards. He could be my mother's nephew. I wanted to ask him about her but I drank him fast instead, and told myself it was for him, not me, so he wouldn't be scared without his people.

I watched three wagon trains pass, and followed them for almost a moon, and this is when I went down to one of them to look at the little cards of paper, but didn't drink any of these napikwans. One of the women had yellow hair, and I thought she might be Yellow-on-Top Woman, dead and sneaking into the napikwan towns, to cut their throats while they slept.

None of these napikwans died, not when I was following.

Weasel Plume still ran to me when I came back to Face Mountain. There were three new calves and one dead one, born that way. I left it on top of Chief Mountain, facing north.

When it was the moon after the first snowfall again, I found a real-bear just going to sleep in its den. It was fat from berries and deer, and it had eaten a Pikuni boy a week or two ago. I could tell from when I bit softly into its back fat after it was asleep.

For the first time since I died, I dreamed Pikuni dreams, boy dreams, sleeping all winter with that real-bear. I was going to grow up like my father and make my enemies cry, I was going to have a herd so big it filled the valley in winter, and I was going to have three wives, but my two friends would live with me too, and our lodge would be so big it would take six horses side by side to pull it.

It made me shake in my sleep like I was dying, it hurt so much to dream something that pure and clean.

When the real-bear woke many moons later, it rolled over onto me all at once, breaking the bone in my chest and pushing my mouth in, because I was still latched on.

I laid there trying to die from that broken bone pushing through my heart, but it finally healed after I ate a long-legs with a Pikuni arrow in its haunch.

I watched another boy fasting in the Backbone, but didn't let myself get close to him. Instead I crossed the Line, drank an old Siksika who was tied up in the back of some hide-hunters' wagon. They were going to kill him anyway, when they needed room for their robes.

Before they could shoot any more blackhorns, I went into their camp while they were sleeping and pushed the rod from one of their many-shots guns into each of their ears.

I skinned them like the rest, painted their faces, dusted them white, cut their tongues out and left them there, all their supplies burning, their guns in that fire melting like the ones you saw the other day. Maybe these are the ones you saw, I don't know. I did it over and over like that, more than I can remember, because the more long-shooter guns I left, the more blackhorns could die by them.

After that, I came back to Nittowsinan, down here by the Yellowstone, and killed two more parties of hide-hunters. The second one was men and women both together. It was the first time I'd seen that. I drank one of the women just to see what it would be like, and then found another mirror, to see if my hair turned orange like hers.

It hadn't. My eyes weren't blue either, even though I think I would have liked that. I would have big-mouth eyes, then, to match my hunger.

Over the summer I fed on a Pikuni woman I found out by herself. She had a short-gun, was trying to make it shoot into her head, but the powder was wet. She was trying to shoot herself because of what a napikwan trader had done to her.

I waited until she was sleeping, and she never woke up.

I built a scaffold for her, and found feathers to hang from it, and sang her songs for ten sleeps.

I no longer thought the dead could lead me to the Sandhills.

Next, starving in the moon when the leaves turn color, I drank a Pikuni hunter who wasn't dying, who didn't want to die. I painted myself like a Crow and fought him like a Crow, not like a Person-Eater or a Cat Man, so he could know he was dying the best way a Pikuni can, fighting his enemy.

Twice I saw a raven high in the sky, following me, but I couldn't do anything about it.

But then one night after Sun Chief went down, the raven was waiting for me on a rock.

It didn't say anything, just flew ahead of me, leading me again.

On the way, behind it, I ran down a prairie-runner and dressed it, carried it over my shoulders like this, because a Pikuni always brings gifts. I didn't have to use that Crow trick to bring it down, either.

I knew we were going to the camp of the Fat Melters by then. Like the Small Robes and the Hard Topknots, they staked their lodges down in the same rings they'd been using for years already.

It was almost time for Sun Chief to come up when we got there, so I sneaked in, left the antelope by Yellow Kidney's lodge, then watched. When his mother came out, her hair was chopped short.

Mine was grown back all the way already, longer than it had

been before, and strong enough to braid a rein from, if I rode a horse anymore.

This mother who had lost her daughter looked all around for who had left this meat, but then she squatted down, started removing the hide. Prairie-runner hide makes good rope, because it's not heavy but it's strong.

I hid in a low place by the creek all day, waiting for Yellow Kidney to come out to the herd after sleeping, because that had to be why the raven had brought me back here. I thought he had remembered the name of that napikwan scout, so I could make him cry and then make him cry some more.

Instead, his mom made two of the men go out looking for him.

I stood and they saw me, yelled, and ran back to camp for their guns.

I didn't care, was already running for the herd, the horses scattering in front of me like a big-mouth moving through whitehorns.

I found the boy on the far side, on a small hill.

He was dead, his neck bitten the same as his sister's had been, right on the front, so he couldn't scream.

I fell to my knees shaking my head no, that it hadn't been me, and then I saw he wasn't lying on a big-head's fur like I'd thought at first.

He had been laid down onto a blackhorn robe, a thick and white blackhorn robe, one still with flesh and fat on the back of it, because I'd been carrying grass up into the Backbone for the herd.

I fell back, couldn't breathe anymore, and already the men from camp were coming in and shooting, and I hadn't fed on this nightrider, I never would have, but my face was red from crying, which meant my mouth was too, so I ran, and I ran, and I've been running ever since then, all the way to here.

I would tell you that my pipe is empty now, but you know now that it's been empty for half of my life.

If that's what you call this.

The Absolution of Three-Persons

May 1, 1912

Good Stab knows who I am, and he knows that I know that he knows, never mind that there can be no proof——the guilty letter is long gone from the kindling, probably burned weeks ago in a sherry induced haze of clumsy inattention.

And yet the farce of this confession continues apace.

Until this day, when I can take no more.

I leave this log now secreted away where even his nose can't find it. I will coat the buckskin pouch he left me with sacramental wafers and what holy wine is left, such that even the wolf he claims to have the senses of would be unaware of its hiding place.

He said I would believe him about what he is, and I fear now that, absent any tangible proof other than his attestation, I begin to, even though the creature he claims to have become is against the natural order, against God Himself.

I begin to dimly hypothesize that Good Stab's visits will persist until he elicits from me the confession he desires.

What he doesn't understand is that it was a different man who did what I adjudge he thinks I'm responsible for. A different man in a different life, and in a different time to boot, with necessities so remote from the contemporary mind as to be practically unretrievable. I am now but a poor Lutheran pastor old in age and weak of mind, Good Stab. Who you claim to see inside me is long dead, is a citizen of another age entire.

I am sorry for your white buffalo, though.

Weasel Plume was the best of us all, was he not?

But of course the horse guard Yellow Kidney need must matter more.

As does his mother, now bereft of two children.

I believe I too, had I done that to her, whether with teeth or with a more mundane blade, would spin a yarn such as you do, Good Stab, to cover the events with a sheen of the impossible, such that my acts could be attributed to a monster dwelling in my blood, rather than my own nature or, worse, volition.

Yet, I saw you drink the blood of that mole without flinching. I've seen blood rim your eyes. I know you can leap down from a crucifix without sound. I know light hurts your eyes, and I have to believe that your nose is as sensitive as you say.

But what does that accumulate towards? Truth, or a convincing charade?

You could prove yourself with a single step. In the moment before you latched onto this old throat, I would see the briefest glimpse of your sharp teeth, and though I would be dying, I would be dying with certainty, which is something I can't even give to my parishioners, who need must accept on faith that a better world awaits.

Well, you could do that if I were to remain here.

But remain here I won't.

I humbly leave this posting for the next pastor.

I hope you drag no sordid past with you to this posting, good man, inheritor of my duties. Would that you were born twenty two or twenty four years ago and so never had to know the world that birthed this one, and would that you have lived your life in safety in one of the cities of the east, and have never committed any acts you have lived to regret, such that that regret finally stands up on two legs, walks down across the Yellowstone, and tells you oblique tales that cause your hand to quake, your chest to tremble, your eyes to fill.

I am sorry, Good Stab.

I know now you won't read this, that you can't decipher these scratching on these pages, but maybe my absence will be enough sign of my guilt to appease you, such that you can leave Miles City be, not make it pay for my trespasses.

We need a new sheriff, yes. The previous one has yet to be found, but we all know he's never to return. The children in the street probably whisper among themselves that the horse of Chance Aubrey's he shot into so many times has risen to seek justice for its mistreatment.

It's a chapter that would slot well into Good Stab's narrative.

As for this chapter of my log, it now draws to a close.

I elect not to include the direction of my retreat, but I trust that my bones will bleach in the sun over the coming years, as I'm too old for a journey such as I intend, that returns me to the site of the greatest among my many sins. I have no food to bring, only the most meager of supplies, and of course I will be walking afoot, not plodding along on a horse, or bouncing in a buckboard. And there is no train where I need to go.

But God never said it would be easy, did he?

If it were easy, then everyone would receive the grace of absolution.

That's the only repast I hope to gorge myself on, now.

Let this be the end of it.

Please.

May 12, 1912

My flock beats on the door of this, my jail cell, but I can't yet face them, though they bloody their knuckles and implore unceasingly whether or not there might be a service——is it even Pentecost yet? If not, then it's still Easter, and either last week or the coming one is the Sunday we would honor Friedrich der Weise for protecting Lutheranism's namesake.

Would that I had a similarly benevolent protector.

But neither should I bemoan my situation. Rather, I should be thankful to those who would entreat me back to decent society, leaving their plates and pots on the stoop like offerings at an altar.

Hesitant to open the door and have one of them see past me to the chapel, I've yet to attempt to retrieve one of those dishes, leaving them for what dogs are now left.

It's only just now that I can rise to the page again, after the previous week's ordeal. My jaw is whiskered and my eyes weak, my throat raw from confessing, my wrists and ankles and ribs yet black with bruise, and my robes drape over my emaciated frame like unto a death shroud, which, I would argue, is both here and there.

All the pews that are yet unencumbered behind me as I write this have been propped against the door, and the windows are now sacrilegiously blacked with a paste made from the wetted pages of all the Bibles and hymnals in what used to be my church, but is now a charnel house most foul.

I've only been to the parsonage once, to reclaim this thin volume. Without it, I have no one to converse with, as God has no reason to hear me anymore. Even Cordelia has abandoned me now, and rightfully so. She can smell what has transpired here.

I can as well, Cordelia.

And, no, I'm not blind to the fact that what I've sat down to record happened on the seventh day after my previous entry——a Wednesday. In spite of that day's pagan derivation, the Seventh Day is meant for rest, is it not? Rest, because a new world has been created. Or, rather, in my case, an old one has been dragged into the present.

Being able to trust my memory less and less with each day that passes, I know not for certainty if Good Stab is what he claims to be, but I can now attest that he is indeed monstrous, his mind and heart spawned from the most sinful part of the Pit.

Perhaps it's such for all of his kind.

If so, then what trespass have I really committed? Or, as Lot said to Zoar, it was but a little sin, and my soul shall live.

So, I troth, shall mine.

But first, this, and this and this and this, as I have no reverend nor preacher nor kindly priest to relay it to in confidence, thus unburdening my soul. But if I capture its nuance and texture in these pages, then I can close this black cover over what I was forced to endure and lock it away, undoing Good Stab's effort to foul the disposition and authority of my flock's shepherd, and thus undo years of God's work.

I record it for them, then, not for myself, who hardly matters. My blood is not Lamb's blood, to wash away sin, but ink, to trace that sin out letter by letter, and so leave it farther and farther behind this nib——I freely submit into evidence that but eleven days ago, under cover of a starless night, I scurried from the church for what I had confidence was to be the last time. I carried a valise with me, but it was only slightly filled, as I knew it would only grow heavier with each step, and a Man of the Cloth's worldly possessions need must always be meager. Even this very log was then buried deeply behind me, away from prying noses.

As it was the warmest garment I had, I was still in these unlaundered robes.

Instead of awaiting a train like would have been expedient if distance were the sole concern, I stepped across the iron tracks that could deliver me from Good Stab's influence and trod into the open prairie to the north, thinking the while that this maychance have been Dove's last walk just the same. By morn, due to my limping progress and my unfamiliarity with the terrain, I could see still the distant shape of Miles City, standing up from the limitless grass.

I slept fitfully through the day, rising at nightfall to gnaw on the crust of bread I had. The stars were out this night, the moon waning, only showing half its face to me.

I waded across the Yellowstone carefully in the dark, holding my valise over my shoulder until I stumbled as I fully expected to, only clawing my way to the northern shore by the grace of God.

My robes soaked through, I proceeded to build a fire, which was a loathsome task for one with no cause to have done it for decades. But I was fortunate to be in a river bottom——there was ample wood. Taking Good Stab's advice, which I know means accepting the truth of his story, I built the fire tall as the buffalo hunters once had, until it was blindingly hot, enough to keep a whole curséd tribe of cat men away, or so I thought.

The robes I was still wearing steamed, and I held my palms out to the heat, and if I slept, then I couldn't draw the line between that and wakefulness. What I do know is that one time when I opened my eyes, there was a pale, naked form sitting across from me.

I startled back but the form didn't move in the slightest.

By degrees, I came to see that this was the headless, naked Body of Christ that had heretofore been hanging on the cross behind my pulpit.

I shook my head no in appeal, but the appeals of men are as mist hissing against the side of a heated kettle. As the Greeks used to say at the dawn of rational thought, each step to avoid your fate is but a step closer to it.

When I looked back to where I had been seated, Good Stab was in my place, in robes so alike mine that I flinched, seeing there a figuration of myself. Good Stab was wearing those darkened spectacles against the pyre I had staged.

"I would welcome you to Nittowsinan," he said with a degree of expansiveness I wouldn't have ascribed to him, "but the Pikuni no longer let you napikwan in like that."

"How did you find me?" I asked, my voice unsteady.

"When was the last time you bathed, Three-Persons?" Good Stab asked back.

As the headless Christ was in the only other seat afforded by my campsite, I went to push Him but slightly to the side as respectfully as I could manage, but found Him too heavy.

"Here," Good Stab said, suddenly alongside me.

He pried Jesus from His place and, instead of laying Him out of the way to the side, he tilted Him forward into the fire. With an exhalation of sparks, the fire swallowed Him, and I prayed that He wouldn't burn, that even these fires of Hell couldn't touch Him.

But they could, they can.

The pale paint on His skin bubbled and burst, and then the flames found the dry wood underneath and roiled into His holy form so He was incandescent, more sparks gouting in a fountain from His neck, as it was slowly developing that this statuary was hollow, unlike the head, hollow and apparently filled with paper or rags or sawdust, which had never expected to escape.

I sagged into this new and regrettable station of my life, stared between my feet.

"When I was a boy, there was an old man in camp who was called Golden Calf," Good Stab led off with, speaking about the Holy thing of wood gulping flames before us. "He was named that when another Black Robe came to the Pikuni and read to us in French from his book."

"Exodus 32," I recited with full abjectness.

"No, Golden Calf," Good Stab corrected. "He cut that Black Robe's throat, but he saved his book. It was his medicine from there on out. He would burn a handful of pages at the Sun Dance each year, less pages every year, and everyone would sing the words they remembered from that Black Robe."

"And so his Mission continued well after his own passing," I muttered, perhaps only to amuse myself.

"We aren't done yet, Three-Persons," Good Stab said to me then, leaning forward to peer up into my downcast face.

"You know that's not my name," I said back to him.

"This is almost where the first of the buffalo men were found," he said back, peering out into the darkness to a hillock or wallow only he and Sheriff Doyle and a few others knew exactly.

"We call them humps, not buffalo men," I mumbled.

"You think I should have called them blackhorn men," Good Stab said with what I would call a leering grin. "They don't deserve a word like that, though. I know where they come from."

I looked up to him about this but couldn't see the relationship he was portending.

"California?" I ventured. "They come from San Francisco, Good Stab. You brought them from there."

"If that's what you say, Three-Persons," Good Stab said, having led me where he wished.

"I was going to die out here," I told him then, like a challenge.

"The Pikuni would carry your bones back across the river," Good Stab said in mild disgust. "To keep them from touching with ours."

"What have I done to you?" I asked.

"You haven't heard my last confession," he said, standing, wincing from the brightness or the heat of the fire, now that it had hold of something Holy. "You don't know the true count of dead I carry."

"I can hear that number now, here," I told him, spreading my hands over the darkened land as if offering the Eucharist.

"No," Good Stab said. "We do it in your holy house, where we started. It's also where we finish."

"But——" I began.

The reason I didn't finish was that Good Stab was rushing at me at last, I thought because he could no longer control his hunger.

As I expected, his open mouth struck at my neck, and I thought to finally feel either sharp teeth or flat ones, and then know, believe like he said I would, but then I noted that his eyes were yet open, as he was watching mine.

When he bit down, his teeth were flat, and clamping down over the main course of blood just under my papery skin, but I believe that he didn't want to puncture and drink, only tighten and hold, such that the blood dammed behind his teeth. My world went dark by slow degrees.

As I fell back, the stars above were scratching lines across the sky, and if I didn't smile from this brief vision, then my soul did.

I was being born anew.

Whether I fell into Good Stab's arms or into the grass, I know not.

Only that, when I woke two days later, perhaps having been lovingly bitten over and over in like manner each time I stirred, my vantage on the chapel was both familiar and strange. The pews and windows and door, dressed in inky shadow, were positioned as they always had been, but the angle I was seeing them from was markedly different, as if I were yet sleeping, and seeing my church through the skew of dream.

I made to move forward, come down to my habitual place at the pulpit, but found myself tied by wrist and ankle and midsection to the cross, such that the wrapping around my ribs carried most of my weight——my brittle shoulders would surely have cracked like grouse wings if asked to support me.

When I lifted my heavy head from where it had been hanging, the muscles at the back of my neck creaked and my throat clenched. When, in the light of the lone candle flickering at the back of the chapel, I saw the dim form of Good Stab standing before me with his hands clasped behind his back, his black robe draped over his frame, I startled, despite the fact that who else could my tormentor have been? How else could I have expected him to be attired?

"Arthur Beaucarne . . ." he said, peering up at me over his darkened spectacles, and hearing my actual name from his lips caused my gut to clench, my heart to spasm.

"What are you——what is this?" I demanded.

"Confession," Good Stab said with the hint of a grin, and then shoved his darkened spectacles up close to his eyes. Whereupon, he struck a match. Even shielded by the dark glass, he still had to turn away from its incendiary first sputters of bright flame and peel his lips back from his teeth to hiss.

For an instant I would rather not remember, either two of his bared teeth seemed to have points or my fears coalesced to grant them such sharpness, but before I could confirm or deny what I was seeing he was swirling around like a stage actor, taking that flickering match to . . .

The front row of pews, it turned out. The left side, from my own personal Golgotha. In my first moments of waking, when this was naught but a dream, I suppose I had the distant notion of worshippers in the pews, but, since this had been mere fancy conjured during my long climb up from the depths of sleep, the shadows out there had just been props, memories, suggestions, a background.

Good Stab would make them particular, and move them into the foreground.

He already had a candle positioned on the seat of that leftmost pew, which caused my eyes to narrow in regret, fixated as I immediately was on the spatter of wax a lonely old pastor would have to be scraping up later, and carrying away in the palm of his hand.

Good Stab held the match's flame to the wick, the candle took it and steadied it, and in the glowing puddle it spread about itself, I couldn't at first accept what I was seeing. But then I had to.

It was Sheriff Doyle's mortal remains. I jerked to occlude this vision from my sight, but there was nowhere to hide.

Doyle was in the early stages of putrefaction. Yet he hadn't been skinned. Judging from the blood pooling on the wooden pew around him, he hadn't even been exsanguinated. The sheriff's badge he had worn on his left breast was now pinned through his right eye, the star jauntily askew, the translucent jelly of his eye crying down his face, and long crusted over.

"Thank you for sending him out to me, Three-Persons," Good Stab said, taking the candle to——

Livinius Clarkson, wrapped tightly in the tattered, waterlogged remains of the American flag he had been so fastidious about. On the dingy white parts of that flag, his putrescent blood was soaking through.

"I would have drank him just so he would know who was killing him," Good Stab said, holding the candle's flame right up against Livinius's muttonchops as if trying to better peer into his dull eyes. "I would have, but he's been touching that flag for too long, and I don't want that inside me, would rather eat another mole, or a wagon train of moles."

Livinius's muttonchop on the right side smoked at first from the candle's sputtering proximity, the outmost hairs singeing and probably curling back on themselves in pain——I couldn't have seen it with that much detail were I sitting right there——then the whole ragged sideburn flared up, turning our former postmaster into Good Stab's next source of illumination.

He held his hand up to shield his eyes and backed away shaking the light from his head.

In the greater glow spreading from Livinius, the rest of the chapel illuminated, and my whole body slackened in defeat.

On the right side of the chapel opposite Doyle were all four of the lodging house Denizens, each fully clothed and showing no obvious wounds, yet each obviously expired and posed in death in the same order they had long occupied their erstwhile pew. What they had done to warrant this treatment is yet a mystery. Perhaps being a resident of Miles City, just south of Blackfeet territory, is enough.

Early Tate's recently acquired bowler hat was in his lap, brim down. It was very proper. No, it was a sacrilegious mockery of propriety. It was a heretic's jovial impulse, run rampant. It was what I should have anticipated a savage mind would conjure from its well of grief and resentment.

Crawling across California Jim's cheek and across his eye was a horsefly of such satiated girth I could even see it clearly from my elevated perch. It made me want to scratch my own eyeball with the back of my knuckle, but neither could my hand reach my face nor my face my hand——meaning, the scent of Livinius Clarkson's face meat slowly cooking was oily in my nose, and the back of my mouth, and my chest.

"Would you preach to them, Three-Persons?" Good Stab said from the shadow he was standing in. "Would you instruct them on how to live a life without sin?"

I closed my eyes to blot all this away, to insist it wasn't happening, but then, in a manner I can't explain unless I had blacked out, my senses retreating along with my tenuous hold on the actual, Good Stab was perched behind me, his mouth right to my ear so he could say, "Would you tell them that killing is . . . wrong?"

I winced, swallowed, closed my eyes tighter yet.

Good Stab's breath smelled of nothing. Of the broken crockery he claimed, I suppose, but Livinius's meat popping was the more overwhelming scent.

One I admit I recognized.

Good Stab took the flap of my ear in his teeth and bit but lightly, affectionately, surely leaving a crescent of bruise, and then he hissed loud enough that I flinched forward.

His hand was on my shoulder in passing, and when I finally deigned to open my eyes again, my vision was all swirling black robe.

Among the pews again, or still, Good Stab took Dove's bowler from Early Tate and used it like a snuffer over Livinius's head, such that smoke billowed out and out around the brim.

The flag swaddling his shoulders was already smoldering, however.

When that thick, sun dried cloth caught with patriotic flame, Good Stab reached forward to gently push Livinius over, and thus, if not dampen the blaze, make it less direct to his night eyes, anyway.

In the resultant glow, the chapel now underlit, which served to deepen the shadowed eyes of all the dead, I felt myself watched now by another corpse, one I didn't recognize from Miles City.

But then I saw this man as Good Stab intended, which is to say

I looked from the grim visage of the face to the open chest of the striped jacket he had been buried in. To save the ruination of a shirt, since there had been no wake, no viewing of the dead, this man had been nailed into his coffin with only the jacket, meaning what I had to look away from between the yawning lapels of his graveclothes was the decomposing muscle and bone of his chest.

This was the hump I had myself helped inter. He was now exhumed, as Dove had intended.

"I know you think I drank his blood," Good Stab said, looking up at me, his dark right hand on this hump's left shoulder, as if greeting an old companion, "but the corruption in him is worse than that other one's flag."

"So you killed him just to kill him?" I had to ask.

"I opened his neck over an empty little grass-eater hole and let his heart push all his blood down into there," Good Stab said, patting this hump in farewell. "But it wasn't empty, the hole, it was only empty of little grass-eaters. A crawls-on-his-belly came up through that blood hissing and striking at the air."

"A snake," I filled in, saying it mostly for myself, to help complete the image now writhing in my head.

"A snake, yes," Good Stab said.

I coughed from the meat smoke in the air and Good Stab seemed to like this.

"Do napikwans taste the same on the air as Pikuni do, Three-Persons?" he asked, and before I could struggle an answer, or resist the question itself, the flame engulfing Livinius's flag and skin burned through to his sheath of fat, the flames spitting and popping with abandon, and I, being of decent stock, not savage, retched, and I long to write in these pages that my revulsion was from the fact of the smell, but that would be a lie. I hadn't eaten since that night on the Yellowstone. What so revulsed me was how my mouth wet itself——and whet itself, I suppose——at the prospect of the food I was smelling.

At the end of this abreaction there was a long string descending from my lower lip, perhaps connecting all the way to the altar floor——I couldn't see directly below me, only knew that I couldn't break this string with my hand or my knee.

I sobbed and each sob made me heavier, so the straps holding me in place cut deeper.

"Why?" I pled, ending it with a wet cough I wasn't certain I would recover from.

Good Stab was drinking this in with his glittering eyes. It was, I believe, the first time I had seen him excited.

On him, it was unholy.

"Why," he repeated back, but not with the same inquiring tone. Rather, he was suggesting that this had been a hollow question—— he was, I see now, whispering to me that this moment we were mired in up to our souls was the culmination of all his devious efforts, and not a word had been wasted in delivering us here. It was where he had been taking me all along, Sunday by Sunday. Even that fanciful story he'd told about the magic turnip opening onto another world hadn't been idle talk, but an indirect way of sketching our burgeoning entanglement out so I could, when it was propitious for his purposes, understand it as he wanted. That time had now come, and I could see at last what our relationship had been. Our whole time together, Good Stab had been a child who had pulled that plump turnip he spoke of up from the prairie, and was, at first, working the caked on dirt and detritus off it, but then he was finding the smallest fleck of that turnip's tough skin and steadily tugging it away strip by careful strip, trying to be careful not to pull too hard, lest that strip rupture partway down, causing him to have to pinch another tatter up.

It was my skin he had been peeling with each chapter of his story, and he was to the last strip now, at which point my fibrous white meat would be exposed, for his teeth to bite into.

"His name was Benjamin Flowers," I managed to get out about the unburied hump, because pronouncing the man's name was a rampart against Good Stab's depredations. "And I don't know why you would do him this indignity, this——this injustice."

"Injustice," Good Stab repeated, as if weighing this term. Considering it.

It made him grin. His face was cast down, but I could yet make out the sharp corners of his mouth.

"You Black Robes can have no children, can you?" he asked, peering up at me.

"Monasticism isn't required," I informed him. "Our founder fought against that."

"So you can take a wife?" Good Stab said back.

"Clerical marriage is not forbidden," I muttered, unsure why we were discussing doctrine, or how else I could frame this for him in respectable terms.

"Did you ever wish you had children?" he asked then, watching my eyes, I believe, for the lie my mouth might give.

"My children are my parishioners," I recited for him——the creed and touchstone of we clergy who never found family life. "The children of our one Father are all brethren with each other. His seed is . . . it's unvergänglich. That means imperishable."

"What does that mean, Three-Persons?" Good Stab asked.

"It never dies," I told him, pride of that rising in my voice.

"Oh," Good Stab said, "they can die." And with that he angled his body to the side and held his hand out wide, presenting the next corpses.

Before I could warn them not to, my eyes fell on three dead bodies seated mutely alongside Benjamin Flowers. The first two were his sons who had been disposed of in like manner, both without the skins of their torsos, which only served to make their faces stand out more, as if imploring me, as if waiting for the service to begin. They were, according to the names penciled on the back of Dove's photographs, Archibald and Milo, though I of course couldn't tell one from the other.

The third in attendance was towheaded and young, perhaps fifteen, and but recently deprived of his skin, adjudging by the wet glisten yet on the scraped raw meat of his torso. This would be Arthur, I knew.

"That one shares my name, I know," I mumbled, trying to snatch that surprise from my tormentor, and tore my gaze away, studied instead some of the other corpses that had been posed in the pews, to be called upon one by one. Now that Livinius Clarkson was providing better light, the chapel was revealed to me entire.

How I wish it hadn't been.

While Good Stab would seem to have respect for cats, little hunters that they are, for dogs he must have no use, as they were all dead but propped upright, their eyelids removed, so I was caught in their hungry, childlike gaze. Perhaps Good Stab had dispatched them en masse because they wouldn't let him alone when he was trundling the dead across the rooftops of Miles City to stage them here——which could explain the Denizens' attendance as well, as their station at the lodging house would have afforded them a clear view of those selfsame rooftops.

As for the dogs, their being intermingled with the corpses of men I had known was perhaps the most damning insult so far.

Good Stab was sitting out amongst all this travesty in his darkened spectacles, giving me time to apprehend this spectacle.

"Was he named after you?" he asked about this child Arthur. "I'm not the first Good Stab among the Blackfeet. Wolf Calf wasn't the first of his name."

"Why would he be named after me?" I asked back, almost with a dismissive chuckle, had levity been remotely possible to broach into in these circumstances.

Good Stab shrugged, studied the boy.

"I'm not the first Pikuni you ever saw, am I?" he said then.

"Do I have to be up here like this?" I asked back.

"Not much longer," he assured me, feigning, I believe, pity for my regrettable situation.

"What do you want from me, Weasel Plume?" I asked.

Good Stab turned away from this name, hiding his face.

"You don't call me that," he said in the other direction.

"Because your cat man killed him?" I pressed. "Your white buffalo, or the child you used to be before——"

Good Stab's hands, each tucked in the opposite sleeve, flung out all at once, and the fists he had made took the opposite sleeve with each hand, baring his dark arms, his black sleeves still drifting across the chapel like discarded wings, his eyes yet hidden behind his darkened spectacles.

"You're asking me to kill you," he hissed. "But I know this game, Three-Persons. Pikuni enemies taunt us like this the same when we have them tied by the fire, and they see the night stretching long before them. Peasy taught us not to listen to their insults."

I looked over to a black sleeve, draped now across California Jim's scraggly head like a Sunday scarf.

"If you won't kill me, then what is it you want from me?" I asked him.

"I would know what happened to your toes," he said, his voice controlled again.

"My toes?" I asked back, leaning forward to see them.

When I couldn't, Good Stab was suddenly there, using either his fingernails or a palmed knife to sever the canvas tie around my forehead.

Instead of watching his agile, soundless descent, I leaned forward to inspect the feet I could already tell were bare. They were crossed just as the statue Christ's had been, a positioning I had always assumed was to save Roman nails——front to back, only a single spike of iron is required.

I started with fright, seeing that my three missing toes were grown back, but were again blackened with frostbite. I waggled them to confirm this was no trick, and the longest one detached, plunked to the wooden floor.

Then, slowly, the next, and the last.

They weren't my toes, but had been clipped, I imagine, from one of the corpses occupying the pews, clipped and somewise adhered to my stumps. Yet? I felt each of them detach, and would have sworn I even felt their slight impacts far below——one, two, the third.

"Yes," Good Stab said in much delayed response. "It was the Cat Man, returned, who killed Weasel Plume. Do not things like this happen in your holy book? He had been living like a weasel in the Backbone, eating small things at first, when he was weak and dead and nothing, and then bigger and bigger things over the years, until he finally found a band of hunters, or trappers, or even Pikuni."

"You said you were going to tell me the number of your dead," I reminded him.

"You first," Good Stab said up to me.

"My toes, then," I said, moving my stumps as much as they will. "That's three."

"But how?" he asked, seeming to play along.

I sucked my cheeks in to my teeth, pursed my lips, then shrugged as best I could, said as I had to, "The cold. Snow. I was walking through the snow, Good Stab. Surely the Blackfeet know about this?"

"We don't know to wrap our legs in your brown sacks," he said back to me. "But, that wasn't enough, was it?"

"Burlap," I muttered. "You're talking about burlap."

"Did it keep you warm, that day?" he asked. "Did Joe Cobell wrap his legs? Did Joe Kipp?"

I breathed in and the air was bitter cold to me. Again.

I turned as far from Good Stab as I could.

From where I was, I could see the ventilation window at last. The cross was the only place in the church it was clearly visible from. Jesus could have told me about my visitor perched up there at any time, but He never did. But He also had to have seen Good Stab rush forward to place that buckskin pouch under Erna Schmid's sausage, mustn't He have?

He, my pale Jesus, was now ash and perhaps a single white foot out on the prairie, just north of the river.

I'm sorry, Father of all fathers. I thought the day Good Stab was bringing back was far enough in the past that it was forgotten like it never happened.

But You see all, I know.

"No," I said, tears flowing freely down my face now, and plunging off my chin into open air.

"No what, Three-Persons?" Good Stab asked.

He was standing between the two frontmost pews, now. The two frontmost pews of this much sullied church I sit in now as I write these selfsame words. But Good Stab would pull me back to the charnel house of my youth, wherein I recognized the Cat Man I carried with me.

"This is your confession, not mine," I objected, but weakly.

"Tell me you weren't there that day on the Bear," Good Stab said, standing directly below me now. "Tell me you weren't there whispering into the coward Joe Cobell's ear that he should shoot Heavy Runner, tell me that here in your holy house and I walk away, Three-Persons."

I was shuddering in my restraints, now.

"We had been walking for days in that blizzard!" I said down to him, my voice loud with resistance. "We had orders from General Sheridan to strike them hard!"

"Them," Good Stab repeated, his lips thin.

"You," I said into my chest, my tears wetting my chin, my chest, my whole damned life. "The Blackfeet."

"The women and children and elders, you mean," Good Stab said, turned away from me again. "And did you strike us hard?" he added, needlessly.

I blinked fast to keep from being pulled back to that day.

"But you're a Black Robe, not a soldier," he said with false misunderstanding. "Were you there to read your holy book over the dead, Three-Persons?"

I opened my mouth in what I would call pain, but it was deeper. It was all my sin trying to find a way out. Yes, I watched women opened from crotch to throat with knives sharp enough to cut through the heart of the world. Yes, axes were used on the few men in camp, once they were taken prisoner. Yes, the infants' heads were collapsed in with the butts of rifles, one blond soldier instructing the rest how less effort was needed if you came down on top of the head, where it was softer, so you just had to snap down and back, fast, like plunking a misbehaving dog away from your horse.

Yes, I remember the pungent smell of the piles of their bodies and lodges and winter stores, burning.

"I wasn't really there," I attempted myself to believe.

"Then Joe Cobell didn't really shoot Heavy Runner," Good Stab said in savage objection.

"But they didn't . . . they didn't even fight," I insisted, which I hear now was the first part of the admission Good Stab had been leading me toward for weeks.

"Because they were sick from the white scabs," Good Stab said, and when he turned halfway around to me, I saw that his cheek on that side was reddened with tears, and his chin was quivering, as was mine.

This is when I screamed, Lord, I know not why, or wherefrom. Just that I had too much inside me for one old man to hold anymore. I had too much inside, and it had been roiling for too long, and this should have been my voice that day, I know, this should have been how I screamed for the soldiers to stop shooting, stop shooting.

Good Stab fell to his knees, pressed his forehead to the floor and he screamed too, and I daresay our screams harmonized, at least in how much they pained us.

This, I believe, is the story of America, told in a forgotten church in the hinterlands, with a choir of the dead mutely witnessing.

"You tore out the heart of my people, Three-Persons," Good Stab said into the floor.

"I'm sorry," I said back, I knew how weakly. "I'm sorry I'm sorry I'm sorry."

"Is it wrong to kill?" he asked then, again, sitting back on his haunches, his bared arms hooked around his knees. "Is this what you tell your people who come each Sunday?"

"Yes," I said.

"Then why did you do it?" he asked, standing again, wiping the blood from his face onto his arms, such that he now had warpaint streaked across his cheeks.

"I didn't," I told him. "It was——it was the soldiers!"

"Why, Three-Persons?" he insisted.

"We were freezing and hungry!" I said back down to him, my bile rising to be forced back to that day again, my toes black and dead in my boot.

"Why?" Good Stab said, his back to me again, so he could walk away, down the aisle.

"Because those were the orders," I explained.

"Why?" Good Stab said quieter, sitting again in his pew, his head down now.

"I don't know," I finally admitted.

"You do," he said.

"They didn't even fight back . . ." I blubbered like a child. Ever since it happened, this has been my balm. And it had heretofore been enough.

Good Stab looked up to me about this, said nothing.

"If it wasn't us, it would have been another regiment," I said, calmer again. "You can't stop a country from happening, Good Stab."

"But we were already a nation," he said up to me. "We didn't ask you to come."

"Didn't you?" I said back. "Did you not want our rifles, our kettles, our——our horses?"

"We just wanted to live," Good Stab said, standing from his pew and approaching, using the back of each pew to support him as he came. "How could you shoot us in our winter lodges?"

"You weren't even there," I told him.

"The best part of me was," he said. "Why did you——"

"Because you were just Indians!" I bellowed at last, my own spit spattering from my mouth, my eyes glaring down at him in all my righteous fury and indignation to even be pressed so on this.

Good Stab held my eyes about this, gauging the truth of it, I think, and then he nodded as if in defeat, though this had to be victory for him.

"You don't understand," I said pleadingly as if to a higher power, longing to use my hands to gesture with, to make him see, to get him to understand that these were different times, with a different breed of men——the kind necessary to forge a new land, a better country, one that made use of its resources rather than letting them lie fallow.

"I understand," he said, however. "You wanted to make us cry. And so you did. You wanted our land, so you took it. You wanted us out of the way, so you killed us in our lodges. Is there more to it, Three-Persons?"

"That's not my name," I mumbled uselessly, swallowing hard.

"Black Toes," Good Stab said then, suddenly chest to chest with me, his teeth brushing my throat. "No, Black Heart."

"Do it," I told him, pointing my chin up to tighten my loose skin for him.

"I wouldn't have the blood of the killer of so many Pikuni in me," Good Stab said directly into my ear, into my soul. "It's why I drained that one's blood into a hole. And the father, and those two."

He was pointing to the men of the Flowers family.

"It was just napikwans," he whispered to me with what sounded like a grin, to be turning my own words against me. "But to you, that's not what they are. Look at them closer, Three-Persons. Look at them with different eyes. Taste their scent on the air like I do."

With that, he dropped down, away, landing so softly I never heard it, staring at the jawline of Benjamin Flowers as I was so intently. And seeing, finally, not my aunt's inborn mischievousness in the eyes and cast of the Flowers sons, but my own mother's.

A new and oppressive silence settled on the chapel, and all its inhabitants. All its denizens.

The dogs waited with open mouths and dry eyes.

The fly rose groggily from California Jim and buzzed heavily over to the fresher meat of Arthur Flowers. My, my . . .

"Your son's son," Good Stab said, making it real.

"What?" I said but weakly. "My . . . grandson?"

"My nose doesn't lie," Good Stab said.

"But——but how?" I asked, already remembering a woman with light red hair at the fort after shooting all those Indians that day. How, with the soldiers yet carousing outside the window, she held me by the hair at the back of my head as I cried and rutted deeper and deeper into her, trying to forget.

When that didn't work, there was a bottle, and another bottle, and three decades of bottles, and then this robe, the Bible, my Book of Concord, this church, my precious flock. Martin Luther waiting to beckon me closer to God, to forgiveness, to another, cleaner life. One in which a man doesn't leave a dead, blackened toe in a prostitute's bed, even when she asks his name, so she can remember him in her prayers that night.

A—Ava? Could that have been her name? The soldiers were calling her Rosy, but, seeing the grief and regret I was in from the week's work, and perhaps recognizing it as a species of her own grief and regret, she shared her real name.

I knew her but for part of an afternoon.

"I never knew . . ." I tried to object, for all that was worth.

"Neither did they when they were bleeding into a little grasseater hole," Good Stab said. "Neither did the Pikuni in their lodges that winter."

"You killed this man and . . . and his children because I fathered them?" I asked.

"Because all of your blood has to spill," Good Stab said, himself again, grim and vengeful.

"When will it be enough?" I asked.

"When will napikwans have enough of our land?" he asked back.

I shut my eyes.

"Kill me," I said. "Let it be over."

"You're ready to eat mice?" he asked with a satisfied grin. Then he added, "It is over, Arthur Black Heart. You walk alone in the world now, as I do. Except I still haven't told you the count of my dead."

"Including them?" I asked about Doyle and the rest, keeping their grim vigil.

"There's still one more," Good Stab said, holding his index finger up. "Did you recognize Yellow Kidney, last time? The young boy guarding the horses on the Bear that morning you killed so many Pikuni?"

"I told the soldiers to let him go," I said. "He was just a child."

Along with Good Stab, I could hear the emptiness of this claim, and it made me wonder whether a sermon would ever be held in this chapel again.

I called this a jail cell a few pages previous, but living tomb is perhaps the apposite term. Yet, after the subsequent relaying of this last chapter of Good Stab's dark gospel, which I record anon, after which I had fallen asleep tied to the cross, Good Stab evidently returned to cut me down, deliver me to the pew I had occupied so many Sundays in while he confessed, Dove's scorched bowler tilted over my swollen eyes.

But, before that tender mercy that wasn't, he had still to regale me with his tempestuous confrontation with the feared and capable Cat Man, and though I'm well enough read in popular literature to guess the word that swarthy, mustachioed soldier had said that violent day in the snow, when the cage finally opened and Good Stab died so he could live again forever, it would serve no purpose to write it down here, for those two corrupt syllables can't be trapped, not in a way that captures the monster they would signify.

Nachzehrer is more fitting for the language spoken here on Sundays.

"I——I listen with my heart on the ground as you want it, Good Stab," I said weakly from my station on the cross.

Good Stab nodded, content it seemed, and patted the left shoulder of Doyle such that the good sheriff slumped forward as if asleep, and so we began again, for the last time.

The Nachzehrer's Dark Gospel

May 5, 1912

I was born the year the stars fell, and I grew up always knowing that there was nothing I could ever see that would be like that.

I was wrong.

I'd seen a bear feeding on one of two long-legs that were locked together by their antlers, feeding while the other one, still alive, watched and snorted and tried to pull away. I'd seen a warrior named Calf Robe pull an arrow from his eye when it was almost as deep as the back of his head, and then walk away. I'd seen a horse born once with two legs between its front and back ones, two legs that it could stand on, and might have run on if Peasy hadn't told us to kill it. But I'd never seen anything like the Cat Man. I know I was one of his kind by then, maybe the only other one, but I never would have killed Yellow Kidney.

Still, I had to run away from the Fat Melters camp. It was easy to get away, even though the men came with horses and guns. I didn't take Weasel Plume's robe, and I couldn't explain to them that it wasn't me. But I knew that now they and all the Pikuni, all of Siksikaitsitapi, would be at war with both of me, The Fullblood and also Takes No Scalps. And probably Good Stab too, if Happy or his raven told them that name. After Yellow Kidney and his little sister, they had to have figured out that was me. The hunting parties and the raiding parties wouldn't just be ready for me, they would be looking for me.

But they didn't know to feed me mice for four or five winters like you know to, Three-Persons. They didn't know that even if they filled me full of greased-shooters and arrows, even if they rode horses across me and covered me in brush and burned me, that would only take my thinking away, leaving just the Cat Man, who would come for them and their blood, and then kill the ones he was too full to drink any more of.

I was banished, like that Snake with his clothes on backwards, but there was no one to give me mercy.

The Cat Man wouldn't, I knew.

I had stood in front of his cage and shot an arrow into him when he was at his weakest, when he was trapped and being traded, forced to take Sun Chief burning down on him, being only fed big dirty-faces.

I don't know if he knew my name, but he had to know my taste on the air. But it wasn't enough for him to be standing over me one night when I woke, so he could claw and bite into me, tear off my arms and legs and leave me burning up in Sun Chief's light for however many moons it would take for something to crawl across my mouth that I could bite into, drink.

From the way he killed Yellow Kidney, I knew that he wanted me to suffer like he had. He wanted me banished from the Pikuni. He wanted me to be a disease to them. And from the way he'd left Yellow Kidney on Weasel Plume's robe, that told me where he wanted me to go.

I showed up on Face Mountain at dawn. My arms and face and legs and chest were scratched open and Sun Chief was going to hurt those cuts, but it didn't matter.

I ran for Weasel Plume, there in the snow. From forty paces, I could already tell that the Cat Man hadn't skinned Weasel Plume's head, had only taken the robe like a hide-hunter. But what I couldn't tell until I got there was that he'd done it while Weasel Plume was alive.

His whole big body jerked when I slid on my knees into him and his nose opened wide in fear, his eyes the same. I pressed my face into his neck, because he was scared of me now. He'd let the Cat Man come close because of that broken ceramic smell, but then that smell had brought him this kind of pain.

I cried red into his white neck, I squeezed him, and I don't know if he ever knew it was me, or that it wasn't me who had done this to him. Weasel Plume was strong, too, would have lived another night or two in the snow like that, even skinned.

I made my hand like this and drove it into his chest, for his heart, and then pushed through it, felt it die around my wrist. I was screaming into his neck to have to do this.

When I stood, I was still screaming.

This was when I saw the rest of the herd, all dead around us. Even the calves. The Cat Man hadn't taken their robes, and didn't even need a long-shooter gun. He had ripped each of their throats out with his hand.

I fell to my knees and hid my face, still crying. It made my hands slick with blood, and I didn't even drink the girl's blood back in when it got to my lips. I spit it back out because I hated myself.

But I hated the Cat Man more.

Sun Chief was straight up in the sky when I finally stood again.

"Well, that was melodramatic," the Cat Man said from behind me.

I hadn't even heard him crunch in on the snow. But then I re-membered that he was quiet like me. I went around like this on my knees, and this is when I saw him for the first time since Peasy had let him out of his cage.

He was sitting on a dead blackhorn, one grown up from a calf I'd taken up here the second year of hunting the hide-hunters, and the sun was behind him so his face and chest were black in shadow.

But his shape was what made me push back.

His chest and shoulders and arms were like mine, but thicker, longer, and coming from his head were long-legs antlers on both sides. Meaning that's what he had been eating the most of.

His face was partway between a man and a long-legs, but his eyes were big and yellow.

"You think I'd want to eat grass, looking like this," he said, step-ping down and standing up. His legs, like what he'd been eating, were long now. He was taller than any man I'd ever seen.

"They didn't do anything to you," I said about Weasel Plume and the rest.

"Stupid animals," the Cat Man said, stepping closer, to inspect me. "But aren't they all? Didn't you just drink that one boy's little sister? She wasn't smart anymore, was she?"

He held his hand down low by his leg, to show he meant Yellow Kidney's sister.

This was when I figured out the Cat Man was speaking my own language to me.

It made me breathe like this, and go forward and backward be-cause I was hurting on the inside.

The only way he could have learned our language was if he went down to a camp for a winter or two and lived in someone's lodge, lived like the Pikuni.

He grinned and looked away, seeing me know this.

When he talked again, it was in napikwan.

"But it's easier to do it this way," he said.

"I don't want to talk to you in either way," I told him.

"Where were you the last two years?" he asked anyway.

I just stared at him.

"He didn't do anything to you," I said again, about Weasel Plume.

"He nuzzled into me like this when I walked up," the Cat Man said, doing his head to show me. "It was quite sweet, really. We didn't have these where I'm from."

"Where you're from?" I said back to him, standing.

He shrugged, didn't answer.

"What are we?" I asked, finally.

"You mean what am I," he said, walking to Weasel Plume to run his hand along his side, over his ribs. He sniffed his palm after, said, "You drank my blood, so you're just a smaller echo of what I am. What I am is four hundred and fifty years old. I know things you don't even know you don't know."

"And the first time I saw you, you were in a cage," I said, showing him my teeth.

"There's nowhere to run on a boat," he said, not worried about my bite.

"The water," I told him.

"Ship, ship, I should have said ship," he said, making a fist from his hand. "Nava, bateau, barco, lod, brod, korabel, ship ship ship." Then he looked up to me, said, "But you don't even know what an ocean is, do you? You can't understand, living up here like this, a mountain peasant."

I know what an ocean is now, Three-Persons. I saw it from the edge of California, like a lake that keeps on going.

"There are fish out there as large as a hill," the Cat Man said. "There are fish with teeth like ours. There are fish that jump up from the water and fly in the air. There are fish that glow at night like stars in the water. The world is bigger than you could guess."

"But you didn't have to kill him," I said again about Weasel Plume.

"Maybe I want to be like him, did you ever think of that?" he said back, and reached down to Weasel Plume's horns, put his knee on Weasel Plume's shoulder, and twisted and pulled and pulled, finally tore the head free, which I couldn't have done without breaking my arms and my shoulders and probably my chest.

The Cat Man held Weasel Plume's dripping head in front of his own like a mask he could put on, to dance.

"Stop," I told him.

"You going to bury him like a person?" the Cat Man asked, flinging the head at my feet so it rolled into my knees, knocked me back a step. It weighed more than a person.

"Since you killed him, you have to kill me too," I said.

I was wearing scratchy napikwan clothes I'd picked up coming to the Fat Melters camp. I pulled them off now, because I wanted to do this like a Pikuni.

"Oh, you're so serious, aren't you?" the Cat Man said, grinning, his yellow eyes flashing. "What if I put you in that, though?"

He tilted his high antlers to the east, which was when I saw what I should have seen before, if I hadn't only been looking at Weasel Plume.

It was the iron cage he had been in. It was brown from rust, but it was still square like a box.

"You can't kill me if I'm like you," I said to him, watching this cage. "If you can come back after being shot in half and then burned, then I can come back from this."

"Oh, we can die," the Cat Man said, taking a long step closer.

Like I'd thought, his taste on the air was the same as mine.

"Yeah, how's that, right?" he said to me, doing his nose like this to show that he saw what I was thinking.

"How do we die?" I asked, hating to need something from him.

"Wouldn't you like to know," he said back.

"Fire?" I asked.

"Fire's not fun," he said.

"We don't starve," I told him.

"There's always something to drink," he said, agreeing with me.

"Sun Chief?" I asked.

"You mean that?" he said, squinting and looking up. "The one that's not killing either of us?"

"The head," I said then. "Pull the head off like that."

I touched Weasel Plume's horn with my knee to show what I meant.

"It does make you wonder where life resides," the Cat Man said. "The heart, or up here?" He tapped his head right here, on the side. "Or, if it's both, do we split into two different people?"

"Two different monsters," I said.

"Monsters," he repeated, and I couldn't tell if he liked the word or if it made him sad. He sat down hard onto Weasel Plume, which made that clear liquid leak out from his broken open spine. "If I wanted to take the time," he said, "if you were worth it, not just an accident, I could educate you, show you the world in all its misery and grandeur. Show you what you are as well, and what you can really do. There are rivers of blood to swim in, little Pikuni. To swim in and drink dry. But I can see in your eyes that what you want is to die. Who am I to deny you that?"

He stood back up and breathed in through his nose, preparing for me.

I think I did want to die, too, Three-Persons. Weasel Plume was dead. The whole herd was. I had no wives, no children. Tall Dog was gone. I couldn't eat real-meat, I couldn't dream my own dreams. My people wanted to kill me. I'd killed women and men and children. I couldn't even ride a horse or smoke a pipe. All I could do anymore was not die. Unless he did that for me.

If you were a Black Robe who could never go into one of your holy places again, or talk standing higher than people, or read from your holy book or sing your wolf songs, your scalp songs, and if other Black Robes hated you and only wanted to kill you because you were killing their families, wouldn't you also want to die?

Or, if you'd killed a whole camp of Pikuni.

But those were just Indians, I know.

"Come on, then," the Cat Man said, holding his arms out to the side.

I rushed at him with all the speed my lightness could give me, and all my anger, all my crying. Instead of jumping for the Cat Man's throat, I slid down at the last step and went along his leg, tearing at it with my hand.

His blood was as red as mine, maybe more red, and he fell to a knee from losing it, turned his face to me to be sure I wasn't already jumping for his back.

I wasn't.

I was already running for the trees. It was so he would chase me there. I could tell from how he'd thrown Weasel Plume's head that he was stronger than me. This meant I would have to bring him down with surprise, not fight out in the open.

Once it was dark under all those limbs, I went up into a tree.

I watched the Cat Man walk under me.

From the top, he looked like a long-legs. It meant I couldn't jump down on him, because his antlers would come up through me, and then it would be over.

I tell you I wanted to die, but I wanted to bring him with me. I would pull him into the Sandhills, and the Pikuni would gather around me and help me pull him apart, carry his pieces to the four directions, so he could never heal back together.

Five breaths after he passed, I dropped down, quiet like you know I can.

I couldn't track him by scent, but this was the Backbone, and I was Pikuni. The land would help me. The waters would rise because they could tell what the Cat Man was. The four-leggeds too. The sky could send a thunderbolt down to burn him. Napi might even come up from a dugout when he heard the trouble going on.

I couldn't track the Cat Man by his taste on the air, but I could hear him. He was ahead of me, by a cliff I liked to sit under. And I was wrong about not being able to track him in the air. I didn't know this when I was in the tree, but on the ground with him now, I could taste the blood from his leg. It was from a real-bear.

I started to run for him, to jump on his back and pull his head to me, but I slowed, stopped.

If he had been alive almost five hundred winters, then he had had many battles.

I nodded to myself, turned to go the other way.

It was for Weasel Plume's head.

I stripped off the face skin, clawed away what meat I could, scraped the insides out to make it light enough for me.

It was bloody, but I held it by one horn and dropped lower on the hill, to come at the cliff from below.

I didn't run this time but went slow, as low as the grass. This was how Hunts-to-the-Side had gotten his name, so many winters ago.

The Cat Man was sitting on the rock under the cliff I liked to sit on. A few paces past him was the wallow I'd scraped out and made a sweat lodge over, to see if I could sweat the Cat Man out of me a few winters ago. All it had done was bring the blood up through my skin everywhere.

The Cat Man was looking up to the cliff like that's where I was going to jump from.

I sang my death song in my head because if I did it with my mouth, he would hear.

The last fifteen paces to him, I ran hard, and for the last five, I jumped, both hands on one of Weasel Plume's horns, his skull above and behind me like this, touching my heels almost, so I could bring it down like the heaviest war club any Pikuni had ever swung against an enemy.

I landed just past the rock the Cat Man had been sitting on.

"Thought they called you Good Stab?" he said, standing over me. "That wasn't a good stab at all, was it? Or were you just, what do your people call it? Trying to count coup? I can understand that. It's something like this, right?"

He held up one of my braids, that I hadn't felt him cut off with his sharp fingernails.

He rubbed the braid apart and opened his fingers, let the hair lift away on the wind.

I screamed then and turned around to swing Weasel Plume's skull harder, as hard as I could, and the Cat Man stepped back but not far enough. One of the horns opened his belly.

He fell to a knee, his mouth open, eyes big.

Swinging the skull that hard had spun me around, but I was still spinning, so I came all the way in a circle again, aiming for his eye this time, to finish him.

This time he caught the skull by the lead horn, was already looking at me in a way that I knew we were a father and his young son wrestling.

He had let that horn open his belly. He had let me cut his leg.

"This is a good stab," he said, and pulled the skull from me with one hand.

He was already holding the wrist of the arm I had been using to swing the skull.

With it he lifted me up, held me there, and drove Weasel Plume's other horn up under my chest bone, into my heart, but grabbing the skull like he did, it cut him too, so some of his blood splashed onto my lip.

I felt it right when it happened, and knew that if drinking Napi's blood had been good, if drinking that girl's blood had been good, then drinking the Cat Man's might be enough to let me kill him.

I used my tongue to pull that drop in, and it made my whole body buck.

Cat Men aren't supposed to drink each other.

Even if he hadn't stabbed me with that horn, I think that drop of blood would have done enough.

He smiled, watching this happen to me.

The sky behind him was going black like Sun Chief was gone, and for me he was.

The last thing I saw were the Cat Man's teeth.

They were white and sharp, and he was smiling.

"See you . . . probably not soon," he said to me after everything was black, and I felt like I was pressing my face into Weasel Plume's side again, and that became the robe I had slept in as a boy, when I would breathe like I was asleep so I could hear my father laughing with his first wife, the only one he had left.

They would talk about other people in camp, he would tell her stories from the hunt that she knew were lies, but the more she listened the more he lied, and I knew that someday I would have a wife like that, that someday I would have a boy and a girl faking sleep in their robes, and in this way the Pikuni would never die, we would always be here.

But all of that was gone for me, now.

I wasn't even in the Sandhills, I didn't think.

It was like a bear dream, but there were no berries.

I was in a den of some kind.

I was sleeping, I could tell that.

When I woke, the world was blue again, like the shadow that had melted in around the Cat Man was being pulled away to show the sky again.

But this was different.

I jerked up because I was on my hands and knees, but when I did, my head hit a hard thing. A hard iron thing.

I blinked, tasted the air, and it tasted like ice. I blinked again and saw the lines of brown in front of me.

I was in the iron cage, but the iron cage wasn't on Face Mountain anymore. I know how the Backbone tastes on the air, and this was the same, but different. It was deeper. It smelled like cold and, again, still, all around, ice. More than I'd ever tasted at once.

Had that one drop of Cat Man's blood kept me sleeping until Coldmaker came again with a big snow?

But it was too quiet.

It was too quiet for how bright it was. And how blue. Blue and dark at the same time.

It was the blue I didn't understand.

I jerked up again to see better, but couldn't go very high.

When I looked down, I could see why. My hands and knees had been set into water, and that water had frozen around them, locking me in.

That same ice, it was all around me.

I was breathing fast now, scared.

The more the taste of this ice got in me, the more I remembered it. It was the slow, giant rivers of ice that are all over the Backbone.

I had walked across these frozen rivers before, but I had never been inside of one.

That's where the Cat Man had taken me. He had made a cave or made a cave bigger, carried the cage in, put me in it, then used a fire to melt enough ice that the cage sank into the water before it froze again.

I screamed but my voice came back to me over and over.

The Cat Man had buried me here. Because it wasn't enough to only kill me.

After the second sleep like this, my left arm broke right here, inside the ice, from how hard I was trying to pull it out. For three sleeps after that, I held my mouth close to where that arm was in the ice and breathed my hottest breath on it, which is your coldest breath. Over and over I kept waking up with my lips stuck to the ice on top I had melted. Pulling away from that tore the skin off my lips and left it there, and then my mouth was bleeding in a long red string.

I dragged that red string onto where my broken arm went into the ice.

Breathing on the ice hadn't worked, but the blood from my lips went down into the space between the ice and my arm, and when that blood ran out I bit through my tongue, spit as much blood as I could down there. It made it slick enough that I could scream and scream more and pull with my legs and other arm so that my broken arm finally came out.

I pushed my mouth back to the hole I'd left, to try and drink that blood back up, but it was already freezing. I had one hand out now, but the arm was broken above it, so the fingers wouldn't grip, and they shook fast like this when I tried to move them. I tried not to cry but did anyway, and then had to tilt my face up like this to balance the blood from my eyes back to my mouth.

After another sleep, my lips got a little skin back. Four sleeps after that, the hand on my broken arm could squeeze like a child squeezes.

I broke the arm again, trying to use it to dig my good arm out.

Finally, after so many sleeps like that, I don't know how many, I bit into my arm at the break that wouldn't heal anymore, I bit and chewed and pulled until the hand fell off. The blood that came out, I drank as much of it as I could to save it, but it was already getting used up and dead.

I needed to feed.

Because I'd pulled the front of my arm off right above where it was broken, there was a sharp bone right here, now. I used it to chip at the ice holding my other arm. Every dig made my eyes stop and my hearing go away.

I cried and grunted and dug and dug and dug. At last my good arm came out.

I opened and closed the fingers, then made a fist and held it. The skin was puckered, it was burned from the ice, but the muscles still worked, and the skin wasn't that torn.

Needing to bite something, anything, I turned to the side and chewed off my other braid as high as I could. I had been wearing two in my hair instead of three because when it's cold, my fingers can only do braids to the side, not behind my head. Two braids right here made me look like the Necklace-People, but I was still Pikuni, because it's not about how many braids you have, or even if you have braids at all.

It's about how bad you want to live.

I wanted to live.

It took two more sleeps to dig my legs out. I could tell it was day and night by how the ice glowed. I didn't know how deep I was in the frozen river, but if I couldn't even chip myself out fast from the ground, I knew there was no pushing up through the rest.

But the Cat Man had to have gotten me into there somehow.

When I stood to see where, I stood into the cage.

He had melted it into the ice with the door under me. I kicked at a bar until it broke out, and then I pushed it back and forth like this until it broke off. Instead of using it to dig the cage out, which would take too long, I kicked the bars beside it out and broke them free the same, until I could crawl through. It was hard from only having one hand, but it was enough.

It wasn't a cave I was in, either. It was a tunnel, not tall enough to stand in. If the Cat Man had made it, then he must have built fire after fire to melt his way through. And if he'd been in here with the antlers he had now, then he must have walked on four legs, not two.

I hunched down a tunnel, and didn't know east from west, north from south. It was the first time I'd ever been without directions. It felt like I was going to float away, even though the roof was touching my head.

It was daylight, so every wall was blue, and the floor, and the roof. I had to squint it was so bright, squint and keep my face down looking at my feet.

It took fourteen sleeps to go down all the tunnels the Cat Man had been living in. I found the dried up bodies of Indians and napikwans he had brought down here to chase and drink. Some were frozen into the walls, some were left on the floor. One was pressed into the top of the tunnel, looking down.

Also there were four-leggeds, all of them.

The Cat Man had been living here for years. I told myself I would clamp onto his neck and drink him until my side burst open, but then I remembered what just one drop of his blood had done to me. How it had knocked me down long enough for him to put me here.

After going into every tunnel and not finding an opening to the Backbone, I came back to the cage to rub the end of the bar I had against the other bars until it was hot enough to melt the ice, so I could draw the lines of the Cat Man's home in the wall.

But he didn't have any plan or shape when he was making them. If he even made them, if he didn't just find them.

The Pikuni never knew anything about the ice-rivers. The four-leggeds didn't even go there unless they were running from something. Otter Goes Back had a story about how they were so cold like that because they had used to come all the way from far north, but when they got cut off from where they started, they didn't have anywhere to go, so were like a worm when the rain pushes it up from the ground, just feeling around slow and without eyes.

I don't know how long I was down there starving when one day a Pikuni my age shook me awake. He was talking but I couldn't understand him. Not because I couldn't speak my tongue anymore, but because I was so hungry.

I drank him before even asking him where he'd come in.

When my nose came back, I followed his taste in the air to a roof in a far tunnel with new ice shutting it closed.

The Cat Man had started a fire up there, let it burn down through, and then pushed this man through and filled the hole with brush and grass. After that he kept pouring water onto the brush and grass, so at first it froze right around the blades and sticks, and then it froze around what was already frozen, and now the hole was shut again, the ice there thicker than my leg is long. Inside the dark blue ice I could see the brush and grass like hair in water, not moving.

I went back to the man who was empty now, dead. I could smell smoke on him, and real-meat, and the broken ceramic smell from the Cat Man. It made me snarl.

From this Pikuni's blood, my hand started coming back.

I'd tried holding my old one in place so the skin could grow together, but it wouldn't work.

Three more times this happened. Two more men, both napik-wan now, and one Snake woman who was related to my mother. I could taste it.

I drank her anyway. It was the only thing I could do.

Finally I had my hand back. The bones in there were even solid. It hurt to make a fist at first, but after a few sleeps, I forgot it had ever been gone.

The Cat Man kept me there for the rest of that winter and then through the next winter too, and then one more winter. I paced the tunnels faster and faster, and then slow, giving up, crying, my hair down to here, now.

The third winter, the Cat Man stopped feeding me Pikuni, started only leaving napikwan trappers and soldiers and wagon people. On every one of them, I looked for their fire makings, or their tobacco pouches so I could smoke and smoke and maybe finally die, but none of them had any. One of the trappers he pushed in through a melt hole came with two elk antlers that were shed off, I was pretty sure. I knew from their shape that they were his, that they were the Cat Man's. Meaning he didn't look like a long-legs anymore. This is what he was telling me.

The trapper tried to use one of the antlers to kill me but I batted it away, held him to the ice by the neck, and asked him in napikwan about the world past the ice.

This is how I learned the Pikuni were starving, that the buffalo had been shot out, that Nittowsinan was getting smaller and smaller, that soon it would be so small we would all fall off the edge of it, into America.

"Why do you care so much about Injuns?" the trapper asked while I was holding him there, and this was how I knew I didn't look Pikuni anymore.

This was what the Cat Man had done to me.

I struck forward with my mouth, drank this trapper while his legs kicked, and I didn't leave even a drop in him. I threw him away but that wasn't enough, so I dove onto him and pulled his head off for making me know what I looked like, and then his arms, his legs, and it was when I split him open in the middle that I saw something that shouldn't have been there.

It was an arrowhead. Made of flint.

I see that you know what this means, Three-Persons. Good.

I took all the hair from the people I'd been drinking and made it into a ball around one of the iron bars from the cage, then pushed my hands into the center of that and scraped the flint fast on the bar until it finally sparked, lit the hair on fire.

I looked like a napikwan now, but I was still Pikuni inside.

When the hair was crackling and smelling and making its bad oily smoke, I started laying clothes on it, and then, with the iron bar still in, I went to one of the holes in the roof the Cat Man had melted. I held the torch to the roof instead of the wall so its own weight could help by pushing down, and so the brush and grass locked in there could help by starting to burn too.

I should have used a leg bone for the torch instead of the iron bar, because the iron bar got hot enough to make my palm smoke, but I bit my teeth together and held on.

After a whole night of doing this, my hand burned black, the ice finally crashed through.

For the first time in three winters, I crawled out into the air of the Backbone. I was crying from happiness. I rolled around on the ice screaming, and then I drew in like this because I was afraid now, from having so much air around me.

Anything could be out there. The Cat Man could be, to put me in another hole, a deeper one. So he wouldn't know I was out, I used his trick to cover the hole back.

After that I ran down a wags-his-tail and drank from her until my side split open again. Usually it hurt when that happened, but this time it felt good.

It was Frog Moon, I thought, because this wags-his-tail had a little one inside, that I drank also, when it lived longer than its mother. It was the first time I'd had that kind of blood. It made me breathe fast but not deep, so I was dizzy.

The snow in the Backbone was starting to melt, and the green was coming back.

This was where I could have crossed at Big Gap or even up at Face Mountain. I could have crossed to the west and kept going, and it would have been many winters until the Cat Man found me, I knew.

But I'm Pikuni.

I had to come down to the east, to the camps, to see the People.

First I went to Face Mountain. I took Weasel Plume's skull, pitted and dry as it was by now, and carried it on my back all the way to Chief Mountain, and climbed it the hard way, on the side where the rock's like this.

I set Weasel Plume's skull down in at the north edge, and sat with him singing a song in my chest, and looking out over Nittowsinan.

Far out there were the fires glowing in lodges, and I knew there were Pikuni moving in them, and from lodge to lodge, and the horses were spread out to the side, and there were nightriders out there with them, and the hunters were out after meat, and the dogs were digging in the ashes of the fires like they know to do, because that's where the grease drips.

A raven settled down up there with me.

"Tell him I'm back," I said to it, and waved it away.

It dropped off the edge then came back up after a minute, riding the wind because doing that is more fun than delivering messages.

Two sleeps later, the first camp I came to and watched was the Hard Topknots. Next I found the Fat Melters, but Happy would know me even in the skin I was in, so I didn't go to there either.

When I found the Small Robes, I watched them for six sleeps.

My napikwan beard was thick and itchy on my face. I didn't have a knife to cut it off, and it was good to hide behind anyway.

After drinking a young long-legs that was by itself when it shouldn't have been, I walked in at dark when all the people would be there. I was making noise on purpose so they'd know I wasn't trying to sneak in. The reason I'd drank the young long-legs was so I wouldn't be hungry. It had made my belly push out and my side too, but it hadn't split open. I had slept in a coulee far from camp, so the long-leg's blood could find where it needed to be.

I had decided my name would be Blackie. It was what Peasy had said he called a napikwan trapper who had lived in his lodge for half a winter when he was young and still had wives.

I didn't have a gun, and the only leggings I had were green buckskin, not even rubbed soft. I hadn't made moccasins or a shirt. But what was important was that I had no gun, no lance, no knife, no horse, no pouches or parfleches.

I walked in like that looking from lodge to lodge, reading their paint. The first boy I saw ran away. The first girl I saw walked beside me, looking at me. And then I felt something hard on the back of my head, here.

I raised my hands and dropped to a knee like this.

The Pikuni man pressing his many-shots gun to my head walked around to in front of me, the gun sliding from the back of my head to between my eyes. When I spoke to him, I did it in our language. His and mine, I mean, not your napikwan, Three-Persons. He opened his eyes wide and mad from me talking like that.

I told him I had been lost in the Backbone for three winters, that I had broken my leg and not been able to come down, that all my supplies were gone.

Soon three more men were there, and one woman.

I didn't know any of them. It had been ten winters since I'd been in the Small Robe camp like this. All the faces were starved and hurting.

"Kill him now," one of the men said.

"Hurt him first," another said, smiling.

I understood. This would have been me, years ago.

"I just wanted to see you," I told them all. It was true.

"Ask Walks Twice," the woman said, flashing her eyes to the men.

They stared at me and finally nodded, didn't kill me. I didn't remember Walks Twice being a Small Robe, I didn't know the name at all, but I hadn't been there in so long.

Two of the men held my arms and walked me to the center of camp. I recognized my father's old lodge, and Hunts-to-the-Side's.

Walks Twice's lodge was new and painted all black, which I'd never seen before. It must make it heavy, hard to pull. Above the doors in white paint on top of the black were two great long-legs antlers, going up like this, almost to the ear-flaps. They were pushing through the sky stripes, even.

The third man, the one leading, called into the lodge, and then the flap pushed out and the Cat Man stood up from it.

He looked like he had that first day in the cage, except his skin was Pikuni now. It meant that we were who he had been feeding on.

He nodded, breathed in deep through his nose, meaning he could see through my beard and hair, knew me for who I was. It made his eyes laugh, like this was what he'd been waiting for.

I jerked away to run but the two men held me, and shook me to be still. One of them hit me with his knee on the side of my leg here, and they had to catch me from falling.

"Let him go if he wants to go," the Cat Man said. "One dirty napikwan can't do anything to us, can he?"

Everyone laughed and they threw me down at the Cat Man's feet.

I looked up to him. He was still tall, even taller than the Pikuni, but only tall like a man now, not like a long-legs. He was the kind of Indian the painters would always pay to stand still so they could put them on your squares of white-cloth.

He grinned down at me and laughed, said with his important voice, "You've been up there for three winters, you say? Not four?"

I wasn't sure anymore but nodded once, holding his laughing eyes.

"Then maybe you're Pikuni now?" he said, smiling his sharp smile so everyone would know he was making a joke. They all laughed. "Maybe we'll let you be, if you prove yourself," he added with a shrug of one shoulder. "Maybe you can stay, if you're good."

"Where is Lone Bear?" I asked.

"Was he chief the last time you knew this camp?" the Cat Man asked, looking around to show how bored he already was with me.

"He left us," one of the men who had been holding me said, and spit after it.

When I looked to the Cat Man about this he did his eyebrows like this, I can't really do it like he did, but what it told me was that Lone

Bear hadn't just walked away from the Small Robes. It told me that the Cat Man knew where his bones were.

"And you showed up to help," I said to the Cat Man.

"My medicine is good for the Pikuni," the Cat Man said, holding his arms out to show me his people. "But to keep it strong, I can't have a wife, and have to stay inside when Sun Chief is out."

"Your medicine keeps you in your night lodge," I said back to him, almost snarling.

He grinned, shrugged, said, "I'm glad you can be out in the daytime, Good . . . good napikwan."

"Blackie," I told him, and everyone.

"Because of your yellow beard," the Cat Man said back to me.

I curled my lips in, hating him. I could only see my beard like this, in shadow.

"Or is that name because of your heart?" the Cat Man said, walking all around me, to look at me better.

"It's just my name," I said. "I don't know why, Walks Twice."

"Is that a question about where my name comes from?" the Cat Man said, coming back around in front of me again.

"Surprised you didn't take Lone Bear's name too," I said. "Along with his blood."

"This was never his lodge," the Cat Man said, holding a hand out to his.

"These were his people," I said back.

"Why do you care so much, napikwan that you are?" the Cat Man asked, reaching forward to touch my hair on the side.

I batted his hand away and all the men watching stood taller, their eyes big.

"You would fight me," the Cat Man said, holding his hands up and away to show how he was right, I was wrong. "For no reason." That second part was louder, for everyone else.

"My medicine isn't as strong as yours," I had to admit.

"A napikwan with medicine?" the Cat Man asked all around, turning and making a face I couldn't see, but didn't have to. "Why should we let you stay?" he asked then, coming back to look at me from my bare, dirty feet to my eyes, which were probably blue. "You probably don't know this, but people keep being taken, like a real-lion is living behind us, eating when it wants. You wouldn't know anything about that, would you?"

I just held his look with mine.

"Trappers have been disappearing in the Backbone too," I said to him. "You don't know anything about that, do you?"

"I know they shouldn't have been there," he said with a shrug. "So who cares about them? Maybe they fell into the ice and a People-Eater ate them."

The Small Robes standing around chuckled, but their eyes were nervous.

"People-Eaters don't live in holes like that," I said back to him. "You should have said that maybe the Inhaler was back, Walks Twice. That it was back and sucking people in. Any Pikuni would know that."

"The Inhaler," the Cat Man said, walking around me and saying this. "I like that."

"If you let me stay," I said then, answering his farback question, "then I can stand guard at night, to keep other people from going missing."

The Cat Man laughed big at this, said, "And where would you stand, Blackie the napikwan?"

I tilted my head behind him, to the flap of his lodge.

"As you can see," he said, "we're hungry this season, can't feed another mouth."

"You don't need to," I told him, and everyone. "I won't eat your food."

"Then what will you eat?" the Cat Man asked.

"Whatever I find," I said.

"Tomorrow we're going out for meat," the Cat Man said. "We'll deal with you when we get back."

"How many days?" I asked back.

He shrugged, said, "Depends how far we have to go."

"You can ride a horse?" I asked him.

"I can do all kinds of things you don't even know about, Blackie," he told me, saying my name louder, like making fun of it. Then he had the men tie me to a thick lodgepole buried in the ground just past the edge of camp. The pole was from when a napikwan family had tried to build one of your houses out here, even before the wagon-roads. They had frozen that first winter, so we didn't even have to kill them, just had to burn their house. This post had been in the part where they kept their horses, so it didn't burn, and because it was buried too deep to pull up, they tied me to it. The rope they used to wrap my wrists behind me were green buckskin, so it would dry hard, and squeeze when it did.

"You'll be dead when we come back singing with meat," one of them said to me, and hit me with the heel of his hand right here, because I didn't matter, and because I was napikwan.

I leaned forward from the pole until my arms burned, and then I leaned back, which made my shoulders hurt. There was no way to sit or stand that didn't hurt.

The dogs kept their distance, but the children squatted far enough away and watched, curious about my beard, my hair, my skin. They laughed and pointed.

A woman brought me a bowl of water. I took it in my mouth, shook my head to her that that was enough, and after she was gone I let the water come out onto the ground.

The girl watching from right in front of me saw this.

"What's your name?" I asked her.

She was eleven winters, maybe twelve. She ran away from me talking to her.

The next morning, after the hunting party left, she was back.

She made a sign with her hands, telling me her name. It was Kills-in-the-Water. When the other children showed up, she still didn't talk, and that was how I knew she didn't speak. I couldn't say anything back to her since my hands were tied, but she saw me keeping my eyes shut against Sun Chief. It took her and the other children most of the day, but they finally found a forked branch they could press against my neck to keep me from moving my head. It was so they could tie a piece of cloth over my eyes.

It was the first nice thing anyone had done for me in years. I would have cried, but it would scare them, and they would get the people from camp.

When it was night, I listened to the sounds from the lodges. The sounds from the fires. The sounds from the horses just over the hill.

The more still I stayed, the farther I could hear. But I needed to feed. I fell away inside myself, which you would call sleep but is really falling and falling inside myself, and then something was touching my lips. I flinched back, spit and spit. Hot broth splashed onto the top of my legs, and I heard the wooden bowl roll away.

Kills-in-the-Water was trying to feed me, was still close enough I could smell her, that there was something different about her, maybe because she talked with her hands.

"I'm sorry," I told her, even though I didn't think my words would mean anything. Or maybe she watched the shape of the words on my lips, I couldn't tell.

"Come here!" an adult said then, and I didn't have to be able to smell this woman to know she was Kills-in-the-Water's mother. I could hear it in her voice.

I hung my head. After they were gone, I rubbed the broth on my shoulder like this, to get it away from my lips.

From ten or twelve paces away, the dogs growled, but they were growling at themselves. They wanted the dirt and grass with the broth on it, but they would have to come close to me to get it, so they were mad at themselves for being scared.

When one of them finally tried, crawling on its belly, I think, pulling forward with its front legs like dogs do, I turned myself into a rock, and let it.

After that, the other dogs came in, some of their tails even hitting into me.

I listened hard for if anyone was standing there, watching this. When I didn't think anyone was, I snapped my mouth forward all at once, bit into a dog's spine, and drank until it flopped away, crying, to die.

It wasn't a meal, but it was better than starving.

Like I told you our first holy day, the Pikuni can eat dogs when we have to.

Three days later, after camp was asleep, I pulled hard enough at the dried buckskin around my wrists that it tore. I pulled the cloth off my eyes and moved to the side, in case an arrow was already coming for me.

Nobody saw me.

I ran out into the darkness and the first thing I saw from a long way off, because of the stars in its eyes, was a young prairie-runner. I wanted to use that Crow trick on it, but that only works in the day-time, so I had to sneak around and jump, then run and grab on to the back of its leg, dig for the big sinew in there. The prairie-runner went down flopping, and I was already on its throat to keep it from screaming. The white tube in there is as big as a long-legs's, even though they're small like the goats people here keep to eat.

A prairie-runner has only a little more blood than a big man, so my side didn't split from having too much in me. Its soft hooves dug into the ground slower and slower the whole time I was drinking.

I cut a strip of its skin loose with my teeth, biting all around like this.

It felt good to not be tied to a pole anymore.

But I couldn't leave the Small Robes to the Cat Man.

I went back to where I was supposed to be, tied the strip of green prairie-runner tight around my wrists and then jumped up high enough to get my arms around the pole again.

When I landed, my hands already behind me, I remembered that the cloth that was supposed to be tied around my eyes was still looped on my neck.

I snarled with anger, hating myself, but then saw Kills-in-the-Water was watching me.

I quit snarling and she walked in, put the cloth back over my eyes.

"Thank you," I said to her. I couldn't see if she heard me, but I said it anyway, and she was close enough I could have gone forward like this, drank her, but I was still full from the prairie-runner.

That blood lasted all the way until the hunting party came back.

They had only found two old bulls with scabby robes, but it was real-meat. Everybody got some. I could hear them dropping it into cooking pots and kettles, because that makes it last longer than cooking it over the fire. The hunting party had only eaten the tongues before coming home, so they were hungry too.

There wouldn't be any left for the dogs. But, there was one less dog, so maybe that made it hurt less for them.

I knew when the Cat Man was standing right in front of me.

I stood, my arms sliding up the pole, my shoulders like this.

"You're a sneaky one," he said, smelling the blood I had in me now, and the prairie-runner skin now tied around my hands.

"I was hungry," I told him, not loud, because camp was busy and I didn't know who was listening.

"Did you hear what else we brought back, Good Stab?" he asked.

I never knew where he had heard my name, but it was before we fought on Face Mountain. Maybe he had asked some Pikuni he was drinking about who went missing the winter Heavy Runner fell, if he knew that's when it was. Maybe I had been talking to myself up in the Backbone. Maybe Weasel Plume had told him. Maybe his nose was old enough and strong enough he could smell my name on me.

"We thought you were the Great White God," I said to him in napikwan.

We could talk your tongue and nobody knew what we were saying.

"Maybe I am," the Cat Man said.

"I don't think that anymore," I told him.

"We brought a forked tree," he said.

"You can't eat a tree," I said back to him.

"But you can dig a hole for it," he said back, and then I heard him walking away.

The next morning there was drumming, but it wasn't strong, and it wasn't steady. In the camp I could hear people crying.

"I had a dream, Good Stab," the Cat Man said from behind me. "The night after we got those two old bulls," he went on, "after the morning when one of our hunters was gone because I was hungry."

"You don't have real dreams like a Pikuni," I hissed to him.

"Does a real-dream leave footprints?" the Cat Man asked. I could hear him smiling. His mouth was close to my ear. "Or are a real-dream's footprints my words?"

I shut my eyes tight even though they were in the cloth.

"Look at those little grass dancers go," he said then, hitting my shoulder with his open hand but soft, like he was Tall Dog.

The grass dance is what the Pikuni do to stomp the grass flat to stand a Sun Dance lodge up. This was Frog Moon, though.

"It's too early," I said to him.

"For the real one, sure," the Cat Man said. His napikwan sounded different than Napi's. It was sort of like yours, Three-Persons, but different, like it had more edges, and different slopes to ride up and down. He kept his hand on my shoulder, moving me back and forth, and said, "But it's not too early for the children's Sun Dance."

"They can't," I said. "It's wrong."

"My dream said they have to do it all themselves, I don't know," the Cat Man said.

He was just doing this to make himself laugh. It was why people in camp were crying.

"But we can bury the sun pole for them," he said, brushing past me. "They shouldn't have to do everything."

It took the children three days to get the arbor built, and do the social dance. The whole time there were people crying in camp. The children were crying too, because they knew what they were doing was wrong. When they blew their whistles all four directions, it wasn't strong.

I wanted to grab each of them and run and run, put them somewhere else. I hated myself for staying trapped in the ice-river so long. It meant the people knew and trusted the Cat Man. And I was napikwan to them, so they wouldn't listen to me. I wouldn't have either.

When the winter count was added to, I knew this children's Sun Dance would be on it now. It had never happened before, even in play. The Sun Dance is our holy time, Three-Persons. And the Cat Man was making water on it. For every part of it he would come behind me and talk napikwan into my ear, to tell me which part was happening.

"And this is the fasting," he said, finally, and hit me on the shoulder with his open hand again. I didn't understand at first, but then I did. It had been many sleeps since the prairie-runner, and Kills-in-the-Water hadn't tried to spoon any broth to me.

I was the one who had been fasting.

Finally someone cut the strap holding me and pulled me forward. My legs didn't work at first and my arms were cold, or I might have run away. But then I felt the hard grip of the Cat Man on this side. He was one of the men holding me, and his hand was like one of your iron rings.

I was pushed ahead sixty paces, then the Cat Man held my head down to get under the edge of the arbor, because it was short, for children.

The drumming stopped and the Cat Man used his important voice to recount the dream he was lying about. It ended with a napik-wan with a yellow beard being made to dance. I shook my head no, no, but then they dragged me stumbling over my feet out to the pole.

When the cloth was pulled away from my eyes, the sky was too bright and the people had soft edges.

"Here, I'll do it, Kills-in-the-Water, you shouldn't have to," the Cat Man said to her with his hands, taking the pegs from her and, when their hands touched, he turned his eyes up to her and opened his nostrils, like tasting her on the air for the first time.

She was wearing an elk teeth dress. It meant she was the medi-cine woman for this. Her face was bad from crying about the wrong-ness of this. But their Walks Twice was telling them it was right.

"Here," I said, pulling the Cat Man's nose away from her by breathing my chest big like this, to make the skin tight. The Cat Man turned back to me and pinched some of my skin right up here.

"I'll kill you," I said in napikwan when he leaned closer.

"Of course you will," he said, pushing the first one through slower than he had to, and deeper than they usually go. "You're the first one to ever say that to me, aren't you? Everyone before you killed me too, can't you tell?"

I gritted my teeth.

The last of the prairie-runner's blood was leaking down my chest.

"Now this one," the Cat Man said, and pushed the other one through.

It hurt, but it was cold.

Then he snapped for the thongs that looped onto both ends of the pegs and tied them up to the rope.

We were standing close to the pole for this.

"Now you can be one of us, Blackie!" the Cat Man said, and pushed me back.

The rope tightened and the pegs pulled against the skin of my chest, and if he hadn't dug them so deep my skin would have torn away then.

I ran at the Cat Man with my mouth open and he smiled and stepped to the side, so that when I fell, the rope pulled against my chest again, yanking me back. I stood to get it slack again and he pushed me back, softer this time, like I was a child.

Blood was on my face now, from my eyes, but, since I'd fallen, the people probably thought it was from the pegs.

"Here, don't forget," the Cat Man said, and pushed the whistle into my lips.

The children were drumming in their way again. Drumming and crying. The people too.

But some were cheering to see me hurt, because I was napikwan.

I breathed in and blew, just trying to blow the pain and shame and wrongness away, out of me, and the Cat Man sat back on the grass with the people and watched and laughed the loudest, and one time when I looked over to him, he was wearing black glasses like these, and that was the first time I had ever seen them.

He made me dance all day, pulling against the pole with my chest, and then I hung there at night and he made the children splash water on me in the morning that was really from three different horses, and I danced and I blew, and I told myself this was real, like the first time I'd done it, when I was proud, and Wolf Calf was watching, proud that his son who had always drank the whitehorn milk was becoming a man now.

Halfway through that second day, the peg on this side pulled through the skin, and then, because all my weight was on the other one now, it gave, but not the same. The peg broke, leaving splinters of its bone inside my skin.

The Cat Man sat on my chest to cut it out.

Before I could drink that blood back in, the children poured water into my mouth.

I let it come back out.

"Let him be," someone said. "Nobody can drink at first."

"I have to take him up to get his helper now," the Cat Man said in joke, and threw me across the back of a horse with a braided mane that didn't even jump away. It didn't make sense that he could ride a horse, but he was doing it.

Every step made my face hit the side of the horse, and I didn't have any blood in me anymore.

We went back to the Backbone under Chief Mountain.

"Now you're a man, Blackie!" the Cat Man said, pushing me down into a shallow creek so I had to roll over to breathe. "You made it through your Sun Dance."

I was breathing hard and crying, but nothing was coming out.

"This is the part that hurts," the Cat Man said, and before I could even look up, he kicked down and broke my leg right here, high up. And then the other one. And then this arm right where it bends.

"I'll leave you that one," he said about the other arm, and stood up from me.

He looked around at the trees and the mountains.

"What do you Pikuni call this?" he asked. "The Backbone of the World? I don't know about that." He looked down to me then, and stepped over closer again. "I do know where your backbone is, though, Blackie."

This is when he stepped down hard and broke my back.

Down the stream from me, a beaver was slapping its tail on the water.

"Hey, dinner," the Cat Man said about the beaver.

Then he squatted down by me.

"I've been like this before," he said. "You left me worse than this, even. You won't be able to come back down until . . . what do you Pikuni call it? Oh, yeah. The moon when the leaves dry up, right? I kind of like that. It's descriptive. Anyway, we can do this all again then if you want. But try to eat some different things this summer? So you can look different the next time the Small Robes see you. I don't want to have to explain Blackie being back. Look like a monster if you can? A bear, or a giant red backed squirrel, or one of those elk, even. Then you'll match my lodge, and I can make up a dream to explain it. If you look like a different monster each time you come back, then you can really live forever, at least in your people's stories. And I can be the hero who kills monster after monster. Maybe I'll even get a new name out of it. I'm getting tired of this one."

He swung back up onto his horse, which was when I saw that its face was painted red like they were going on a raid. Then he looked down at me and made the horse ride across me back and forth, breaking more bones, so I was a skin bag of slivers and rocks, that prairie runner blood all leaking out of me, going down to the beaver lodge.

For three days after he left me I couldn't move at all, and then the only reason I could, finally, was a silver fish hit into me right here and my arm that wasn't broken clamped down on it.

It tasted worse than anything, worse than the time Tall Dog and me cooked one, but I drank its thin iron blood while its mouth was opening and closing in the air, looking for the water its kind breathes.

Over the next seven sleeps, I drank the blood of twenty more of them.

It was finally enough that I could crawl to the bank.

I knew I could float down and dig into the beaver lodge and eat them, drink their blood that's the most red of any of the four-leggeds, but I knew not to.

The Cat Man was right, too. It took me all those moons until the leaves dry up until I could walk and run again. It meant eating dirty-faces at first, and then more and bigger, until I finally pulled down a big moving-shadow bull. That's like a long-legs, but taller even, with flat antlers like two big hands opening, like this. They hardly ever come down to the Bear, so I don't know if you've seen one, Three-Persons, since I don't think you went farther into Nittowsinan than there.

It felt right to drink it in until my side burst open again, because moving-shadow hooves are tied to Feather Woman's digging stick, and Morningstar let her down through her turnip hole on strips of blackhorn hide, one of which had a tail, and that's why we tie tails to the real sun pole.

The moon when the snakes go blind, a party of Blue Mud People came up to the Backbone with two riders for each horse. They were running from the soldiers. I wanted to talk to them, not kill them, but I didn't want to be a monster like the Cat Man wanted, so I drank one of them every eight sleeps until the moon when the geese leave, and I put on one of their leggings, another one's shirt, a third one's moccasins, and I tried to tie my hair into three braids but couldn't, so made it into two braids again, like the Necklace-People.

I was Indian again, and Pikuni on the inside. My bones were together at last. In a piece of ice I could see that I still had one eye that was blue, but that would be my medicine eye, I told myself.

I was going to go down and kill the Cat Man, but first I walked along the ridge of the Backbone in the freezing rain to see Weasel Plume on the Great Chief, so he could give me power. Or, so I could say goodbye to him, and tell him again I was sorry for not being there when the Cat Man came.

It was when I came down from the slick rocks to walk in the high-up snow out of the wind that I saw Kills-in-the-Water and her brother holding the Small Robes' winter count over their heads, Otter Goes Back's paint dripping down onto the crust of snow. Around them were three dead Pikuni, two women and a man called

Lone Horn, who would have known me even with my medicine eye. They had been running away, I could tell. No Pikuni comes that high in the winter unless they're running from something.

This was how I knew the Cat Man had gotten tired of playing chief. The Small Robes were scared of him, and the camp had broken up to try to live.

I ran a few paces to Kills-in-the-Water to help her and her brother, to explain to her that it wasn't her fault she'd had to be the fake medicine woman for that Sun Dance of the children, but this is when she brought her knife up, like I told you the first time I was here.

I thought she was doing it because I looked like the Blue Mud People, from wearing their leggings. Even if she didn't know that, she knew I wasn't Pikuni, and if I wasn't Pikuni, I was an enemy. This is how it's always been.

But then I looked down to my feet, understood what she was seeing. My feet weren't pushing down through the snow enough. To her I was a wrong thing, I was something cursed to live up here where nobody was like the Cat Man had been telling the Small Robes, which meant, Pikuni or not, I was a Person-Eater.

I'm not, but she wasn't wrong, either.

Instead of scaring her more by speaking words she would know, or by telling her I was Blackie with different skin and hair, I backed off while holding my hands up like this, and that night I built a lean-to for them in the dry part where the trees started down the steep slope, and I left three wags-his-tails there for her, with the guts already out.

The way I made her find the shelter was I started a fire in it. Her and her brother followed the smoke. I watched from the trees until it was night. Her arms were cut on top, and her brother's were too.

I went back to the two women and Lone Horn, frozen where they were. I pried the first woman up and it was New Robe Woman. We had played together when we were children. I didn't know the other woman.

There were no holes in them, so they had died either from cold or starving or fever, I couldn't tell.

Before I left again I dragged dead wood that wouldn't smoke close to Kills-in-the-Water and her brother's camp, so they would find it when they looked, and not have to walk far. They should have gone down lower if they wanted to live, because only white big-heads can stay up here, white big-heads and the Cat Man and me, and Weasel Plume, but if I tried to talk to her she might run away and hurt herself.

The next night I was up on Chief Mountain.

I looked down across Nittowsinan and I told Weasel Plume about my wives and my children, whose names I never say, and how Kills-in-the-Water and her little brother were like my two had been, so it was like they'd come back from the Sandhills. I told him that after I killed the Cat Man, I would come help them, save them. I knew I couldn't save all the Pikuni. I hadn't even been able to save the black-horns, and there were so many more of them. But I could save these two children at least.

That was how I knew I had to survive the Cat Man.

But I didn't know how to do that.

He was stronger than me, and smarter than me. I had lived almost fifty winters, and he had lived almost five hundred. He said he got caught on a boat on the ocean, so that meant he was from where all the napikwan were. If they'd never started coming over, then he never would have either.

It made me wish the Pikuni had been there when those first boats landed, waiting on the shore of that ocean with its great toothed fish swimming in it.

But we wouldn't have known, would we? We would have wanted the iron kettles like you said. And it just would have been one boat-load of you, so what would that even matter? Except now your shiny-wheels are cutting the land up into smaller and smaller pieces.

I don't even know what to fight anymore, Three-Persons. The Backbone is a playground now, for napikwan to come look at. The Pikuni live in lodges at the gates and the Bear isn't the Bear anymore, so even Heavy Runner is being forgotten.

But not by me.

There's a grave by Old Agency where Pikuni ghosts dance in green light, because they can't dance anywhere else.

I cry still about it, and Heavy Runner, and Tall Dog, and my family, but I sit alone, far away, so no one sees the blood on my face.

More and more, I talk to no one.

I don't want to live as long as the Cat Man, Three-Persons.

My time to eat mice is almost here.

The only reason I haven't yet is that the wife the scout Joe Cobell left behind after he died, who was Pikuni, Buffalo Stone Woman, whispered your name to me when I sat by her bed while she was sleeping and dying. I told her I was a ghost of the Pikuni her husband had killed, and that I needed to know why he had shot Heavy Runner.

It was your name she said, Three-Persons.

But I didn't know how to find you, not until one of the people driving through Old Agency to their new playground said your name, and how good it had been to hear a service in the right tongue, all the way out here where the blackhorns used to be.

That's how I got your taste on the air the first time. It was still on them, just barely, but enough. And it was the same taste I'd already smelled while sitting on the Big Gap, when the shiny-wheels was stopped because of snow in front of it.

This is how I found your son, Three-Persons. The one you didn't know about. He had been coming to see the mountains before they were gone, because he had enough money to do that. You can write that in your book if you want, and then hide it again after I'm gone for the last time. I don't need it. I just need you. No one else can confess me for what I've done.

Which is about to happen.

I don't want to tell it, but I have to.

Don't be afraid if there's blood on my cheeks for this last part. You know I can catch you if you pull down from there and run away. Even if your foot had all its toes, I could still catch you. I can run down a wags-his-tails. A whole pack of big-mouths can't catch me. The only thing faster than me now is a prairie-runner, but they don't chase, they just run away from things that want to eat them.

But in this holy house of yours, there's nowhere to run anyway.

Can you see my hand? I didn't think it could shake anymore from being afraid.

This is my last fight with the Cat Man, Three-Persons.

I told this to Weasel Plume on Chief Mountain, and then I held his forehead to my forehead before setting him down facing north, because blackhorns always look into the cold wind, not away from it.

The first place I went was the Small Robes' winter camp.

They weren't there anymore, but there were six lodges fallen down, and dead Pikuni all around. Two of their throats had been bitten, and the rest had been killed.

It smelled of broken ceramic and decay.

There was a dog moving among the dead. It did its tail like this between its legs when it saw me, and then it curled down while standing up, because it thought I was going to kill it.

"Go on," I told it, and turned away.

I walked out in circles, tasting the air, and the Small Robes had gone every direction like grouse bursting up from the brush when you almost step on them.

On a hill just past seeing but not smelling, I found the Cat Man's tall black lodge all by itself, and empty.

Inside was another Pikuni, this one a girl. She was dead, and wearing the same elk tooth dress Kills-in-the-Water had had to wear to be a medicine woman for the children's Sun Dance.

I set the lodge on fire and watched it burn, the paint making bubbles it was so thick, the two long-legs horns on the front lasting the longest. The smoke was thick and black, and I waited, and finally the Cat Man was there behind me. He's the only one who can do that.

"Why did you kill them all?" I said without turning around.

"Because they kept hiding her from me," he said back. We weren't talking your napikwan anymore. My language was normal to him now.

I turned around to him.

His chest was black with old blood, and his hair was down.

I looked at the Blood Clot Hills like far away ghosts.

"The one in there?" I said, about the girl burning in the lodge.

"They tricked me with her," he said. "They put her blood on all of them, and on the horses and dogs, and then went every direction."

I thought of the cuts on Kills-in-the-Water's arm, and on her brother's arm.

"The one who talks with her hands," I said.

"That's the one," the Cat Man said.

"Why?" I asked.

"Did you not smell her?" the Cat Man asked back.

"I smelled her," I told him.

"You didn't like I did," he said. "You don't know this yet, but once a generation, once a century, someone is born with a kind of blood no one else has. If you drink from that person . . . how to explain it? It's like the difference between an animal and a person. But the person is the animal now, and this new one is above them. Their blood, you do anything for it. I've only tasted it twice so far in all my years. She's going to be the third time."

"Her brother too?" I asked.

He shook his head no, said, "Just her."

"And if you get her, do you leave Nittowsin forever?" I asked him.

He stared hard at me, then said, "Why do you still call it that, Good Stab? It's not Pikuni territory anymore, and it never will be again. Can't you see what's happening? Your time is over. It's the age of the napikwan, now."

I lowered my face, my eyes filling with red, and then I couldn't stop myself, I was jumping at him with my teeth out.

We fell back and I was tearing and biting and screaming, but he was just laughing, hitting me away. Finally he rolled us over and held me down with his knees on my arms, and leaned his face down over me.

"You could have been a good one," he said to me. "But you care too much, Good Stab. You still think people are people, that they matter. You still think you can save the Pikuni. You can't. It's over."

I bucked and pushed but he held me down.

"I can at least save them from you," I finally said up to him.

"You don't even know what I can do when I really want to," he said, grinning. "I've destroyed villages, towns, cities. There are whole peoples forgotten to history because of me."

"I can bring her to you," I said then, just loud enough for him to hear.

This stopped him.

"You know where she is?" he asked, opening his nose to smell me better. He pulled his lips back from his teeth when he smelled one single trace of her on me.

"Did your precious white buffalo tell you where they've hidden her?" he said, his eyes big and angry, his teeth coming out, so much longer than mine. He'd smelled Weasel Plume on me too.

"If I bring her, do you leave Nittowsin forever?" I asked. "Do you leave the Pikuni alone?"

"One girl for a whole people?" he said, then finally nodded. He stood, offered a hand to pull me up.

I got up myself instead.

"Once you smell her blood, you'll want her for yourself," he said. "I'll follow you to her."

"I said I'll bring her," I told him. "She's far away."

"I'll keep up," he said.

"I go alone," I told him. "They told me they'll kill her if they see you again. But they know me."

"They know Blackie?" the Cat Man said with a grin.

"They remember Good Stab," I said back. "Wolf Calf's son, Curly Hair Woman's son, Tall Dog's friend."

"Your names," the Cat Man said, shaking his head because they were funny to him. "But," he went on, "how do I know you don't come back with your warriors?"

"Because you would kill them," I said.

"You really know where she is?" he asked again.

I nodded, said, "You tasted her on me."

"One day," he said, holding his finger up. "If I don't have her by then, I kill every Pikuni I find, no matter how long it takes. And I don't kill you, Good Stab. You'll be the last one, so you can mourn forever."

"Over there in the dead lodges," I told him, pointing with my lips to where they were.

The Cat Man held my eyes for longer and longer, and finally nodded that that was where we'd meet.

I walked away, moving north, and then I ran and ran and ran, eating a wags-his-tail on the way because I was using my blood up. I wasn't running for the Backbone this time. I was going north, and then more north, fast. I found some little grass-eaters, apologized to them, and spread their blood all over my arms and legs and face, then kept running. I didn't know if he could smell through them or not.

By night, I was coming back fast, and the whole world was thunder.

When it was almost morning, I saw the lodges of the dead.

The Cat Man heard me coming, and the thunder I was bringing with me.

He shook his head, impressed I think, and then I turned to the side and dove into a coulee so the last herd of blackhorns in all of Nittowsinan could run over and over him, pounding him into the ground.

There were three hundred of them, and they kept going and going, hated him as much as I did.

I had been run over by horses two times before, maybe three, and each time it was hard to rise again.

After they were gone and the dirt was still hanging in the air, I walked in.

The Cat Man was broken, mixed in with a lodge of the dead, one that had had an otter painted on it. I knew whose it had been, when I was a boy. That otter had been painted going backwards to the water over and over through the winters.

I fell to my knees, crying again.

In all of my stories I'm crying, Three-Persons.

But I couldn't wait too long, I knew.

He had a taste of that girl's blood in him, the one I'd burned in his lodge, and from when I'd had a child's blood in me, I knew he'd be able to stand again soon.

I went down over him with my knees on his arms like he had been on me, and I grabbed his head behind the ears and leaned back to pull, but his leg came up and hooked around my neck and threw me back.

He was already starting to stand again in his broken way, like a child's dream he wakes screaming from.

I shook my head no, no, and then I was running and falling and getting back up and running again.

I went to the west at first, to the Backbone, but then I looped around into the chewed up grass the herd was still running through, and when that trail got close to the Backbone, I went up into the trees.

But I knew the Cat Man could follow me anywhere. I could run west and keep running, and maybe he would follow me. But he wanted Kills-in-the-Water worse than he wanted me. So I went higher and higher, up to her but going half up the slope above the tangles of brush and dead four-leggeds I'd been making for years, so the Cat Man would take the lower part that's supposed to be easier and then get slowed down, and this is what I need confession for, Three-Persons. This is what I need you to wash away with your holy book, so I can finally eat mice until I forget I'm not one of them.

When I crashed into Kills-in-the-Water's lean-to, she was combing her dead brother's hair back from his eyes. He was frozen, dead.

She looked up to me with scared eyes and I took her by the wrist fast, and was running again, first to Lone Horn frozen in the hard-snow, because I needed his parfleche, and then back down the ridge, my feet sure like a white big-head's, because if I fell with her she would die, and I needed her to be alive, and smelling like she did.

Finally she started holding on to me like my daughter used to, and I don't like to think about that part of it, Three-Persons. But when her hands found each other behind my neck, I knew I was still a father, and I hated myself, and I still hate myself, and I'll always hate myself, because this wasn't the Cat Man inside me or behind me making me do this. This was me doing this.

I came down Face Mountain going fast, sliding and running, her weight letting me push through the crust of snow finally, letting me be a man again, and then I came to the edge of the lake and was splashing in even though it was cold. Kills-in-the-Water screamed and held on tighter, and I swam us out to that Wild Goose Island.

I let her go once we were there.

"What are you doing?" she asked me, crying and scared. "Only lost spirits live here!"

I nodded that she was right about that.

I dumped out Lone Horn's parfleche, got his short pipe ready, and started a small fire. Then I felt around and found the traps I used to throw here, so the trappers couldn't use them anymore.

I didn't think this could work, what I was doing, but it had to. This is the only time I used Tall Dog's Crow trick, which is just to wave a strip of wags-his-tail belly skin or white-cloth torn from your wagons until a prairie-runner has to come close enough to see what it is, so you can put an arrow in it, don't need a gun at all. It's a way of bringing what you want to you instead of going to it to kill it. But now I was using it for the Cat Man.

I went fast, getting everything ready, and was only just done when Kills-in-the-Water heard it like I did. The Cat Man was calling my name across the water. I was Good Stab again. It felt right to be myself at the end. The Cat Man was still crooked and not standing right from the blackhorns running over him so hard, and one part of his face and head was caved in, but that only made him worse. He started walking into the lake until he had to swim, and when he swam it wasn't like Pikuni do, it was like he had been taught to be afraid of the water when he was a boy, and never forgot that.

But when he came up dripping onto the island, he was smiling, his eyes only looking at Kills-in-the-Water. She was the belly skin I'd been waving in the air, so he would taste her in the air.

"This is how you bring her to me?" he said, stepping closer and closer, one leg dragging. "All the way out here?"

The girl jumped to me and clung to me with her arms and her legs. She was shaking but not with cold.

This is why I'm here, Three-Persons.

It's because I can't carry her anymore.

The Cat Man had told me he wanted me to be a monster when I came down from the Backbone again, and I was, now. And I still am, and I always will be. Not because of the Cat Man part of me, but because of what I'm doing right now in what I'm telling you. This is my confession, Three-Persons.

Since then, I've told myself I did it to save the Pikuni, but every time I ask back if it was really because I hated the Cat Man, because he was what I'll be, if I live as long as him.

What I need is for you to use your holy book and tell me it's all right. That what I did is good. That I had to do it.

"So you're going to hold her for me?" he said. "How polite, all the way out here where there's no civilization, no manners."

I closed my eyes, nodded.

I opened them when, stepping to us in his crooked way, he dragged one of his feet across a trap. It bit onto the air only.

He hissed and I opened my eyes, but he was only still looking at her, now that he was this close.

His next step, with his good foot, was into the middle of another trap, and he screamed now like a real-lion screams at night, and the girl clutched on to me tighter.

"Do it, do it," I said to the Cat Man, because I didn't know if I could hold her here for him any longer. My teeth were out now too, from smelling her blood, so close.

"This isn't over, Blackfeet," he said in napikwan. "These traps won't mean anything, once I have her in here." He touched his chest to show what he meant.

"I know," I said back to him in napikwan so the girl wouldn't have to hear, and while I said it I was biting through the end of my tongue. I held Kills-in-the-Water's hair up from the back of her neck, with my hand on the back of her head like keeping her safe, my lips tight to keep the blood in my mouth.

I know you hate yourself for your son and his children out there because of what you did on the Bear that day, Three-Persons, but you don't hate yourself like I do. Nobody can.

The Cat Man nodded about her bare neck, not able to look at or smell anything else, and then he placed a hand on her shoulder to be sure this wasn't a trick, and he bit into her deep.

Her whole body shuddered against me hard, and she made a noise of being afraid that I've never heard so close to my ear before, that I still hear every time I close my eyes, and then he was drinking deep, his eyes open to watch me, to be sure this wasn't a trick.

But then, like happens with the best blood, his eyes rolled back, seeing nothing, and he was just feeding, and that's when I bit into her just like he was doing, Three-Persons.

Not into him, because that would knock me down, but into the girl's shoulder that was right under my mouth. And he was right. Her blood, her taste, it made even Pikuni blood taste like it was from a silver fish. This blood would let me go a year without feeding, I could tell. She was a taste I didn't even know could be real.

I didn't let myself swallow, though.

It's the hardest thing I've ever done.

For this to work, I couldn't.

And also I had to keep the blood from my tongue in my mouth.

When her blood came in, it mixed with mine.

Instead of swallowing, I pushed what I had back into her.

If one drop of the Cat Man had knocked me down for two days or two moons or however long it was, then a whole mouthful would have to hurt him.

She was starting to jerk and die in my arms by the time he got to it.

When he did, when he tasted my blood in his mouth like poison, his eyes rolled back to me, and he knew what I had done, but it was too late.

He threw Kills-in-the-Water to the side like an empty doll and charged me, pulling hard enough that he left his good foot behind in the traps all the way up to his knee. It didn't matter to him. He had me down on the ground and was roaring into my face like a real-lion before the blood spasmed his body, made him fall over to the side, shaking, my blood frothing on his lips like a mad big-mouth. He was still reaching for me but his fingers were blind, his eyes were going grey like clouds, and he was weak like a puppy, weak enough I could kick him away, into two of the other traps. They bit into his arm and his hip and he screamed, and then he didn't scream anymore.

I stood, stumbled to the fire, lit Lone Horn's pipe and came back to him, jammed it into his mouth so that the next breath he took, it was napikwan tobacco.

This made my blood in him even worse.

I gave him the pipe over and over for the rest of the day, until all the rivers and streams of blood in him went hard and black through his skin, even though it was Pikuni skin.

His cheeks went in like he was dead and his eyes didn't move anymore, and I used a rock to knock all his teeth out, and I used the other traps for his arms, and I threw his broken off foot and leg into the lake, and he was dead enough that I went back to the ice-river for the bars of the cage to use for stakes on the traps, and drove them deep so that not even a real-bear could pull them up.

The Cat Man was no real-bear.

But when I put my ear to his chest, he wasn't quite dead. There was still a small, small sound in there.

I spent the next two days making a scaffold for Kills-in-the-Water up in one of the trees on the island, and when I buried her after washing her in the lake, my face was so red I hardly had any blood in me at all. It was how I'd cried when I buried my own children and wives. It was crying with my whole body, with everything that makes me Pikuni.

But Pikuni fathers don't kill their daughters.

On the third day, the Cat Man coughed and turned his head to the side, threw something up, and I saw that it was a ring with a horn design on it, a ring he had probably been swallowing over and over for almost five hundred winters, to keep from losing it.

I threw it in the lake and hammered the iron bars of his traps deeper.

On the fifth day, I used a net I wove to catch an omkomi, the big-fish. Because it was snowing the first snow, the big-fish was hungry, easy to trick.

I cut it open and let the blood go into the Cat Man's mouth.

He drank it deep and opened his mouth for more.

Over the next four winters, I fed him more big-fish than I can count. Every moon it was twenty or thirty more. All I did was fish, and feed myself. By now I was going down to Old Agency and Badger Creek and only eating the Pikuni who were dying. It wasn't good, but they weren't little girls, I told myself. And I only did it when I was starving.

Slowly, fish by fish, the Cat Man stopped being the Cat Man.

I had been telling myself that eating mice would be like dying, but eating fish is worse, because once you finally become one, you're in the water, and the other fish you eat only make you more and more an underwater person. Muskrats and otter and beaver go in the water, but a muskrat is the only one small enough for a big-fish to eat. Maybe a baby white-cheeks, but I've never seen that.

At first the Cat Man's skin went silver, and then his eyes changed, went to both sides of his head, and then thin mouths opened on his neck in flaps, so he was drowning in the air. This is when I used a digging stick to carve a channel to him, so the lake water could come in and he could breathe, because there were more big-fish he needed to drink from.

By the fourth winter, he was as long as he had been tall, but he was a big-fish. I think you call this a sturgeon. It's a boss fish, and mean, but it's still just a fish, trapped in the water.

I finally let him go during the moon when the jackrabbits whistle at night, and he swam away, I think without any memory of having lived four hundred and fifty winters. He was just a big-fish now, in a big lake, and if he ever saw his ring down there, he didn't know what it was.

I walked across the ice back into the Backbone, and because I needed to be Neetsetupi, even just for a day, I came down at last.

Crossing a creek, there was a roan horse using its hoof to break the ice. It still had red paint on its haunch and an eagle feather tied in its mane. This is how I knew it was Pikuni.

I came in behind it, ran my hand on its back to its mane, and lowered to a knee to push through the ice with my hand.

The horse reared and turned away when I did, but I was already there on the other side holding its forehead to mine hard. I was crying again, and when I pulled away to let the horse go, to let it run away like it wanted to, my blood was around its eyes and in its nose, and this is a thing about being a Cat Man I never knew. It's that our blood can make a horse not afraid.

Maybe dogs and people too, I haven't tried, don't want to know.

But it works with horses. I don't like to do that to them, but I can.

Calmed now, this horse came back to the new hole in the ice and drank, its sides swelling out like this from it, making me miss water, and when it was done I climbed on and rode for the first time in fourteen winters, for the first time since you killed Heavy Runner, Three-Persons, and this horse took me along the creek, into the frozen grass. I was hoping to find a camp to watch. Not the Small Robes, because they had to be still broken up from the Cat Man, but maybe the Fat Melters or the Black-Patched Moccasins or the Gopher-Eaters. It didn't matter, I just wanted to see a Pikuni.

I had been gone too long, though.

There were no lodges anymore, no camps.

All the Pikuni now, they were at Old Agency starving.

I rode through in a striped blanket I found blowing away across the hard crust of snow and there were dead people the whole ride, frozen, nobody to tend to them.

This was what we call Starvation Winter, Three-Persons, and I say it like that because I don't want you to write the sounds down in your book and trap it, make them small like all the other words. Because this winter isn't small for us. Six hundred Pikuni died in the snow because rations never came. Even more people than died on the Bear.

Finally I couldn't look at it anymore, so I rode north, into the whiteness.

After almost a day of it, I saw another rider through the blowing snow. He was on a small pony. He saw me back and lifted his
hand.

I let him ride up but stayed in my blanket, pretending the cold
mattered to me.

He explained that he was making a count of how many Pikuni
were left on the reservation.

This was the first time I heard that word, Three-Persons.

We used to call our home Nittowsinan.

Now we don't.

I sat up higher on the horse, because this new word hurt me.

The funny little napikwan said he was the Indian agent here. He
was leaning in to try to see my face in the blanket.

"Are you Piegan?" he asked.

I looked at him from the darkness of the blanket, and then I
looked north, to where Chief Mountain and Weasel Plume would be.

"Am I Amskapi Pikuni," I repeated, thinking about it.

The little Indian agent nodded, waiting and waiting, but I finally
couldn't lie to him. After everything bad and wrong I had done, I
couldn't add one more thing.

I shook my head no, touched my heels to the horse under me,
and we pushed past this scared little Indian agent, and my number
isn't on that count, and I know I'll never be Kills-in-the-Water standing in front of her brother with that knife, to stab the world until it
kills her back.

But I tried, Three-Persons.

I tried as hard as I could.

And so I rode in my blanket on that horse through the blowing
snow Coldmaker was throwing at us to make the world new again,
and it was so thick and fast that at first I didn't see the large brown
four-legged moving slow through the trees to the side of this steep
uphill we were on. At first I knew it was a real-bear, but then I

remembered they were all dreaming about berries in their dens, and also the horse wasn't scared.

This meant it had to be Beaver Chief, out getting sticks for his lodge under cover of the storm.

I was back where Tall Dog and Peasy and Hunts-to-the-Side had died.

Where I had died too.

I reined us around, through the taller trees on the other side, and when I came back, I had as many big sticks as I could hold on my lap. Good ones I had broken off from high up on trees, from the back of the horse.

I left them stacked on the top of the snow for Beaver Chief, and then I turned, taking us uphill again.

It felt good for the horse's hooves to go through the snow to the ground.

It made it like I was a person again.

We went higher and higher, colder and colder, the ice frozen on my face and in the horse's mane and tale, and then Chief Mountain was there between gusts of white, so close and huge that we stopped, had to suck our breaths in. It's always been there, but each time it's new again.

I held my hand up to it in greeting, and in honor. I held my hand up but my face was down, because behind me was a whole camp of the dead, their throats red and open.

But I was home at last.

This is where my confession is over, Three-Persons.

I leave you now with your dead.

The Absolution of Three-Persons

May 26, 1912

The mice are back.

I don't know whether this is a good thing or a bad one.

It does mean Cordelia has yet to return. I think of the calloused, dirty hands of the rough men who visit her current residence more than I should, I know. I don't like the way they touch her, at least in my imaginings, but there's naught an old Lutheran pastor can do to remedy the situation and finally calm his nerves. Would I dart in through and amongst, tuck her under my arm, and run my limping run out the door whilst patron and prostitute alike watched this frantic effort, a grin of benevolent amusement creasing some of those weathered faces?

It would be the talk of Miles City. The number of my congregation would swell again, as it did when the humps were being left out on the prairie. And perhaps the new sheriff, whenever one is elected, would finally come to my door to make certain inquiries. About which I would tell him it's my assigned duty to save souls, isn't it? Even the lowliest, and most feline.

Or perhaps I would try to convince him that I spirited Cordelia away to solve my rodent problem.

It's very much as if the mice can smell the rot and decay that but previously occupied the pews of the chapel. It's redolent enough to their sensitive noses that they also come here to worship, even though I've washed and scrubbed and scrubbed again, such that I had to discreetly ask a parishioner for stain with which to color again the pews, the floor.

Would but that I could equally take my memory down to the grain as such. But so says this whole nation, I know.

I'm just now unlimbering this log from its clandestine nook, which I'm satisfied my savage visitor was apparently unable to sniff out. I'm only just now unlimbering it after a fortnight, as I fear these pages falling open to the entry before last, forcing me to be again in this chapel with the dead all around.

Good Stab must be eminently satisfied with this.

While it would have been simple for one so young and vital as he to dispatch this pastor, it's, to him, more fitting torture to instead leave me endlessly mulling over my misdecisions. Either that or, having strongly suggested my coming execution, he denies me the day it's actually to occur, meaning I wake each morning affrighted with certainty, knowing that it will be this day, and then the next, and the next, and suchwise do all my remaining days become polluted with a mix of certainty and narrow escape, which, in accumulation, serves to grind my frailty unto dust, which I cough up continually, and wipe on the lower portions of my robes.

I have to presume that my parishioners know full well, in spite of my avoidance in addressing it from the pulpit, what transpired here but recently. The deputies who removed the corpses from the chapel were sworn to secrecy, but that amounts less to word of the spectacle not leaking out than it does to that leak having no clearly named source.

I of course did give those grim faced deputies all of Good Stab's aliases, including even the temporary appellation Blackie. As well, they know he was the one responsible for the humps, the postmaster, the erstwhile sheriff and his boon companions, and a large portion of the town's population of dogs, but his motivations, being pagan and savage——look upon his works and despair!——are well beyond decent civilization's ken.

This old man won't be enlightening them, concerning that. The infestation of mice is more of a concern, currently.

If I knew no better, I would suspect they're being delivered by the bucketful as some sort of message.

Perhaps their creeping presence is due to my unanticipated lack of appetite. Though the women of the congregation persist in delivering sweets and victuals with each visit, be it Sunday or no, I find myself no longer desirous of that which but previously compelled me. I now eat only enough to keep shuffling forward through the day, and I do so with a distaste that would be an affront to the person I was but weeks previously.

Leaving, of course, the mice to swarm my pantry.

Instead of leaving them to feed thusly, I now, after dark, have become the old man who feeds the new generation of local dogs off his back stoop. I know it doesn't make of them allies, that they only use me to fill their bellies, but, watching them gorge themselves mindlessly as they do, I can tell myself that they are the sinners, choosing their own gluttony over decent behavior to their fellow man.

Them, not I.

It's a ruse that surely will crumble in the doing, but for the moment, it suffices.

As do the eggs.

Where I formerly had no cause to keep them on hand, as I'm no baker, Frieda Zimmerman's paganistic method for ferreting out the proximity of servants of the Pit provides me a bit of solace——as well as my dwindling congregation.

Each Sunday, so as to assuage their lingering suspicions about the sanctity of the chapel they again sit in, I make a demonstration of breaking a singular egg into a clear chalice. The yellow of the yolk shot through with a thread of blood is the gateway through which we walk together, into the service, and about it no one would ever utter a word, making mummers of us all, in hopes God doesn't notice the superstition we now entwine with his Holy Word.

Such is life on the frontier. Such is life in Miles City, Montana, in this year of the Lord, 1912.

Including, though I wish it weren't so, as it was the immediate cause of my sermon slipping completely from my mind, the unexpected presence of an Indian visage at the back of the chapel once more, wearing those selfsame darkened spectacles.

My heart rose beating into my throat, my hand trembled near the bone, but then by degrees I realized it was only Amos Short Ribs, and that the light hurt his eyes, yes, but that was from overconsumption of spirits, not the presence of a human hunger.

That he now wore a black feather on his forehead, licked wet on its backside, can mean nothing, of course, save that he also wishes to torment me for his own twisted amusement, which is perhaps a predilection shared by all Blackfeet.

After worship, I walked him down to Mose, whereupon I gifted this Indian visitor with a bottle, and told Mose, in private, to keep him stocked in such manner, and to place it on my tab, so long as it was nothing from the top shelf.

Better I accrue a debt I can never pay than that a second Blackfeet come to tell me his story. They are a curséd people, and the quicker they become tillers of the soil and tenders of cattle, the better, not only for Montana, but for the sanity and sanctity of this old man, who longs only to till the soil of his parishioners' hopes and fears, and tend after their souls in whatsoever manner I best can.

As my confession, I here confess that it feels good to return to this practice of expelling my thoughts in delicately traced ink, line by line. It means those thoughts can stop swirling behind my forehead, and in the tremble of my fingers. Perhaps now I may yet even sleep unfitfully, never mind the distinct sound of mice breeding in the walls.

I go now to attempt such sleep, lest this legion of rodents rise and carry me away.

June 2, 1912

I trust that these be my last words, save the ones I entreat my savage abductor with on our long walk out into the nighttime prairie, where my bones will bleach unceremoniously, with no witnesses.

It's Sunday now, again, interminably, and Sun Chief yet blazes across the sky.

With the fall of night, I know the darkness in the street will be matched by the darkness standing behind me when I least expect it.

I feel I have failed in whatever vague task Good Stab left me with. Was I to burn the church with myself in it? Were the mice supposed to have gnawed on my ankles and so infested me with their nature? Was I to have, as Good Stab repeatedly suggested he himself is soon to do, eaten their small bodies one after another until whiskers extend from above my lip, out past the limits of my face? Would all of this count as apology enough? Could it buy me passage into what I intended to be my last years of service to my parishioners, my Faith, or is there no effort that could wring the sin from my past?

I have to think the latter is, to Good Stab, the case, at least as pertains to me. Would that I were like he claims to be, so that he could kill me over and over for what I've done.

I have but one life to use as recompense, however.

Tonight, I spend it.

Leaving me this afternoon to mull, to dwell, to pace, to dust, to straighten, to hunch again over these pages, attempting either vainly or in vain to follow a line of ink to Truth, to Revelation.

None from my congregation has inquired after their pastor after today's failed sermon, either. For which I take no umbrage. The leper should be left to his isolation, n'est-ce pa?

On my simpering way out the rear door, which I should just go ahead and admit was a retreat from the quick into the land of the dead, I could feel the congregation shuffling and whispering amongst themselves, confirming with each other that I was indeed abandoning them. When the door to the parsonage shut with finality, I have to assume they themselves left as well. Either that or one of them rose to the moment and delivered a sermon of such vigor and persuasiveness that their previous pastor's meager efforts were immediately forgotten.

I know not.

And all this after I again broke the egg into its chalice, to show that we were yet in the presence of God, not his opposite.

The egg lied, however.

I know because I made it do so.

In the antechambers behind the altar, where I prepared the Eucharist the night before, I took from the basket the egg I intended to break for them, beginning us again. My hands not being so steady anymore, however, the egg shook loose and fell to the ground, cracking open between my feet.

Its innards were corrupt, rotten, black.

As was the next, and the next, and the last one.

My vision dulled such that I was floating in near blackness myself. Better in that pernicious moment that I would have teetered over and cracked my head on a sharp corner than do what I did—— scurry out the back door to the parsonage.

There in the cooling rack were the other eggs my parishioners supply me more of than I can use, now. I need but one a week, for the service, but they bring me a bounty each Sunday, such that I'm aswim in eggs.

I tested one nearby the window, and when it cracked yellow, guaranteeing no nachzehrer had been in the parsonage, I took the next for the chalice.

It was subterfuge of the most rank and regrettable kind, but I was desperate, and thought God would forgive such chicanery if it meant His flock waiting in the chapel could be appeased.

I should have known the attempt would result in abject failure.

Standing finally at the podium, broken egg shell betwixt my fingers, the faces of the congregation beatific, ready to be chastised and chastened closer to God, I chanced to look up to the ventilation window to assure myself there was no Indian gentleman sitting up there, his naked brown legs hanging from the rafters among his black robes.

Again, there wasn't.

However, that window I had propped open so as to take advantage of the midday breeze had admitted another visitor.

A raven sat up there now, its head turned to the side so as to see me with one black marble of an eye. I drew my breath sharply in, and, recovering somewhat, attempted a pleasant mien for those in the frontmost pews.

"Let us begin," I said, guiding them all to standing, which is how we've always commenced a service.

Following my habit, I then leaned down over the top of the podium, to turn the page of my breviary with the appearance of measured thoughtfulness——the previous night, as always, I had left it as such, so that the congregation could know the last week was over, and we were now, together, broaching into the subsequent one, and after that, there would be another page, another week, and on and on into Eternity, as it should be.

My hand turning the page, however, was already whispering to me that something was amiss.

The backs of my fingers, accustomed to the velvety softness of the purple stole draped thereupon, were instead feeling something more coarse, with more depth.

It was a buffalo robe, draped over my podium.

I looked quickly away from it, certain that when my eyes came back, it would be the purple stole, but when I gazed into the pews, they were full again, as they hadn't been a moment before.

Sitting out there now were my son and his sons, dead but alive enough to look up to me. Livinius Clarkson was in attendance, watching me as well, and Sheriff Doyle was in there, and also Dove, both of them with their hats in their laps. Dove had been stitched together after his time under the train, and his seams were yet suppurating.

In every other empty space were the dark faces of the women and children and old people who had been sick in their lodges that cold, cold day on the Marias.

They were each looking directly at me, into me.

And, as 173 people can't fit amongst my congregation, they were also standing along the wall three and four deep, and I knew if I counted that the number would climb higher than that recorded.

These Blackfeet's hair was icy with snow, and their hands were crossed in their laps, and they were waiting for me to breathe in and intone The Word.

"I'm sorry, I'm sorry I'm sorry I'm sorry," I said, quietly at first but then louder and with more desperation, not speaking so much to my congregation as to these unexpected visitors, and then, after carefully closing my breviary one final time, I proceeded to scuttle off through the rear entrance, my robe catching awkwardly in the closing door, such that I had to open it again slightly so as to make my shameful escape.

Now, these hours later, the chapel is empty again.

The front door is unlocked, for whomsoever is posted here after my disappearance.

My hand shakes, writing this, or trying to, so I need must stop, and await my inevitable visitor.

By the time he arrives, I will have hidden this log in such a way that it will never be uncovered. Not in the chapel or even the church, but whereso I know he doesn't set foot, as the yolks over there are as yet yellow.

I think it's best these words fade and blow away. Or, as is more likely the case, it's best that the mice in the walls feast on them.

At least they'll be of some use, then.

My time in this world draws to a close.

I now long only to scream and scream when the parchment of my skin is removed from my back while I yet live.

Perhaps, while doing it, I will finally see the sharp teeth Good Stab professes to have, and then I will know for certainty that he wasn't lying to me, and I will finally, as he portended, believe him, and his story.

But, too, it will be dark out on the prairie, I know.

As it is in my heart.

My pipe is empty, now.

I believe it has been since January 23rd, 1870.

THE
BEAUCARNE
MANUSCRIPT

part 2

12 January 2013

A dayworker in Communication and Journalism reaches into the crumbling past and pulls a piece of history up, *laboriously* transcribes it *while* teaching two survey courses over the fall semester, and . . . this effort isn't "meritorious" enough get her over that promotion hump, into the promised land of tenure.

Never mind that, just before Thanksgiving, I had to up the magnification of my readers from sacrificing my eyes to that spidery old script, the gall ink long bled through to the back of its pages, which Lydia Ackerman's scanner seems bound and determined to pack into each high-res image.

To make it all stupider?

Arthur Beaucarne, my great-great-great-not-so-great grandfather, is still just as gone—mystery *not* solved.

He just ends it right there, with the date of that massacre, hides the journal in the wall of that parsonage for that construction worker to find, and . . . who knows. I get that his behavior was erratic those last few weeks—I'm pretty sure mine would have been too—but still, even in 1912, if someone's just suddenly not there . . . did anybody wonder where the doddering old pastor went?

These and other questions, never to be answered by yours truly, as the project's now, officially, dead. There won't be a book contract. I won't call campuses my home for the next few decades, like my dad did. And I might, depending on if he wakes back up or not down in his facility in Denver, and if the snow clears so I can get down there, have to tell him this. Because who doesn't need even more disappointment on their deathbed.

I am sorry, Dad, for whatever that's worth.

I probably should have gone into chemistry like you wanted for me, yes, okay. Is there less sniping over there? More objectivity? How about department politics? Associate professors so entrenched in the way it was when *they* were junior faculty that they can't allow that this might just be a new world happening all around them? Do women over there not get plugged into every service obligation, *keeping* them from having time to publish?

Never mind, never mind. Just venting. Again. But, no worries, anyone who hacks my laptop—getting this document ready for the committee, I went back and burned away all the half-ass footnotes I'd tagged in, promising to flesh them out later. No great loss, there. They were just me trying to figure out if my "greatest"-grandfather was good or evil, wondering if Good Stab was Socrates to Arthur Beaucarne's Plato, some deep dives into the microfichy waters, and a lot of notes chasing down antique vocabulary—which, I don't know, this last one seems pretty meritorious to me, and not *un*fitting for a "Communications" professor.

One of my anonymous committee members even played that word-game *with* me in the report, via a comment I guess they thought they'd deleted, but, being a citizen of the scary new world, I could toggle it back into visibility: *if Dr. E continues pursuing this unique project, she should consider the term "tresayle" instead of "great-great-great-grandfather." The French are so much more efficient when discussing lineage.*

Of course, as there's only one member of my T&P committee who did their graduate work in Paris, her identity isn't as much of a *mystère* as she might hope.

But, I can't say I'm not fascinated by the superficial harmony of using a French term for someone with such a decadently Gallic name. "Beaucarne" *does* translate out to "beautiful meat," I mean—which, okay, I'll admit is suspicious. And I have no way to disprove their other comment about the possibility that the project I printed and bound for them isn't the transcription of an early twentieth century Lutheran pastor at all, but—more of their unhidden comments—*a spurious work of early twentieth-century fiction owing a certain something to its contemporary,* Dracula*, but being traipsed out under a nom de plume surely meant to be seen through.*

Your French is showing, madame.

But, if I can be allowed a reply, I did actually look into that dubious nom, which took no small amount of campus resources and "scholarly rigor." Apparently my *grandfather*, whom I also never knew, carried the family name "Flowers" until he was sixteen—surprise.

Born in 1913 in San Francisco to a chambermaid who died delivering him in secret, Artemis Flowers is the product of a brief union between Arthur "Arty" Flowers and a young woman who helped keep his father's house—the maid the Pinkerton agent Harrison Dove (I found him too, yes) mentions as being distraught over the disappearance of her young paramour, presumably right after she had unwittingly conceived my grandfather.

What the esteemed Harrison Dove failed to mention, however, was that Arty Flowers's *grandmother* was still alive in 1913. Alive and well-established both.

Ada Neismith, née Murray, was then fifty-eight years old. Born in Arcadia, Missouri, in 1855 and both orphaned and dispossessed by the Civil War—I've got a blurry PDF of the birth certificate—she found herself in Montana Territory that pivotal winter of 1870, having had to resort to prostitution in order to keep moving west, a fact she refused to be shamed by in a bracingly candid interview near the end of her life in 1928.

She was the redheaded woman Arthur Beaucarne was with immediately following the Marias Massacre, I guess at . . . Fort Benton? Doesn't matter.

What does is that the child born the following October in San Francisco was Benjamin Flowers, the first "hump"—*ugh*—my great-great-grandfather mentions. As to how Ada was so certain this child was a result of her union with Arthur Beaucarne, she says in that last interview ("Available, T&P Committee, in three serialized installments through the California Digital Newspaper Project" . . .) that he was the only gentleman caller with which she failed to use the pessary she was otherwise insistent about (hackers, please, image-search that one up). This was due to the fact that Arthur Beaucarne, nicknamed "Holy Joe" due to the Bible he always carried, assured her that his intended vocation meant he carried no social diseases, which I guess is a claim that could pass muster in the Wild and Woolly West.

Anyway, for the first sixteen years of his life, Artemis Flowers, my grandfather, so named to honor his missing father Arty, went by the florid name his missing father and grandfather had carried. However, as outlined in this brief article from the December 12th, 1928, edition of the *The San Francisco News* (a four-page daily specializing in stories of one or two paragraphs), that was a mistake that had been compounding already then for nearly six decades:

Oh but to be young and unlettered in the Wild West! Such was the case for the recently passed San Francisco matron Mrs. Ada Neismith, widow of none other than J. T. Neismith, whom everyone reading these pages is of course familiar with, as he was one of the early investors in The Call & Post. According to a recent series of interviews posted by the Chronicle, it was Mrs. Neismith's lack of literary familiarity that resulted in her son and his subsequent family living under a name coined on the spot.

What happened was Mrs. Neismith, fresh from the birthing room, was asked who the father was. When she mumbled the only name she had known him by other than his soldierly nickname, what was heard by the scribe of a nurse entering the information was Bouquet. As this medical officiant, having been herself wooed, knew this French term but thought it beneficial to copy it down in English, she translated it to Flowers when it should have been the meatier term Beaucarne. And that, faithful readers, is how Benjamin Flowers and his progeny, all absconded from these environs probably due to impending scandal or ruin, became known as such. As for myself, I prefer the mis-heard name, as navigating the spelling of the historically accurate name feels unpatriotic, so thanks are due to that American hero of a nurse who altered it. I hope she got some flowers for her effort.

On her deathbed the week before this, attended by her only grandchild Artemis, then sixteen years old, Ada Neismith, having suffered some irreparable rupture with her deceased husband, returned Artemis's lost family name to him, and with the last of her fortune had her attorney make that name legal, such that my father was the first born under it since Arthur Beaucarne himself in 1839—1839 being a mere six years after Good Stab claims to have been born (*no* birth certificate), if his birth indeed shares a year with the Great Leonid Meteor Shower of 1833.

Phew.

That's one footnote sort of recovered. Don't expect more, hackers.

Anyway, what all of this means is that I'm now the *second* to have been born with that name in the shiny new twentieth century. Second and presumably the last *ever*, my prospects for motherhood being not exactly promising.

But I have Taz My Cat, currently in my lap. Taz, six months' lease on this apartment, a PhD draped in cobwebs, a dead pastor's complicated confession about a massacre nobody remembers, and seven years of teaching experience, which, come the end of spring semester, won't matter at all, as . . . find a new life, Etsy! It'll be fun! An adventure at forty-three years old!

Yeah.

Okay, I'm back.

Where I was: out on the balcony being dramatic, burning all those card stock journal pages. Open flames are explicitly forbidden according to The Social Laramie, this apartment complex, but it was worth Marcie from the front office's censure to watch that paper writhe and twist in agony under those yellow flames, and then crumble to ash. It made my dark balcony feel like the chapel of the church I picture Arthur Beaucarne writing in, even, which was kind of neat at first.

It wasn't neat at second.

Staring into those flames dialed my pupils down to specks, meaning when I looked out into the Big Dark—I'm on the north side of the property—I couldn't *clearly* see the shape I'm sort of sure was maybe standing out there, but I could . . . sort of see it?

Him, I mean.

I dropped the last burning page and it lifted away like a prayer.

There was definitely a man behind a tree out there where there's no sidewalk, no trail. I could only see him from the chest down, but that was enough to make me step back fast, against the sliding door, hard enough to shatter that cold glass all around me.

I pushed forward away from that even though I didn't understand what it was I'd done yet, what was falling around me. I jerked ahead and grabbed onto the balcony railing, still desperately trying to see that man out there, but the snow did its skirling, powdery thing, and in a sweep of whiteness, he was gone.

My first thought, the one I still can't shake, who cares about what's rational, was that this was that wooden Jesus that was supposed to have burned in that fire above the Yellowstone. That he's still out there lumbering around in his stiff way, naked, pale and headless, his grasping fingers charred to ash, his neck stump trailing smoke.

But I'm being dramatic.

It was Arthur Beaucarne, I know.

He haunts the prairie still, my tresayle.

Or, me.

17 January 2013

Just when I think I'm done with this file.

The same way I was able to un-invisible my T&P committee's comments, I was able to find this whole huge document in the trash, recover it. Like a certain legendary monster, it refuses to die.

Unlike my dad.

She said glibly, the bad daughter. The worst daughter. The newly minted orphan. The last of the Beaucarnes.

I got the news about him five days ago. He passed peacefully in his sleep down in Denver. His ashes should be here today, which seems like a scary fast turnaround. The facility he was in, I guess eager to fill the bed—death is a volume business—they sent his belongings Priority the day-of, like I'm supposed to furnish his eternal resting place with the stuff, make an altar or something.

I loved you, Dad, but, please, let's be real.

It was one banker's box. One banker's box for seventy-seven years.

Inside was a framed photo of my father and my mother at some lake in Yellowstone, before her cancer; an incomplete set of Zane Grey novels I know he cherished and had always been looking for the rest of, so he could live in them; a small painting of a terrier he had a different story for each time I asked—it was our game, and I'm glad he never told me anything approaching the truth; his secret pack of cigarettes that I think all the nurses knew about; three DVDs, all westerns of course; his worn-thin wedding band, which I admit I cried over, and now wear on my left thumb; a yellow Case pocket-knife with the smaller blade broken but reground to a chisel point; and a Bible with letters tucked inside, suggesting he used it less as spiritual inspiration, more as a folder for important stuff.

I can't tell if the Bible is Lutheran. I don't know how to tell.

I opened the box on the same day I got the call from Lydia Acker-man at the "Rolling Wren Library" in Bozeman—that's not the spell-ing, but I don't feel like looking it up. Anyway, after asking about my progress with the transcription, which they still think I've yet to complete, this special collections breathed in to tell me the real reason for this call.

She's had to call the police.

That mouse-gnawed buckskin Arthur Beaucarne's day journal had been in for so long had, upon forensic inspection meant to iden-tify the subspecies of deer, revealed itself to be not from a deer at all, but a person—that was how she phrased it: "person," not "human."

I know this Lydia Ackerman kept speaking, assuring me that po-lice involvement was just to be sure this "artifact" was indeed older than any cold case on the books in Miles City, but her voice was small and distant.

Much closer was Good Stab, telling Arthur Beaucarne that there would come a point where he, "Three-Persons," would believe this fantastic, unlikely life story.

It was as if he were speaking across the generations, directly to me.

And my dad was still dead, turned to ash.

Lydia Ackerman finally managed to reel me back into the conversation by asking if I'd decided yet on the fate of this journal. Was I going to donate it, perhaps—emphasis on her hopefulness? Auction it—*not* her recommendation? Reclaim it for my personal collection, so long as I have a climate-controlled space to keep it in, and am trained in preservation, and want to hoard this one-of-a-kind knowledge away from the world until it crumbles to dust?

What I answered back was "How far back do cold cases go, do you know?"

"Excuse me?" she asked back, switching ears on the phone, it sounded like—giving me *all* her attention.

I told her I would let her know about the fate of the journal, and gently ended the call.

Human skin.

And not just any human. Benjamin Flowers's probably, if my searches on how long it takes to treat a hide are halfway right, and can apply to people. Benjamin Flowers, Arthur Beaucarne's son. My great-grandfather. I don't know what the French word for his tanned skin might be.

When sleep wouldn't come a couple of nights ago, maybe three, I decided to say goodbye to my father the way he would have wanted: by watching his movies before lugging them down to the thrift store, which I'm going to count as his memorial service.

The first was *Jeremiah Johnson* with Robert Redford, which I remember always being in the VCR when I was eleven—I *hated* that guy who kills all the bears. The second was *Rio Bravo* with Dean Martin and John Wayne. I was in and out through most of it. The musical numbers probably weren't meant to put the viewer to sleep, but that's what they did to me. The third was a Kevin Costner one I had also seen before, on a forever-ago date: *Dances with Wolves*.

Given what I had spent the fall transcribing—was I ready to see Indians yet?—I paused to brew a pot of coffee and watched this one through to the raised hands at the end, where the Indian guy with the great hair acknowledges the white soldier as a friend. It was touching. My father the hard sciences guy had always been more sentimental than he let on, as the letters he saved in his Bible suggests.

I thanked him, ejected this last disc and put it by the door with the rest.

It was coming on dawn, and I told myself I wanted to wait for Taz to get back before giving in to the pillow, maybe see Sun Chief glimmering through the clouds, but I didn't make it.

That was yesterday, I guess. Or maybe the day before? Time feels like it's passing differently in this white-out. It's moving in spurts and clumps. But, what I do know for sure is that Taz wasn't there for my movie marathon. Which was cool. It was night, and that's when he roams, does his cat stuff. He clocks in for his shift at about my bedtime. But, if he came back after I fell asleep on the couch, I didn't know it. And—I don't want to say this, don't want to make it real—I haven't seen him now for something like thirty-six hours? Maybe longer. He's a survivor, no doubt, but it's January in Wyoming, and he can't have too many lives left.

I've left the taped-over sliding glass door open enough for him to slide through, who cares about heating all of Laramie, Dad, but, with no proper cat door, does he think he doesn't live here anymore? Taz, is that it? You think someone else moved in and you don't have a home? A person?

You do, you so do.

Lydia Ackerman is still calling, eager for my decision, but I haven't made it yet. I have to assume she's also struggled through some of my tresayle's handwriting, but, since she didn't key on me asking about cold cases, I bet she's still in the first few years, when he was the new pastor in town, and just writing daily junk—not under tenure pressure, she hasn't pushed through as far as I have, to Good Stab, has been more concerned with getting it all scanned in, posted in that directory she made me co-"owner" of, like I care.

Just today, she finally got me on the line again by dialing in from her personal phone. Hers was the first call to come in after I put the flyers for Taz up, so I answered before the first ring was done.

The excuse I gave her for not having made a decision yet is my father's passing.

Sorry, Dad. But, thanks for the assist, I guess?

Your cremains are waiting at the front office now, since they won't fit in my mailbox. I just got the courtesy call from Busybody Marcie, up there. She didn't offer condolences, because that would mean she'd read whatever warning label's on the Priority Express package, but it was there in her voice.

I hate her.

I don't even know why I'm still writing in this file, to be honest. I think it's because I don't have Taz to talk to anymore?

Where are you, bud?

I can't do this without you, man.

Classes start next week—delayed due to this winter storm—but, instead of manically prepping the opening-day salvo for my survey lecture, quoting this speech, that speech, threading some McLuhan through it all like any Communications prof is legally bound to, I've been walking the grounds of the apartment complex with the digital recorder I use to record my lectures, which has a little speaker you can actually hear a few feet away.

The sound on it is a can of cat food being sumptuously opened.

My feet are frozen, my cheeks blistered with cold, but it's got to be worse for Taz out there, doesn't it?

Now I'm back from doing what I knew I shouldn't have done, but can't help: peeling through photos of him as a kitten with his then-favorite toy; him with stitches in his ear; him covered in this or that adventure, him being the most perfect scamp to ever scamp.

Desperate, I even opened Dad's Bible at last. Is there a chapter on lost cats? A prayer for lost pets?

The first thing I was surprised by was that, handwritten on the front endpapers—silk, I think?—were a few lines of encouragement from his grandfather to my dad's dad "Art," both of whom, I guess, attended a certain Lutheran church up in Miles City, minus their skin. It's unsettling to be suddenly touching actual history, isn't it? Reading about them in Arthur Beaucarne's spidery script is one thing; running my fingers over the slight indentations left on marbled pink silk is another thing altogether.

As was the third letter tucked into the pages, the first two having been from my mother—one from when they were dating, one from her hospital room, both of which reduced me to a sobbing mess on the couch. For them. For Taz. For me.

This third letter, however, had never been opened, which I found odd. Until I put my new glasses on to study the logo in the return-address corner at the upper-left. It was an official seal. One ringed with feathers, I guess like looking down the stovepipe part of a chief's headdress, down to an outline of what I first took to be a state.

It's a nation, actually. The Blackfeet one.

I don't know what's worse: where this letter's from, or the fact that it's not opened.

Now that I'm sitting on the couch with it, though, there's something I like even less.

There's no postmark. There's not even a stamp.

This isn't to my father at all.

It's to me.

Left by someone who stood over my father's deathbed.

20 January 2013

I'm in no mood for it this week, Marcie.

All my lost-cat flyers on my doormat, along with a note citing the procedure for getting permission, and "the necessary stamp," to distribute materials around the complex?

I'll show you a stamp.

Taz is gone, can't you see?

I admit to spending the last twenty-four hours in the fetal position on my couch, alternately bawling my eyes out and punching the cushions. I also admit to pacing back and forth from the kitchen to here, sneering and showing my teeth to that letter from the Blackfeet Nation, which I don't think I can handle opening yet, maybe ever.

Why couldn't that construction worker have just crumbled that journal when he first touched it, before he even knew what he was touching? Then maybe I'd do something actually on-track to bolster my tenure portfolio. Then I don't have to know what blood's in my veins. That massacre can just stay in the past where it belongs.

That parsonage is going to be a battered women's shelter now, I read.

Good for it. Good for those women. Good for Miles City—for all of Montana, and its hard-handed men with their oh-so-fragile egos.

I hope every egg that breaks on the kitchen floor in that shelter is bright yellow.

Maybe that's where I'll go, even, when this lease is up. Etsy Beaucarne, ready to volunteer, or help finish painting the walls, whatever. I can even teach Journalism, Communication. I can quote from a variety of speeches. Which are practically sermons. It's where my inheritance and my education meet.

Ugh.

That's a convergence I don't need, thanks.

What I also don't need anymore of ever: what I just saw in the hall, coming back from the bathroom. Which—I know what antihistamines do to me, I know I shouldn't take them, but all this crying, my nose, and who cares anyway.

What I'm saying is Benadryl always leaves you a little loopy, Etsy, so, don't freak out.

Still?

I either saw or thought I saw a tiny grey shadow scurrying across the carpet in front of me and into the kitchen, where its tiny claws found the faux-tile and scrabbled furiously, like a cartoon in the making.

You don't have to run, little fellow, don't you know?

The cat no longer lives here.

And, if I shouldn't take a single Benadryl, then I probably shouldn't double-dose it either, but I've got to sleep at some point. My dreams will be goopy and I'll wake with medicine-head, my sinuses either flowing or dry as the tomb, but checking out is checking out.

Until it isn't.

It's now four in the dark-ass morning, a different date I guess, but who cares if this document's calendar is right anymore. My heart is POUNDING, and I'm using the light from this screen to at least light me up, if not the rest of the bedroom.

It's not because of the sea of mice I had to step over in the hallway to get to the bathroom—I'm fairly certain those were paranoia and antihistamine—but because, when I heard the lightest tapping coming from the dining room table, I groggily stepped in to see if I was hearing what I thought I was hearing.

I was.

This keyboard. These keys I'm using right the fuck now.

Hunched over my laptop in this very chair was the shape from outside, which I'd convinced myself I'd dreamed up, stitched together from shadow.

The man, but not a man.

I saw him first from the side, and—my throat clenched, made a little choking noise, and I stepped back hard again, this time into the wall, which didn't break.

But I wish it would have.

Then I could have run screaming the other way.

I can't believe I'm even going to commit this to figurative paper, as saying it sort-of out loud may very well get *me* committed.

Yes, I slowed down to italicize that, and that trick there, of using "commit" in two senses, that's pure rhetoric, baby. It's how you get an audience on your side, class. It's inviting them into your circle of confidence, how you create an in-group.

Just, now I'm doing it so I can put off what I saw a line longer.

And a line longer now.

Please.

But no more. Here goes.

When I saw this man that wasn't a man from the side, in profile, typing on my laptop, his head wasn't human.

What it was was LARGE, *over*large, and his shoulders were somehow involved—it was a man's body, I could tell that, he was wearing jeans and boots with blocky safety toes, and probably a tight t-shirt, but it was definitely a man's body with a bison's head.

"What have you been eating, Good Stab?" I heard myself ask, either in my sleeping voice or my actual one, and he turned sharply to face me, his horns pointing up and up, his eyes these large black marbles, no human sclera at all but an intelligence there all the same, and—and this is where I screamed and screamed and ran back down the hall, locked myself in the bedroom and called 911, yelled to them about monsters and history, ghosts and justice.

The officers and firemen must have found me by my phone number, as I don't think I was ever able to get my address out. Marcie showed up a moment later in her robe. It took them all of thirty seconds to assure me I was the only person, or thing, in the apartment.

No one said "just lost her job," "father's ashes on the kitchen table," "over-the-counter drug packaging by the sink," "extended isolation in this winter storm," but it was there in their eyes all the same. I was, so far as they were concerned, hysterical. Which is itself hysterical.

"So what happened here?" a fireman just out of junior high, it looked like, asked about the tape and paper that are my sliding door, now.

"Is the carpet wet from it?" Marcie, being Marcie, asked.

"My cat is missing," I said back to all, not really in reply.

"Cat?" a police officer asked, skating her eyes around the place in question.

I didn't say anything else, just sat on the couch hugging a pillow to my chest.

They're all gone now.

I don't know why I even called them. Did bringing Sheriff Doyle and his deputies to Sunday service help Arthur Beaucarne any?

I have the manual for what I'm experiencing right here, higher in this document, a whole stack of century-old entries, but still I resist what it has to tell me. Probably because it's so much easier to call it a lonely old man's fancy, or an Indian's devious narrative torture.

But, there will come a day I believe, won't there?

There will come a day I can't not.

I might already, I mean.

Left behind by the laptop so his fingers could press a single key, not two or three at once, is a pair of leather work gloves.

Meaning someone, some*thing*, will be coming back for them.

21 January 2013

Welp, here we are three weeks into January somehow.

The 23rd looms—the day all those Blackfeet died in the snow. I don't think that's any accident.

And, sure, "welp" is my dad's word, how he used to pre-announce some announcement he was about to make, and me using it is just a daughter calling down the hall for her daddy, because the boogeyman's in the closet again, but . . . what if he is?

The last twenty-four sleepless hours, I've been compulsively reading everything I can on the Marias Massacre, can go verse and chapter on it. I delivered my father's DVDs to the thrift store, making myself walk instead of drive so I could experience the cold like the survivors of that massacre, being pushed into the storm like a death sentence. The cold stung, the chill was bone deep even in my Patagonia jacket and ski pants, but the whole time I knew I had a warm apartment to return to, so it's more like I went through the motions of penance than actually paid anything real. My tresayle named the entries that were just him "Absolution," and I think I get that now.

Okay, I'm just in from standing on my balcony as long as I could in the blowing cold, wearing my ski goggles so I don't have to blink, because I don't want to miss the fleeting image of a man standing out there, watching me back.

Clicking through page after page of Blackfeet material, I even fell into a Chief Mountain hole, if that's not an oxymoron. Apparently when the first white surveyors scaled Chief Mountain, they found a much-weathered bison skull up there.

Weasel Plume.

I never knew you, but *God* do I miss you.

It's two nights until the anniversary of Marias.

My Benadryl isn't just in the trash, but that trash has been delivered to the dumpster.

I expect my visitation will be tomorrow night, the "eve" I guess I should call it. Better go write my last will and whatever. I hereby bequeath my career to _____

Forget it, Etsy.

Just

Okay, OKAY, this ISN'T a will, it's not a suicide note, it's a—I don't know what you call it, it's nerves, it's fear, it's terror, it's unfair, it's . . . it's when the person left to die on the warehouse floor writes the name of their killer in blood on the concrete before they die? There a name for that? "Dying declaration"?

I'm shaking so bad, God. GOD!

It wasn't a dream. I know that. What it was, was a nightmare. One I guess I'm trapped in, now, SHIT!

Okay, you can do this, Etsy.

Now, do it.

In, out. Calm.

Okay, okay.

When I rose from bed to make sure the light tapping I was hearing wasn't my laptop—my laptop was in bed with me, thank you—that it was just some flashing on the roof, blowing in the wind, or a dirty-face in the walls, chewing on matchsticks—a mouse, I mean, a mouse a mouse a MOUSE—I drew to a slow stop, realizing something was wrong, but it was something vague, only slightly wrong.

Usually in the hallway at night, I don't need any light, as, in complete darkness, the steady green light of the smoke detector at the far end, by the living room, casts its sickly glow on the beige carpet, giving me an oatmeal-looking path to step into.

Now I was stepping into *darkness*, though? Not complete darkness, but some sort of . . . shadow? Blocking the smoke alarm?

I tracked it up, and up, and—

He was standing just inside the hallway, his bison head ponderous, giant, grand, especially in contrast to his human legs and arms and torso, his pearl snap shirt untucked, work boots still on.

"Etsy Beaucarne," he said, or, really, *pronounced*.

How he spoke with the mouth of a bison, I had no idea. And it was ridiculous, I know, to be looking a bison-man in the face and be wondering about his throat structure.

"Good Stab," I said back, and he nodded, seemed to like hearing that after all these years.

"It's hot in here," he said.

I made a little noise I don't know how to spell, a kind of gulp and a chirrup at once, a little girl noise, a dying animal noise, the kind you make not because it'll do any good, but because you're giving up, you know your mom or dad isn't there and that this is it, this thing is really happening. Good Stab's huge bison head looked sharply to the side, away from me and my mewling. Or: no. He wasn't looking away from me, he was looking at . . . at something I couldn't see, in the living room. But then he came back to me, his head ponderous in the tight confines of the hall.

"Your hair isn't like his," he said, as if impressed.

"I think it's from my three-times-great grandmother?" I said.

He just stared with his marble eyes.

"You're here to finish it?" I had to ask, even though I didn't want to know.

"Finish what?" he asked back, leaning into the wall beside him like, of all people, James Dean? I know that image from an album cover, a poster, a magazine.

Minus the bison head, of course.

"What you started in 1912," I mumbled, my chin pruning up.

Good Stab considered this, considered it some more, using the side of his hand to rub at the pendulous Adam's apple the same way I would try to rub the certainty of spittle from the corner of my mouth while delivering a conference paper.

"Can I hurt him more, by hurting you?" he finally asked, maddeningly calm.

"I'll—I can destroy that journal!" I blurted out all at once, trying to save my life. "I can, I promise!"

Good Stab snapped his head to the side again, as if keeping track of something.

"What?" I had to ask, wanting to lean forward, see, but also not wanting to be even one step closer to him.

"Your little hunter," he said with a shrug, and held his hand out, snapped his fingers once.

Taz jumped into his arms, his face crusted with something.

I steepled my hands over my mouth, fell to my knees, the tears already coming, even though that had to be exactly what Good Stab wanted. Some things you can't help, though.

And, what was on Taz's face . . . it wasn't exactly red, but black? Flaky?

It hit me all at once: dried blood.

Because that's how nachzehrers make horses, and I guess cats, docile.

"Just let him go, *let him go*!" I begged, reaching my arms out, fingers spread. "Take me, drink my blood, I don't care, I don't have anything anymore! But let him go, please. *Please*, Good Stab. He hasn't done anything to you."

"Neither have you," he said, running a human hand down Taz's spine—Taz, hedonist that he is, luxuriating in this, his purring filling the hall.

"Here," he said, holding Taz out.

Tentatively, so tentatively, knowing this was the end of me, I stood and crept forward inch by inch, finally drawing close enough to take Taz all at once and bury my face in his fur, my chest hitching and falling, hitching and falling.

He smelled of Lysol and winter.

"He already ate this morning," Good Stab said like he was just the cat sitter, like I was just back from a ski trip.

"Thank you, thank you," was all I could say back, both to Taz for being alive and to Good Stab, for giving him back to me.

"Family reunion, yeah?" he said, his delivery so much more contemporary than his diction in the journal would suggest. But he's had a lot of years between then and now, I suppose.

I nodded, kept nodding, not wanting to pull my face away from Taz, the traitorous scoundrel.

"No, I mean this," he said, stepping back and having to duck so as to not catch his black horns on the arched doorway into the living room.

He was holding his arm to the side, presenting . . . what?

"Family reunion," he repeated, softer but with more meaning, his black marble eyes watching me.

Slowly, clutching Taz so close, I edged down the hall, watching Good Stab the whole time because this had to be when the jaws of the trap were going to close, the same as they'd closed over the Cat Man, over Arthur Beaucarne.

I surged past him, trying to stay out of reach of his arms, but he had them crossed, was somehow tilting his bison head forward, like that's where I was meant to be focusing my attention.

I turned that way, ready for, I don't know, a dollhouse-sized Lutheran church I was expected to duck into. Even just a single flickering candle on my dining room table would have made me scream.

What was there, though—I couldn't even scream, and I still can't.

My breath is still hitching.

How can your eyes and your mind and your heart hold something that's impossible, that's fundamentally incomprehensible?

There was a seven-foot-long rodent of some kind, light brown like a camel, trying to claw its way up onto the couch. And I was close enough to it that it turned its face to me, its huge yellow incisors top and bottom keeping its mouth chocked open inquisitively, *hopefully*, its eyes . . . its eyes were were large and old enough to be sagging into ovals, like the skin was drooping down from its own weight, and, cupped in those lower lids were tears, and those tears were watery red, rimming the whole eye, and the way those eyes looked at me . . .

"A hundred years of drinking little-grass-eaters will do that to a Black Robe, won't it?" Good Stab said, seemingly from the end of a long tunnel. "A little-grass-eater is a—"

"Prairie dog," I finished for him, my face so warm, the breath in my chest so, so cold.

"Yes, that," Good Stab said.

"Arthur," I said, just to try to accept this.

He was pelted head to tail in dusty-brown, close-cropped hair, and his arms were short, his hands sharp at the fingertips, his rear legs perhaps longer than an actual prairie dog's, and still beholden to a pelvis meant to be upright, but the stubby, stiff tail wagging between them made the structure of the hip not that important, finally.

But his face, that was what kept pulling my eyes back.

There was something human there yet. Something human, tortured, pleading for help behind the jaunty-long whiskers. His ears were rotated around maybe halfway higher than they should have been, and seeing them made me want to touch my own ears, to be certain of their placement.

And then my great-great-*great*-grandfather reached for me with his right foreleg, the one he needed to support himself on the couch, and this caused him to slough down onto the coffee table, not breaking it but pushing it over.

He thrashed between it and the couch, screaking in terror and then the man trapped in that huge prairie-dog body gave up, laid his great brown head back in defeat, and panted shallowly but congested, because I don't think prairie dogs are meant to be on their backs like that.

I fell back against the doorframe, dropping Taz.

He hit the floor and bounded immediately for Arthur Beaucarne, jumping onto his chest.

My monstrous tresayle, who had himself once loved a cat named Cordelia, stolen from an Old West whorehouse, managed to use his forepaw that wasn't pinned against the couch to stroke Taz between his shoulders, his head coming up as far as his neck could bring it to see Taz at least a little. His missing chin—I guess it's a prairie dog thing, one I'd never paid attention to—made his overbite more pronounced, his expression even more imploring, more forlorn. More lost.

"How could you—?" I said to Good Stab, already picturing Arthur Beaucarne trapped in a cellar on the reservation for the last century, only seeing light when the next prairie dog was dropped down to him, but when I turned, my knee-jerk reaction was that my *other* monstrous visitor had somehow sunken into the floor.

His bison head was sitting on my carpet, I mean.

When I finally made myself approach, touch a black horn, the whole head fell over, was hollow.

A mask. He'd had a mask pulled over his head like a mascot.

And he'd left me with . . . with a Lutheran pastor sentenced to a hell that had never been in his Bible.

Of course I ran away.

To here, my bedroom, the door locked, the dresser pushed against it. I have my laptop with no charger and I have Taz with no litterbox, and there's giant prairie-dog claws scratching slowly at the door, leaving gouges a hundred years deep.

And the moaning sounds out there.

I thought I knew what pain was.

Wrong, Etsy.

Just now, with dawn, Taz using my closet for his business like he hasn't since his kitten days, I'm off the phone with Marcie.

There have been complaints about noise, presumably from my new downstairs neighbors—grad students, I think, though it's hard to keep track. Evidently the sounds of a century-old monster suffering are, what? Slightly bothersome? Is that it?

Or, is it the sounds of me tap-tap-tapping my keys, each keystroke thunder, each revelation another anvil falling into my life, upending everything I thought I knew? No, no, it was probably when I searched up how the Blackfeet say "prairie dog," like getting all the accent marks right is going to be the thing that saves me.

Yeah, that's probably what the complaint's about.

Anything remotely scholarly or academic I do: *instant* wrist-slap.

Here, then, downstairs douchebags, I'll use my digital recorder, then, just embed its MP3s into this file. Battery on this laptop's throwing warnings anyway.

And . . . here I am again, live and in, I don't know. Mono?

I'm not even sure what that means. Less sure I care.

And I'm sorry, Taz, that was the sound of your cat food opening, bud. But I'm recording over it now.

We all have to make sacrifices.

So, now that I'm not typing, I don't know what else to say.

Okay, now it's noon, and I think I understand what Good Stab is doing, here.

If I want, if I have the nerve, the pluck, the whatever, I can feed my greatest-grandfather back to human over the course of a few years, can't I? I can rent a house instead of an apartment, and I can come home every week with another two-legged meal for him to bite into with his big teeth, and drink down.

I think Good Stab is testing whether I'm a killer or not. If I'm like him, like Arthur Beaucucarne, if that name even still applies.

Shit, is this even recording?

Okay, back. Don't freak out, Taz. That was my voice, yeah, yes, but this is me too, Mommy's still here.

But I can't live in my bedroom.

Here goes.

I'm in the hall, I'm in the hall, Arthur Beaucarne isn't here, isn't here.

Oh, shit.

Hey, um, hey, yeah. It's me, Granddad. I'm just going to . . .

Not getting this to stab you. It's just for in case.

No, no, stay over there, stay over . . . stay, stay, how do you say that in German? Verboten, verboten.

Shit! No no no!

STILL 21 January 2013

Okay, laptop'd in again, *with* the charger. In the bedroom again. But this time it was for a cry session that's mostly over now, I think.

It's because of what I just had to do.

No, my tresayle didn't eat me.

Taz did wind through his legs, though, and then vault in his silky way up to my arms, to nuzzle my neck to tell me it's feeding time—he didn't know Good Stab had told me that had already happened.

Arthur Beaucarne was watching all this so intently.

"Ku, Ku, Ku," he finally managed to say, sort of, like doing sound effects or something.

I shrank away, squinting, protecting Taz, but then, slowly, probably too slowly, I heard that front letter for what it was.

"*Cordelia*," I over-enunciated, holding Taz even closer. "Cordelia's gone, Granddad. I'm sorry."

For a long time, maybe even a minute, he looked down at the floor.

When he came back, his whiskers still for once, his mouth hanging open, his eyes directed right at mine, I knew he had finally translated that word, "Granddad."

He shook his head no, no, red collecting at the corners of his big eyes again.

But I had to nod yes.

"Arty had a son before he was taken," I told him, shrugging it true. "Good Stab never knew. Until . . . recently, I guess? When they found your journal? I mean, you called it a . . . what? A logbook?"

Arthur Beaucarne turned away, pivoted back into the living room, falling down onto his forelegs. On all fours, he has a sort of hump in the middle of his back like a weasel's, or a ferret's.

I followed, hugging the far wall, still holding Taz.

Arthur Beaucarne was leaning into the corner of the room, softly hitting his head against the wall, which Marcie was probably already getting a call about.

"I don't know any . . . any Lutheran stuff," I said to him apologetically, but then inspiration hit: I knelt, dug my dad's Bible up from that banker's box, held it out, my elbow straight like a little kid's trying to feed a dog they're afraid is going to bite their hand.

My great-great-great-granddad looked at that Bible a long time, then turned away from it, his lips pressed together over those long teeth now.

Taz jumped out of my arms, trotted across the room to the giant prairie dog—I guess they'd been prisoners together—and I put my hand down to push with, to stand, and . . . what crinkled under my hand, in the banker's box, was my father's last pack of cigarettes.

I looked from them to the monster across the room, and I finally pulled them up, worked the matchbook in the cellophane up.

Arthur Beaucarne looked up sharply when the match flared, and lurched over to the kitchen doorway like scared of what I was doing. To stand, he had to hold on to the doorframe, as he apparently doesn't know how to sit back on his tail as I'm fairly certain I've seen prairie dogs do. With his human pelvis, it hurts to sit back?

Shit.

I mouthed the smoke enough to get the cherry going, knew better than to breathe in. I'm no Cat Man, but I know I am a cougher.

"I'm sorry, I really am," I said, and licked my lips, held my tresayle's eyes with mine, and started forging across the living room, stepping through all the junk spilled off the coffee table.

When I edged up sort of close to Arthur Beaucarne, I felt like a kid taken to the nursing home to see their dying grandparent, only they're scared of them lying there, they're scared of death, they don't understand it, they don't want to be here.

My grandparent helped me by reaching his stubby arm out to me, black claws splayed.

Shaking my head no, and sort of already blubbering but not wanting to, I worked the cigarette between the first and second of his claws, having to arrange them to get the cigarette situated.

As far as I knew, the last time Arthur Beaucarne had smoked, it had been a Chesterfield from a bartender with a single name. I just had to tab over and do a search to pull "Chesterfield" from the ether, yes.

I'm not sure that matters.

I do know what's up with Cat Men and cigarettes, though. I think. Google tells me it's the *nicotine*. It constricts the blood vessels. Simple as that. For monsters that burn oxygenated blood like fuel, siphoning the redness out until only the plasma is left to pee, dialing the blood flow down to nil via a vasoconstrictor is about as bad as it gets.

Benadryl's my kryptonite, cigarettes are his.

So, knowing full well what he was doing, my greatest-grandfather drew his great-great-grandson's cigarette to his lips, closed his huge eyes, and breathed in deep-deep, then did it again, exhaling smoke through his nose, and, before it could take him all the way down, he dropped to all fours beside me, startling me a step back.

He wasn't trying to run away from the pain, though. He had dropped down to stagger across the living room, curl his long, stubby body around that bison head as best he could, and pass out, his chest shuddering at the end, not with physical pain, I don't think, but the other kind.

Then, after he was conked, he sort of threw up in his sleep. It was bloody hair either licked from his own coat or swallowed on accident, from the prairie dogs he'd sucked dry.

Taz sniffed the mess, sniffed it better, finally wasn't interested.

I had to run——*run*——down here, press my door shut as quietly as I could, and scream and cry into my pillow.

Yes, Great-Great-Great-Grandfather, I'm using your long-ass Victorian dashes. It's just an autocorrect setting, here in the new world.

Not everything you did was bad, sir.

And that makes what I have to do now so much harder.

22 January 2013

Parting is such sweet bullshit.

She said from a rest stop in southern Montana. Well, she typed into her faithful laptop, which is literally *in* her lap. It makes doing italics trickier, what with elbow room and a giant prairie dog sleeping in the backseat, but not nearly as tricky as getting out of Laramie in all this snow.

But a lot of shit's happened since yesterday. Too much for one day, but that's my life now, isn't it?

Classes start in . . . who cares. I'm not going to be there.

Who am I even writing to now, with this? Taz, you're here with me. You too, Tresayle. Hackers? I don't warrant that kind of attention. I think I am actually tracing words in blood on the concrete floor of the huge empty warehouse that's my life. Too, though, that's not really here or there, is it, as all the cool kids were saying in 1912?

Do I want someone to find a record of what happened to me after I didn't get tenure, is that it? My sad descent, my death spiral? Do I email this to the department listserv so they can blame the stupid university system that's *actually* responsible? Is this to be my first and last monograph? Will someone else get a book contract out of this, after they transcribe my voice recordings?

No, bury it in a wall, Etsy. Just drag it to the trash again.

I don't know.

I'm afraid to sleep, here, afraid of waking with my throat in a set of giant, yellowy teeth——the eyes looking into mine would be the worst part——but I'm afraid that if I don't keep my fingers doing something, I'll *fall* asleep. Let's say that's why I'm still in this document. Not that I'm like my greatest-grandfather, addicted to his journal.

So: yesterday.

First, thinking step-by-step, I needed something to lead a monster with by the neck, but, when nothing in the apartment would work, I knew I needed to get down to . . . not the pet store, because I needed other junk, didn't want to be gone from the apartment too long. Murdoch's, then. Murdoch's has hardware, pet stuff, ranch supplies, hunting stuff——some real one-stop shopping, at least for this zip code. But, once I got geared up to go outside, it was pretty obvious what my problem was: a giant prairie dog curled up around a bison head, right by where the front door would swing if I opened it.

Like Taz, then, I took the balcony, hung off the frozen railing and counted to three and then to three again and finally fell into a drift of snow, the downstairs douchebags, as luck would have it, standing at their sliding door to watch the big slow flakes drifting down over the neat-to-them winter wonderland.

The flakes were big, yes, Jim and Terry, or whatever your names are, but the biggest one that ever fell, that got documented? I just stumbled on it, when looking up Miles City, Montana. The biggest flake ever recorded fell there. Fifteen inches across.

Picture *that*. It'd have been like it was snowing lace doilies.

So, after that powdery drift of just normal-sized flakes under my balcony swallowed me, I stood up, raised a gloved hand to Jim and Terry and shrugged, each of us, I think, accepting that there really was no explanation for this scene.

Where I went after that was my Subaru, to scrape it and get the engine started for the first time in days. While the car was warming, I waded to the front office to make nice with Marcie, whose voice and posture were so fake-concerned for whatever I was obviously going through that I really wanted to explain it to her, just to watch her blanch.

Instead, I told her my brother, about whom she'd never heard, probably since he never existed, is taking my father's passing hard.

As in, *drinky*-hard. Where I was going, why I was all suited up was . . . it was to find his sponsor, bring him back, because this situation couldn't go on——he was going to get me evicted, lose me my security deposit, endanger my standing at the university.

"So that was him the . . . other night?" Marcie asked, and mimed clomping footsteps which for some reason involved a dour expression.

I nodded and attempted a grin, she squeezed my upper arm on the left side, her right, and then she was off to deal with the undergrads in the hot tub with glass bottles, who probably weren't even old enough for that beer, and I was in my trusty Outback churning to Murdoch's, where I did indeed find a leash sized for Labradors and Great Danes. But what I have can pull harder than that. I ended up just getting a lead for a horse. But I did pick up a light, retractable leash for Taz. It makes me a freak in Wyoming, in Montana, in the West, walking a *cat* at rest stops and gas stations (italics suck), twenty-five feet of slack fed out for him to do his business. It's weird for me, it's weird for Tazzy Boy, but it's better than him running away into the storm.

But, if you want weird, Montanans? Check out my backseat, here. It's where this braided, blue horse lead looped on my emergency brake goes.

Yeah.

Arthur Beaucarne wakes, sits up, the leash around his neck pulls that ratchety handle, and my rear tires are going to lock, no regard for how fast I'm going, what's behind me, what hairpin turn I'm praying I don't slide off. Fun stuff.

So, when I got back to the apartment forty-five minutes later, Murdoch's run complete, one corner of the couch had been gnawed into deeper than Taz has ever done. The big chunks of foam were scattered all over the living room. Flecks of it were in my greatest-grandfather's chin whiskers. My brief foray that morning into the care and feeding of prairie dogs had already told me that, when nervous or scared, they chew up whatever's close.

None of those care and feeding pages said not to give them cig-arettes, though, so I lit another up to share——I needed time to pack up, clear enough snow off the balcony to dig Taz's cat carrier out from the storage closet, and was doing that when, through the butcher paper that's my sliding door, I heard the knocking.

I stepped back into the apartment and stood there, appraising my disaster of a living room.

The giant prairie dog, not as sedated as I'd wanted, had retreated from the sound, was over in the front corner by the fireplace, his eyes locked on mine because I was the one who could make the scary knocking go away. Taz, tomcat that he is, was nosing the bottom of the front door, looking for a fight. Me, I was dropping the cigarette I'd been holding and grinding it into the carpet.

That was when the knocking graduated from three-polite-knocks-and-wait to *banging*.

"Shh, shh," I told everyone, and crossed the living room.

Through the peephole, Marcie had two police male officers with her, in the winter versions of their police jackets, with the high blue collars.

I shook my head no, no, not when I'm so close, but, because she had the master key, I hauled the door open at last and stood in the doorway, trying to block the living room as best I could.

"Ma'am," the first officer said, as if apologetic about his presence there.

"You know the rule on guests that stay longer than four days . . ." Marcie said, equally apologetic, but a sort of thrill to her demeanor all the same.

"We just need to——" the second officer said, planting his hand to the jamb to pull himself in.

"Wellness check," Marcie said primly.

I stepped over to block this officer.

"Wellness check?" I asked, looking down at myself to see if I was bleeding, or overdosed, or unstable.

"There's been concern about your safety," the first officer said. "Ms., Ms. . . . how do you say that?"

"My name is Etsy," I said back, to make this easier.

"That a real name?" the second officer asked.

"I'm fine," I told them. "Wellness check, *done.*"

"You're obviously not fine, Ms. Boquet," Marcie said, and the way I flashed my eyes to her about this casual catachresis——if it *was* casual, and not hostile——she actually held the fingertips of her right hand to the hollow of her throat.

"If we can——" the second officer said, trying to slide past again, but I blocked him out.

"Isn't it only family who can instigate a wellness check?" I asked, then, to Marcie, "Are you my aunt, my cousin, my *mother*?"

"Property manager," she said back, puffing herself up with it.

"Exactly," I said, stooping quickly to pick Taz up, which gave the second officer a quick glimpse behind me, I guess.

"Is that——?" he started.

I stood back up fast.

"Cat?" I interrupted, hitching Taz higher like show and tell.

"Buffalo," he said.

We all looked back to the bison head, upright on the carpet.

"My brother's a . . . a team mascot," I said quietly, like embarrassed.

"Did you find his sponsor?" Marcie leaned in to ask, touching my forearm like activating a cone of silence around us.

"It's all . . . in-process," I told her, not having to fake how flustered I was. "Sorry it's, you know, taking longer than *four days*."

To my right, I could sense my greatest-grandfather struggling to stand, lumber into view, touch his great nose to an officer's blue thigh.

"Is that *smoke*?" Marcie asked, nosing in.

I looked around again, fully expecting my tresayle to be there. But it was just his droppings, some unsquashed into the carpet, some not.

"Taz doesn't like the snow," I explained, holding him up again, drawing their eyes to him, the obvious shitter. "And I'm *fine*, thank you, thank you," I added, and then, directly to Marcie, "If you'll let me out of my lease, I'm gone by the end of the week, how does that sound to you?"

Marcie considered this.

"And the security deposit?" she finally asked.

"Yours," I told her flatly.

"Where will you go?" the first officer asked, genuinely concerned, I think.

"I've got a volunteer thing lined up," I said to him, still holding Marcie's eyes. "Well?" I asked her.

"Done," she said, and took a neat step back to signal that this was over.

"Ma'am?" the second officer asked her.

"We have cookies in the front office," she said. "They won't make up for this . . . inconvenience. But I made them myself. They're supposed to be for potential residents, but——"

After she was gone, my greatest-grandfather's nose nudged into the back of my right calf and I shrieked forward, into the cold.

When I looked back to him, he was bleeding from the eyes. It must be some automatic defense mechanism: when attacked or hurting or scared, they want to calm the situation down the only way they can.

Either that, or he was crying.

"Here," I said to him, and got another cigarette going, held it down for him to inhale.

I blew my own smoke out the front door, as if smoke in the walls and carpet was something I still needed to worry about.

When my greatest and saddest grandfather was down again, I

covered him with a blanket, and when he was awake enough to follow the lead, and there were no other residents braving the snow on a Saturday afternoon, I walked him downstairs, packed him into the backseat, and shut the door firmly.

I left the bison head on my living room floor. It's real. No skull, but it's not mascot-grade, is from an actual animal.

I'm sure it'll make its way to the thrift store. Everything does eventually. Ask Robert Redford, John Wayne, Kevin Costner.

"Ready?" I asked Taz in the passenger seat in his carrier, Grand-dad in the backseat, and eased us down to the ice rink 80 was, past the hill I used to sit on my first few years here, to watch the big rigs slide in slow motion and sometimes roll, great roostertails of snow climbing into the sky in slow motion, at a distance.

The bored trooper there waved us back with his flare, shook his head in amusement.

That's Snow Chi Minh Trail for you, from November until about March.

So, another route. An even dicier route.

But before that, a cigarette break for the backseat passenger, which doesn't feel right. I don't like him doing this to himself, sucking on these things so willingly, like reaching for death, for escape. But I'm afraid if I sleep, I'll miss a smoke break, and then this ends bad.

Okay, back again. Ended up driving and driving and driving some more. So much coffee. I can't listen to anything with a good heart anymore. All I have left is this rabbit heart in my chest, kicking to get out.

We're now in . . . in Nittowsinan, which I also had to look up from higher in the document, to paste here. I'm spelling it like the man sleeping behind me wrote it down, which I guess is how it sounded to him from Good Stab. Sorry if it's wrong, all Blackfeet. I know it means "our land," and I'm not part of that "our," but I don't know how to change it.

Nittowsinan looks very much like Wyoming, it turns out.

It was snowy enough on the small backroads that I'm not even sure when or where in the night the state line was. But we finally found 25 around Wheatland, then crossed the Yellowstone into Blackfeet territory around Custer, but didn't hook it east for Miles City. Instead we booked it west towards Bozeman, making a quick but important stop there and then angling up through Montana and parking by a coffee shop so I can type all this in, get enough free signal to send it to myself——email's the best backup.

And now, hours later, which I should measure either in gallons of coffee or complete lack of sleep, it's dawn of the 23rd, everything frozen and blowing and white, and we're here: the Marias River, as Lewis and Clark named it once upon an expedition. Just east of the Blackfeet Reservation.

The bolt-cutters I bought at Murdoch's will get me through the gate——the site of the massacre is on private land, some ranch, and it requires special permission to visit.

Fine.

I give *myself* permission, thanks. It's what we white folk do.

January 23. 2013

Okay, back to the recorder, as long as its battery lasts. It was taking too long to fix all the typos numb fingers make, and, doing it this way, I can wear my gloves and keep my elbows tight by my side. Less heat escapes that way.

This matters because the Subaru's bogged down in the snow maybe ten yards past the gate.

Shit.

I'm just waiting for dear old Great-Great-Great-Granddad to wake from his last cigarette so we can do this, I guess.

It made a lot more sense from my apartment in Laramie. Take the monster back to where it was made. The drifts out there are up to my hip, though, and visibility's about two inches and then your eyelashes freeze, and the cold reaches in through your mouth, wraps its hand around your spine, and that's when you know Montana's got you.

Fun times ahead, Etsy.

You must be this stupid to ride this ride.

And no, shaking your cell phone doesn't make that one little bar any more than a square dot. I don't think AT&T knows about this kind of cold.

I'm sorry, Taz, I really am. I just . . . I don't know what else to do.

What started 143 years ago ends today, one way or another.

If there's an entry after this, then I made it back somehow. If there's not, though, then, shit. I guess I should. I didn't bring it to NOT read it, right? And maybe what the Blackfeet Nation left in my dad's Bible for me will be instructions on how to survive in extreme winter conditions. They've been doing it since forever, they've got to know something.

Okay.

Oh.

OH.

No. No.

Shit.

Are you listening back there, Three-Persons?

You wrote this in 1912, back when you had hands. It's got your dashes that look like fill-in-the-blanks, I'd know them anywhere. It's that letter you sent in 1870, that was waiting for you when you came back east to brush up on your Latin and get sober, maybe in the opposite order. That letter you dug up after Good Stab's first visit?

But, hey, surprise, it's not burnt up in your church's fireplace. Good Stab must have stolen it when you weren't looking. Stolen it and saved it for a hundred years, in whatever the Indian version of a safe deposit box is. Which is maybe just a safe deposit box, I don't know.

Okay, okay, here's where . . .

Reading, reading, old paper crumbling, history dying, Lydia Ackerman back in Bozeman feeling a disturbance in the Force . . .

Okay.

Why would you even KEEP this?

She said, flashing on her prom photo from 1988.

But you did, didn't you? And Good Stab wanted me to read it bad enough to drive all the way down to Denver, probably in three pairs of sunglasses. He maybe didn't mean for me to read it out loud like this, but, if I've got enough memory left on this thing, I'll do it. It's not long, just three, okay, four pages, and if I don't save them here in this voice memo, then they're gone forever, with the way this paper's falling apart. Maybe if the rancher who owns the gate I just busted finds this recorder frozen in my glove, he can give it to the Blackfeet, I don't know. Maybe they don't even want it.

Here goes.

When we marched out under Major Baker's command, it was an adventure. I wasn't a soldier, just happened to be milling around with soldiers, but that was good enough to get caught up in the mission. I grandly told myself we were the Greeks at Thermopylae going out to resist the Persians, who, unless my readings misled me, are complected similarly to the red Indians of America. Everyone longs to be in a storybook, do they not? The morning we left, I was in the kitchen stealing one more spoonful of the rich, warm pudding I'd discovered that was better than anything I'd ever imbibed, which I admit may have been a judgment made due to scarcity. I scurried to my horse with a mouthful of it yet, and savored it the first mile or two, and I won't bore you with the long and torturous route we took out into the field after these Indians in need of federal scolding, but trust that it was seventy miles between Fort Ellis and Fort Shaw, and it was seventy below zero for most of it, which was rapidly disenchanting me from the romance I had previously felt I was in, this affaire du cœur I suffered then from, that affair being with Experience, Blake's version, of which you once instructed me. Every iota more of it I consumed, the better I could eventually shake off my own impulse to judge, when on my side of the act of Confession. In order to better flense my eventual flock of their sin, I first needed to understand what it was to carry the burden of that sin myself, no?

I had neither rifle nor spurs for this expedition, however, and the castoff cavalryman's uniform I had taken when my New Haven finery turned to rags was no protection from the elements. Yet I had no training, no sea legs for an effort such as this. I was like the man in the play who wakes with donkey ears, and so must bray around hopelessly.

When we slept under a formation of rock called Priest Butte, I took that as a sign that my presence here was Providence. But when we began riding only at night, and left the supply train behind us so as to increase our already hurried pace, and were only allowed the smallest of fires, I admit I began, like Thomas, to doubt.

I was the first to begin wrapping my extremities in burlap sacking to fend off the cold. I also continually recalled that pudding to mind, to warm at least my thoughts. I also became friendly with the pair of scouts, the two of them sharing the sobriquet the soldiers had taken to calling me by. Since they also weren't cavalry, thus not beholden to the various etiquettes of soldierkind, we fell in together, and they came to share their bottle with me. Everyone in the column was drinking just to stay warm, Major Baker the most, I believe, as leaders of course lead by example. With each stop I would mumble to my scout companions of the pudding, relishing its memory such that they could almost taste it themselves, I warrant. Three separate times I begged the officers for permission to return to the supply train for provender, and, three times I was denied, the last time with belligerence sufficient to forewarn me away from asking again, on threat of violence.

In the saddle, I swam through a sea of warm pudding, ducking my head under continually, to gulp.

My left foot——for I was on the left side of the column——continually dragging through unbroken snow, finally froze through solid. The toes there are yet blackened with frost, and feelingless, though not without scent.

Perhaps the salve for these eventual stumps will be pudding, of which, from desperate overindulging on our earlier return, I've already thrown up twice. We were heroes, however, so no one pulled that warm kettle out from under me, and the spectacle I was making of myself, for which I now feel only the direst shame, and hereby swear off all sweet victuals from this point forth, as they will only serve to remind me of my weakness.

On the trek into the featureless wastelands these savage and learnéd Piegan have somehow occupied for time immemorial, the day before we found them camped on the dry fork of the Marias River, the scouts became parsimonious with their bottle, refusing to let me warm myself at its neck, as the liquor only made my talk of the pudding more swoonful.

I doubted whether I would ever know warmth again.

On the morning of the 23rd, we finally came across a scrawny Indian boy working a herd of horses. A large portion of the soldiers dismounted and arrayed themselves along the bluff, lying prostrate on their bellies, leading with their rifles, and Baker's second in command sent other units this way and that, as morning had caught the good Major colder than usual, thus his fully inebriated state. Joe Kipp finally used pig string to bind Baker's wrists to the horn of his saddle to keep him astride his mount, as it would be disheartening for the august commander to reel down to one side or the other by incremental degrees, until the cap on his head touched the snow.

As I had no assignment to fulfill, I attached myself to the less resentful of the two scouts, Joe Cobell. Him being a scout, I thought to remain out of the action, as his job was now completed. Shortly thereafter, Joe Kipp had to be forcibly restrained when he wouldn't quiet himself about which camp this actually was. According to him, who himself had some tincture of Indian blood, these were peaceable Indians, not the marauding sort. But no one cared. Indians were Indians, and the sooner we punished them, the sooner we could get back to the fort, and my pudding.

So, attached to the scout Joe Cobell as I was, I found myself suddenly coming down the slope alongside the bluff, I thought to parlay with the chief, and so be part of history as it was happening.

In part, this was true.

However, due to my persistent cold and the insistent hunger which corrupted my heart, the whole way down that slope I had my chin on Joe Cobell's shoulder, whispering to him about the pudding I knew he could feel in his mouth now as I did, so well had I described it. My lips were brushing his very ear such that my sibilance had to be tactile to him, and in this way did I become even lower than the snake whispering to Eve, and I can't deny this, nor will I ever——which is why I send this to you now, so I will forevermore have to own this, my foulest act.

"They're naught but savages," I hissed to his innermost, weakest self, making it so.

"If you don't stop them now, then you're as guilty of killing Malcolm Clark as are they," I added.

"This one is surely Owl Child's own father," I lied. "Whatever he tells you or shows you will be a lie to save his son."

And, lastly, damning my immortal soul, "God looks the other way when men must dole out justice. I can show you in the Bible whereof it speaks that. No forgiveness is necessary when those you punish are naught but savages. Would you feel guilt for shooting the fox that stole your hens? No, the fox, by his acts, is compelling you to take his life, even as downy feathers line his foul mouth. So it is with these Piegan. And, in this cold, they won't even survive the winter, will they? How could they, with their limited means, and no culture? Killing them now will be mercy, an act which the Father who sees all will look kindly on, recognizing in you a man made in His very mold, and following His tenets and teachings."

I can be convincing when allowed to paint with words, as you know from our many classroom discussions. I aver that I was perhaps even more desperate to convince this day, such that, when the chief came out carrying his useless paper, Joe Cobell, driven into a frenzy of hunger by my savory descriptions, and made immune to Divine reprisal by my assurance that any sin would be hastily forgiven, raised his rifle and put this chief down with a single shot.

As this was what we had been ordered to do, I thought little of this other than that, finally, we could get back to warmth, and civilized company.

But then, once that first shot was fired, all the men on the bluff commenced firing as well, perforating the lodges below as with grapeshot. It was roughly 200 rifles against thirty some lodges, and it was over by noon, and please understand that, though I fired not a single shot into Indian flesh that day, I also, in a sense, fired them all. No, I wasn't one of the ones slicing into lodges to use pistols and axes against those who had escaped the shooting from the bluff, but I may as well have been. Neither did I aid in pulling the bodies into a pile and setting them and their lodges and supplies alight——though I did thaw my hands at that enormous fire, its columns of black smoke sinuous and oily, and redolent of nothing so much as guilt.

On the ride back, after the weather broke, I convinced myself that the scout Joe Cobell already had it in his heart to shoot that chief for personal not immediate reasons, which is why I pen this to you now, sir. Any man can ratiocinate his own deeds and thereby cleanse his conscience, but doing so when evidence to the contrary, such as this to you, exists, must need be an act of futility.

As well, I also now have the reminder of a Piegan face looking out at me from the fire of bodies and lodges that day. A visage looking up pleadingly from the flames of Hell I had sparked. And, as I watched, there was then another, and another, and all of their eyes were open, indicting, and I vow not to come home again until those eyes have shut themselves, which is to say, goodbye henceforth, sir.

This will be my last dispatch.

I now fold myself into this hostile land, away from the world which would judge me, and rightly so. I implore you not only not to burn this, but to frame it for all to see, such that such darkness in Man can be known, and then avoided. In this way will my life at least have served some small purpose.

——*A. Beaucarne.*
Jan 26, 1870

Yeah, well, Three-Persons, I didn't burn your letter, but, goddamn you, it is all in crumbles in my lap.

Now, the floorboard of the Subaru.

Which, as anyone listening to this can probably hear, is now dead dead dead. I can't even see outside anymore, from my breath frozen on the inside of the windshield, and all the windows.

Well, my breath and Taz's and yours, Great-Great-Great-Granddad.

Did you hear any of that? Did you remember?

And, yes, Taz, I can smell the warm pudding you left just now. Thanks, bub. Always willing to pitch in and make a bad scene shittier, aren't you?

But I love you.

And, you know what? Fuck it, you didn't come this far to die, Etsy Beaucarne, last of your cursed name.

Hell no.

Don't worry, Taz, Mommy's got this.

Here, buffalo jerky, you like that.

Me too. Okay, if you don't want it, I'll just, I can——

I know, I know.

I'm not crying.

These are tears of joy. I think this is where I've been going my whole life. I just never knew it. And don't worry, I'll walk us the fuck out of here if I need to, I'll show up in Shelby or Cut Bank carrying a cat crate, my hair frozen stiff, nose bleeding from the cold, eyes wild, ALL my toes frozen off, and if anybody asks if I'm all right, if I need anything, I'll just glare them down, take another slurp of coffee.

I'm talking to you too, Tresayle. I see you moving back there, don't think I don't, you with your groggy eyes and ashtray breath.

My heart's broken, yeah, and you're the one who just broke it.

Let's do this.

Okay, shit, I'm back, I'm here, it's after, it's done, I'm alive, I don't know how, I know I shouldn't be, I don't know if I will be in five minutes, in two minutes, it's blowing again, even harder, so I have to say this all fast into my hand, my glove, the battery light's already having a panic attack, and the memory's almost full.

I know how you feel, little recorder.

Okay, okay. Get your breath.

You're okay, Taz. Mommy's got you. Come here, yeah, keep me warm, I shouldn't have brought you, I know, I should have left you for Marcie, but I'm glad you're here, I don't know what I'd do without you, you big little man.

We can do this. We have to.

But, rancher man, when you find me it's going to be a mystery, I know.

Why would a person do this to themselves?

What the hell even happened?

Here, let me tell you.

My great-great-great-grandfather, see, this monster from legend turned him into a giant prairie dog because he'd done a massacre up here on your land. So I brought him, my tresayle, which is the French way for saying who he is, I brought him up here because what else could I do?

Thing was, though, it turned out his stubby legs weren't long enough to reach through to the ground, so his belly sort of slid on top of the snow, and he paddled with his legs like an otter, I guess. One going back to where it all started, sure.

You can figure that out with the document open on my laptop. The password is T A Z Z.

So, anyway, I got the cat crate hooked under my left arm, the horse lead looped around my right wrist, I already had my backpack on, and there I went, out into the storm.

It was noon when we finally reached the bluff. Down below us, just like the time my great-great-great-grandfather was here, were the Blackfeet, surprise. They were packing a big drum up, and their horses were standing around, each on three feet, their manes and tails frozen.

I'd read about the memorial ride the Blackfeet make every year to here, with your permission to be on their land, but I never thought they would do it in a storm like this. I guess I don't really know the Blackfeet, though.

I backed off from the lip of the bluff to give them their privacy, and then I set Taz's crate to the side and peeled out of my backpack one arm at a time, the straps taking the top layer of my Patagonia with it, which I know I can get warrantied, if I live through this.

I think my great-great-great-grandfather recognized this place too, Mister Rancher. His name is Arthur Beaucarne. He was a Lutheran pastor a century . . . who cares, look it up if you want.

For the whole car trip north, anyway, he had been game for whatever, but now, remembering this place I guess, he was trying to pull away.

I finally had to plant my knee down over my end of his lead to keep him in place long enough for me to unpack what else I'd bought at the hardware store.

First was the nail gun, which is heavy as fuck. Air-driven would have been better, but they have electric models too, surprise. I would have bought an actual pistol, but even in Wyoming, purchasing a firearm can take a bit. More info than you need, sorry. Guns are great, rah-rah, more guns, more guns!

As for my having an airgun instead of an actual gun, though, now that the Blackfeet were down there doing their thing, I was glad to have something that wouldn't make a lot of noise.

"I'm sorry," I said to my tresayle, holding the business end of the nail gun to his forehead, his big dark eyes looking up to me like I didn't have to do this.

I did it anyway.

After reading his letter, I mean, I knew that the monster he was had just been coaxed to the surface. But it had been there the whole time.

The first nail planted up to its head between his eyes, and the second one as well, not half an inch away.

His kind are hard to kill, though.

When he bucked away, the lead I had stepped through spilled me on my ass.

My Great-Great-Great-Grandad was humping away through the snow.

I walked up behind him and laid a line of coppery nails down along his spine, trying to hit something that mattered enough to slow him down.

I finally found it at the base of his tail.

It took his rear legs away and he rolled over as four-leggeds do when it's time to claw and fight.

Here I am talking like an Indian, yeah. Guessing you hate Indians, living this close to them.

Screw it.

This is an Indian story, I think, rancher man, and you're on Indian land whether you admit it or not. We all are.

I stayed out of reach, loaded another belt of nails like the nice man at the hardware store had taught me, and shot into my kindly old tresayle again and again, and yeah, I was crying and sputtering each time I pulled the trigger. I talk tough now, but I'm not, I know.

In his crate in the snow, Taz was yowling. I was killing his friend. Bad Mommy.

I think he's probably going to run away the first time I give him the chance, and that'll be fair. I deserve it. I understand.

He's seen a thing in me he didn't know was there. A thing I didn't know was there.

I stitched another belt of nails into this giant prairie dog's front-side then, each shot like a shot into my own chest, I swear, and, slower and slower, those claws scratching at the air stopped scratching.

Next was what I'd happened to walk by at Murdoch's. It was something I hadn't even known was real. Do you know about these, rancher man? Thirty-six-inch cable saws? It's this three-foot-long somehow sharp cable with padded loops at each end to hold on to, for pulling back and forth.

You can cut through a tree trunk with one of these faster than you'd think.

They also work on necks.

I rolled my greatest-grandfather over and I planted my knee in his back, the nailheads there tearing through my layers of pants, which I paid for on this long-ass walk back to the car, and I looped this sharp cable around his neck and started sawing back and forth, putting all my weight into it.

Arthur Beaucarne woke when it cut through his windpipe, I think. And I say his name like that here because it really was him, finally. That was how deep I'd cut. This wasn't a prairie dog scream-ing, it was a man. His short arms tried to reach his claws up to this new pain, but the cable just cut those fingers off too.

I couldn't stop, but I had to scream to get through it. I had to scream with each pull. Dragging a cable through the meat of a living creature, it's not as easy as you might think, at least for a city girl. Dragging it through the neck of someone's whose book you've read sucks even more, I think.

When I was halfway through, he quit fighting.

That was the worst part. It's the part where I sort of loved him. It's why I'm sort of crying now, I guess you can hear it.

But I kept going. I had to.

His camel-colored head toppled forward into the snow like the heavy, awkward thing it was and I fell back, chest heaving, arms burning, tears freezing on my face.

I thought I was done, that this would be enough.

Wrong.

I heard the snow crunching before I saw what was coming for me.

My greatest-grandfather's body was flopping through the snow, his neck stump raw and open, his hands stump-fingered, his chest stitched with nailheads that I swear were like the copper or brass or whatever buttons on a horse soldier's jacket, which I think an Indian in 1870 would have taken a fancy to.

I kicked back through the snow until my hand, reaching behind me, clawed into open air.

This headless body was still coming.

I shook my head no, no, and dove to the side, floundered through the snow to my backpack, for another thing I'd picked up from Murdoch's.

Spray-foam.

I pulled it from my backpack, rolled over onto my back, shook it as hard as I could, and when this giant prairie dog body rose over me, I coated its front side with it until the can sputtered, empty.

It didn't slow the body down at all, so I was still having to kick back, along the edge of the cliff.

And then I got the lighter fluid out.

I sprayed it on the foam all at once in a big spurt. The warning on the can says the foam is flammable at seven hundred degrees, but I didn't have a thermometer, wanted to be sure it would light.

When the lighter fluid was empty, I lit the multi-purpose lighter. It was one of those with a long neck, for lighting fires and candles and backyard grills, I don't know.

I lit it and shoved it into my greatest-grandfather's chest.

I was screaming again. Not for him, or it, its ears were on the head, and the head was in the snow ten feet way, but for me.

The foam went up like toilet paper and the body stood up, away from the flames, and it was really kind of wondrous, and the term that popped in my head was real-bear, because that's what this looked like. Just, one that's on fire, and trying to swipe that fire away.

Arthur Beaucarne, my great-great-great-grandfather, tresayle to the end, Lutheran pastor somewhere along the way, he stumbled forward, I rolled out of the way, and . . . and he went tumbling over the cliff, fell down and down through the blowing snow, his short arms still trying to reach those flames, and I had my face hanging off the edge so I saw it all.

He got smaller and smaller, dimmer and dimmer.

And then I pushed away from falling just the same.

When I came back I was standing there on the edge the soldiers had lain belly down on all those years ago, and I had his head gripped in my hand by an ear. It was hanging by my leg, the mouth still moving. I was about to toss it down when I remembered the memorial riders.

Through a long gust of snow, I saw them riding away, heading home.

All but one.

He had wheeled his horse around, and his horse's face, it was painted red, I shit you not.

You don't know what that means, do you, rancher man?

It means a lot is what it means.

This Blackfeet was maybe forty years old still, thirty-seven to be exact I guess, and he had black hair, chiseled cheekbones, and I can't say about his eyes because he was wearing dark sunglasses, because the snow is bright.

I fell to my knees, seeing him at last.

I fell to my knees and let the giant prairie dog head go tumbling into open air, and what I wanted worse than anything was to tell this Indian about that stop I'd just made in Bozeman, to keep my promise to him.

I'd called ahead, see, so Lydia Ackerman was waiting for me.

I'd told her she could have the journal, that it belonged there, with her, in Montana.

She almost cried. Really.

And, people like that, that happy? They make allowances.

I told her all I needed in trade for this was a few minutes alone in the conservation lab. With the journal. Pretty pretty please. When she looked down to the Priority Express package under my arm, I lowered my face, licked my lips, and told her that my dad had never met his great-grandfather. I told her that he would have really liked to.

Lydia Ackerman let me in.

I had ten minutes.

It was more than I needed.

The glass case the journal was buried in just had a simple latch, like on my old lunchboxes from elementary. And, I hadn't been all that interested in Lydia Ackerman's lecture about paper and ink and dust the last time I was in Bozeman, but I was listening. Well, the girl who was still the daughter of a chemist was listening.

And that's who did what I did.

Trick is, when acid meets something basic, the results are pretty much vinegar and baking soda, just, not quite as science-fair exciting. They sort of just meet halfway, trying to balance in the middle of the pH scale, and just leave behind table salt. And, now my dad's cremains, they were mostly calcium phosphate, that being what's left over from bones and teeth, everything else having burned away, gone up the exhaust pipe as smoke.

All I had to do to keep my promise was open the case, use a stray probe to puncture the cardboard box and the bag underneath that, and sift some of those alkaline ashes down into the acid currently being stopped in its tracks by the climate-controlled display case.

Just like was supposed to happen, probably taking into account the butter and pork grease and tears and sherry and cake and candle smoke and sweat and yellow and black paint and the homemade ink soaked into the pages night after night, the paper writhed the slightest bit with oh-so-heavy ashes being sifted down onto it, as if the pain of the story it had held for so long was finally being released, one ion at a time. And then I sifted more onto the next set of facing pages, and the next, most if not all of them, some of them crumbling at the edges just from my clumsy fingers, like waiting to transubstantiate, just like Lydia Ackerman had promised.

I didn't even stop to watch the reaction, I was so sure of it, of the rightness of it, the unavoidable goodness of it, could already see it happening in my mental rearview mirror, the individual letters of my greatest-grandfather's journal separating at a nearly microscopic level, the tiniest plate tectonics, and then the sepia tone little expanses between those words pocking with nearly invisible craters, like a hundred mouths bubbling open, gasping to try to suck in some more of that good climate-controlled air, escape this slow reaction. And then those mouths opened slightly wider, and then wider yet, a choir singing in this little glass church, and even if those pages don't quite decompose into table salt like a Bible story, still, just the slight weight of my father's ashes will have been enough to punch the letters out. This hundred-year-old journal, by the time I was pulling out of the parking lot, might look okay to Lydia Ackerman through the glass, but it had to have less integrity than the Dead Sea Scrolls, only, it won't be handled that carefully, that expensively.

On my way out, because of my academic credentials, I had been able to talk my way to a computer terminal on the first floor to "send a fast email to my chair about a family situation." Deleting all the images in the directory I was co-owner of was easy as anything, since I was on the same network it was——why *not* trust my administrative presence there? There may be more copies, I don't know, but, without anything physical, they're just Photoshop curiosities now.

And anyway, a name like "Beaucarne" on a story with monsters like this in it? Respectable scholars are supposed to take this seriously?

Not if they care about their precious jobs, their vaunted "tenure."

This is what I wanted to tell the Indian down there, because I needed him to know that this could be over between me and him now, but all I really had to show him to prove that was a giant prairie dog head pulled off a 173-year-old Lutheran pastor——yes, I, the Communications prof, did the math. I know how old Arthur Beaucarne was, when his birthday was, and how many Blackfeet the Army said died down the road from here. And I can guess that it's no accident that I'm right here where I am.

Maybe that head tumbling down and down and down was enough, though. Maybe it told Good Stab what I need him to know.

The reason I think maybe it was, was that, all the way down there by the river, the Bear as he calls it, he nodded once that this was finally done, yes, and then, because I knew this is what you do——I'd just seen it in one of my dad's westerns——I held my fist up high to him in farewell, in acknowledgment, in friendship, and, his horse fighting under him from side to side, Good Stab looked up to me for long enough for me to be sure he was really seeing me, and then he turned his horse around and I saw that the bright yellow at his knee, hanging from his saddle, it wasn't a ceremonial shield made of buffalo hide painted bright yellow, it was a hard hat, which, added together with the work gloves he'd left on my table, with the job site boots he'd been wearing when sitting there, told me who'd sniffed out your journal in the wall of that parsonage, Three-Persons.

I grinned, knowing this, grinned and winced both at the same time, still holding my hand up as high as I could, waiting for him to hold his up too, but he didn't. He didn't and he wouldn't, and he never will.

Instead he spun around, giving me his back like his father Wolf Calf probably should have in 1806 when he encountered William Clark of the Lewis and Clark Expedition on the Two Medicine, a short walk from where we were. He turned his back on me and he fell in with his people, riding west for the Backbone, and within a few paces, the storm had folded the nachzehrer into itself.

No, not the vampire.

The Blackfeet.

ACKNOWLEDGMENTS

On a plane to California on December 1st, 2023, right after reading the opening of a friend's novella for him and making some changes to the second issue of *True Believers*, barely able to stay awake but also in half a panic because I'd somehow left my wedding ring in a pair of gloves I'd taken off well before dawn, I decided to hide from all of that for at least a few minutes, so I did what I do: opened a new file, wrote the first three paragraphs of . . . of what turned out to be *The Buffalo Hunter Hunter*. I was, at that point, nearly two-thirds through a super early version of Paul Tremblay's *Horror Movie: A Novel* and I was maybe two hours shy of finishing the audiobook of Craig Johnson's *Next to Last Stand*. I had just turned in the last script for *Earthdivers* and was in the last two weeks of a graduate seminar I'd led called "Writing the Vampire." All of which is to say: of *course* I started this and no other novel, right?

I wasn't expecting Etsy, though. I wasn't expecting this academic wrapper at all, really. But, I'm not the boss. I just run along that splintery, decrepit fence between worlds and write down what I can see from the cracks and holes along the way. I don't think this is how Tolstoy did it, no.

I'd be lying if I didn't admit to jumping that fence some nights, too. I didn't grow up reading Conan the Barbarian for nothing, I mean. But I always make it home before dawn.

I didn't just come up with the premise for *The Buffalo Hunter Hunter* in the boarding area that morning, though. It had congealed over that whole semester, talking vampires in that seminar room with a bunch of writers. And, before that, I'd been thinking about vampires for years and years. Just like the werewolves in *Mongrels*, I had a list in my head of "My Vampires." This was mostly just a way to make them make sense. For me to write about a thing, a monster, a creature, a person, I have to believe in them, and for me to believe in them, they have to make sense. And, then? Writing *The Buffalo Hunter Hunter*, I didn't look at that list even once.

Also, to contend with: Why even bother to write a vampire novel, when Christopher Buehlman's *The Lesser Dead* is already out in the world? Seriously, that book. It's one of the Great Feats, right up with there with D. M. Thomas's *The White Hotel*, Martin Amis's *Time's Arrow*, Virginia Woolf's *To the Lighthouse*. But, too, I was like a kid at recess just wanting to play with the same toys the rest of the—no, I *am* that kid, what am I even saying: at Kiddycorner in Stanton, Texas, about four years old, I always had to sit inside at the window watching the other kids outside on the fun equipment, a glass of white milk set before me on the windowsill, which I refused to drink. If I would drink it, I could go to recess like everyone else. But Blackfeet, we didn't come up milking buffalo, so, as a result, a lot of us are lacking the necessary enzyme to digest the evil lactose is.

Anyway, before starting *The Buffalo Hunter Hunter*, I was still that kid sitting in the window, watching all the other writers out there playing with vampires, and having such a great time. And I wanted to play too. My heart was already out there on the jungle gym, the merry-go-round, that see-saw everyone was laughing so much to be riding.

As for the title for this one, though: thank you, Maggie Howell, my editor at IDW. With *Earthdivers*, we'd decided to do one-off arcs between 1492 and 1776 and then before the last run, 1890. Which meant two of these standalones. The first was *The Ice Age*, and the second? I pitched it to Maggie as "The Buffalo Hunter Hunter." Maggie's enthusiastic response to this is what keyed me onto the title having something to it. We ended up scrapping that standalone, meaning

I could now use that title for something else. And, no longer under that *Earthdivers* logo, I could now nudge the pages a little to the left, into the darkness, which is where the blood is. But, I should slow down to say: to me, *all* vampire stories are time-travel stories, in that this person, this monster, they're not beholden to that big hourglass anymore, are they? Just, instead of a device or a magic cave, they use an infection to cross the centuries.

Just as important to this novel, though, is my dad, Dennis Jones. In July 2023 I was up on the reservation with him and my sisters and all our families, and the whole time we were looking for the buffalo the tribe had just let loose, so they could be buffalo again, not fluffy cattle behind a fence. We never saw them, but, the day after I had to get back to Colorado, my dad texted a snapshot he'd taken: that little herd, hanging out right under Chief Mountain.

Things were connecting for me and this story, like it was surging right under my skin, looking for any way out, and fast. Or, to say it in a horror way, the story was Frank under the floorboards in *Hellraiser*: thirsty for blood, coming together one red string at a time.

As for the books in my head and my heart, Louise Erdrich's *The Last Report on the Miracles at Little No Horse* was and is vital for *The Buffalo Hunter Hunter*. But the vocabulary, Good Stab's diction, and his way of thinking, that's completely James Welch's *Fools Crow*. And I'd just spent the spring hanging out with Lois Welch, sitting at James's desk, peeling through his old photographs and research, teaching at the school he taught at, hearing all the old stories about him—most of *The Buffalo Hunter Hunter* was even written under the same "Super" sign that was over James's desk for thirty years! But, of course, snaking some vocab will only take you so far. For the rest, I'm forever indebted to Robert Hall. Dude knows the component parts of all the Blackfoot words, and is endlessly helpful. I mean, I mess up in here, and everywhere, and that's all on me. The stuff I manage to get halfway right, though, that pertains to speaking Blackfoot? I owe Robert for that.

Thanks, man. You kept me straight in *The Only Good Indians*, and now you've done it again, here. Also, I'd like to say it was intentional, but I was halfway through a development near the end before I realized this could very well be the result of having read and taught Rebecca Roanhorse's "Welcome to Your Authentic Indian Experience™." Thanks, Rebecca. And I've also got to thank a novel I can't remember the title of, as it's locked in a box in my heart, never to be opened again. I found this novel in a *Reader's Digest* condensed book at my grandparents' house one summer when I was maybe twelve, and it's got this scene forever etched on my fear wall, of someone sleeping in a guest bedroom, and the painting over the bed sliding back so this longhaired woman could extend herself from that now-open passage, and sort of loom over the sleeper. And Percival Everett's *Erasure* is a big part of this, too. I lived in that book twenty years ago, and I'm not sure I ever made my way out of it. The Good Stab sections of this one, what I kept asking myself was if I was doing a knock-off of *My Pafology*, just, minus the irony. And what that might mean, if I didn't spread the irony on? I can't say I ever figured it out, except that it makes me wonder if the writers Everett was sending up now include me.

It wasn't only books in my head and my heart, though. Very big here was the second installment of *The Fly*—especially that ending. Just as important was *No Mercy*, the South Korean crime/horror movie from 2010. Without it, I probably don't get a terrible development in *The Buffalo Hunter Hunter*. And big thanks to Ken Burns's *The American Buffalo*. I hated watching that, but only because I so, so hate that whole long, senseless attempt at an extinction. It fueled me for this novel, I mean. It fuels me still. And, of course, there's no way to avoid it: *The White Buffalo*, that 1977 Charles Bronson vehicle. The way Will Sampson as Crazy Horse rides that buffalo, man. I watched that movie so many times as a kid, until I was right there in it. One of the very first stories I ever published, even, "Last Stand"—*Cutbank*, maybe 1997—it's got a white buffalo in it. I can't get away from them.

At least in stories. In real life, I sort of feel sorry for them, as they don't get to just hang out, be normal, always have to be "sacred."

I miss you, Weasel Plume. Still a mystery to me how you even got that name. Of everything in this novel, I think that you getting called who Good Stab used to be is somehow the key that unlocks it all. I'll never understand the mechanism, but who cares, so long as the story opens, right?

And, many more thanks. Nobody writes a novel alone. Thanks to Billy Stratton, for a perceptive, insightful article he wrote on the film *Butcher's Crossing*. Thanks to Adam Johnson, for that bit about cats carrying moles indoors. I've never had a cat, but when you told me that story in grad school, Adam, I knew I was going to be using it somewhere. Thanks to Vladimir Nabokov, for Beaucarne's loooong em-dashes. I forget in which of your early-translated books this happens—could be *Invitation to a Beheading*?—but your em-dashes, man, they get so carried away, just swooshing from left to right, like an actual hand is writing them, not a machine. I fell immediately and irrevocably in love with them. And, Saga had just let me stack two en-dashes side by side for the length of *I Was a Teenage Slasher*, so I thought that they might also let me fake these Nabokovean em-dashes. If this is still here in the acknowledgments, then that means they did let me. And thanks once more to Candace, Phineas and Ferb's intractable big sister. I never would have thought that your phrasing and intonation when leaving a scene would mark me this indelibly, but . . . surprise? I stole a line from *The Holdovers* too, I guess, some little bit of trivia from history that I wouldn't have otherwise stumbled on. Thank you, *The Holdovers*. Thanks also to the way *Mr. Monk's Last Case: A Monk Movie* ends. The instant I saw all those dead people walking behind you, Monk, I knew I was plugging that into this, which I was then writing (had to wait until winter break to watch it, so my daughter could be home from school, as we're a *Monk* family). Thanks to Scott Crossley, who passed not long before I started writing this. You were big on my mind, and that package of your cremains, it's buried in this book now, man. Good travels. Thanks to Koda, my son's dog of fifteen years—a Great Dane mix who held on and held on, because he needed to keep his boy safe from the big scary world. I remember how it hurt for you to sit, your whole life, because of your hips. I gave that pain to a certain giant prairie dog in here, Koda, but I'll always see you in that scene. Thanks to the poet Paisley Rekdal, for telling me about sitting on that rise just out of Laramie in the winter to watch the big rigs slide around on 80—I think I've used that in two books now, actually, the other one forthcoming soon, here. But, it imprinted on me, I guess, the way you said it? But, that's what poets can do with language, isn't it? Use it like a stamp, to press things into our souls. And, I altered a line of Joe Lansdale's to use in here, too. Thanks, Joe. For everything. You've been a model and an exemplar for all of us for so long, man. I also stole a line from William Goldman, as we all do whether we know it or not. Thanks too to Ryan Hall, of Colgate. Had dinner with you years ago, and you told me you'd written a book on the Blackfeet. To write *The Buffalo Hunter Hunter*, I looked up your *Beneath the Backbone of the World*, and, wow, this book. Man. It's got everything, and it says it so well. And thanks too for all the primary research materials you sent that informed the book. They informed mine as well. Billy Stratton: thanks in the same way, for the back-when newspaper clippings, the yellowy reports, the old letters. Without you and Ryan and Robert Hall, I don't feel like I'm standing on firm enough ground to write this novel. Guess I also stole a line—well, a construction, but pretty much the line—from Tony Earley's forever-amazing and perfect story "The Prophet from Jupiter." It's been one of the most important stories of my life. Thanks also to Grady Hendrix, for introducing me to the term "overserved." It'll never not crack me up, especially when someone who was drinking alone uses it. Thanks to a big rattlesnake I tried cooking in a pan in my friend Steve Woods's trucker-dad's house when I was seventeen and that dad was on the road. Not because you, this rattlesnake, tasted good, but for the way you kept rising up from the pan with your neck-stump, to strike at me. I had to use that in here, didn't I? I appreciate the fight you had in you, I mean. Appreciate and respect. I still remember the day I shot you, too. It was when Steve and Randy and Jeff and me were living on whatever doves we could poach, because we were on our own, had no money for groceries. So, your meat might have been trouble, but it was necessary to keep on living, too. Thanks also to Kafka, for "The Wish to Be a Red Indian." That used to be the epigraph for my first novel, in its dissertation stage . . . I guess this would be 1997? Anyway, the jealous, reverential, demeaning way you intoned the term "red Indian" is with me yet, in this novel. Thanks to a person I won't name, too, who, while I was writing this, sort of indirectly taught me about wellness checks? Thanks also to Jesse Lawrence, the first person to read this and touch it up for me. And thanks to all the Thor comics I inhaled in sixth grade. I think I get a lot of Beaucarne's diction from you? All that "verily" stuff, which I had to learn the hard way isn't how people on the playground want to be spoken to (I finally got to go to recess, yes). And thanks as always to my mountain bikes: it was December and January while I was writing this, but every day it was possible, and some that weren't that possible, I was out there on the trails, in the snow, pedaling and letting this novel simmer on the back burner. Without my bike, I have no idea how I write anything. All work and no play . . . we all know how that one goes, especially this close to Sidewinder. Thanks also to a car I was sitting behind in traffic, one snowy day. Your vanity plate was simply "sdf." This is what I type as placeholder at the end of each writing session—this left-handed flourish of a temporary farewell. Always lowercase like that, and usually with some dramatic sound effects as well, courtesy me, and my need for drama. Seeing those three magical letters like a doorway in traffic that day, it felt . . . it's hard to explain: it was like the world was telling me to get home fast, write write write. I did. I still am. Thank you.

And, when Beaucarne suddenly became Lutheran in here, as I found that the Lutheran church in Miles City had been built at the right time, I did what research I could on Lutheranism, but . . . there's just so much I don't know. However? I have known Gay Zimmerman for some thirty years now—and she's a Lutheran pastor! My Big and Secret Plan while writing this was to send you an early draft, so you could tell me what-all I'm getting wrong. But then . . . lost my nerve. Or: I decided, since there's terrible stuff happening in here, in the actual church, and since this Lutheran pastor's not exactly a sterling dude, that, when asking you for details and the like, I'd also be, around the side, asking for approval, for something like permission. And that's wrong to ever ask. I'd rather be wrong like I'm sure I am in here than to put someone in that position. Still? Thanks for being there, to remind me to not be That Person. And, I'm sure you would have read and helped with this, even though horror's not your thing. And, I wish I knew if "chapel" was an accurate or even acceptable word, if this or that sermon or Bible-part actually fits with Lutheranism, but . . . oh well. And, sure, I probably could have found the right kind of church around Boulder, gone to a service. But it wouldn't have been a 1912 service, in German. And it feels weird and wrong, going to someone's place of worship just to steal facts and feels and details, and I don't like feeling wrong.

All of which is to say: yeah, some of the Lutheran stuff in here's probably jacked. Sorry? But, if it were Catholic, Protestant, Muslim, Buddhist, it would also be wrong. The Blackfeet stuff, though, fingers crossed I can still do that, anyway. This doesn't mean it was anything like easy to find the pre-Glacier names for all the places Good Stab goes. But: I tried. That's all you can do, finally. Try and hope.

Thanks also to Francis Dalimpere, for wanting to get that census right back in 1884. And to a couple of Texas Rangers who, in an early draft of *Seven Spanish Angels*, had learned at the feet of this guy named "Dove." Thanks also to a kid named Nolan, who, in his way, taught me epistolary stuff. Sorry about your dad, Nolan. This goes for you too, Tolly.

Thanks as well, big time, to Amanda Rybin Koob, librarian at CU Boulder. You connected me to Special Collections, to Hillary Morgan, the Book and Paper Conservator for CU Boulder Libraries. Hillary, wow, thank you. And when I was desperate in the final hours for some chemistry help, my friend and the chair of English, William Kuskin (a medievalist who also slipped me a couple of old terms I needed . . .), connected me to Susan Marie Hendrickson here at CU, who knows chemistry inside-out and upside-down. I do take dramatic liberties, but, I try to play at least somewhat within the periodic table? And, for hyphen-usage and mis-usage in late-nineteenth century and early twentieth century diaries: Nicole M. Wright. You were so helpful, Nicole. Thank you forevermuch. How else would I know anything, other than asking my brilliant friends and colleagues?

Thanks also to Ozzy, for always being the first song of the playlist I wrote this novel to. You were perfect, man. I'll never hear "Crazy Train" without dropping back into Good Stab's story, I don't think.

And thanks, as ever, to BJ Robbins and Joe Monti. You each told me that Etsy's frame story as it used to be wasn't working, which made me have to look into that opening and closing, see at last that she wasn't just a story-deliverer, she *was* the story. That's a big difference. And, Joe, if you hadn't pushed me to make Good Stab and Beaucarne's final encounter an actual confrontation, then . . . then I don't know if this novel's heart ever actually starts beating. Thanks, y'all. And thanks to Caroline Tew, who was part of these early reads, these formative suggestions. Thanks to Camryn Johnson and Rane Jones, for some last-minute copyediting and proofreading saves, which you each had to cash in a lot of sleep for. Typos, man, they're survivors, aren't they? They're Superman's Doomsday, surviving round after round, until they finally achieve invisibility. Except for the discerning eyes of people like you. And thanks just to *everyone* at Saga and Simon & Schuster, from copyediting all the way to cover design—maybe we can have some credits in this book, like should happen in all books? Because it takes a team, a village, is never just one person alone in a room. I'm so lucky to work with such talented people. And, Christine Calella and Savannah Breckenridge, thanks so much for getting this title in front of the world's eyes, and then filling its hands with early copies, and doing so much more that I don't even know. Thanks as well to Michael Noble and everyone at Simon & Schuster Audio: once again, your production kills it, brings it alive, makes it sound and feel amazing.

And, most sincere thanks to my wife, Nancy. Writing *The Buffalo Hunter Hunter* it was . . . it was weird for me. I felt like, after *The Angel of Indian Lake* tore me down and made me forget all-what I thought I knew, I was having to re-figure out how to write a novel. Like, from scratch. What are they even made of? How to get from here to there? Why start at this place and not somewhere better? What to say and what to let the reader fill in? But, again, as always, you kept my world running so I could hide on the page, and when I stumbled out into the bright light, like a mole delivered by cat-mouth to a new world, you were always there to walk me along, teach me that it's this foot first, then that foot. Without you propping me up time and again, Nan, I've long since fallen on my face and just stayed there, lying to myself that the floor is a pretty good place to watch the world pass by. But you keep me standing, and you stand beside me, and, with you, I can walk across whatever's in front of us. There's a reason in here Good Stab never says his dead wives' names, I mean, and it's not an Indian reason. It's because it would hurt me too much to make them, her, you that kind of real, and really *gone*——to have to imagine standing alone out here in the elements without you. It's been, what, thirty-plus years now? Better than thirty years since I first saw you when we were freshmen at Texas Tech, thirty years since you first threaded your hair out of your eyes and smiled at me, made me whole, and, like that, we stepped forward into the future holding each other's hand, and the adventure starts all over again every day.

Thank you, Nan. None of this without you.

Stephen Graham Jones
Boulder, Colorado
1 Dec, 2023 – 10 Feb, 2024